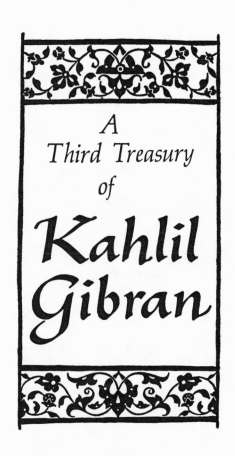

A
Third Treasury
of
Kahlil
Gibran

EDITED BY
ANDREW DIB SHERFAN
THE CITADEL PRESS, SECAUCUS, NEW JERSEY

Second paperbound printing

Published by Citadel Press
A division of Lyle Stuart Inc.
120 Enterprise Ave., Secaucus, N.J. 07094
In Canada: George J. McLeod Limited
Don Mills, Ontario
Copyright © 1975, 1973, 1966, 1965 by Philosophical Library, Inc.
Manufactured in the United States of America
ISBN 0-8065-0648-2

CONTENTS

INTRODUCTION

No VOICE has ever roared from the top of the snowy mountains of the land of the cedars and been heard in the Western world as has that of Kahlil Gibran, the Lebanese poet-philosopher. His pen was sharp, thorny and precise, throwing its critical venom at the strong as well as at the weak, chastising the former for their cruelty and urging the latter to shake off the yoke of slavery, the result of their meekness and passivity. In his romantic writings, Gibran tries to unravel the mystery of love while acknowledging that the more he tries to understand love the more it becomes mysterious to him. This state of confusion makes Gibran fond of paradoxical statements that do not fail to arouse the reader's curiosity as well as his perplexity. The overall thrill which he gives to his readers is a mixture of Oriental sensitivity and Western analytical thinking.

Gibran Kahlil Gibran was born in 1883 at the village of Bsharreh in Mount Lebanon, perched over 3000 feet above sea level. Gibran had to face a rugged physical environment and a culture dominated by old and rigid customs by which the individual is trained to treat the past as his only guide for the future. He must continue the sacred traditions and customs woven by a rigid patriarchal society forcing its members to toe the line in thought and behavior. The young Kahlil learned Arabic, Syriac (which was then a moribund language), the catechism, and the Psalms of David. His mother, who seems to have been an exceptionally well-read woman, was fond of reading to him tales of Antar, El-Zir, Abu Nuwas and Harun El Rashid.

Gibran's country was at that time subject to the ruthless Ottoman Empire, which exploited the Middle East for more than four hundred years. The economy of the land was at a very low ebb as the Turkish authorities unscrupulously gathered food and materials from the starving people to feed and support ragged armies. Religious authorities, according to Gibran, were not only subservient but were also in connivance with the civil authorities, thus accepting *de facto* the state of oppression that the people suffered. Although it is very hard to see how far the Church could afford to go against the Muslim Ottoman Empire, Gibran nevertheless did not seem to be satisfied with the performance of the gospel preachers when a bishop snatched his beloved Salma Karamy from him, for his nephew. This seems to have antagonized Gibran against Church authorities of that time.

When life in Lebanon became very hard, the Gibrans, like many other families, emigrated to the United States to find a better living. The young Kahlil was sent to a public school, and it was there incidentally that the spelling of his name was changed from Khalil, meaning "friend," to Kahlil, as it was hard for his American classmates to pronounce his name. In his late teens his mother sent him back to Lebanon because she felt that he had become the prey of a wicked woman almost twice his age. Back in Beirut, the young Gibran continued his college studies, even editing the school paper, and came to know the real plight of his native country. His first work, *Spirits Rebellious*, attacked oppression, tyranny, and various customs of the land. The book was swiftly condemned by the Maronite Catholic Church of Lebanon and burned in the marketplace of Beirut.

With that background in mind, the reader will be able

to understand the state of frustration in which Gibran found himself during his stay in his enslaved country. His works reflect fully his rebellion against both civil and religious authorities. He considered himself a kind of "prophet," with a special mission to speak up for the masses and liberate them from the various evils that had befallen them as a result of their inertia, customs and traditions. Had the Ottoman authorities been less ruthless, we would probably have seen Gibran leading demonstrations, and writing in the local press to awaken a social consciousness in the minds of his countrymen. But he knew that his voice would have fallen on deaf ears, for ignorance and passivity were paralyzing their thinking.

Family problems brought Gibran back to the United States, where he continued to paint and write. He spent some time in Paris studying art. Later he opened a studio in New York, where he painted much and wrote most of his works.

His untimely death came on April 10, 1931, while he was at the peak of his powers. Gibran was then forty-eight. After much respect was paid to his remains in the United States, the coffin draped in the Stars and Stripes and the Lebanese flag was taken to Lebanon aboard the ship *Providence.* The reception given in his native land was unprecedented, and ironically he was buried in the grounds of the convent of Saint Sarkees in his home village of Bsharreh, although it is doubtful whether his excommunication by the Maronite Church had ever been lifted. To this day, people visit his tomb as a place of pilgrimage. Even after his death, Gibran continued to be a paradoxical figure to the readers.

Gibran's works are many and have been translated by different scholars under varying titles. It is enough for us to review some of them rapidly. As said earlier, *Spirits Rebellious,* his first publication, created a sensation in the

Middle East. He labels those who are in office corrupt and tyrannical with no right to condemn other people, as they are judges appointed to office by corrupt hands. In *The Broken Wings* he narrates the facts of his own life under the various borrowed names; it mainly concerns his frustrated love for Salma Karamy, whom he wanted to marry, but who was taken from him to be betrothed to a bishop's nephew. This work also caused a stir in the Arab world. *A Tear and a Smile* paints love as always being associated with pain. It was inspired by his many meetings with Hala Dhaber, whom he saw one day weeping. To Gibran's inquiry she answered simply, after smiling: "It's a tear and a smile." She knew that she would never be wed to Gibran, her real love. In *The Madam* Gibran praises strength but chides cowardice and surrender. In *The Procession* Gibran accuses people of being slaves to the ambitious. In *The Tempests* he praises the strong, but also urges the weak to get stronger. He ridicules those who think that they are the only people to know the truth in *The Forerunner*. *The Garden of the Prophet* shows Gibran the naturalist admiring the dew-drop, the falling snow and the vineyards. *Jesus, the Son of Man* was written at the end of Gibran's life and he considered it as the crowning of his life and mission. He stresses the human qualities of Jesus to the extent that he strips him of his divinity and makes him a superman. In *The Nymphs of the Valleys* Gibran attacks those in authority, whether civil or ecclesiastical, since they make laws but do not observe them. *The Prophet*, which is considered his masterpiece, speaks of his inner life, feelings and beliefs. He follows the pattern of Nietszche's *Thus Spake Zarathustra*. Gibran considered Nietszche the best mind that ever came into this world; but while Nietszche was an atheist, Gibran was a deeply religious man. Almustapha is Gibran's spokesman, who answers all the questions from the people who came to see him off after his stay among them for a few years. Gibran considered *The Prohet* as 'part of myself.' He kept the manuscript for four years, for he wanted "to be sure, very sure, that every word of it was the very best I had to offer."

Gibran's works are fascinating and deal with many topics. But in this short introduction we shall attempt only a brief summary of his outlook on his favorite topic: love. We shall try to use his own words most of the time.

Gibran is at once very poetic and extremely analytical when he writes about love. He dissects this highest of human feelings with superb perception, although he remained a bachelor to the end of his life. He considers love as sacred and before he gives himself the pleasure of writing about it, he purifies his lips with what he calls a sacred fire.

When Gibran came to know love, the songs in his heart became a deep silence, and he needed to ask for advice from someone to tell his heart about his heart and himself about himself. Love, according to Gibran, consumes our emotions and passions. Its hand is rough and sweet, takes hold of us in our loneliness and pours into our heart a drink in which bitterness and sweetness mingle. The real feelings of love are made of tears and laughter, of sorrow and happiness. It is a strange force that brings to our soul both death and life, sorrow and happiness, generating a dream stronger than life and deeper than death. When love touches our soul with the tips of its fingers we gather enough energy and strength to cross valleys, climb mountains to meet the one we love, and travel from afar to meet the beloved who is our life.

Gibran divides life into two halves: one half is frozen and the other half burning, and love is that burning half. This divine flame comes from the throne of divinity and

Gibran prayed that he be consumed by it. Love, according to Gibran, is not created by us but is sent from above and directs everything in our life, as it sees fit. We are merely a plaything in its hands, knowing not where to go or what to do. Gibran adds than when we love we should not say that God is in our heart, but rather that we are in the heart of God.

Real and genuine love for Gibran is a self-consuming and self-nourishing fire. The flame is as strong as death, which changes everything and gives nothing but itself and takes nothing but from itself. Therefore, the idea of reward or self gratification is unknown in Gibran's idea of love, for he adds that love possesses not, nor would it be possessed, for love is sufficient unto love.

Gibran affirms that love is a divine call that directs our course, but the subject must be worthy of this call. If we must have desires, Gibran stresses, we should have only one desire—that we be melted like snow and become like a running brook singing its melody to the night. The painful side of love, Gibran adds, is found in too much tenderness. We must be willing to be hurt, wounded and punished by our own understanding of love and then suffer willingly and joyfully. Love is a word of light, written by a hand of light upon a page of light. Love, being as strong as death, changes everything without changing itself. Without its consuming fire our life will remain like a blank sheet in the book of existence.

Gibran goes so far as calling love a blessed crucifixion. At times it is cruel and savage, because it plants a flower and uproots a field; revives us for a day and stuns us for an age With one hand it offers pleasure and with the other sorrow and bitterness. Love is sorrow and sorrow is love. The desire for certain pleasure is part of our pain. We seem to like the sword that strikes us and the arrow that pierces our breast. We feel comforted to be wounded and only when we drink of our own blood can we be intoxicated. When our heart is bleeding within ourselves we call our offenders tender names. Love must kill our desire so that we may live freely and virtuously. False love, or limited love, asks for possession of the beloved, but real or unlimited love asks only for itself. Love gives us the only freedom in the world because it so elevates the spirit that the laws of humanity and the phenomena of nature do not alter its course.

Gibran has a very interesting way of looking at women. He recognizes that they have been very influential in his personal life. He feels indebted for all that he calls 'I' to women, ever since he was an infant. Women opened the windows of his eyes and the door of his spirit. They play an important role in every man's life. For Gibran "one look from a woman's eyes can make you the happiest man in the world." For those who complain of not being able to understand their lovers and accuse them of telling lies, or changing their minds Gibran seems to feel sorry, for they have never understood the psychology that makes a woman as she is. He urges them to "listen to the woman when she looks at you, but not when she talks to you." For Gibran it seems that we are asking too much of a woman to expect her to express her feelings verbally, as she is usually better qualified to communicate through her looks and affections. Gibran adds that a woman has many great faults, but to enjoy her virtues we must first forgive her faults.

Beauty in a woman is not only physical, for what makes her beautiful is dependent on our attitudes. The accord between a man and woman makes one love the other. Every visit that Gibran made to his adored Salma Karamy gave a new meaning to her beauty and a new insight into her sweet spirit, until she became to him, in his words, like a book whose pages he could understand but which he could never finish reading.

According to Gibran, a woman whom Providence has

provided with beauty of spirit and body is a truth, both open and secret, which could be understood only by love and can be touched only by virtue. Silence, love and beauty dwell together and make the beloved an idol which the spirit could worship and before which the heart could kneel to pray.

As for marriage, Gibran gives many interesting insights, and he tries to liberate it from what he calls man-made laws, whether civil or religious. The history of man, for Gibran, is birth, marriage and death. Marriage is the climax of love in this world. Marriage is either death or life, there is no in-between. Gibran compares the partners in marriage to the strings of a lute: although each stays alone, they nevertheless quiver with the same music. He considers marriage divine and any man-made law interfering with it is an affront to its sacredness. A real love is the union of two hearts that no brokers or matchmakers should meddle with. Whenever there is interference Gibran gives full freedom to the partners to divorce and seek the one their heart yearns for. In many stories, Gibran attacks false marriages and calls them living hells. The story of Wardeh El Hani (in *Spirits Rebellious*), who left her imposed husband with his wealth and riches to live in poverty with the man she loves, is only one of the many stories that Gibran narrates to illustrate his philosophy. Gibran sums up by saying that when a woman through ignorance finds herself living with a man whom she does not love, although he may shower her with money, and jewelry, decides to leave him, this means that real love was nonexistent and there was no way of satisfying her spirit with the divine wine that God makes to flow from a man's eyes into a woman's heart.

Gibran's overall philosophy on love and marriage might be disturbing to deeply religious readers, since he

rejects the laws of the Church. But let us assure them that
although Gibran's outlook is not orthodox in all aspects,
laymen as well as churchmen can learn a great deal from
him about human nature and the serious problems resulting from marriages contracted without real love.

ANDREW SHERFAN

BOOK
1

TRANSLATOR'S DEDICATION

To my dear and beloved wife,
Florence, I dedicate this work.

JOSEPH SHEBAN

MIRRORS OF THE SOUL
IS IT ALL POSSIBLE?

$\mathbf{K}$AHLIL GIBRAN was born in the shadow of the holy Cedars of Lebanon but spent the mature years of his life within the shadows of the sky-scrapers of New York. Gibran has been described as The Mystic, The Philosopher, The Religious, The Heretic, The Serene, The Rebellious and The Ageless. Is it possible to accumulate all these contradictory characteristics in one man?

Is it possible for some to burn his books because they are "dangerous, revolutionary and poisonous to youth," while others, at the same moment, are writing: "Gibran, at times, achieves Biblical majesty of phrase. There are echoes of Jesus and echoes of the Old Testament in his words."

One of Gibran's books, *The Prophet*, alone has been on the international best-seller lists for forty years; it has sold more than a million and a half copies and has been translated into more than twenty languages.

The Prophet is Gibran's best work in English, but *The Broken Wings*, his first novel, is considered his best in Arabic. It has been on the international best-seller list longer than *The Prophet*.

Biographers of Gibran, to date, have been his personal friends and acquaintances; they have thus been unable to separate his work from his personal life. They have written only of what they had seen of the Gibran with whom they lived; they were concerned only with the frailties of his life. Biographers, until now, have not tried to explain why the Gibran family migrated to America or

3

to explain the effect of such a migration upon Gibran's work, upon his revolutionary thought or upon his mysticism.

Gibran revolted against law, religion and custom. He advocated a society peaceful and mystical; but the world lacks the procedures and the formulae through which man can discard his present social orders to move into a Utopia full of love and eternal happiness.

Gibran wrote in two languages: Arabic for Lebanon, Syria and the Arabic world; English for the West. His admirers have translated his Arabic works into English, his English works into Arabic. Often, however, the translations have been like transporting an automobile to a country without roads or like training a horse to travel highways and expressways. To understand and justify some of Gibran's writing, a reader must study the unusual environment which influenced the dual Gibran. For example, his biographers have stated that he was exiled from Lebanon, but they have failed to explain that the Lebanese government did not expel Gibran. It was the Turkish Sultan who feared the rebellious Gibran and the introduction of modern Western ideas and Western methods of government into the Arab world which would accelerate the rebellion which was already fermenting agains Turkish rule in the Middle East.

THE ENVIRONMENT THAT
CREATED GIBRAN

Even before the birth of
Gibran, many men had fled from Syria and Lebanon,
some settling in Egypt, some in America, others in
Europe. Those who were not lucky enough to escape or
to be exiled were hanged in the public squares as examples to those who might have been tempted to revolt
against the Sultan.

Turkey had conquered Syria as early as the year 1517,
over 350 years before Gibran was born (1883). However,
the mountains of Lebanon were too treacherous to be
assaulted by the Turkish army; hence, Turkey occupied
the seashore and the plains and left the mountains and
their stubborn inhabitants in control of their own government under the supervision of an agent appointed by
Turkey, providing that they paid taxes to the treasury of
the Sultans.

The French Revolution

One of the ramifications of the French Revolution in
1789, nearly a century before the birth of Gibran, was the
expulsion of the Jesuits from France. Many of these religious were accepted, as refugees, in Lebanon.

The Christians of Lebanon are predominantly Maronites, who are Catholics with extraordinary privileges,
which are traditions preserved from the early practices of
the Church. The Patriarch, the head of the church in
Lebanon, is authorized to appoint bishops, an authority

5

which, of course, is not granted to even Cardinals in the Roman Rite. The Maronite Church uses Syriac, or Aramaic, in its liturgy, the same language spoken by Christ. A Maronite priest may marry. Gibran's mother was the daughter of a Maronite priest, educated in Arabic and French because the Jesuits who had settled permanently in Lebanon had opened schools and taught the French language and Western history, which had not been available in Arabic since the Turks took over three hundred years earlier.

The Sultans, Beautiful Women and Taxes

Turkey was once one of the mightiest nations on earth; it controlled all of the Arab World, North Africa and a great part of Europe. Proud of its military might, Turkey granted its army one-third of the spoils of war. The Sultan, according to law, owned the Empire. In return for good service or for a favor the Sultan was able to bestow an estate upon many of his subjects. This practice recreated and revitalized the feudal system in the Empire. All this favor and practice did not induce the Arab world to become a part of the Turkish Empire; local uprisings and small rebellions continued for many years. In 1860 Youssif Bey Karam, a member on the maternal side of this writer's family and from Gibran's district, led a great revolution for the independence of Lebanon. Although lacking manpower and ammunition, he outmaneuvered and defeated the Turkish Army in several engagements. In the end, however, the revolution failed.

The Sultans, generally speaking, did not help the economy of the Empire; their agents were busy selecting and transporting beautiful girls to the palace. If the girl did not suit the Sultan, she pleased the Wazir or a secondary officer. If she happened to displease her benefactors, her hands were tied, she was placed in a sack and thrown in the sea to drown.

Tax collectors were not regular salaried employees of the government. They would submit bids to the Sultan for the privilege of collecting the tax in a certain country or countries. The tax rate was supposed to be 10 percent of the gross income. However, through intimidation and force those agents collected more than this percentage. If a farmer happened to harvest his wheat before the arrival of the tax collectors, he was accused of having disposed of some of the wheat. If the farmer waited for the tax collector, the wheat was estimated to have a higher yield and collection was made on the higher estimate. Tax collectors often walked into barns, seizing the livestock, and into houses, taking mattresses, cooking utensils and clothing, and selling them for payment of tax. This practice made the Turkish tax rate the highest in the world, without a single benefit accruing to the taxpayer.

The Sultan, as owner of the Empire, had full control of all mineral resources, which remained buried in the ground while the citizens remained in poverty.

The Suez Canal

A French engineer, Ferdinand de Lesseps, was in love with a beautiful girl who abandoned him to marry the Emperor Napoleon III. The Empress, to save her former lover from the Emperor's wrath, induced him to leave France.

The wandering lover, de Lesseps, went to Egypt, where he obtained from the Viceroy (who ruled in behalf of the Turkish Sultan) a charter to open a canal from the

Mediterranean to the Red Sea. This was not a new idea. Canals had been opened by the Pharaohs, the Arabs, and other rulers of Egypt, but in time they had become useless, being filled by sand drifts from the desert.

After many turbulent years, amid complications and financial difficulties which brought Egypt to the verge of bankruptcy, the Suez Canal was finally ready to be opened. The wandering lover, de Lesseps, anxious to impress his former sweetheart with his magnificent work, induced the Viceroy, Khedive Ismail, to invite the royalty and the dignitaries of Europe to attend the opening of the Canal.

The Khedive, not lacking in gaiety, pomp, or imagination, ordered the building of a new palace to house the guests, and since there was not time to grow trees around the building he ordered grown trees to be moved at a tremendous expense and replanted in the gardens of the new palace. As if this were not enough, he ordered the building of an opera house in which to entertain the guests; this building is the world's oldest opera house still in continuous use.

The Khedive commissioned Verdi, the Italian operatic composer, to set an Egyptian story to Western music. The opera was *Aida*.

What has all this to do with Gibran's life?

In 1869, just fourteen years before Gibran was born, the Empress Eugénie and her Emperor husband, Napoleon III, boarded the first ship at Port Said and the Canal was formally opened. While the emperors, kings and dignitaries of Europe sat in the opera house listening to the *Aida*, the bugle was sounding the death march for all caravan routes in India, Arabia, Syria, Lebanon, Turkey and even Egypt itself.

The hundreds of thousands of people who raised and sold horses and camels, managed inns and operated caravans, and the merchants who carried on trade between the East and Europe (and all their attendant employees) were out of business. All these routes were within the domain of the Turkish Empire.

It was the straw that broke the camel's back. Until the present day, the Arab world has not recovered from this economically fatal blow. The Sultans of Turkey faced revolutions within their own palaces and brought about their own destruction. Egypt, in bankruptcy, surrendered to the English Army which came to protect English investments in the Canal, received no revenue from the Canal, and its economy never recovered. The Middle East became, theoretically, a sinking ship, its inhabitants abandoning their homes without life preservers.

It was not the poor but the majority of the intellectuals who migrated, the intellectuals who could understand that the economic upheaval was the disastrous result of the canal. Many of them were familiar with the idea of freedom and the Western world through their Jesuit education; many anticipated the permanency of the conditions created by the opening of the canal. Others rebelled against the tax collectors and the tyranny of the Turkish rulers.

Many Syrians and Lebanese migrated into Africa and opened the interior to white European settlers. Many simply boarded ships at Beirut and ended their migration wherever the ship left them, whether it was Australia, South America, New York or Boston.

The Gibran family was among them.

THE BIRTHPLACE OF GIBRAN

Man is neither consulted about his birth nor about his death, and he will not be consulted about his eternal abode. Man registers his complaint about his arrival by crying at birth and registers his complaint about leaving this earth by his fear of death.

Gibran registered his birth complaint on the sixth day of December, 1883, at Bcherri in the Republic of Lebanon.

The city of Bcherri perches on a small plateau at the edge of one of the cliffs of Wadi Qadisha. Today there is a paved road to Bcherri, but in Gibran's day there was only a trail which led up the mountain, past the outskirts of the city, then, almost retracing itself, descended to the entrance of the city with its compact homes, built of ivory-hued stones and with rusty, red-tiled roofs.

Before the advent of the helicopter and modern transportation, no army or invader could have entered Bcherri; it was like an unwalled fortress.

Gibran's ancestors millennia ago must have angered the gods, particularly Baal, whose thunder, storm and roaring threw up the ocean bottom and created the chain of mountains from Europe to the Red Sea in Arabia. In the museum at Beirut, there is a rock imbedded with a fish eight or ten million years old. This fish was found in the mountains, not far from Bcherri. This work of the gods left deep canyons and cliffs, the deepest of which is Wadi Qadisha, meaning holy or sacred valley. It begins by the seashore and it ends near the summit, traveling along this great valley. Gibran as well as modern tourists

10

could not but ponder the force that raised the strata of rocks on its side thrusting toward the sky, and created out of the ocean floor a wave-like ribbon of mountains stretching out for miles.

Barbara Young, a friend and biographer of Gibran, wrote: "To visit the Wadi Qadisha is to leave the modern world and to be plunged body and spirit into an atmosphere both ancient and timeless.

"It is a beauty of a wild and unbridled quality, and it has a mighty force that compels the mind to dwell upon the words we have for eternity."

These mountains of Lebanon for centuries were covered with cedars, mentioned in the Bible more than 103 times. They are called the "cedars of God" and "the cedar in the paradise of God." Now the cedar forest near Gibran's home is called the holy cedar. If the guardianship of this forest were awarded to the nearest large city, Bcherri would be entitled to the honor. Gibran's grandfather being a priest, the family would have had the first claim to the keys of the "cedars of God." Gibran's ancestors, the Phoenicians, celebrated their religious rites among these cedars.

The oldest recorded stories, like those of Gelgamish, Eshtar and Tamuz, took place in the forest of the cedar.[1] Gibran walked, slept and meditated in the shadow of the cedars. He read about ancient gods and the history of the cedar and how it was used in the palaces of the ancient empires of Assyria, Babylonia and in the temples of Jerusalem and in the coffins of the Pharaohs. It was cedar wood that gave the Phoenician ships extra strength, resilience and resistance to the elements.

Gibran, living in the shadows of the skyscrapers of New York, never forgot the cedars in the paradise of

1. See the chapters on Gelgamish, Eshtar and Tamuz in the author's book *One White Race*.

God, and never forgot the gods who lived and played in that paradise. It was reflected in the mirror of his soul; it was reflected in his work. In a letter to his cousin Gibran wrote: "The things which the child loves remain in the domain of the heart until old age. The most beautiful thing in life is that our souls remain hovering over the places where we once enjoyed ourselves. I am one of those who remembers those places regardless of distance or time."

In his book *Jesus the Son of Man* in the chapter "The Woman from Byblos" Gibran wrote:

Weep with me, ye daughters of Ashtarte, and all ye
     lovers of Tamouz.
Bid your heart melt and rise and run blood-tears,
For He who was made of gold and ivory is no more.
In the dark forest the boar overcame Him,
And the tusks of the boar pierced His flesh.
Now He lies stained with the leaves of yesteryear,
And no longer shall His footsteps wake the seeds
     that sleep in the bosom of Spring.
His voice will not come with the dawn to my
     window,
And I shall be forever alone.
Weep with me, ye daughters of Ashtarte, and all ye
     lovers of Tamouz,
For my Beloved has escaped me;
He who spoke as the rivers speak;
He whose voice and time were twins;
He whose mouth was a red pain made sweet;
He on whose lips gall would turn to honey.

Weep with me, daughters of Ashtarte, and ye lovers
     of Tamouz.
Weep with me around His bier as the stars weep,

And as the moon-petals fall upon His wounded
    body.
Wet with your tears the silken covers of my bed,
Where my Beloved once lay in my dream,
And was gone away in my awakening.

I charge ye, daughters of Ashtarte, and all ye lovers
    of Tamouz,
Bare your breasts and weep and comfort me,
For Jesus of Nazareth is dead.

Byblos was not one of the mightiest Phoenician cities,
but it was the greatest religious center. The Old Testament was called the Book of Byblos. The head deity of
that city was El, the father of all gods. El is the name in
the Bible often called Elohim, and in Arabic is called Elah.
The earliest alphabetical writing was discovered in Byblos. Gibran, attending school in Beirut, must have
passed through Byblos and Tripoli each time he went
home on visits. Byblos is on the seashore, north of
Beirut, and a full day's journey on horseback from
Bcherri.

Gibran's knowledge of geography and history was not
limited to his home town or the school route. His de-
scription of places, events, customs and history of the
Middle East prove that he had visited those places.
Gibran was twelve years of age when he came to the
United States. After two years of schooling in Boston he
was back in Lebanon finishing his education. During the
summer his father took him all over Lebanon, Syria and
Palestine. After four years of studying Arabic and
French, he left for Greece, Rome, Spain and then Paris to
do more studying. After two years of study in Paris,
Gibran returned to Boston.

Among the places Gibran visited were Nazareth, Bethlehem, Jerusalem, Tyre (Sidon), Tripoli, Baalbek, Damascus, Aleppo and Palmyra. These names are but small dots on the map of the world, but they must have had profound effect on the thinking, the writings and philosophy of Gibran. They are reflected in the mirrors of his soul and in every word he wrote. It is reasonable to assume that while Gibran's feet were stumbling on the stones of Nazareth, he decided to write his book *Jesus the Son of Man*.

Baalbek is one of the wonders of the world; among its strewn stones and columns a man stands in humility, bowing his head to the skill, might and devotion of its builders to their gods. Baalbek was built east of one of the highest summits of the chain of mountains confining the Mediterranean; the cedar forest is on the west side of this summit, and Gibran's humble home was a short distance from both of them.

Baalbek was the oldest and the greatest religious center of the white man; the Egyptian Pharaohs placed boats of cedar wood near their tombs to transport them, on the day of resurrection, across the Mediterranean into Baalbek. The god Baal was found in all of the holy places of the white man, from Babylonia to the Baltic Sea.[2] The greatest competition to Jehovah came from Baal and his mother, Eshtar. Baal created the rain for everything living; but he was also temperamental and in his anger created storms, lightning and earthquakes. How could Gibran remove him from the mirrors of his soul when he gazed daily at Wadi Qadisha, created by the anger of this god? Who is to say that Gibran's book *The Earth's Gods* was not conceived on the cliffs of Bcherri, or amid the ruins of Baalbek? Within this book, Baalbek was the setting for many articles dealing with religion and mystic life.

2. See chapter on Baal in the book *One White Race*.

Damascus, the oldest continuously inhabited city in the world, was the capital of the golden period of Islam. While Europe was in its dark ages, its rulers unable to sign their own names, and while numbers and science were considered the work of the devil, the Ommiad dynasty at Damascus was gathering learned men from the four corners of the empire, which stretched from Spain to India, an area greater than any empire preceding it. These men translated the works of the Persians, the Greeks and the Romans and added their own. The outcome of this labor was preserved and translated into the modern languages after the Crusades. In other words, the works of the Greeks were translated into Arabic and from Arabic into English.

Wandering in the streets and mosques of Damascus, Gibran realized the absence of pictures of the great Arab leaders. This was due to the fact that Islam prohibits the use of images. Before he reached the age of sixteen, Gibran studied the works of the Arab philosophers and poets, and to match the written characters, he etched a set of pictures depicting those men and women.

Among the cities near the birthplace of Gibran were Tyre and Sidon. They were the main Phoenician cities which carried trade and civilization to the known world; they colonized and civilized Greece; they founded the city of Rome; they colonized North Africa and developed constitutional government in Carthage (this system originated in Tripoli, which is on the road between Bcherri and Beirut). It was carried thence into Carthage, and from that great Phoenician city was copied in America and became the great document known as the United States Constitution, under which Gibran lived to write in freedom for both Arabic and English readers. This small piece of land, the birthplace of Gibran, was the birthplace of Western Civilization and constitutional government, and Gibran was one of its blessed sons and the latest contribution to this great United States of America.

WORDS OF CAUTION

Lebanon or Syria?

GIBRAN is known as the man from Lebanon, but he wrote *My Country Syria*. This discrepancy creates a most vexing problem for anyone writing about the Middle East.

As guideposts we offer the following:

As rivers bring sediment into the sea, new areas of land are created and new cities follow the land; in that case one city is older than another. In the Middle East the bottom of the ocean rose, carrying its petrified fish to the summit of a mountain. All the land east of the Mediterranean was created at the same time; no one section of it is older than another.

Man roamed the land as a hunter in the Middle East and North Africa for hundreds of thousands, if not millions of years. During this period of hunting there were no political subdivisions and man needed no passport to migrate.[1] Europe was covered with snow until twenty-five thousand years ago. Hence it was not conducive to human habitation; a few hardy savages lived in caves until the glacier receded. Then man changed his residence from a cave to a sur, or enclosure, and became a city dweller; this sur became the name of a city on the seashore known to the West as Tyre. This city, Sur (Tyre), and its goddess Suria, which is still worshiped in

1. See the book *One White Race*.

17

India, gave its name to the whole area east of the Mediter-
ranean. As Sur was Latinized into Tyre, Suria was
Latinized into Syria and included the mountains of
Lebanon.

Those city dwellers developed a philosophy of the
existence of the soul, its immortality and resurrection,
along with the premise that the soul needed help or
guidance in order that it might reach paradise (heaven).
This idea was adopted by St. Augustine. Those city
dwellers of Sur or Tyre traveled with their philosophy to
Egypt, Babylonia, North Africa and Europe; they conquered the seas, colonized and founded the great cities
of Europe, including London. They were nicknamed the
Phoenicians or "the believers in immortality."

In the caves men developed the idea of fighting in
groups to overcome the mighty animals; in the city they
fought in groups to destroy each other.

The cave dwellers grouped together to protect a cave
or a spring of water; the Suri or city dwellers built a sur to
protect a city and an army to protect a country. Even now
every country keeps an army.

What has all this to do with the nationality of Gibran?

It affects us in this respect: wars create new bound-
aries, new administrations and new philosophies of
government. Hence the administrative divisions of
Gibran's country during the Roman period varied
greatly at different times. The Roman Emperor,
Hadrian, divided it into three provinces: Syria, Syria-
Phoenicia and Syria-Palestine. Gibran was born in
Syria-Phoenicia; Christ was born in Syria-Palestine.

One historian writing about the birth of Christ has
said: "It did not appear that one born in obscurity of a
Syrian provincial village would be able to give a new date
to history and change the religious belief of mankind."

After the Romans came the Arabs, after the Arabs

came the Turks, after the Turks came the French and the English. None of the armies of these invaders ever assaulted the mountains because they were treacherous, impregnable and not worth the cost. These mountains were like a besieged city; the armies would occupy the plains on the east and the cities along the seashore, and after a period of time the mountaineers would come down to join each new invader, bargaining but reserving for themselves certain rights and privileges.

When the Arabs conquered that part of the world from India to Spain and converted it to Islam, the mountaineers, Gibran's ancestors, were able to preserve their Christian religion, a tiny island of Christians in an ocean of Islam.

When Turkey overran the country, it divided Syria into districts (*Wilayah*), naming for each one a governor with the title of Pasha. The people, during the Turkish rule of four hundred years, refused to be assimilated by their conquerors. Hence the country of Gibran remained its Achilles' heel, and its numerous revolutions were supported by one European country or another until 1860, when a civil war broke out. England sent her fleet and France disembarked on Lebanese soil an army of six thousand men. After the landing of these armies, a special committee composed of diplomatic representatives of France, England, Russia and Austria convened in Beirut with the First Minister of Turkey. The outcome was the conferring upon Lebanon of an internal autonomy guaranteed by these European powers. The Sultan was to appoint a Christian governor for Lebanon and the European powers were to approve the appointment. This autonomous area included neither the plains of Bekka on the east nor the cities along the seashores, nor even Beirut, which is now the capital of Lebanon.

Therefore, the people who came to America from the

eastern shores of the Mediterranean were classified as
Syrian nationals regardless of whether they came from
Damascus or from the mountains by the cedars.

After the First World War Turkey was ousted and
France received from the League of Nations a mandate
over Syria and Lebanon, while England took over Palestine. Even then, people arriving in America were listed
as Syrian nationals.

During the Second World War, Lebanon and Syria
overthrew the French mandate and became separate,
independent countries with full representation in the
United Nations.

Therefore the words in Gibran's book *My Countrymen
the Syrians* include both the Syrians and the Lebanese.

Youth

"During the days of my youth I wrote enough prose
and poetry to fill many volumes, but I did not, and shall
not, commit the crime of having them published."

Thus wrote Gibran to a friend. However, the admirers
of Gibran are publishing anything and everything they
can find. As a matter of fact, his best friend did the same
thing while Gibran was still alive. Gibran protested,
"Don't mention to me my past deeds, for the remembrance of them makes my blood into a burning fire."

This does not mean that all the early works of Gibran
were trivial or unimportant, especially when we consider that Gibran died at the age of forty-seven (December 6, 1883–April 10, 1931).

A word of caution: Keep in mind that many items now
in book form were originally written in a letter to a friend
or in an article to a newspaper.

Reprints

Most, if not all, of Gibran's works have been through numerous reprints. Some of these reprints fail to carry the date of the original publication or the date and source of the material, particularly the Arabic editions, whose front page carries the year of reprint.

How can future biographers determine the time and circumstances under which a newspaper article was written?

For example, the Arabic edition reads: *"Spirits Rebellious* by Gibran, 1959." The English edition, published by Heinemann, reads: "The Spirits Rebellious by Gibran, translated from Arabic; first published 1949." But the introduction explains that the stories were completed in 1908.

Barbara Young wrote that the book was written and burned in the market place in Beirut between 1901 and 1903.

Quotation Marks

There are no quotation marks in Arabic writing. However, Arabic students of English or French do use quotation marks, often haphazardly.

One Lebanese biographer wrote some paragraphs in Arabic, using quotation marks, describing them as the work of Gibran. In reality, the quotation marks were meant to signify that they were figments of the biographer's own imagination. In translation these marks were not removed. A biographer writing in English, especially one who is not familiar with the Arabic language, accepts the quotation marks as an indication that the statements are Gibran's own sayings and beliefs.

This confusion is unfair to Gibran, unfair to future writers and unfair to the reader. Therefore these words of caution become imperative.

GIBRAN'S DUAL PERSONALITY

MAN is the product of his environment. When Gibran was born, the economic conditions of the Middle East were bad and political conditions were even worse. For many years Turkey had been involved in wars, of which she was always the loser. Thus, the boundaries of the Empire were shrinking. Meanwhile, inside Turkey, the government grew more and more tyrannical. Minority groups in all parts of the Empire were abused and persecuted. It was true that the Lebanese were exempt from military service because of the local autonomy granted them in 1860 under pressure of the European nations, but it was also true that many families were moving from the cities into the mountains to avoid the dreaded military service. Many Moslem families changed to Christianity.

The whole Arab world became honeycombed with secret societies working to throw off the Turkish yoke. The Turkish government, trusting no one, systematically discharged non-Turks from government offices and replaced them with Turkish citizens; even judges were removed from their high offices. These secret societies even dared to send delegates to an Arab conference held in Paris. Many Syrian and Lebanese men from America attended the conference and made demands for reform. Many of the leaders paid with their lives. They were hanged in public squares for others to see and take heed.

Gibran, a young man in the United States and beyond the rope of the hangman, called his countrymen to revolt. He wrote articles for Arabic publication, using the

words, "my countrymen." These articles translated into
English without benefit of explanations gave the impression that Gibran was calling the people of his adopted
country of America to rebellion. Hence we find in Gibran
a dual personality; he wrote in Arabic calling for arms,
and in English calling for contentment and peace.

The following is an example of Gibran's writing to his
countrymen, published in translation without explanation:

My Countrymen

by Kahlil Gibran

What do you seek of me my countrymen?
Do you wish that I falsely promise to build
For you great palaces out of words, and temples
    roofed with dreams?
Or would you rather I destroy the work of liars
    and cowards and demolish the work of
    hypocrites and tyrants?
What would you have me do, My Countrymen?

Shall I coo like a pigeon to please you,
Or shall I roar like a lion to please myself?
I sang for you but you did not dance;
I lamented but you did not cry.
Do you wish that I sing and lament at the same time?
Your souls are hungry and the bread of knowledge
    is more plentiful than the stones of the valleys,
    but you do not eat.
Your hearts thirst, yet the springs of life pour around
    your homes like rivers, and you do not drink.
The sea has its ebb and tide, the moon its crescent

and fullness, and the year has its seasons of
summer and winter, but Justice never changes,
never falters, never perishes.
Why, then, do you attempt to distort the truth?

I have called you in the quietness of the night
    to point out to you the beauty of the moon and
    the dignity of the stars. You arise, frightened,
    and unsheathing your swords, cry, "Where is the
    enemy—to be struck down?"
At dawn, when the horsemen of the enemy arrived,
    I called again, but you refused to rise. You
    remained asleep, at war with the enemy in your
    dreams.

I told you, "Let us climb to the summit of the mountain
    where I can show you the kingdoms of the world."
    You answered saying, "In the bottom of the valley
    of this mountain our fathers and forefathers lived;
    and in its shadows they died; and in its caves
    were they buried. How shall we leave and go to
    places to which they did not go?" I told you,
    "Let us go to the plains and I will show you
    gold mines and treasures of the earth."
You refused, saying, "In the plains lurk thieves
    and robbers."

I told you, "Let us go to the seashore where the sea gives
    of its bounties." You refused, saying, "The tumult
    of the abyss frightens us to death."

I loved you, My Countrymen, yet my love for you
    distressed me and did not benefit you.

Today I hate you, and hate is a flood that carries away the
  dead branches and washes away crumbling
  buildings.
I pitied your weakness, but my pity encouraged your
  sloth. . . .

What are your demands from me, My Countrymen?
Rather what are your demands from Life,
Although no longer do I consider you children of Life.
Your souls cringe in the palms of soothsayers and
  sorcerers, while your bodies tremble in the paws of
  the bloody tyrants, and your country lies prostrate
  under the heels of the conquerors: what do you
  expect as you stand before the face of the sun? Your
  swords are rusty; the points of your spears are
  broken; your shields are covered with mud. Why,
  then, do you stand upon the battlefield?
Hypocrisy is your religion; Pretension, your life; dust,
  your end.
Why do you live? Death is the only rest for the wretched.

Life is determination in youth, strife during manhood,
  and wisdom in maturity. But you, My Countrymen,
  were born old and feeble, your heads shrunk,
Your skin withered, and you became as children, playing
  in the mire, and throwing stones at one
  another. . . .

Humanity is a crystalline river, singing, in a rippling
  rush, and carrying the secrets of the mountains to
  the depths of the sea. But you are as a swamp with
  worms in its dregs and snakes on its banks.

The soul is a sacred, blue-burning flame, illuminating the
  faces of the gods. But your souls, My Countrymen,
  are ashes for the wind to scatter over the snows, and
  for the tempest to dispel into the deep abysses.

I hate you, My Countrymen, because you despise glory
and greatness.

I vilify you because you vilify yourselves.

I am your enemy because you are enemies of the gods
and you do not know it.

The day of reckoning came during the First World
War. Turkey entered the war on the side of Germany and
the troops of both countries occupied the shores east of
the Mediterranean. This action was to prevent a landing
by the Allies and, more important, it was to protect the
railroad line that carried food to Turkey and Germany,
preventing a complete blockade of Germany.

Lebanon, demanding autonomy, had finally been
given that privilege. To start with, Lebanon was not
self-sufficient. Now that it was being blockaded, it was
deprived of the importation of food. Then the locusts
came, for two solid years, to eat everything from the
smallest blade of grass to the old oaks. The inhabitants
died of starvation on the roads and sidewalks and inside
their houses. The leaders were picked up and hanged in
the public squares; if the war had lasted longer the ex-
termination would have been complete and no one
would have been left to tell the story.

Gibran, reacting to this tragedy, wrote in Arabic the
article "My People Died," part of which follows:

My People Died

by Gibran

My people died of starvation and I came here alive,
lamenting them in my loneliness. . . .

I am told, "The tragedy of your country is only a part of the tragedy of the world; the tears and the blood shed in your country are only drops in the river of blood and tears pouring night and day in the valleys and the plains of the world."

This may be true, but the tragedy of my people is a silent one conceived in the heads of men, whom we should call snakes and serpents. The tragedy of my people is without music and without parades.

If my people had revolted against the tyrants and died in defiance, I would have said that death for liberty was more honorable than the life of servitude.

Whoever reaches eternity with sword in his hand lives as long as there is justice.

If my countrymen had entered the World War and were destroyed in battle to the last man, I would have said it was a wild hurricane destroying the green and the dead branches; I would have said death under the force of a hurricane is better than life in the arms of old age.

If an earthquake had swallowed my people and loved ones, I would have said it is the law of Nature directed by a power beyond the comprehension of man. It is foolish to attempt to solve its mysteries.

But my people did not die in rebellion, did not die in a battle and they were not buried by an earthquake.

My people died on the cross. My people died with their arms stretched toward both East and West and their eyes seeking in the darkness of the skies.

They died in silence because the ears of humanity had become deaf to their cry.

They died but they were not criminals.

They died because they were peaceful.

The died in the land that produced milk and honey.

They died because the hellish serpent seized all their flocks and all the harvest of their fields.

After the war France took over Syria and Lebanon, through a mandate from the League of Nations, to help them organize governments and become independent within three years.

The three years dragged into six, into twelve, and it appeared as though the French were to stay in Lebanon forever.

Gibran, in reaction to this situation, wrote his article, "You Have Your Lebanon and I Have My Lebanon."

"You Have Your Lebanon and I Have My Lebanon"

by Gibran

You have your Lebanon and its dilemma. I have my Lebanon and its beauty.

Your Lebanon is an arena for men from the West and men from the East.

My Lebanon is a flock of birds fluttering in the early morning as shepherds lead their sheep into the meadow and rising in the evening as farmers return from their fields and vineyards.

You have your Lebanon and its people. I have my Lebanon and its people.

Yours are those whose souls were born in the hospitals of the West; they are as a ship without rudder or sail upon a raging sea. . . . They are strong and eloquent among themselves but weak and dumb among Europeans.

They are brave, the liberators and the reformers, but only in their own area. But they cowards, always led backward by the Europeans. They are those who croak like frogs boasting that they have rid themselves of their ancient, tyrannical enemy, but the truth of the matter is that this tyrannical enemy still hides within their own souls. They are the slaves for whom time had exchanged rusty chains for shiny ones so that they thought themselves free. These are the children of your Lebanon. Is there anyone among them who represents the strength of the towering rocks of Lebanon, the purity of its water or the fragrance of its air? Who among them vouchsafes to say, "When I die I leave my country little better than when I was born?"

Who among them dare to say, "My life was a drop of blood in the veins of Lebanon, a tear in her eyes or a smile upon her lips?"

Those are the children of your Lebanon. They are, in your estimation, great; but insignificant in my estimation.

Let me tell you who are the children of my Lebanon.

They are farmers who would turn fallow field into garden and grove.

They are the shepherds who lead their flocks through the valleys to be fattened for your table meat and your woolens.

They are the vine-pressers who press the grape to wine and boil it to syrup.

The are the parents who tend the nurseries, the mothers who spin silken yarn.

They are the husbands who harvest the wheat and the wives who gather the sheaves.

They are the builders, the potters, the weavers and the bell-casters.

They are the poets who pour their souls in new cups.

They are those who migrate with nothing but courage in their hearts and strength in their arms but who return with wealth in their hands and a wreath of glory upon their heads.

They are the victorious wherever they go and loved and respected wherever they settle.

They are the ones born in huts but who died in palaces of learning.

These are the children of Lebanon; they are the lamps that cannot be snuffed by the wind and the salt which remains unspoiled through the ages.

They are the ones who are steadily moving toward perfection, beauty and truth.

What will remain of your Lebanon after a century? Tell me! Except bragging, lying and stupidity? Do you expect the ages to keep in its memory the traces of deceit and cheating and hypocrisy? Do you think the atmosphere will preserve in its pockets the shadows of death and the stench of graves?

Do you believe life will accept a patched garment for a dress? Verily, I say to you that an olive plant in the hills of Lebanon will outlast all of your deeds and your works; that the wooden plow pulled by the oxen in the crannies of Lebanon is nobler than your dreams and aspirations.

I say to you, while the conscience of time listened to me, that the songs of a maiden collecting herbs in the valleys of Lebanon will outlast all the uttering of the most exalted prattler among you. I say to you that you are achieving nothing. If you knew that you are accomplishing nothing, I would feel sorry for you, but you know it not.

You have Your Lebanon and I have My Lebanon.

[As Gibran bitterly assailed the politicians in Lebanon he tenderly expressed his hopes and belief in the young people of Lebanese and Syrian origin in America. The following message is often found, framed and displayed on the walls in the homes of Gibran's countrymen:]*

*Sections in brackets are editor's interpolations within Gibran's text.

I Believe in You

by Gibran

I believe in you, and I believe in your destiny.

I believe that you are contributors to this new civilization.

I believe that you have inherited from your forefathers an ancient dream, a song, a prophecy, which you can proudly lay as a gift of gratitude upon the lap of America.

I believe that you can say to the founders of this great nation, "Here I am, a youth, a young tree whose roots were plucked from the hills of Lebanon, yet I am deeply rooted here, and I would be fruitful."

And I believe that you can say to Abraham Lincoln, the blessed, "Jesus of Nazareth touched your lips when you spoke, and guided your hand when you wrote; and I shall uphold all that you have said and all that you have written."

I believe that you can say to Emerson and Whitman and James, "In my veins runs the blood of the poets and wise men of old, and it is my desire to come to you and receive, but I shall not come with empty hands."

I believe that even as your fathers came to this land to produce riches, you were born here to produce riches by intelligence, by labor.

I believe that it is in you to be good citizens.

And what is it to be a good citizen?

It is to acknowledge the other person's rights before asserting your own, but always to be conscious of your own.

It is to be free in word and deed, but it is also to know that your freedom is subject to the other person's freedom.

It is to create the useful and the beautiful with your own hands, and to admire what others have created in love and with faith

It is to produce by labor and only by labor, and to spend less than you have produced that your children may not be dependent upon the state for support when you are no more.

It is to stand before the towers of New York and Washington, Chicago and San Francisco saying in your heart, "I am the descendant of a people that builded Damascus and Byblos, and Tyre and Sidon and Antioch, and now I am here to build with you, and with a will."

You should be proud of being an American, but you should also be proud that your fathers and mothers came from a land upon which God laid His gracious hand and raised His messengers.

Young Americans of Syrian origin, I believe in you.

[Gibran did not live long enough to enjoy the realization of his hopes and dreams. The Lebanon of Gibran succeeded finally in becoming an independent nation.

In the summer of 1964, the Lebanese Government dedicated a four-lane boulevard stretching from Beirut to the gracious International Airport, the name of the avenue being Jadat Al Mogtaribeen (Lebanese Overseas). This boulevard is the path Gibran walked to meet his first love, and it encompasses the dreams toward which Gibran prodded his beloved homeland: the graceful resorts, modern skyscrapers and luxurious hotels of Beirut and the jet-age accommodations at the airfield. Each day, the emigrants born here in poverty travel Gibran's path. "The young trees, rooted in the hills of Lebanon, transplanted to various parts of the world, return, and they are fruitful."

In my mind's eye, I see Gibran watching this new passing parade. For did he not write:

"A little while, a moment to rest upon the wind, and another woman shall bear me."]

GIBRAN'S PAINTING AND POETRY

T HE RELIGION of Islam prohibited the use of images and idols, even the image of Mohammed. In the Christian countries it conquered, Islam converted many of the churches into mosques. Statues and paintings were easily removed; mosaic walls were covered with plaster. Hence the art of painting and carving vanished from the Islamic world. To enhance the appearance of new buildings, architects and decorators resorted to lines, geometrical designs and scenery.

As a young student in Lebanon, Gibran was not influenced by the art of one particular man or school of painters. Studying the work of the Arab philosophers, Gibran imagined their appearances and for the first time etched likenesses of these men appeared in books. Gibran created these at the age of seventeen. In the early days of his career as a painter, he exhibited his work in a studio in Boston. A fire destroyed the building and the entire collection of drawings and paintings. This was a great shock to a young man who needed to sell his work for a living. In later years he remarked that it was just as well that they were destroyed because he was not fully mature when he painted them. The paintings and drawings of Gibran are now scattered all over the Middle East, Europe and America.

Early in his career, Gibran wrote books, poetry and articles in Arabic. He created a new era in style, influenced by Western thought, and a revolution in the minds of the younger generation of his country. But all this did not give him a living income; therefore in his art he concentrated on portraits of famous or rich people. The illustrations for his books consisted basically of naked bodies, shadows drawn in gray and black. Their movements and the settings were a clear attempt to relate the known to the unknown, to depict love, sorrow, and life in their relation to man and God. He used no clothes, no trees, no buildings, no churches, and nothing to identify the scene with any section of the earth or any religious denomination. What is revealed is Gibran and his own connection with the handiwork of God. Gibran's ancestors conceived of God as an ancient father with long beard and flowing clothes; this conception remained with the church which supported and financed the work of the great men of the Middle Ages. Gibran, not supported by the church, not affected by any specific style in his childhood, remained free to develop his own style.

Gibran left few poems because he learned how to write Arabic poetry before he knew how to write English. This has been the case of other Arabic writers in Gibran's circumstances. According to the rules of Arabic poetry, what we call a poem in English is considered only a rhymed phrase. In other words, if we accept the Arabic rules as standard, the English language has no poetry.

Gibran wrote most of his Arabic poetry in the early years of his life. Arab poets prided themselves in using words that could be understood only after consulting the dictionary. Gibran's Arabic poetry opened a new era and new horizons by using short and simple words.

In his later years, Gibran wrote for English readers. As we have said, according to Gibran's education, writing poetry in English would be like taking the work of Shakespeare and rewriting it in ordinary language. Hence, we find very little poetry among the voluminous work of Gibran.

In what poetry he wrote, the philosophy was the same as in his prose. The following translation gives an example of this philosophy:

During the ebb, I wrote a line upon the sand,
Committing to it all that is in my soul and mind;
I returned at the tide to read it and to ponder
   upon it,
I found naught upon the seashore but my
   ignorance.

One of Gibran's Arabic poems, "The Procession," has been translated into English by two different writers. Comparing the two works we find great variation and we feel that something is missing. If I were to attempt a translation, I could probably do no better. There remains something inherently untranslatable in the basic use of words and language. One of the translators wrote: "By reason of the nebulous, untranslatable character of the Arabic language . . . it required occasional departure from strict translation in order that Gibran's mighty message be captured intact."

A commentator who knew Arabic has said: "Arabic is a forceful language with a prolific vocabulary of pregnant words of fine shadings. Its delicate tones of warmth and color form with its melodies a symphony, the sound of which moves its listeners to tears or ecstasy."

Though we lose some of the forcefulness and melody, even a translation conveys the basic philosophy of Gibran, which reached its peak of expression in the later work, *The Prophet*.

The translator, G. Kheirallah, said of this work: "The poem represents the unconscious autobiography of Gibran: Gibran the sage, mellowed beyond his years, and Gibran the rebel, who had come to believe in the Unity and Universality of all existence and who longed for simple, impersonal freedom, merged in harmony with all things."

THE PHILOSOPHY OF GIBRAN

"**A** PHILOSOPHER is an ordinary person who thinks more deeply and obstinately than other people."

The American philosopher William James defines philosophy as "an unusually stubborn attempt to think clearly."

The word "philosophy" comes from Greek and means "love of wisdom." It is the process of observing the facts and events of life, in both the mental and the physical worlds, with intelligent analysis of their causes and effects, and especially laws that govern them, for the purpose of deducing sets of general principles and concepts, usually with some practical application of these as a final goal.

Because we live in a such a complex and distracting world, few of us see the effect of the principles of the great philosophers upon our lives, our relations with each other and indeed upon the very concepts we take for granted. For example, even hunger is a much more sophisticated process to man today than in the past: he measures his desire for food not merely by his appetite and the accessibility of foodstuffs, but also by his ability to pay for it and his peculiar tastes. This self-control is the result, of course, of thousands of years of legal, religious and political training.

Our world is so complex that we take for granted engineering processes that would dwarf any of the ancient Seven Wonders of the World; we ride railroad tracks that do not follow faithfully the curvature of the earth, for the train would jump the tracks if they were level. We pass skyscrapers whose stress and strain are figured to the millionth of an inch, yet take for granted the fact that the Empire State Building actually sways constantly many feet. If we are religiously inclined, we take going to the church of our choice for granted; if we are non-believers, we give no second thought to the fact that we do not have to attend religious services if we do not choose. Yet the very privilege of non-belief represents the victory of philosophy; otherwise the non-churchgoer would still face the lions or the stake.

Gibran did not write treatises about philosophy, but as soon as he began his great book *The Prophet*, dealing with the question of birth and death, he placed himself within the Socratic maxim: "Know thyself."

A woman hailed him, asking, "Prophet of God . . . tell us all that has been shown you of that which is between birth and death."

As soon as Gibran wrote, "I did not love man-made laws and I abhor the traditions that our ancestors left us," he placed himself in the sphere of the theologians, illustrating particularly one of the principles of St. Augustine: "One could not doubt unless he were alive and thinking and aware that there is such a thing as truth."

Before man was able to read or write he pondered the meaning of his existence on earth. He came from where? He was going where? And why?

And as man learned to write, though in a simple and crude manner, he left for us his conception of life and death. Modern writers called this writing philosophy.

However, in these few pages, we cannot explore at length this great and vast subject, examples of which fill the shelves of libraries throughout the world. We will attempt to determine only the belief and reflections in the heart and soul of Gibran. Much of his writing reveals that he asked himself the same perplexing questions as ancient man. He did accept the premise that there is a God, but was criticized for his definition of God.

Gibran's ancestors in Lebanon and the Middle East described God as a merciful Father and hewed His image from rock in the likeness of an old man with a long beard. This conception was expressed in the three great religions of the West: Judaism, Christianity and Islam.

Some philosophers, particularly the Arabic ones, searched for a more comprehensive definition of God.

Averröes (1126–1198), a great Arabic philosopher, wrote that a simple-minded believer would say, "God is in heaven." However, he said, "A man of trained mind, knowing that God must be represented as a physical entity in space, would say, 'God is everywhere, and not merely in Heaven.'

"But if the omnipresence of God be taken only in a physical and spatial sense, that formula, too, is likely in error.

"Accordingly, the philosopher more adequately expresses the purely spiritual nature of God when he asserts that God is nowhere but in Himself; in fact, rather than say that God is in space he might more justly say that space and matter are in God."

Gibran, educated in Lebanon, must have accepted the explanation of Averröes. In his *Garden of the Prophet*, he has one in a group of men ask, "Master, we hear much talk of God hereabout. What say you of God, and Who is He in very truth?" Gibran answered saying: "Think now, My Beloved, of a heart that contains all your hearts, a love that encompasses all your loves, a spirit that encompasses all your spirits, a voice enfolding all your voices, and a silence deeper than all your silences, and timeless.

"Seek now to perceive in your self-fullness a beauty

more enchanting than all things beautiful, a song more
vast than the songs of the seas and the forest, a
majesty. . . .

"It were wiser to speak less of God, Whom we cannot
understand, and more of each other, whom we may
understand. Yet I would have you know that we are the
breath and the fragrance of God. We are God, in leaf, in
flower, and oftentimes in fruit."

When it came to questions about the soul the biographers and critics of Gibran were at a loss. Some biographers said that Gibran believed in the transmigration
of the soul, which is better known as the doctrine of
Nirvana. Others, because Gibran assailed the activities
of some religious men, accused him of being a heretic.

Therefore, to understand the philosophy of Gibran,
we must discard part of what his biographers have written and consider objectively what Gibran himself wrote.
He wrote many articles in Arabic about the great
philosophers, among them Avicenna, Al Farid and Al
Ghazali. Gibran regarded the belief of Avicenna nearest
to his own. The following are Gibran's words translated
from the Arabic:

"A Compendium on the Soul" by Avicenna

by Gibran

There is no poem written by the ancient poets nearer
my own beliefs and my spiritual inclination than that
poem of Avicenna, "A Compendium on the Soul."

In this sublime poem, the old sage embodies the
greatest hopes engendered by man's aspiration and

knowledge, the deepest well of imagination created by man's thinking; and he raises those questions which are the first in man's quest and those theories which result from great thought and long meditation.

It is not strange for such a poem to come from the awareness of Avicenna, the genius of his age; but it is paradoxical for it to be the manifestation of the man who spent his life probing into the secrets of the body, into the peculiarities of physical matter. I believe he reached the mystery of the soul by studying physical matter, thus comprehending the unknown through the known. His poem, therefore, provides clear proof that knowledge is the life of the mind, and that practical experiments lead to intellectual conclusions, to spiritual feelings and to God.

The reader is bound to find, among the great writers of the West, passages which remind him of this sublime poem. For example, there are lines in Shakespeare's immortal plays similar to this one of Avicenna:

"I despised my arrival on this earth and I despise my departure; it is a tragedy."

There is a resemblance to the writing of Shelley in the following:

"I dozed, and in a revelation, I saw what it is not possible to see with open eyes."

There is in the writing of Browning this parallel thought: "It shone like lightning, but it vanished as if it had never shone."

Nonetheless, the sage preceded all these English writers by centuries, yet he embodied in a single poem ideas which have appeared in a variety of writers of many ages. This is what confirms Avicenna as the genius not only of his century but of the centuries following and makes his poem "A Compendium on the Soul" the most sublime poem ever composed upon this most glorious subject.[1]

Al Farid

Al Farid was a devout poet. His unquenchable soul drank the divine wine of the spirit, wandering intoxicated through the exotic world where dwell the dreams of poets, lovers and mystics. Then, sobered, his soul returned to this earth to register what it saw and heard in words of beauty.

If we examine the merit of Farid's work, we find him a holy man in the temple of free thought, a prince in the great kingdom of the imagination and a general in the mighty army of mysticism. That mighty army inches steadily, nevertheless, toward the kingdom of God, conquering on its way the petty and mean things in life, ever seeking the magnificent and the majestic.

Al Farid lived in an era (1119–1220) void of creativity and original thinking. He lived among a people who parroted tradition, energetically commenting upon and explaining the great heritage of Islamic learning and philosophy.

He was a genius; a genius is a miracle. Al Farid deserted his times and shunned his milieu, seeking seclusion to write and to unite in his universal poetry the unknown with the known in life.

Al Farid did not choose his theme from daily events as

1. In the field of medicine, the books of Avicenna remained basic textbooks of the universities of Europe almost until the present day. About a hundred treatises are ascribed to him. He was great not only in his medical work, but in mathematics and astronomy, as well as philosophy. See *One White Race* by Joseph Sheban, page 241.

Al Mutanabbi[2] had done. He did not busy himself with the enigma of life as Maary[2] had done. Rather, he shut his eyes against the world in order to see beyond it, and he closed his ears against the tumult of the earth so that he could hear the eternal songs.

This, then, was Al Farid, a soul pure as the rays of the sun, a heart aflame, a mind as serene as a mountain lake, his poetry reaching beyond the dreams of those who came before and after him.

Al Ghazali

There exists between Al Ghazali and St. Augustine a spiritual unity. They represent two eras, but one idea despite the difference in the time, the religion and the society of their days. That idea is that there is a desire deep within the soul which drives man from the seen to the unseen, to philosophy and to the divine.

Al Ghazali gave up a life of ease and a high position to follow a life of asceticism and mysticism.[3] He searched for those thin lines which join the end of science to the beginning of religion. He searched for that hidden chalice in which the intelligence and experience of man is blended with his aspirations and his dreams.

St. Augustine had searched for the same chalice more than five centuries earlier. Whoever reads *The Confessions*

---

2. Both Matanabbi and Maary are great Arab poets.

3. Al Ghazali was a professor at the college in Bagdad. He gave up his chair suddenly, left his family and devoted himself to the ascetic life. He left 69 works, one of them in thirteen volumes. Al Ghazali wandered through Damascus, Jerusalem, Hebron, Mecca, Medina and Alexandria, but returned to Tas, Arabia, where he died.

of St. Augustine finds that he used the world and its fruit as a ladder to climb to consciousness of eternal truth.

However, I have found Al Ghazali nearer the secret and the heart of the matter than St. Augustine. This could be attributed to the difference in their eras; also to Al Ghazali's inheritance of the teaching and philosophies of the Arabs and Greeks who preceded him, as well as St. Augustine's bequest. By this I mean the matters that one mind hands down to another just as customs and dress represent certain eras.

I found in Ghazali a golden chain linking those mystics of India who preceded him with the deists who followed him. There is something of Al Ghazali in Buddhism and there is some of Ghazali's thinking in Spinoza and Blake.

Al Ghazali is highly respected among learned Orientalists of the West. The religious among them consider his the greatest and noblest concepts born of Islam. Strange as it seems, I saw on the wall of the fifteenth-century church in Venice a mural including Al Ghazali among the philosophers, saints and theologians whom, in the Middle Ages, the Church considered the cornerstones and pillars of its spiritual temple.

*   *

Gibran, in his articles about Avicenna, Al Farid and Al Ghazali, left no doubt about his admiration for these great Arabic philosophers and made clear his belief in the philosophy of Avicenna: "There is no poem . . . nearer my own beliefs and my spiritual inclination than that poem of Avicenna."

Gibran followed the definition of Averröes: "Space and matter are in God." Gibran said: "We are the breath and the fragrance of God." Gibran believed in the existence of God, in the existence of the soul and its rebirth, but not according to the doctrine of Nirvana.

Those who follow the doctrine of Nirvana believe that after death the soul enters the bodies of lower animals or the bodies of other human beings; and that it passes from one body to another until it is purified. It then returns to the dwelling place of its god.

Gibran did not accept the purification process. He believed that the soul comes back to finish what the man abandoned when he left the earth.

In an article about reincarnation and Nirvana, "The poet from Baalbek," written in Arabic, Gibran stated that the soul returns to an equal status. He wrote: "And the prince inquired, saying, 'Tell us, O sage, will the gods ever restore me to this world as a prince and bring back the deceased poet to life? Will my soul become incarnated in a body of a great king's son and the soul of the poet in the body of a great poet? Will the sacred laws permit him to face eternity composing poetry about life? Will I be able to shower him with gifts?' And the sage answered the prince saying: 'Whatever the soul longs for it will attain. The sacred laws which restore the spring after the passing of the winter will reinstate you a prince and will reinstate the poet as a poet.' "

Gibran wrote in *The Prophet*:

Fare you well, people of Orphalese
This day has ended.

Forget not that I shall come back to you.
A little while, and my longing shall
    gather dust and foam for another body.
A little while, a moment of rest upon
    the wind, and another woman shall
    bear me.

Gibran wrote in the last page of *The Garden of the Prophet*:

O, Mist, my sister, my sister, Mist,
I am one with you now.
No longer am I a self.
The walls have fallen,
And the chains have broken;
I rise to you, a mist,
And together we shall float upon the sea until
   life's second day,
When dawn shall lay you, dewdrops in
   a garden,
And me a babe upon the breast of a woman.

In the late eighteenth century, materialism gained wide hold in Europe. The economic life of society became more important than religious ethics. The theory of natural selection was held to justify might against right, whether between individuals or nations.

Nietzsche and many other writers made the "self" the center of something approaching worship. Nietzsche even proclaimed that God was dead.

John A. T. Robinson maintained that Nietzsche was not an atheist, that he was trying to free man from the God who is a tyrant, who impoverishes, enslaves and annihilates man. He was trying to get rid of the kindly old man who could be pushed into one corner while men "got on with business."

One of Gibran's biographers has claimed that Gibran became acquainted with the work of Nietzsche and was even influence by it.

Gibran demanded that his people in the Middle East should revolt against Turkish rule. But at no time did he ever deny the existence of God.

We know that Gibran believed in God and in the immortality of the soul. But did he believe that man and his soul required guidance and, if so, what kind of guidance?

It is essential that we know the traditions and auspices of Gibran's background to answer the questions raised by his works. Gibran was born to the daughter of a Maronite priest, was baptized by his grandfather in rites employing Syriac, or Aramaic, the language Christ spoke. The Maronite Church is typical of Lebanon's tradition of being not only physically but philosophically and intellectually at the crossroads of the world. The Maronite rite came to Lebanon directly from the Church of Antioch, but it is Roman Catholic, preserving its ancient language and rituals through the Patriarch of Antioch and the Middle East, but preserving also its allegiance to Rome. Maronite priests are often married, for a married man may become a priest. A man may not, however, marry after he takes the Maronite vows of the priesthood.

At the age of five, Gibran was sent to a village school under the auspices of the Maronite Church. When he was eleven, he had memorized all the Psalms. At thirteen, he entered Al Hikmat, a church college, where he remained for five years. At Al Hikmat, he studied with Father Joseph Haddad, whom Gibran described as "the only man who ever taught me anything."

In his maturity, after he had written *The Prophet*, Gibran wrote *Jesus, the Son of Man*, a book which reflects Gibran's deep knowledge of the Bible and of both Western and Eastern thought; for Gibran wrote not only of Arab philosophers but also of such men as St. Augustine, whom the West considers the Father of Latin theology. Augustine, nevertheless, was of Lebanese origin (Punic or Phoenician); he had been educated in the

Phoenician schools of Carthage and was 33 before he accepted Christianity. Augustine accepted St. Paul's belief in man's original sin, but defined evil as that evil that man does voluntarily; St. Augustine wrote that only with help and through grace could man attain salvation, a premise which is now an orthodox doctrine of the Church.

Also, even a cursory review of Gibran's works reveals that he had familiarized himself with the works of the ancient Lebanese, the high priests of Eshtar, Baal and Tamuz; he knew, too, Moses, the Prophets, the Beatitudes, and had read deeply of both Christian and Islamic theology. Gibran's thirst had taken him to the fountains of Buddha, Zoroaster, Confucius, Voltaire, Rousseau, Nietzsche, Jefferson, Emerson and even to Lincoln. Gibran recognized that our religions advocate discipline and guidance, first through ceremonial practices, and secondly through prescribed ethical conduct.

Although religious rites vary greatly, Western ethics today are still those codified by Gibran's ancestors along the eastern shore of the Mediterranean, rules which advocate prudence, temperance, courage, justice, love, mercy and self-sacrifice.

Gibran was a rebel, but only against ceremonial practice, not against the ethos of his ancestors. Barbara Young, Gibran's secretary in the latter years of his life, has written, "Organized religion had no attraction for this man." But careful reading proves that Gibran was not agnostic; his anger was against religion as it was practiced, not against the religious man.

When Gibran was growing to manhood, the Turks ruled Lebanon, and the Maronite church accepted a feudal role in order to survive within an Islamic society. Buttressing the feudal position of the church, the Christian Lebanese, the Maronites, zealously donated more lands to the church than it could cultivate; therefore, as the church turned more and more to the practice of sharecropping, it became increasingly a feudal master and employer of its own members. As the Church's secular power grew, some of its hierarchy, its bishops and priests, used their position and the Church's power to advance and enrich friends and relatives.

Gibran grew up too near the Church not to recognize its worldliness. He lost his first love to the nephew of a rapacious bishop. Then, leaving his own land, he saw the contrast provided by liberty, tolerance and freedom in America. His rebellion against the religious, then, was not only personal, but grew from the very ethos he had first learned from the religious.

Gibran later wrote a story in Arabic called "Kahlil the Heretic," in which a novice tries to convince the monks to distribute all their possessions and to go preach among the poor. "Let us restore to the needy the vast lands of the convent and let us give back the riches we have taken from them. Let us disperse and teach the people to smile because of the bounty of heaven and to rejoice in the glories of life and of freedom.

"The hardships we shall encounter among the people shall be more sanctifying and more exalting than the ease and serenity we accept in this place. The sympathy that touches a neighbor's heart is greater than virtue practiced unseen in this convent. A word of compassion for the weak, the criminal and the sinner is more magnificent than long, empty prayers droned in the temple."

The monks, of course, unable to make Kahlil obey their rules, throw him out of the monastery.

"The feudal lord proclaims from his castle that the Sultan has appointed him as overlord to the people and the priest proclaims from his altar that God has appointed him as guardian of their souls.

"The feudal lord binds the poor 'fellah's' arms while the priest filches from his pockets. Between the lord representing the law and the priest representing God, the bodies and the souls of the people of Lebanon wither and die."

In another story, also written in Arabic, "John the Madman," Gibran tells of John's reading the New Testament, which ordinary men were forbidden to read.

One day, reading and meditating, John neglected his herd, the heifers slowly wandering into the monastery's pasture. The monks kept the heifers and demanded payment for damages. Unable to pay, John's mother ransomed the herd by giving the monks her heirloom necklace in payment. Thus John became a crusader against the church, a preacher in the public square:

"Come again, O Jesus, to drive the vendors of thy faith from thy sacred temple. . . . They fill the skies with smoke from their candles and incense but leave the faithful hungry."

The monks had John arrested and refused to free him until his father testified that he was insane. Therefore no one listened to John because the public was led to believe he was a madman.

Gibran, writing a friend about "John the Madman," said, "I found that earlier writers, in attacking the tyranny of some of the clergy, attacked the practice of religion. They were wrong because religion is a belief natural to man. But using religion as an excuse for tyranny is wrong. That is why I made sure that John in my story was a powerful believer in Jesus, in his Gospel and in his teaching."

The ethics of the West are, of course, the products of religion. It is true that much of the Western world has separated the state from religion;[4] but our laws recognize

4. See *One White Race*, by Joseph Sheban.

Mosaic law in the prohibition against murder, theft and adultery and in recognition of each individual's property rights. Gibran, recognizing the traditions and ethos of religion, also urged prudence, temperance, courage, justice, love, mercy and self-negation. Nowhere, however, does he answer the question, "Is it possible to believe in God, to practice the ethics of religion and to admit salvation without the rites of religion?" He does, however, recognize the question in his short poem in Arabic, "O Soul":

O Soul

by Gibran

O Soul, if I did not covet immortality, I would never have learned the song which has been sung through all of time.

Rather, I would have been a suicide, nothing remaining of me except my ashes hidden within the tomb.

O soul! if I had not been baptized with tears and my eyes had not been mascaraed by ghosts of sickness, I would have seen life as through a veil, darkly.

O soul! life is a darkness which ends as in the sunburst of day.

The yearning of my heart tells me there is peace in the grave.

O soul! if some fool tell you the soul perishes like the body and that which dies never returns, tell him the flower perishes but the seed remains and lies before us as the secret of life everlasting.

"ASK NOT WHAT YOUR COUNTRY CAN DO FOR YOU"

THE FEUDAL system disappeared in both the political and religious life of Lebanon. It is now an independent state with its president and parliament elected by the people. Some of the stories and articles written by Gibran fifty years ago are a matter of history, but others are as modern as today's political situation, remaining timeless.

On the walls of many American homes hangs a plaque commemorating the statement of the late President John F. Kennedy:

Ask not what your country can do for you,
but ask what you can do for your country.

This statement appeared in an article written by Gibran in Arabic, over fifty years ago. The heading of that article can be translated either "The New Deal" or "The New Frontier."

The article was directed to Gibran's people in the Middle East, but its philosophy and its lesson will continue as long as man lives in a free society. Hence we offer the translation of the whole article:

"The New Frontier"

by Gibran

There are in the Middle East today[1] two challenging ideas: old and new.

1. Fifty years before this translation.

52

The old ideas will vanish because they are weak and exhausted.

There is in the Middle East an awakening that defies slumber. This awakening will conquer because the sun is its leader and the dawn is its army.

In the fields of the Middle East, which have been a large burial ground, stand the youth of Spring calling the occupants of the sepulchers to rise and march toward the new frontiers.

When the Spring sings its hymn the dead of the winter rise, shed their shrouds and march forward.

There is on the horizon of the Middle East a new awakening; it is growing and expanding; it is reaching and engulfing all sensitive, intelligent souls; it is penetrating and gaining the sympathy of noble hearts.

The Middle East, today, has two masters. One is deciding, ordering, being obeyed; but he is at the point of death.

But the other one is silent in his conformity to law and order, calmly awaiting justice; he is a powerful giant who knows his own strength, confident in his existence and a believer in his destiny.

There are today, in the Middle East, two men: one of the past and one of the future. Which one are you? Come close; let me look at you and let me be assured by your appearance and conduct if you are one of those coming into the light or going into the darkness.

Come and tell me who and what are you.

Are you a politician asking *what your country can do for you* or a zealous one asking *what you can do for your country?*

If you are the first, then you are a parasite; if the second, then you are an oasis in a desert.

Are you a merchant utilizing the need of society for the necessities of life, for monopoly and exorbitant profit? Or a sincere, hard-working and diligent man facilitating the exchange between the weaver and the farmer? Are you charging a reasonable profit as a middleman between supply and demand?

If you are the first, then you are a criminal whether you live in a palace or a prison. If you are the second, then you are a charitable man whether you are thanked or denounced by the people.

Are you a religious leader, weaving for your body a gown out of the ignorance of the people, fashioning a crown out of the simplicity of their hearts and pretending to hate the devil merely to live upon his income?

Or are you a devout and a pious man who sees in the piety of the individual the foundation for a progressive nation, and who can see through a profound search in the depth of his own soul a ladder to the eternal soul that directs the world?

If you are the first, then you are a heretic, a disbeliever in God even if you fast by day and pray by night.

If you are the second, then you are a violet in the garden of truth even though its fragrance is lost upon the nostrils of humanity or whether its aroma rises into that rare air where the fragrance of flowers is preserved.

Are you a newspaperman who sells his idea and his principle in the slave market, who lives on the misery of people like a buzzard which descends only upon a decaying carcass?

Or are you a teacher on the platform of the city gathering experience from life and presenting it to the people as sermons you have learned?

If you are the first, then you are a sore and an ulcer. If you are the second, then you are a balsam and a medicine.

Are you a governor who denigrates himself before those who appoint him and denigrates those whom he is to govern, who never raises a hand unless it is to reach into pockets and who does not take a step unless it is for greed?

Or are you the faithful servant who serves only the welfare of the people?

If you are the first, then you are as a tare in the threshing floor of the nations; and if the second, then you are a blessing upon its granaries.

Are you a husband who allows for himself what he disallows for his wife, living in abandonment with the key of her prison in his boots, gorging himself with his favorite food while she sits, by herself, before an empty dish?

Or are you a companion, taking no action except hand in hand, nor doing anything unless she gives her thoughts and opinions, and sharing with her your happiness and success?

If you are the first, then you are a remnant of a tribe which, still dressing in the skins of animals, vanished long before leaving the caves; and if you are the second, then you are a leader in a nation moving in the dawn toward the light of justice and wisdom.

Are you a searching writer full of self-admiration, keeping his head in the valley of a dusty past, where the ages discarded the remnant of its clothes and useless ideas?

Or are you a clear thinker examining what is good and useful for society and spending your life in building what is useful and destroying what is harmful?

If you are the first, then you are feeble and stupid, and if you are the second, then you are bread for the hungry and water for the thirsty.

Are you a poet, who plays the tambourine at the doors of emirs, or the one who throws the flowers during weddings and who walks in processions with a sponge full of warm water in his mouth, a sponge to be pressed

by his tongue and lips as soon as he reaches the cemetery?

Or have you a gift which God has placed in your hands
on which to play heavenly melodies which draw our
hearts toward the beautiful in life?

If you are the first, then you are a juggler who evokes
in our soul that which is contrary to what you intend.

If you are the second, then you are love in our hearts
and a vision in our minds.

In the Middle East there are two processions: One
procession is of old people walking with bent backs,
supported with bent canes; they are out of breath though
their path is downhill.

The other is a procession of young men, running as if
on winged feet, and jubilant as with musical strings in
their throats, surmounting obstacles as if there were
magnets drawing them up the mountainside and magic
enchanting their hearts.

Which are you and in which procession do you move?

Ask yourself and meditate in the still of the night; find
if you are a slave of yesterday or free for the morrow.

I tell you that the children of yesteryears are walking in
the funeral of the era that they created for themselves.
They are pulling a rotted rope that might break soon and
cause them to drop into a forgotten abyss. I say that they
are living in homes with weak foundations; as the storm
blows—and it is about to blow—their homes will fall
upon their heads and thus become their tombs. I say that
all their thoughts, their sayings, their quarrels, their
compositions, their books and all their work are nothing
but chains dragging them because they are too weak to
pull the load.

But the children of tomorrow are the ones called by
life, and they follow it with steady steps and heads high,
they are the dawn of new frontiers, no smoke will veil

their eyes and no jingle of chains will drown out their voices. They are few in number, but the difference is as between a grain of wheat and a stack of hay. No one knows them but they know each other. They are like the summits, which can see and hear each other—not like caves, which cannot hear or see. They are the seed dropped by the hand of God in the field, breaking through its pod and waving its sapling leaves before the face of the sun. It shall grow into a mighty tree, its root in the heart of the earth and its branches high in the sky.

SOLITUDE AND SECLUSION

by Gibran

L IFE is an island in an ocean of solitude and seclusion.

Life is an island, rocks are its desires, trees its dreams, and flowers its loneliness, and it is in the middle of an ocean of solitude and seclusion.

Your life, my friend, is an island separted from all other islands and continents. Regardless of how many boats you send to other shores or how many ships arrive upon your shores, you yourself are an island separated by its own pains, secluded in its happiness and far away in its compassion and hidden in its secrets and mysteries.

I saw you, my friend, sitting upon a mound of gold, happy in your wealth and great in your riches and believing that a handful of gold is the secret chain that links the thoughts of the people with your own thoughts and links their feeling with your own.

I saw you as a great conqueror leading a conquering army toward the fortress, then destroying and capturing it.

On second glance I found beyond the wall of your treasures a heart trembling in its solitude and seclusion like the trembling of a thirsty man within a cage of gold and jewels, but without water.

I saw you, my friend, sitting on a throne of glory, surrounded by people extolling your charity, enumerating your gifts, gazing upon you as if they were in the presence of a prophet lifting their souls up into the planets and stars. I saw you looking at them, content-

58

ment and strength upon your face, as if you were to them as the soul is to the body.

On the second look I saw your secluded self standing beside your throne, suffering in its seclusion and quaking in its loneliness. I saw that self stretching its hands as if begging from unseen ghosts. I saw it looking above the shoulders of the people to a far horizon, empty of everything except its solitude and seclusion.

I saw you, my friend, passionately in love with a beautiful woman, filling her palms with your kisses as she looked at you with sympathy and affection in her eyes and the sweetness of motherhood on her lips; I said, secretly, that love has erased his solitude and removed his seclusion and he is now within the eternal soul which draws toward itself, with love, those who were separated by solitude and seclusion.

On the second look I saw behind your soul another lonely soul, like a fog, trying in vain to become a drop of tears in the palm of that woman.

Your life, my friend, is a residence far away from any other residence and neighbors.

Your inner soul is a home far away from other homes named after you. If this residence is dark, you cannot light it with your neighbor's lamp; if it is empty you cannot fill it with the riches of your neighbor; were it in the middle of a desert, you could not move it to a garden planted by someone else.

Your inner soul, my friend, is surrounded with solitude and seclusion. Were it not for this solitude and this seclusion you would not be you and I would not be I. If it were not for that solitude and seclusion, I would, if I heard your voice, think myself to be speaking; yet, if I saw your face, I would imagine that I were looking into a mirror.

THE SEA

by Gibran

In the still of the night
As man slumbers behind the folds,
the forest proclaims:
   "I am the power
   Brought by the sun from
   the heart of the earth."
The sea remains quiet, saying to itself,
   "I am the power."

The rock says,
   "The ages erected me as a monument
   Until the Judgment Day";
The sea remains silent saying to itself,
   "I am the monument."

The wind howls
   "I am strong,
   I separate the heavens from the earth."
The sea remains quiet, saying to itself,
   "The wind is mine."

The river says
   "I am the pure water
   That quenches the thirst of the earth";
The sea remains silent saying to itself,
   "The river is mine."

The summit says,
   "I stand high like a star

In the center of the sky."
The sea remains quiet saying to itself,
   "The summit is mine."

The brain says,
   "I am a ruler;
   The world is in those who rule";
The sea remains slumbering saying, in its sleep,
   "All is mine."

HANDFUL OF BEACH SAND

by Gibran

When you tell your trouble to your neighor you present him with a part of your heart. If he possesses a great soul, he thanks you; if he possesses a small one, he belittles you.

Progress is not merely improving the past; it is moving forward toward the future.

A hungry savage picks fruit from a tree and eats it; a hungry civilized man buys it from a man who, in turn, buys it from the man who picks it.

Art is one step from the visibly known toward the unknown.

The earth breathes, we live; it pauses in breath, we die.

Man's eye is a magnifier; it shows him the earth much larger than it is.

I abstain from the people who consider insolence, bravery and tenderness cowardice. And I abstain from those who consider chatter wisdom and silence ignorance.

They tell me: If you see a slave sleeping, do not wake him lest he be dreaming of freedom.

I tell them: If you see a slave sleeping, wake him and explain to him freedom.

Contradiction is a lower degree of intelligence.

Bravery is a volcano; the seed of wavering does not grow on its crater.

The river continues on its way to the sea, broken the wheel of the mill or not.

The greater your joy or your sorrow, the smaller the world in your eyes.

Learning nourishes the seed but it gives you no seed of its own.

I use hate as a weapon to defend myself; had I been strong, I would never have needed that kind of weapon.

There are among the people murderers who have never committed murder, thieves who have never stolen and liars who have spoken nothing but the truth.

Keep me away from the wisdom which does not cry, the philosophy which does not laugh and the greatness which does not bow before children.

O great intelligent Being! hidden and existing in and for the universe, You can hear me because You are within me and You can see me because You are all-seeing; please drop within my soul a seed of Your wisdom to grow a sapling in Your forest and to give of Your fruit. Amen!

THE SAYINGS OF THE BROOK

by Gibran

I walked in the valley as the rising dawn spoke the secret
   of eternity,
And there a brook, on its course, was singing, calling and
   saying:
Life is not only a merriment;
Life is desire and determination.
Wisdom is not in words;
Wisdom is meaning within words.
Greatness is not in exalted position;
Greatness is for he who refuses position.

A man is not noble through ancestry;
How many noblemen are descendants of murderers?

Not everyone in chains is subdued;
At times, a chain is greater than a necklace.

Paradise is not in repentance;
Paradise is in the pure heart.

Hell is not in torture;
Hell is in an empty heart.

Riches are not in money alone;
How many wanderers were the richest of all men?

Not all the poor are scorned;
The wealth of the world is in a loaf of bread and a cloak.

Beauty is not in the face;
Beauty is a light in the heart.

Perfection is not for the pure of soul;
There may be virtue in sin.

This is what the brook said to the tree upon its banks;
Perhaps what the brook sang was of some of the secrets
of the sea.

FOR HEAVEN'S SAKE, MY HEART!

by Gibran

For heaven's sake, my heart, keep secret your love,
  and hide the secret from those you see
  and you will have better fortune.
He who reveals secrets is considered a fool;
  silence and secrecy are much better for him
  who falls in love.
For heaven's sake, my heart, if someone asks,
"What has happened?" do not answer.
If you are asked, "Who is she?"
Say she is in love with another.
And pretend that it is of no consequence.
For heaven's sake, my love, conceal your passion;
  your sickness is also your medicine because love
  to the soul is as wine in a glass—what you
  see is liquid, what is hidden is its spirit.
For heaven's sake, my heart, conceal your troubles;
  then, should the seas roar and the skies fall,
  you will be safe.

THE ROBIN

by Gibran

O Robin, sing! for the secret of eternity
is in song.

I wish I were as you, free from prisons and
chains.

I wish I were as you; a soul flying over
the valleys,
Sipping the light as wine is sipped from
ethereal cups.

I wish I were as you, innocent, contented
and happy,
Ignoring the future and forgetting the past.

I wish I were as you in beauty, grace and
elegance
With the wind spreading my wings for
adornment by the dew.

I wish I were as you, a thought floating
above the land
Pouring out my songs between the forest
and the sky.

O Robin, sing! and disperse my anxiety.
I listen to the voice within your voice
that whispers in my inner ear.

THE GREAT SEA

by Gibran

Yesterday, the far and the near yesterday,
   my soul and I walked to the Great Sea to wash
   from ourselves, in its waters, the dust and dirt
   of the earth. Arriving at the shore, we searched
   for a secluded place far from the sight of others.

As we walked, we saw a man sitting upon a gray rock,
   in his hand a bag of salt from which he took one
   handful at a time and threw it into the sea.
      My soul said, "This man believes in bad omens;
      He sees nothing of life except its shadows.
      No beliver in bad omens should see our naked
         bodies.
      Let us leave; we can do no bathing here."

We left that spot and moved on to a bay.
There we saw a man standing on a white rock,
   and in his hand was a vase ornamented with precious
   stones.
From the vase he was taking cubes of sugar
   and throwing them into the sea.
      My soul said, "This man believes in good omens,
      and he expects to happen things which never
      happen.
      Beware, for neither should we let him
      see our naked selves."

We walked on until we came to a man
   standing by the shore,

picking up dead fish and throwing them
back into the sea.
    My soul said, "This man is compassionate,
       trying to bring back life to those
       already dead. Let us keep away from him."

We continued on until we saw a man
    tracing his own shadow on the sand.
The waves rolled across his sketches and erased them,
    but he continued to retrace his work.
    My soul said, "He is a mystic, creating
       images to worship in his own imagination.
       Let us leave him alone also."

We walked on again until we saw a man
in a quiet bay skimming the foam off the waves
    and putting them into an agate jar.
    My soul said, "He is visionary like
       one who tries to weave a garment from
       spider threads. He is not worthy of
       seeing our naked bodies."

We moved ahead until suddenly we heard
    a voice calling, "This is the sea!
    This is the frightful sea!" We looked for
    the source of the voice, and we found a
    man with his back turned to the sea. In his
    hand he held a shell over his ear, listening
    to its murmur.
    My soul said, "He is a materialist,
       who closes his eyes to those things
       in the universe which he cannot understand
       and occupies himself with trifles."

My soul was saddened, and in a bitter voice said:
    "Let us leave these shores. There is no
      secluded place here for us to bathe.
      I will not comb my hair in this wind,
      nor will I open my bosom in this open space,
      nor will I undress and stand naked in this
      bright light."

My soul and I then left this great sea in search
   of a greater sea.

SEVEN REPRIMANDS

by Gibran

I reprimanded my soul seven times!

The first time: when I attempted to exalt
  myself by exploiting the weak.

The second time: when I feigned a limp
  before those who were crippled.

The third time: when, given a choice,
  I elected the easy rather than the difficult.

The fourth time: when I made a mistake
  I consoled myself with the mistakes of others.

The fifth time: when I was docile because of fear
  and then claimed to be strong in patience.

The sixth time: when I held my garments upraised
  to avoid the mud of Life.

The seventh time: when I stood in hymnal to God
  and considered the singing a virtue.

DURING A YEAR NOT REGISTERED IN HISTORY

by Gibran

. . . In that moment appeared from behind the willow trees a beautiful girl with hair that touched the ground. She stood beside the sleeping youth and touched his tender brow with her silken soft hand.

He looked at her through sleepy eyes as though awakened by the rays of the sun.

When he realized the Emir's daughter was standing beside him he fell upon his knees as Moses had done when he saw the burning bush.

He attempted to speak. Words failed him but his tearful eyes supplanted his tongue.

The young girl embraced him, kissed his lips; then she kissed his eyes, drying his copious tears and lips with her kisses.

In a voice softer than the tone of a reed, she said: "I saw you, sweetheart, in my dreams; I looked upon your face in my loneliness. You are the lost consort of my soul and the other better half from which I was separated when I was ordered to come into this world."

"I came here secretly to join you, sweetheart. Do not fear; you are now in my arms. I left the glory which surrounds my father and came to follow you to the end of the world, and to drink with you the cup of life and death."

"Come, sweetheart, let us go into the wilderness, away from civilization."

And the lovers walked into the forest, into the darkness of the night, fearing neither an Emir nor the phantoms of the darkness.

THE WOMEN IN THE LIFE OF GIBRAN

Gibran's Mother, Kamila

G IBRAN recognized the influence of women in his life. He once wrote: "I am indebted for all that I call 'I' to women ever since I was an infant. Women opened windows of my eyes and the doors of my spirit. Had it not been for the woman-mother, the woman-sister and the woman-friend, I would have been sleeping among those who disturb the serenity of the world with their snores."

There were many women in Gibran's life, his biographers agree.

Gibran's mother was especially important in his life because of circumstances which directed her own life. After she married, she and her husband migrated to Brazil, where he took sick and died, leaving her with her infant son, Peter. The mother returned with her son to the home of her father, Stephen Rahmy, a Maronite priest.

The man who was to become Gibran's father heard her singing one day in her father's garden, fell in love with her and soon they were married.

Kahlil Gibran was born December 6, 1883, followed by two sisters, Mariana and Sultana. Their mother taught them music, Arabic and French. As they grew older a tutor was brought into the home to teach them English.

Later they were sent to city schools. They were often taken to church, where their grandfather, a capable priest, served Mass and preached.

In the Maronite church, in certain ceremonies, the whole congregation participates, chanting in Syriac, the

73

language Christ spoke. The effect of the Maronite ceremonies remained with Gibran the rest of his life; a letter
he wrote in later years acknowledged his debt to the
church.

The religious bent of Gibran's mother, her beautiful
voice in church and the religious atmosphere of the family molded Gibran's character. This effect is apparent in
Gibran's book, *Jesus, the Son of Man.*

As Gibran reached the age of twelve, his half-brother,
Peter, reached the age of eighteen.

Peter was thus ready to go out on his own and, like all
the Lebanese (Phoenicians) who have used the seas as
their highways for thousands of years, set his heart on
America.

Gibran's mother, unwilling to have her children separate, brought Peter, Kahlil and the two girls to Boston.
Kahlil's father protested, for he owned large properties,
collected taxes for the government, and in season did
business as a cattle dealer. However, the fables from
America—that the streets were paved with gold and the
prospect of immediate riches—overwhelmed Peter,
and he decided to bring the family to America, Kahlil's
blond, blue-eyed father remaining in Lebanon.

Some of Gibran's biographers did not know that a
cattle dealer in the Middle East is actually a sheep dealer,
because sheep are imported to Lebanon, from Syria,
from Iraq and sometimes even from Turkey. Actually,
transporting sheep from Turkey without benefit of
trucks, with few rail facilities, with little feed and water,
is harder and more speculative than cattle droving in the
United States. Kahlil's biographers, in their confusion,
wrote that his father was a shepherd.

In Boston, Peter opened a grocery store, the other
children being sent to school. At the age of fourteen
Kahlil decided to go back to Lebanon to complete his

education in Arabic. His mother, realizing the talent and ambition of her son, consented to have him return to Beirut to enter the College of Al Kikmat.

Gibran remained in the college five years, spending the summers near the cedars and traveling with his father through the Middle East. After his five years were over, Gibran visited Greece, Italy and Spain on his way to Paris to study art (1901–1903).

Gibran was called back to the States because his younger sister, Sultana, had died and his mother was very sick. His mother remained bedridden nearly fifteen months before she died. During this time his half-brother Peter also died. It was the greatest shock in Gibran's life. The family was very close and its members had made great sacrifice to educate him. Mariana miraculously survived the tuberculosis which decimated Kahlil's family. Gibran's feelings toward his mother are more eloquently expressed by his own words from *The Broken Wings*:

"Mother is everything in this life; she is consolation in time of sorrowing and hope in time of grieving and power in moments of weakness. She is the fountainhead of compassion, forbearance and forgiveness. He who loses his mother loses a bosom upon which he can rest his head, the hand that blesses, and eyes which watch over him."

Micheline

One biographer has stated that Gibran met, in Boston, a beautiful and vivacious girl named Emilie Michel, nicknamed Micheline. He also stated that Micheline followed Gibran to Paris, that she asked him to marry her and when he refused she left Gibran's apartment and vanished forever. Some biographers accepted this story; others did not mention the girl by name. Offered as proof by some who mentioned Micheline were two items: first, that Gibran had painted her before he left for Paris; second, the dedication of one of his books to Micheline.

I made a special effort to determine the existence of this beautiful girl. I visited the Museum of Gibran in Lebanon, where I asked the curator to direct me to the painting of Micheline. Pointing to one of the paintings on the wall he said, "This is what is considered to be the painting of Micheline."

This painting has no identifying marks whatsoever. It is not even signed by Gibran. But then only a few of his paintings are signed. I found no facts to show that this was the painting of Micheline; I found no correspondence between Gibran and Micheline.

The reprints of Gibran's Arabic books, as stated earlier, lack information as to the date of first publication. They also lack dedications. After a long search I obtained copies of the earlier editions which contain dedications; I found that Micheline was not mentioned.

The dedication I found read thus:

"To the soul that embraced my soul, to the heart that poured its secrets into my own heart, to the hand that kindled the flame of my emotions, I dedicate this book."

In Paris Gibran lived and worked with a close friend, Joseph Hoyek, who wrote a book about their two years together. The two young men did not live in the same apartment; however, they met daily and often shared the cost of a model for the sake of saving money. Hoyek wrote about the girls they met, the restaurants in which they ate. He named Olga, a Russian girl, another named Rosina, and an Italian girl who was the most beautiful model they hired, but Hoyek made no mention of Micheline.

Therefore, until further evidence is available, I withhold my decision that Micheline ever existed.

Mary Haskell or Mary Khoury?

In 1904 Gibran borrowed twenty dollars and arranged for an exhibition of his paintings. One of those who visited that exhibit was a Miss Mary E. Haskell, who became his friend. Later, she paid his way to Paris to further his art studies. One biographer said that Gibran thereafter asked her to check each of his manuscripts before he submitted it to his publisher.

Gibran's novel *The Broken Wings* was dedicated to M. E. H. However, the administrator of Gibran's estate insists that the woman who helped Gibran financially was a wealthy woman named Mary Khoury. The executor of the estate was the personal physician of Mary Khoury, and had seen in her apartment several of Gibran's paintings and statues on which Gibran had written in Arabic: "Do not blame a person for drinking lest he is trying to forget something more serious than drinking." The doctor further reports that she, Mary Khoury, agreed to have her letters from Gibran published. He also claims those letters were given to a friend for editing, and that both the friend and Mary Khoury have since died. Thus the letters and paintings fell into unknown hands.

According to Mary Khoury, Gibran spent many evenings, in the later days of his life, at her apartment.

The existence of letters from Gibran to Mary Khoury was verified independently by a reliable Lebanese reporter who explained that he had read some of them and that Mary Khoury had promised to have letters released after they were edited. When I asked the newsman if the letters were business or love letters, he emphasized that they were love letters.

Nevertheless, the mystery remains about the benefactress in Kahlil Gibran's life: Was she Mary Haskell or Mary Khoury—or both?

Barbara Young

Barbara Young knew Gibran the last seven years of his life, during which time she became the first of his disciples to shout his praise in a biography, *The Man From Lebanon*.

"If he, Gibran, had never written a poem or painted a picture, his signature upon the page of eternal record would still be inerasable. The power of his individual consciousness has penetrated the consciousness of the age, and the indwelling of his spirit is timeless and deathless. This is Gibran," wrote Barbara Young.

In 1923 Barbara heard a reading from *The Prophet*.

She wrote to Gibran expressing her admiration. She received "his gracious invitation to come to this studio 'to talk about poetry' and to see the pictures."

"So I went," she wrote, "to the old West Tenth Street building, climbed four flights of stairs and found him there, smiling, welcoming me as though we were old friends indeed."

Barbara was taller than Gibran, of light complexion, beautifully built. Her family came from Bideford, in Devon, England. By profession, she was an English teacher, she operated a book store, and she lectured about Gibran the rest of her life after that first climb of the four flights of stairs. After Gibran's death, she assembled and put together the chapters of his unfinished book, *Garden of the Prophet*, and arranged for its publication.

Barbara Young and other biographers have described Gibran as being slender, of medium height, five feet-four inches, as having large, sleepy, brown eyes fringed by long lashes, chestnut hair, and a generous mustache framing full lips. His body was strong and he possessed a powerful grip. In some of his letters he mentioned that the beating of his heart was becoming normal again.

Barbara Young was with Gibran at the hospital when he passed away. Soon afterward she packed the precious paintings and effects left in the studio where Gibran had lived for eighteen years, and sent them to his home town of Bcherri in Lebanon.

During her speaking tours Barbara exhibited more than sixty paintings of Gibran's work. What became of this collection or any unfinished work, papers or letters she may have had depends on the generosity of those who bought, received or inherited these objects. Until they come forward, there will never be a complete biography of Gibran, particularly that part dealing with Barbara Young.

How close a relationship existed during these seven years can be answered, in part, by excerpts from Barbara's own writing.

Barbara never lived with Gibran. She kept her own apartment in the city of New York.

One Sunday, Barbara wrote, accepting an invitation from Gibran, she went to the studio. Gibran was writing a poem; he was at his desk when she arrived. While composing Gibran usually paced the floor and then he would sit down to write a line or two.

"I waited while he repeated his writing and his walking again and again. Then a thought came to me. The next time he walked I went and seated myself at his table and took up his pencil. When he turned he saw me sitting there.

" 'You make the poem and I'll write it,' I said."

After much protest Gibran consented to try it. He was pleased with the experiment.

" 'Well, you and I are two poets working together.' He paused. Then after a silence, 'We are friends,' he said. 'I want nothing from you, and you want nothing from me. We share life.' "

As they worked together and as she became more acquainted with his manner of thought and his work, she told him of her determination to write a book about him. Gibran was pleased and "it was from that time on that he talked often of his childhood, his mother and family, and some events in his life."

One day Gibran asked, "Suppose you were compelled to give up—to forget all the words you know except seven—what are the seven words that you would keep?"

"I named only five," Barbara wrote. "God, Life, Love, Beauty, Earth . . . and asked Gibran what other words would he select and he answered, 'The most important words to keep are: You and I . . . without these two there would need to be no others.' Then Gibran selected the seven words: You, I, Give, God, Love, Beauty, Earth."

"Gibran liked a frugal supper in the studio," Barbara wrote, "particularly during a period of his life when he was entertained and being feasted. This one evening Gibran said that 'in the East there is a custom of eating all from one huge vessel. Let us have our soup tonight in one bowl.' So we did and Gibran humorously drew an imaginary line through the soup and said, 'This is your half of the soup and this other is my half. See to it that we neither one trespass upon the soup of the other!' Then laughter and a thorough enjoyment, each of his own half of the soup."

In another chapter Barbara wrote: "One evening when we were doing the book 'Sea and Foam,' I piled cushions on the floor and sat upon them instead of occupying my usual chair. Then I had a strange feeling of a familiarity about the gesture, and I said: 'I feel as if I've sat like this beside you many times—but I really haven't,' and Gibran answered, 'We have done this a thousand years ago, and we shall do it a thousand years hence.'

"And during the writing of the book 'Jesus, the Son of Man' the drama of some incident, now and again, was so overwhelming that I felt, and said, 'It is so real. It seems as if I had been there.' And his answer came, almost like a cry, 'You were there! And so was I!' "

It is appropriate, here, to tell that two years after the death of Gibran, Barbara Young and this author met in the city of Cleveland. She asked: "How long would it take to learn the Arabic language?" I explained to her that for the purpose of translating any of Gibran's works it would take many years to learn the classical version of the language; just to speak Arabic would be a different matter. In any event Arabic is a difficult language.

At that time I was studying for my law degree. I was neither interested in teaching Arabic nor contemplating the writing of a book about Gibran. She also told me that whenever Gibran painted a hand it was hers.

The most famous hand Gibran painted is the one with an eye in its palm. This painting was meant to represent the Phoenician Goddess Tanit. In honor of this Goddess, there are two cities in Lebanon called Eyetanit meaning "Eye of Tanit."

This pose, the eye nestled in the palm of the hand, appeared in Carthage in North Africa, carried there by Gibran's ancestors (the Phoenicians). The Phoenicians left one of these carvings of the hand of Tanit in Alabama before the arrival of Columbus.

Did Gibran see one of these hands in Lebanon, was the similarity a coincidence, or were Gibran and Barbara there when the Temples of Tanit were being built in Lebanon and Carthage long before the birth of Christ?

Barbara Young wrote that once when some women came to visit Gibran, they asked why he did not get married. He replied: "Well . . . you see it is like this. If I had a wife, and if I were painting or making poems, I should simply forget her existence for days at a time. And you know well that no loving woman would put up with such a husband for very long."

One of the women, not satisfied with the smiling answer, prodded still deeper, "But have you never been in love?" Controlling himself with difficulty, he said, "I will tell you a thing you may not know. The most highly sexed beings upon the planet are the creators, the poets, sculptors, painters, musicians . . . and so it has been from the beginning. And among them sex is a beautiful and exalted gift. Sex is always beautiful, and it is always shy."

Barbara Young wrote the following paragraph, which we quote, without comment, leaving it to the reader to determine her place in the life of Gibran:

"It is always wise to be wary of the woman who appears out of nowhere and claims a great man for her own when he is dead. But if there be those who never say, 'Lord, Lord,' but who maintain a silence, doing his works, may it not be that these are the hands that have indeed ministered unto him, these the hearts that have perceived the intricacies of his myriad being? And for myself, I do not doubt that through the turbulent years of this man's life the ageless and universal cry for woman-comfort went out from his great loneliness, and that in the goodness of God, the cry was answered. To conclude otherwise would be the essence of stupidity."

Mariana

Mariana, being a younger sister of Gibran, was not consulted about her family's migration.

She was not asked whether her brother should be sent to Lebanon and Europe. However, when tragedy struck, and her mother, her sister and brother Peter, who was the breadwinner, died of tuberculosis within two years, Mariana found herself alone with her brother Kahlil, whose literary work was awakening the Arab world and upsetting the Ottoman Empire. Mariana realized that literary greatness and money do not often meet until, and if, late in life. Gibran's education was in Arabic; thus his articles and books were not bringing in sufficient cash to furnish the necessities of life.

Mariana refused to let her brother alter his plans or to take a job which would interfere with his literary and art career. She sewed and knit to keep a home for herself and for her brother. She encouraged him to paint until he had a collection ready for showing. Mariana did not have the money to pay for the display of his works, but Gibran managed to borrow twenty dollars from a Lebanese woman, who lived in Boston then, and is still living now, in Lebanon, and considers Gibran's note her greatest possession.

The investment in Gibran's education paid dividends, not only to the literary world but in money as well. The estimate of the royalties from Gibran's books is over a million and a half dollars. These royalties are sent to his home town, Bcherri. However, he left to his sister, Mariana (Mary), who still lives in Boston, sufficient money for her to retire with security for the rest of her life. She was on very good terms with Barbara Young, who dedicated the book *The Man From Lebanon* to her.

May Ziadeh

May Ziadeh was Gibran's love on paper only; he never saw her. May was a Lebanese girl, whose family had moved to Egypt. An only child, she was educated in the Middle East and later went to Europe to study; later she wrote articles in her father's magazine and in other French and Arabic publications. Her parents' home was a meeting place for most of the prominent literary men in Egypt. Gibran's articles, appearing at this time, in many papers and magazines, were often a topic of discussion.

May, admiring Gibran's articles, decided to write to him. Fearing that he might disregard her letters as simply those from another admirer, she wrote, in the beginning, an introduction of herself. She explained that she wrote articles and books, and that much of her work appeared under the nom de plume, Isis Cubia. Then she proceeded to tell him the great effect his writing was having upon the Egyptian community.

Gibran was prompt in his answer. He wrote admiring her courage and thanking her for working toward the liberation of women in the Middle East. He told her that he was mailing her, in a separate package, a copy of his new book, *The Broken Wings*. And he tried to explain how he came to give it that title:

"I inherited from my mother ninety percent of my character and my disposition. This does not mean that I inherited her beauty and her humility, or her big heart. I recall that she told me once, when I was twenty years old, that it would have been much better for me and the people had I become a monk in one of the monasteries.

"I said, 'It is true except that I took you as a mother before I came into this world.'

"She replied, 'If you had not come, you would have remained an angel.'

"I answered, 'I am still an angel.'

"She smiled and asked, 'But where are your wings?'

"I placed her arms on my shoulders and then said, 'These are my wings.'

"She responded, 'But they are broken.' "

Gibran added in his letter: "My mother, since passed beyond the blue horizon, but her words, 'the broken wings' remained with me and I used them for the title of the novel I am sending to you. I appreciate your personal opinion."

May sent her opinion, admiring the book, but sharply disagreeing with Gibran, because in the story he condoned a married woman meeting with her former lover.

"Regardless of how innocent it was," May wrote, "it is a betrayal of the husband, it is a betrayal of the name she carries and it is a betrayal of society."

In the meantime, the intelligentsia of Egypt were planning to honor a Lebanese poet and Gibran was to be one of the speakers. Unable to attend, mainly because he didn't have the money, Gibran sent an article "The Poet of Baalbek"[1] to be read at the affair. The toastmaster, knowing about the correspondence between Gibran and May, asked her to read the article.

Even though it was May's first attempt at public speaking, her reading earned an ovation. Thus, she had auctioned her heart to Gibran. They corresponded until his death. May's letters were not all of love, for she criticized his writing frequently and prodded him to write on certain subjects.

Once May wrote:

"The new Turkish governor arrived in Lebanon, and as usual, he began removing people from their jobs. He is following in the footsteps of his predecessors. The Lebanese people are prostrating themselves before his feet. When are we going to have among us men of courage? When are the Lebanese going to shake off the dust of insult? Why don't you write on this subject? The people respect your ideas, Gibran. Remind them they are men and men should not humble themselves."

1. Baalbek was the hometown of the poet being honored.

Writing on the subject Gibran said:

"Woe to the nation that receives her conquerors beating the drums. Woe to the nation that hates oppression in her sleep and accepts it in her awakening. Woe to the nation that raises her voice only behind a coffin and prides itself only in the cemetery. Woe to a nation that does not revolt until her neck is placed on the scaffold."

Gibran wrote and asked May to come to the United States. She refused because she was a woman and custom did not permit her; she asked him to come to Egypt. Part of Gibran's letter said: "What can I say about my economic condition?

"A year or two ago I had some peace and quiet. But now the quietness has turned into tumult and peace into struggle. The people are demanding my days and nights. I am overwhelmed by their demands. Every once in a while I leave this great city to elude the people and to escape from myself. The American public is mighty. It never wearies or gets tired, is never exhausted, never sleeps and never dreams. If it dislikes you it destroys you with neglect and if it likes you it destroys you with its affection and demand.

"The day may yet come when I can escape to the Middle East. If it were not for this cage, whose bars I have wrought with my own hands—I would have taken the first ship going East. What man would desert a building whose stones he had hewn and polished his entire life even though it had become a prison?"

In one of her letters May wrote:

"I do not know what I am doing but I know that I love you. I fear love. I expect too much of love, and I fear that I never will receive all my expectations. . . . How dare I write this to you . . . ? However, I thank God I am writing it and not saying it. If you were present I would have vanished after such a statement and disappeared until you had forgotten what I said.

"I blame myself for taking even this much liberty. Nevertheless, right or wrong, my heart is with you and the best thing it can do is to hover over you and guard you with compassion."

May's heart needed to hover only for a short time because Gibran's health was failing. He wrote:

"You know, May, every time I think of departing, that is, in death, I enjoy my thoughts and am contended to leave."

Gibran departed in 1931 at the age of forty-seven after nearly nineteen years of his love affair, on paper, with May Ziadeh.

Salma Karamy

Gibran was eighteen "when love opened his eyes by its magic rays and Salma was the first woman" to do it.

Gibran wrote a novel in Arabic about his first love. No other author could have narrated the events better than Gibran. However, biographers and Gibran's neighbors insist that Gibran's first girl was called Hala El-daher and that the events of the story took place in Bcherri instead of Beirut.

Gibran intended to buy the monastery of Mar Sarkis where Salma once met him. This monastery was actually carved in a cliff for a safe refuge. To enter it in the old days required either a rope or a ladder. Mariana, Gibran's sister, bought it. A footpath was built later for the convenience of visitors who now bow humbly before the resting place of Gibran, who had wished to retire there in life but reached his refuge only in death.

Among his last letters exists evidence of Gibran's desire to "to go to the Middle East, to Lebanon, to Bcherri, to Mar Sarkis, that hermitage carved in the rock and overlooking the most astonishing sight the eye could ever see of the whole valley." Gibran was longing for the "new life in the heart of nature; among the golden fields of wheat, the green meadows, the flocks of sheep being led to pasture, the roaring falls and the rising mist reflecting in the rays of the sun."

Salma is presented to the reader in *The Broken Wings*, Gibran's own love story which has been on the best-seller list in Arabic for more than forty years.

BOOK
2

To my children,
Jeneen, George and Faram,
I dedicate this work.

JOSEPH SHEBAN

KEY

BW-ST: *Broken Wings* by Kahlil Gibran, in *A Second Treasury of Kahlil Gibran*, trans. by Anthony R. Ferris, Citadel Press, 1962.

KG-P: *Kahlil Gibran: A Biography* by Michael Naimy, in *The Parables of Gibran* by Annie Salem Otto, Citadel Press, 1963.

P: *The Procession* by Kahlil Gibran, trans. by George Kheirallah, Philosophical Library, 1958.

MS: *Mirrors of the Soul, Kahlil Gibran*, by Joseph Sheban, Philosophical Library, 1965.

S: In conversation and correspondence.

SH-P: *Secrets of the Heart* by Kahlil Gibran in *The Parables of Gibran*.

SH-T: *Secrets of the Heart* by Kahlil Gibran in *A Treasury of Kahlil Gibran*, trans. by Anthony Rizcallah Ferris, edited by Martin L. Wolf, Citadel Press, 1947.

SP-P: *Kahlil Gibran: A Self Portrait*, trans. by Anthony R. Ferris, in *The Parables of Gibran*.

SR-T: *Spirits Rebellious* by Kahlil Gibran in *A Treasury of Kahlil Gibran*.

T: *A Treasury of Kahlil Gibran*.

TL-T: *Tears and Laughter* by Kahlil Gibran in *A Treasury of Kahlil Gibran*.

VM-P: *The Voice of the Master* by Kahlil Gibran in *The Parables of Gibran*.

WM-ST: *The Words of the Master* by Kahlil Gibran in *A Second Treasury of Kahlil Gibran*.

THE WISDOM OF KAHLIL GIBRAN

INTRODUCTION

Kahlil Gibran, whose books have been international best-sellers for more than fifty years, was born near the Holy Cedars of Lebanon. While Kahlil was a young boy, his family migrated to the United States. After several years in Boston schools, Gibran's family sent him back to Lebanon to be educated at a college in Beirut. Later, he was sent to Paris for further education. Gibran then returned to the United States, where he applied his brush to painting and his pen to writing in Arabic. Through his first art exhibit, in Boston, he met Miss Mary Haskell, who became patron of his further art studies in Paris.

Because of his cosmopolitan background and education, Kahlil Gibran became first a student of and then an interpreter of the Middle East, Europe and America. Thus, through him, the twain, East and West in great fulfillment, met. He brought to his readers of Arabic the simplicity of English expression, a refreshing freedom of thought and a frankness which demanded reform. In Arabic, his style and concepts were revolutionary. To his readers in English, he brought the poetry, family traditions, sagacity and philosophy of the Middle East: the great sweep of Christianity, Islam and Judaism, as well as their ancient roots.

Kahlil Gibran's songs were of the earth; he loved his fellow man, to whom he carried the torch of freedom for all peoples alike:

"I love you, my Brother," he wrote, "wherever you are, whether you kneel in your church, worship in your synagogue or pray in your mosque."

Gibran's essays, poems and stories are salted with nuggets of wisdom; thus his writing, although simple, is unique and immortal. Within the covers of this work there is a collection of those nuggets, reflecting his philosophy and his unique expression. For example, in a love story, he wrote:

"The first kiss is the beginning of the Song of Life. It is a word uttered by four lips proclaiming the heart as a throne and love as a king. It is the first flower at the tip of the branch of the tree of life."

Writing of government, he urged, long before John F. Kennedy was to repeat his words: "Ask not what your country can do for you, but ask what you can do for your country."

Of tyrants, he wrote: "You may chain my hands, you may shackle my feet; you may even throw me into a dark prison; but you shall not enslave my thinking, because it is free."

As a young man in Lebanon, Kahlil Gibran loved a beautiful girl, but her parents refused their permission for marriage because of Kahlil's poverty. Later, through letters they exchanged, Gibran came to love another woman, but he was too poor and too ill to travel to Lebanon to marry her. Yet the paradox is that, though Gibran lost the two loves of his life because of his poverty, his books have earned more than two million dollars in royalties.

Gibran lived all his mature life in a small, fourth-floor walk-up studio in New York but he dreamed always of returning to the beautiful mountains of Lebanon, the homeland of his heart which he described thus:

"Lebanon, among Western poets, is an imaginary place, whose real existence vanished with the passing of David, Solomon and the Prophets, as the Garden of Eden was hidden through the fall of Adam and Eve.

Lebanon is a poetical expression and not the name of a mountain."

And:

"Spring is beautiful everywhere, but it is more than beautiful in Lebanon. Spring is the spirit of an unknown God speeding through the world, which, as it reaches Lebanon, pauses, because now it is as at home with the souls of the Prophets and Kings hovering over the land, chanting with the brooks of Judea the eternal Psalms of Solomon, renewing with the Cedars of Lebanon memories of an ancient glory."

The body of Kahlil Gibran now rests in the shadow of the Holy Cedars, his soul, as his Spring in Lebanon, hovering and chanting, in his own words:

"The river continues on its way to the sea, broken the wheel of the mill or not."

JOSEPH SHEBAN

A

ACTION

A little knowledge that *acts* is worth infinitely more than much knowledge that is idle.
WM-ST-63

Believing is a fine thing, but placing those beliefs into execution is a test of strength. Many are those who talk like the roar of the sea, but their lives are shallow and stagnant, like the rotting marshes. Many are those who lift their heads above the mountain tops, but their spirits remain dormant in the obscurity of the caverns.
SH-T-17

ADOLESCENCE

It is said that unsophistication makes a man empty and that emptiness makes him carefree. It may be true among those who were born dead and who exist like frozen corpses; but the sensitive boy who feels much and knows little is the most unfortunate creature under the sun, because he is torn by two forces. The first force elevates him and shows him the beauty of existence through a cloud of dreams; the second ties him down to the earth and fills his eyes with dust and overpowers him with fears and darkness.
BW-ST-18

ADVICE

He who does not seek advice is a fool. His folly blinds him to Truth and makes him evil, stubborn, and a danger to his fellow man.
WM-ST-67

AFFECTION

The heart's affections are divided like the branches of the cedar tree; if the tree loses one strong branch, it will suffer but it does not die. It will pour all its vitality into the next branch so that it will grow and fill the empty place.

BW-ST-93

AGE

Seek ye counsel of the aged, for their eyes have looked on the faces of the years and their ears have hearkened to the voices of Life. Even if their counsel is displeasing to you, pay heed to them.

WM-ST-68

AMBITION

What good is there, pray thee tell me,
    In jostling through the crowd in life,
'Mid the argumental tumult,
    Protestation, and endless strife;

Mole-like burrowing in darkness,
    Grasping for the spider's thread,
Always thwarted in ambition,
    Until the living join the dead?

P-73

AMERICANS

The Americans are a mighty people who never give up or get tired or sleep or dream. If these people hate someone, they will kill him by negligence, and if they like or love a person, they will shower him with affection.

SP-ST-82

ANCESTRY

A man is not noble through ancestry;
How many noblemen are descendants of murderers?

MS-74

ANTHROPOMORPHISM

The mountains, trees, and rivers change their appearance with the vicissitudes of times and seasons, as a man changes with his experiences and emotions. The lofty poplar that resembles a bride in the daytime will look like a column of smoke in the evening; the huge rock that stands impregnable at noon will appear to be a miserable pauper at night, with earth for his bed and the sky for his cover; and the rivulet that we see glittering in the morning and hear singing the hymn of Eternity will, in the evening, turn to a stream of tears wailing like a mother bereft of her child.
BW-ST-78

APPEARANCE

The appearance of things changes according to the emotions, and thus we see magic and beauty in them, while the magic and beauty are really in ourselves.
BW-ST-51

> The purpose of the spirit in the
> Heart is concealed, and by outer
> Appearance cannot be judged.
> T-372

ART

Art must be a direct communication between the artist's imagination and that of the looker. For that reason, I avoid, so much as possible, busying the looker's eye with too many details in order that his imagination may roam wide and far. As to the physical molds, art is forced to create for expressing itself; they must be beautiful molds. Otherwise, art defeats its purpose.
KG-P-102

Is it really God that created Man, or is it the opposite? Imagination is the only creator, its nearest and clearest

manifestation is Art; yes, art is life, life is art; all else is
trite and empty in comparison.
KG-P-97

Art is one step from the visibly known toward the
unknown.
MS-71

ARTIST
I should be a traitor to my art if I were to borrow my
sitter's eyes. The face is a marvelous mirror that reflects
most faithfully the innermost of the soul; the artist's
business is to see that and portray it; otherwise he is not
fit to be called an artist.
KG-P-97

AUTHORITY
Selfishness, my brother, is the cause of blind superiority, and superiority creates clanship, and clanship
creates authority which leads to discord and subjugation.
The soul believes in the power of knowledge and
justice over dark ignorance; it denies the authority that
supplies the swords to defend and strengthen ignorance
and oppression—that authority which destroyed Babylon and shook the foundation of Jerusalem and left Rome
in ruins. It is that which made people call criminals great
men; made writers respect their names; made historians
relate the stories of their inhumanity in manner of praise.
TL-T-8

B

BARRENNESS
How many flowers
Possess no fragrance from the day

Of their birth! How many clouds
Gather in the sky, barren of rain,
Dropping no pearls!
T-373

BEAUTY

Beauty is that which attracts your soul, and that which
loves to give and not to receive. When you meet Beauty,
you feel that the hands deep within your inner self are
stretched forth to bring her into the domain of your
heart. It is a magnificence combined of sorrow and joy; it
is the Unseen which you see, and the Vague which you
understand, and the Mute which you hear—it is the
Holy of Holies that begins in yourself and ends vastly
beyond your earthly imagination.
TL-T-407

Are you troubled by the many faiths that Mankind
professes? Are you lost in the valley of conflicting beliefs? Do you think that the freedom of heresy is less
burdensome than the yoke of submission, and the liberty
of dissent safer than the stronghold of acquiescence?

If such be the case, then make Beauty your religion,
and worship her as your godhead; for she is the visible,
manifest and perfect handiwork of God. Cast off those
who have toyed with godliness as if it were a sham,
joining together greed and arrogance; but believe instead
in the divinity of beauty that is at once the beginning of
your worship of Life, and the source of your hunger for
Happiness.

Do penance before Beauty, and atone for your sins, for
Beauty brings your heart closer to the throne of woman,
who is the mirror of your affections and the teacher of
your heart in the ways of Nature, which is your life's
home.
WM-ST-33

Only our spirits can understand beauty, or live and grow with it. It puzzles our minds; we are unable to describe it in words; it is a sensation that our eyes cannot see, derived from both the one who observes and the one who is looked upon. Real beauty is a ray which emanates from the holy of holies of the spirit, and illuminates the body, as life comes from the depths of the earth and gives color and scent to a flower.

BW-ST-34

Beauty is that harmony between joy and sorrow which begins in our holy of holies and ends beyond the scope of our imagination.

KG-P-93

Beauty is not in the face;
Beauty is a light in the heart.

MS-75

BEING

It is impossible for the mirror of the soul to reflect in the imagination anything which does not stand before it. It is impossible for the calm lake to show in its depth the figure of any mountain or the picture of any tree or cloud that does not exist close by the lake. It is impossible for the light to throw upon the earth a shadow of an object that has no being. Nothing can be seen, heard, or otherwise sensed unless it has actual *being*.

SH-T-149

BELIEVER

When you *know* a thing, you *believe* it, and the true believer sees with his *spiritual discernment* that which the surface investigator cannot see with the eyes of his head, and he understands through his *inner* thought that which the outside examiner cannot understand with his demanding, acquired process of thought.

The believer acquaints himself with the sacred realities through deep senses different from those used by others. A believer looks upon his senses as a great wall surrounding him, and when he walks upon the path he says, "This city has no exit, but it is perfect within." The believer lives for all the days and the nights and the unfaithful live but a few hours.
SH-T-149

BODY
He who endeavours to cleave the body from the spirit, or the spirit from the body, is directing his heart away from truth. The flower and its fragrance are one, and the blind who deny the colour and the image of the flower, believing that it possesses only a fragrance vibrating the ether, are like those with pinched nostrils who believe that flowers are naught but pictures and colours, possessing no fragrance.
SH-T-139

Life is naked. A nude body is the truest and noblest symbol of life. If I draw a mountain as a heap of human forms and paint a waterfall in the shape of tumbling human bodies, it is because I see in the mountain a heap of living things, and in the waterfall a precipitate current of life.
KG-P-102

BOSTON
This city was called in the past the city of science and art, but today it is the city of traditions. The souls of its inhabitants are petrified; even their thoughts are old and worn-out. The strange thing about this city is that the petrified is always proud and boastful, and the worn-out and old holds its chin high.
SP-ST-53

BOUNTY

An eternal hunger for love and beauty is my desire; I know now that those who possess bounty alone are naught but miserable, but to my spirit the sighs of lovers are more soothing than music of the lyre.
T-413

BRAVERY

Bravery is a volcano; the seed of wavering does not grow on its crater.
MS-72

BROTHERHOOD

I love you because you are weak before the strong oppressor, and poor before the greedy rich. For these reasons I shed tears and comfort you; and from behind my tears I see you embraced in the arms of Justice, smiling and forgiving your persecutors. You are my brother and I love you.
TL-T-7

I love you, my brother, whoever you are — whether you worship in your church, kneel in your temple, or pray in your mosque. You and I are all children of one faith, for the divers paths of religion are fingers of the loving hand of one Supreme Being, a hand extended to all, offering completeness of spirit to all, eager to receive all.
WM-ST-69

C

CHAINS

Not everyone in chains is subdued;
At times, a chain is greater than a necklace.
MS-74

CHARITY
>The coin which you drop into
>The withered hand stretching toward
>You is the only golden chain that
>Binds your rich heart to the
>Loving heart of God. . . .
>SH-T-345

CHATTER
I abstain from the people who consider insolence, bravery and tenderness cowardice. And I abstain from those who consider chatter wisdom and silence ignorance.
MS-71

CHILDHOOD
The things which the child loves remain in the domain of the heart until old age. The most beautiful thing in life is that our souls remain hovering over the places where we once enjoyed ourselves.
SP-ST-27

CHURCHES
Oh Jesus, they have built these churches for the sake of their own glory, and embellished them with silk and melted gold. . . . They left the bodies of Thy chosen poor wrapped in tattered raiment in the cold night. . . . They filled the sky with the smoke of burning candles and incense and left the bodies of Thy faithful worshippers empty of bread. . . . They raised their voices with hymns of praise, but deafened themselves to the cry and moan of the widows and orphans.

Come again, O Living Jesus, and drive the vendors of Thy faith from Thy sacred temple, for they have turned it into a dark cave where vipers of hypocrisy and falsehood crawl and abound.
SH-T-81

CITIZENSHIP

What is it to be a good citizen?

It is to acknowledge the other person's rights before asserting your own, but always to be conscious of your own.

It is to create the useful and the beautiful with your own hands, and to admire what others have created in love and with faith.

It is to create the useful and the beautiful with you own hands, and to admire what others have created in love and with faith.

It is to produce by labor and only by labor and to spend less than you have produced that your children may not be dependent upon the state for support when you are no more.
MS-35

CITY

Oh people of the noisome city, who are living in darkness, hastening toward misery, preaching falsehood, and speaking with stupidity . . . until when shall you remain ignorant? Until when shall you abide in the filth of life and continue to desert its gardens? Why wear your tattered robes of narrowness while the silk raiment of Nature's beauty is fashioned for you? The lamp of wisdom is dimming; it is time to furnish it with oil. The house of true fortune is being destroyed; it is time to rebuild it and guard it. The thieves of ignorance have stolen the treasure of your peace; it is time to retake it!
TL-T-403

CIVILIZATION

The misery of our Oriental nations is the misery of the world, and what you call *civilization* in the West is naught

but another spectre of the many phantoms of tragic deception.
SH-T-25

Inventions and discoveries are but amusement and comfort for the body when it is tired and weary. The conquest of distance and the victory over the seas are but false fruit which do not satisfy the soul, nor nourish the heart, neither lift the spirit, for they are afar from nature. And those structures and theories which man calls knowledge and art are naught except shackles and golden chains which man drags, and he rejoices with their glittering reflections and ringing sounds. They are strong cages whose bars man commenced fabricating ages ago, unaware that he was building from the inside, and that he would soon become his own prisoner to eternity.
SH-T-26

CLERGYMAN

The clergyman erects his temple upon the graves and bones of the devoted worshippers.
SR-T-269

CONCEALMENT

Conceal your passion; your sickness is also your medicine because love to the soul is as wine in a glass— what you see is liquid, what is hidden is its spirit. . . .

Conceal your troubles; then, should the seas roar and the skies fall, you will be safe.
MS-76

CONSCIENCE

Conscience is a just but weak judge. Weakness leaves it powerless to execute its judgment.
TM-ST-118

CONTENTMENT

Be not satisfied with partial contentment, for he who engulfs the spring of life with one empty jar will depart with two full jars.
SH-T-136

Fortune craves not Contentment, for it is an earthly hope, and its desires are embraced by union with objects, while Contentment is naught but heartfelt.
TL-T-92

CONTRADICTION

Contradiction is a lower degree of intelligence.
MS-72

COUNSEL

My brothers, seek counsel of one another, for therein lies the way out of error and futile repentance. The wisdom of the many is your shield against tyranny. For when we turn to one another for counsel we reduce the number of our enemies.
WM-ST-67

My soul is my counsel and has taught me to give ear to the voices which are neither created by tongues nor uttered by throats.

Before my soul became my counsel, I was dull, and weak of hearing, reflecting only upon the tumult and the cry. But, now, I can listen to silence with serenity and can hear in the silence the hymns of ages chanting exaltation to the sky and revealing the secrets of eternity.
MS-V

COUNTRY LIFE

We who live amid the excitements of the city know nothing of the life of the mountain villagers. We are swept into the current of urban existence, until we forget

the peaceful rhythms of simple country life, reap in autumn, rest in winter, imitating nature in all her cycles. We are wealthier than the villagers in silver or gold, but they are richer in spirit. What we sow we reap not; they reap what they sow. We are slaves of gain, and they the children of contentment. Our draught from the cup of life is mixed with bitterness and despair, fear and weariness; but they drink the pure nectar of life's fulfillment.
TM-ST-53

COURAGE
The spirit who has seen the spectre of death cannot be scared by the faces of thieves; the soldier who has seen the swords glittering over his head and streams of blood under his feet does not care about rocks thrown at him by the children on the streets.
BW-ST-106

COURSER
My soul, living is like a courser of the night; the swifter its flight, the nearer the dawn.
WM-ST-69

CREEDS
People's creeds come forth, then perish
Like the shadows in the night.
P-46

CRIMINAL
For the Criminal who is weak and poor the
Narrow cell of death awaits; but
Honour and glory await the rich who
Conceal their crimes behind their
Gold and silver and inherited glory.
T-364

108 THE WISDOM

D

DARKNESS

God has bestowed upon you intelligence and knowledge. Do not extinguish the lamp of Divine Grace and do not let the candle of wisdom die out in the darkness of lust and error. For a wise man approaches with his torch to light up the path of mankind.
WM-ST-62

DEATH

Man is like the foam of the sea, that floats upon the surface of the water. When the wind blows, it vanishes, as if it had never been. Thus are our lives blown away by Death.
WM-ST-31

The Reality of Life is Life itself, whose beginning is not in the womb, and whose ending is not in the grave. For the years that pass are naught but a moment in eternal life; and the world of matter and all in it is but a dream compared to the awakening which we call the terror of Death.
WM-ST-32

The soul is an embryo in the body of
Man, and the day of death is the
Day of awakening, for it is the
Great era of labour and the rich
Hour of creation.
T-373

Death is an ending to the son of
The earth, but to the soul it is
The start, the triumph of life.
T-374

Death removes but the
Touch, and not the awareness of

All good. And he who has lived
One spring or more possesses the
Spiritual life of one who has
Lived a score of springs.
T-375

A child in the womb, no sooner born than returned to
the earth—such is the fate of man, the fate of nations and
of the sun, the moon, and the stars.
S

DESPAIR
Despair is an ebb for every flow in the heart; it's a mute
affection.
SP-ST-57

Despair weakens our sight and closes our ears. We can
see nothing but spectres of doom, and can hear only the
beating of our agitated hearts.
BW-ST-98

DESPOT
The ignorant nations arrest their good men and turn
them into their despots; and a country, ruled by a tyrant,
persecutes those who try to free the people from the yoke
of slavery.
SR-T-274

DESTINY
Man possesses a destiny
Which impels his thoughts and
Actions and words, and that not
Sufficing, directs his footsteps to
A place of unwilling abode.
T-376

DESTRUCTION
I am indeed a fanatic and I am inclined toward destruction as well as construction. There is hatred in my heart

for that which my detractors sanctify, and love for that which they reject. And if I could uproot certain customs, beliefs, and traditions of the people, I would do so without hesitation. When they said my books were poison, they were speaking truth about themselves, for what I say is poison to them. But they falsified when they said I mix honey into it, for I apply the poison full strength and pour it from transparent glass. Those who call me an idealist becalmed in clouds are the very ones who turn away from the transparent glass they call poison, knowing that their stomachs cannot digest it.
TM-ST-91

DEVIL

Remember, one just man causes the Devil greater affliction than a million blind believers.
WM-ST-62

DICHOTOMY

He who does not see the angels and devils in the beauty and malice of life will be far removed from knowledge, and his spirit will be empty of affection.
BW-ST-20

DIVINITY

Remember that Divinity is the true self of Man. It cannot be sold for gold; neither can it be heaped up as are the riches of the world today. The rich man has cast off his Divinity, and has clung to his gold. And the young today have forsaken their Divinity and pursue self-indulgence and pleasure.
WM-ST-65

DOCTORS

Since the beginning of the world, the doctors have been trying to save the people from their disorders; some

used knives, while others used potions, but pestilence spread hopelessly. It is my wish that the patient would content himself with remaining in his filthy bed, meditating his long-continued sores; but instead, he stretches his hands from under the robe and clutches at the neck of each who comes to visit him, choking him to death. What irony it is! The evil patient kills the doctor, and then closes his eyes and says within himself, "He was a great physician."
SH-T-23

E

EARTH

The earth that opens wide her mouth to swallow man and his works is the redeemer of our souls from bondage to our bodies.
WM-ST-79

EAST AND WEST

The West is not higher than the East, nor is the West lower than the East, and the difference that stands between the two is not greater than the difference between the tiger and the lion. There is a just and perfect law that I have found behind the exterior of society, which equalizes misery, prosperity, and ignorance; it does not prefer one nation to another, nor does it oppress one tribe in order to enrich another.
SH-T-25

EDIFICE

What man is capable of leaving an edifice on whose construction he has spent all his life, even though that edifice is his own prison? It is difficult to get rid of it in one day.
SP-ST-83

EQUALITY

> One hour devoted to mourning and lamenting the
> Stolen equality of the weak is nobler than a
> Century filled with greed and usurpation.
> TL-T-412

ETERNITY

Each thing that exists remains forever, and the very existence of existence is proof of its eternity. But without that realization, which is the knowledge of perfect being, man would never know whether there was existence or non-existence. If eternal existence is altered, then it must become more beautiful; and if it disappears, it must return with more sublime image; and if it sleeps, it must dream of a better awakening, for it is ever greater upon its rebirth.
SH-T-143

> Only those return to Eternity
> Who on earth seek out Eternity.
> TL-T-410

EVOLUTION

The law of evolution has a severe and oppressive countenance and those of limited or fearful mind dread it; but its principles are just, and those who study them become enlightened. Through its Reason men are raised above themselves and can approach the sublime.
TM-ST-99

EXCESS

In battling evil, excess is good; for he who is moderate in announcing the truth is presenting half-truth. He conceals the other half out of fear of the people's wrath.
TM-ST-96

I will not be surprised if the "thinkers" say of me, "He

is a man of excess who looks upon life's seamy side and reports nothing but gloom and lamentation."
TM-ST-95

EXILE

He who does not prefer exile to slavery is not free by any measure of freedom, truth and duty.
SR-T-224

EYE

I feel pity toward those who admit of the eternity of the elements of which the eye is made, but at the same time doubt the eternity of the various objects of sight which employ the eye as a medium.
SH-T-144

Man's eye is a magnifier; it shows him the earth much larger than it is.
MS-71

F

FACE

A look which reveals inward stress adds more beauty to the face, no matter how much tragedy and pain it bespeaks; but the face which, in silence, does not announce hidden mysteries is not beautiful, regardless of the symmetry of its features. The cup does not entice our lips unless the wine's color is seen through the transparent crystal.
BW-ST-67

FAITH

God has made many doors opening into truth which He opens to all who knock upon them with hands of faith.
SH-T-138

FAME

There is something in our life which is nobler and more supreme than fame; and this *something* is the great deed that invokes fame.
SP-ST-32

FATE

Circumstances drive us on
In narrow paths by Kismet hewn.

For Fate has ways we cannot change,
While weakness preys upon our Will;
We bolster with excuse the self,
And help that Fate ourselves to kill.
P-74

Life takes us up and bears us from one place to another; Fate moves us from one point to another. And we, caught up between these twain, hear dreadful voices and see only that which stands as a hindrance and obstacle in our path.
WM-ST-46

FEAR OF DEATH

Fear of death is a delusion
Harbored in the breast of sages;
He who lives a single Springtime
Is like one who lives for ages.
P-71

FERTILITY

The body is a womb to soul
In which it dwells until full term,
When it ascends once more to soar,
While womb again recedes to germ.
P-67

FIRST LOVE

Every young man remembers his first love and tries to recapture that strange hour, the memory of which changes his deepest feeling and makes him so happy in spite of all the bitterness of its mystery.
BW-ST-12

FLOWERS

The flowers of the field are the children of sun's affection and nature's love; and the children of men are the flowers of love and compassion.
BW-ST-122

FOLLY

The fool sees naught but folly; and the madman only madness. Yesterday I asked a foolish man to count the fools among us. He laughed and said, "This is too hard a thing to do, and it will take too long. Were it not better to count only the wise?"
WM-ST-55

I once heard a learned man say, "Every evil has its remedy, except folly. To reprimand an obstinate fool or to preach to a dolt is like writing upon the water. Christ healed the blind, the halt, the palsied, and the leprous. But the fool He could not cure."
WM-ST-56

FORBIDDEN

When you behold a man turning aside from
Things forbidden that bring
Abysmal crime to self, look
Upon him with eyes of love, for
He is a preserver of God in him.
T-372

FREEDOM

I love freedom, and my love for true
Freedom grew with my growing knowledge
Of the people's surrender to slavery
And oppression and tyranny, and of
Their submission to the horrible idols
Erected by the past ages and polished
By the parched lips of the slaves.
But I love those slaves with my love
For freedom, for they blindly kissed
The jaws of ferocious beasts in calm
And blissful unawareness, feeling not
The venom of the smiling vipers, and
Unknowingly digging their graves with
Their own fingers.
  SH-T-100

Dying for Freedom is nobler than living in
The shadow of weak submission, for
He who embraces death with the sword
Of Truth in his hand will eternalize
With the Eternity of Truth, for Life
Is weaker than Death and Death is
Weaker than Truth.
  SH-T-342

The free on earth builds of his strife
    A prison for his own duress,
When he is freed from his own kin,
    Is slave to thought and love's caress.
  P-55

Life without Freedom is like a body without a soul, and
Freedom without Thought is like a confused spirit. . . .
Life, Freedom, and Thought are three-in-one, and are
everlasting and never pass away.
  TM-ST-62

Freedom bids us to her table where we may partake of her savory food and rich wine; but when we sit down at her board, we eat ravenously and glut ourselves.
WM-ST-47

You may chain my hands and shackle my feet; you may even throw me into a dark prison, but you shall not enslave my thinking because it is free.
S

FRIENDSHIP
Friendship with the ignorant is as foolish as arguing with a drunkard.
WM-ST-62

G

GENTLENESS
> The gentleness of some is like
>   A polished shell with silky feel,
> Lacking the precious pearl within
>   Oblivious of the brother's weal.

> When you shall meet one who is strong
>   And gentle too, pray feast your eyes;
> For he is glorious to behold,
>   The blind can see his qualities.
> P-59

GIANTS
We live in an era whose humblest men are becoming greater than the greatest men of preceding ages. What once preoccupied our minds is now of no consequence. The veil of indifference covers it. The beautiful dreams that once hovered in our consciousness have been dis-

persed like mist. In their place are giants moving like tempests, raging like seas, breathing like volcanoes.

What destiny will the giants bring the world at the end of their struggles? . . .

What will be the destiny of your country and mine? Which giant shall seize the mountains and valleys that produced us and reared us and made us men and women before the face of the sun? . . .

Which one of you people does not ponder day and night on the fate of the world under the rule of the giants intoxicated with the tears of widows and orphans?
TM-ST-97

GLORY

> One hour devoted to the pursuit of Beauty
> And Love is worth a full century of glory
> Given by the frightened weak to the strong.
> TL-T-411

I have seen you, my brother, sitting upon the throne of glory, and around you stood your people acclaiming your majesty, and singing praises of your great deeds, extolling your wisdom, and gazing upon you as though in the presence of a prophet, their spirits exulting even to the canopy of heaven.

And as you gazed upon your subjects, I saw in your face the marks of happiness and power and triumph, as if you were the soul of their body.

But when I looked again, behold I found you alone in your loneliness, standing by the side of your throne, an exile stretching his hand in every direction, as if pleading for mercy and kindness from invisible ghosts—begging for shelter, even such as has naught in it but warmth and friendliness.
WM-ST-42

GOD

Man has worshipped his own self since the beginning, calling that self by appropriate titles, until now, when he employs the word "God" to mean that same self.
SH-T-391

Most religions speak of God in the masculine gender. To me He is as much a mother as He is a Father. He is both the father and the mother in one; and Woman is the God-Mother. The God-Father may be reached through the mind or the imagination. But the God-Mother can be reached through the heart only—through love. And Love is that holy wine which the gods distill from their hearts and pour into the hearts of men. Those only taste it pure and divine whose hearts have been cleansed of all the animal lusts. For clean hearts to be drunk with love is to be drunk with God. Those, on the other hand, who drink it mixed with the wines of earthly passions taste but the orgies of devils in Hell.
KG-P-94

It were wiser to speak less of God, Whom we cannot understand, and more of each other, whom we may understand. Yet I would have you know that we are the breath and the fragrance of God. We are God, in leaf, in flower, and oftentimes in fruit.
MS-43

GOLD

Gold leads into gold, then into restlessness, and finally into crushing misery.
TL-T-403

The life that the rich man spends in heaping up gold is in truth like the life of the worms in the grave. It is a sign of fear.
WM-ST-65

GOOD

> The good in man should freely flow,
>   As evil lives beyond the grave;
> While Time with fingers moves the pawns
>   Awhile, then breaks the knight and knave.

P-41

GOVERNOR

Are you a governor looking down on those you govern, never stirring abroad except to rifle their pockets or to exploit them for your own profit? If so, you are like tares upon the threshing floor of the nation.

Are you a devoted servant who loves the people and is ever watchful over their welfare, and zealous for their success? If so, you are a blessing in the granaries of the land.

WM-ST-35

H

HANDS

How small is the life of the person who places his hands between his face and the world, seeing naught but the narrow lines of his hands!

SH-T-150

HAPPINESS

> I sought happiness in my solitude, and
> As I drew close to her I heard my soul
> Whisper into my heart, saying, "The
> Happiness you seek is a virgin, born
> And reared in the depths of each heart,
> And she emerges not from her birthplace."
> And when I opened my heart to find her,
> I discovered in its domain only her

Mirror and her cradle and her raiment,
And happiness was not there.
SH-T-101

Happiness is a myth we seek,
    If manifested surely irks;
Like river speeding to the plain,
    On its arrival slows and murks.

For man is happy only in
    His aspiration to the heights;
When he attains his goal, he cools
    And longs for other distant flights.
P-57

Happiness on earth is but a fleet,
Passing ghost, which man craves
At any cost in gold or time. And
When the phantom becomes the
Reality, man soon wearies of it.
T-371

HARDSHIP
    Braving obstacles and hardships is nobler than retreat
to tranquility. The butterfly that hovers around the lamp
until it dies is more admirable than the mole that lives in a
dark tunnel.
BW-ST-89

HATE
    I use hate as a weapon to defend myself; had I been
strong, I would never have needed that kind of weapon.
MS-72

HEAVEN
    The angels keep count of every tear shed by Sorrow;
and they bring to the ears of the spirits hovering in the
heavens of the Infinite each song of Joy wrought from
our affections.

There, in the world to come, we shall see and feel all the vibrations of our feelings and the motions of our hearts. We shall understand the meaning of the divinity within us, whom we contemn because we are prompted by Despair.
WM-ST-32

HELL

> Hell is not in torture;
> Hell is in an empty heart.
> MS-74

HERD

> Say not, "There goes a learned man"
>   Nor, "There a chieftain dignified."
> The best of men are in the herd,
>   And heed the shepherd as their guide.
> P-41

HONORS

> Honors are but false delusions
>   Like the froth upon the wave.
>
> Should the almond spray its blossoms
>   On the turf around its feet,
> Never will it claim a lordship,
>   Nor disdain the grass to greet.
> P-55

HOPE

> Hope is found not in the forest,
>   Nor the wild portray despair;
> Why should forest long for portions
>   When the ALL is centered there?
>
> Should one search the forest hopeful,
>   When *all nature* is the Aim?

For to hope is but an ailment,
So are station, wealth and fame.
P-58

HUMANITY

Humanity is the spirit of the Supreme Being on earth, and that humanity is standing amidst ruins, hiding its nakedness behind tattered rags, shedding tears upon hollow cheeks, and calling for its children with pitiful voice. But the children are busy singing their clan's anthem; they are busy sharpening the swords and cannot hear the cry of their mothers.

Humanity is the spirit of the Supreme Being on earth, and that Supreme Being preaches love and good-will. But the people ridicule such teachings. The Nazarene Jesus listened, and crucifixion was his lot; Socrates heard the voice and followed it, and he too fell victim in body. The followers of The Nazarene and Socrates are the followers of Deity, and since people will not kill them, they deride them, saying, "Ridicule is more bitter than killing."
TL-T-5

My soul preached to me and showed me that I am neither more than the pygmy, nor less than the giant.

Ere my soul preached to me, I looked upon humanity as two men: one weak, whom I pitied, and the other strong, whom I followed or resisted in defiance.

But now I have learned that I was as both are and made from the same elements. My origin is their origin, my conscience is their conscience, my contention is their contention, and my pilgrimage is their pilgrimage.

If they sin, I am also a sinner. If they do well, I take pride in their well-doing. If they rise, I rise with them. If they stay inert, I share their slothfulness.
TM-ST-31

HUNGER

A hungry man in a desert will not refuse to eat dry bread if Heaven does not shower him with manna and quails.
BW-ST-40

HUSBAND

Are you a husband who regards the wrongs he has committed as lawful, but those of his wife as unlawful? If so, you are like those extinct savages who lived in caves and covered their nakedness with hides.

Or are you a faithful companion, whose wife is ever at his side, sharing his every thought, rapture, and victory? If so, you are as one who at dawn walks at the head of a nation toward the high noon of justice, reason and wisdom.
WM-ST-35

I

IDEAS

How blind is the one who fancies and plans a matter in all true form and angles, and when he cannot prove it completely with superficial measurement and word proofs, believes that his idea and imagination were empty objects! But if he contemplates with sincerity and meditates upon these happenings, he will understand with conviction that his idea is as much a reality as is the bird of the sky, but that it is not yet crystallized, and that the idea is a segment of knowledge that cannot be proved with figures and words, for it is too high and too spacious to be imprisoned at that moment; too deeply imbedded in the spiritual to submit yet to the real.
SH-T-148

Every beauty and greatness in this world is created by a single thought or emotion inside a man. Every thing we see today, made by past generations, was, before its appearance, a thought in the mind of a man or an impulse in the heart of a woman. The revolutions that shed so much blood and turned men's minds toward liberty were the idea of one man who lived in the midst of thousands of men. The devastating wars which destroyed empires were a thought that existed in the mind of an individual. The supreme teachings that changed the course of humanity were the ideas of a man whose genius separated him from his environment. A single thought built the Pyramids, founded the glory of Islam, and caused the burning of the library at Alexandria.
BW-ST-49

IGNORANCE

In the house of Ignorance there is no mirror in which to view your soul.
SH-T-87

During the ebb, I wrote a line upon the sand,
Committing to it all that is in my soul and mind;
I returned at the tide to read it and to ponder upon it,
I found naught upon the seashore but my ignorance.
MS-39

ILLNESS

I have found pleasure in being ill. This pleasure differs with its effect from any other pleasure. I have found a sort of tranquility that makes me love illness. The sick man is safe from people's strife, demands, dates and appointments . . . I have found another kind of enjoyment through illness which is more important and unmeasurable. I have found that I am closer to abstract things in my sickness than in health.
SP-ST-84

I have pleasure in being ill. This pleasure differs with its effect from other pleasure. I have found a sort of tranquility that makes me love illness. The sick man is safe from people's strife, demands, dates and appointments, excess of talking and ringing of telephones. . . . I have found that I am closer to abstract things in my sickness than in health. When I lay my head and close my eyes and lose myself to the world, I find myself flying like a bird over serene valleys and forests, wrapped in a gentle veil. I see myself close to those whom my heart has loved, calling and talking to them, but without anger and with the same feelings they feel and the same thoughts they think. They lay their hands now and then upon my forehead to bless me.

SP-P-34

ILLUSION

> Man's will is a floating shadow
> In the mind he conceives,
> And the rights of mankind pass and
> Perish like the Autumn leaves.

P-51

IMAGINATION

Thoughts have a higher dwelling place than the visible world, and its skies are not clouded by sensuality. Imagination finds a road to the realm of the gods, and there man can glimpse that which is to be after the soul's liberation from the world of substance.

TM-ST-74

With one leap it [the imagination] would reach the core of life, divest it of all excrescences, then burn these excrescences and fling their ashes into the eyes of those who brought them into being. So must all imaginations be.

KG-P-24

IMITATION

> The people of the city feign great
> Wisdom and knowledge, but their
> Fancy remains false forever, for
> They are but experts of imitation.
> It gives them pride to calculate
> That a barter will bring no loss
> Or gain. The idiot imagines himself
> A king and no power can alter his
> Great thoughts and dreams. The
> Proud fool mistakes his mirror for
> The sky, and his shadow for a
> Moon that gleams high from the
> Heavens.
> T-368

IMMORTALITY

> Death on earth, to son of earth
>   Is final, but to him who is
> Ethereal, it is but the start
>   Of triumph certain to be his.

> If one embraces dawn in dreams,
>   He is immortal! Should he sleep
> His long night through, he surely fades
>   Into a sea of slumber deep.

> For he who closely hugs the ground
>   When wide awake will crawl 'til end.
> And death, like sea, who braves it light
>   Will cross it. Weighted will descend.
> P-70

If I did not covet immortality, I would never have learned the song which has been sung through all of time.

Rather, I would have been a suicide, nothing remaining of me except my ashes hidden within the tomb. . . .

Life is a darkness which ends as in the sunburst of the day.

The yearning of my heart tells me there is peace in the grave.

If some fool tells you the soul perishes like the body and that which dies never returns, tell him the flower perishes but the seed remains and lies before us as the secret of life everlasting.
MS-58

IMPERMANENCE

Mankind is like verses written
Upon the surface of the rills.
P-35

INDICTMENT

I will gladly exchange my outcries for cheerful laughter, speak eulogies instead of indictments, replace excess with moderation, provided you show me a just governor, a lawyer of integrity, a religious hierarch who practices what he preaches, a husband who looks upon his wife with the same eyes as he looks upon himself.
TM-ST-96

INFINITE

We are naught but frail atoms in the heavens of the infinite; and we cannot but obey and surrender to the will of Providence.

If we love, our love is neither from us, nor is it for us. If we rejoice, our joy is not in us, but in Life itself. If we suffer, our pain lies not in our wounds, but in the very heart of Nature.
WM-ST-23

INHERITANCE

The man who acquires his wealth by inheritance builds his mansion with the weak poor's money.
SR-T-269

INTOXICATION
> The human turns to drugging,
> As to nursing from the breast;
> Coming to the age of weaning
> Only when he's put to rest.
>
> P-39

ISLAND

Life is an island in an ocean of loneliness, an island whose rocks are hopes, whose trees are dreams, whose flowers are solitude, and whose brooks are thirst.

Your life, my fellow men, is an island separated from all other islands and regions. No matter how many are the ships that leave your shores for other climes, no matter how many are the fleets that touch your coast, you remain a solitary island, suffering the pangs of loneliness and yearning for happiness. You are unknown to your fellow men and far removed from their sympathy and understanding.

WM-ST-41

J

JESUS

Humanity looks upon Jesus the Nazarene as a poor-born Who suffered misery and humiliation with all of the weak. And He is pitied, for Humanity believes He was crucified painfully. . . . And all that Humanity offers to Him is crying and wailing and lamentation. For centuries Humanity has been worshipping weakness in the person of the Saviour.

The Nazarene was not weak! He was strong and is strong! But the people refuse to heed the true meaning of strength.

SH-T-154

Jesus came not from the heart of the circle of Light to destroy the homes and build upon their ruins the convents and monasteries. He did not persuade the strong man to become a monk or a priest, but He came to send forth upon this earth a new spirit, with power to crumble the foundation of any monarchy built upon human bones and skulls. . . . He came to demolish the majestic palaces, constructed upon the graves of the weak, and crush the idols, erected upon the bodies of the poor. Jesus was not sent here to teach the people to build magnificent churches and temples amidst the cold wretched huts and dismal hovels. . . . He came to make the human heart a temple, and the soul an altar, and the mind a priest.
SH-T-155

Surely you have prayed enough to last you to the end of your days, and hence forth you shall not enter a church as a worshipper; for the Jesus you love so dearly is not found in churches. Many are the places of worship, but few indeed are those who worship in Spirit and in truth.
KG-P-19

JOURNALIST

Are you a journalist who sells his principles in the markets of slaves and who fattens on gossip and misfortune and crime? If so, you are like a ravenous vulture preying upon rotting carrion.
WM-ST-35

JUDGMENT

The learned man who has not judgment is like an unarmed soldier proceeding into battle. His wrath will poison the pure spring of the life of his community and he will be like the grain of aloes in a pitcher of pure water.
WM-ST-54

JUSTICE

> Justice on earth would cause the Jinn
>   To cry at misuse of the word,
> And were the dead to witness it,
>   They'd mock at fairness in this world.
>
> Yea, death and prison we mete out
>   To small offenders of the laws,
> While honor, wealth, and full respect
>   On greater pirates we bestow.
>
> To steal a flower we call mean,
>   To rob a field is chivalry;
> Who kills the body he must die,
>   Who kills the spirit he goes free.
>   P-47

What justice does authority display when it kills the killer? When it imprisons the robber? When it descends on a neighbouring country and slays its people? What does justice think of the authority under which a killer punishes the one who kills, and a thief sentences the one who steals?
   TL-T-9

When a man kills another man, the people say he is a murderer, but when the Emir kills him, the Emir is just. When a man robs a monastery, they say he is a thief, but when the Emir robs him of his life, the Emir is honourable. When a woman betrays her husband, they say she is an adulteress, but when the Emir makes her walk naked in the streets and stones her later, the Emir is noble. Shedding of blood is forbidden, but who made it lawful for the Emir? Stealing one's money is a crime, but taking away one's life is a noble act. Betrayal of a husband may be an ugly deed, but stoning of living souls is a beautiful sight. Shall we meet evil with evil and say this is the Law? Shall we fight corruption with greater corruption and say

this is the Rule? Shall we conquer crimes with more crimes and say this is Justice?
SR-T-315

The gifts which derive from justice are greater than those that spring from charity.
WM-ST-65

K

KIN
He who understands you is greater kin to you than your own brother. For even your own kindred may neither understand you nor know your true worth.
WM-ST-62

KINDNESS
From a sensitive woman's heart springs the happiness of mankind, and from the kindness of her noble spirit comes mankind's affection.
SR-T-262

> The kindness of the people is but an
> Empty shell containing no gem or
> Precious pearl. With two hearts do
> People live; a small one of deep
> Softness, the other of steel. And
> Kindness is too often a shield,
> And generosity too often a sword.
> T-367

KINGDOM OF HEAVEN
Vain are the beliefs and teachings that make man miserable, and false is the goodness that leads him into sorrow and despair, for it is man's purpose to be happy on this earth and lead the way to felicity and preach its gospel wherever he goes. He who does not see the king-

dom of heaven in this life will never see it in the coming
life. We came not into this life by exile, but we came as
innocent creatures of God, to learn how to worship the
holy and eternal spirit and seek the hidden secrets within
ourselves from the beauty of life.
SR-T-256

KINGDOMS
Humans are divided into different clans and tribes,
and belong to countries and towns. But I find myself a
stranger to all communities and belong to no settlement.
The universe is my country and the human family is my
tribe.
Men are weak, and it is sad that they divide among
themselves. The world is narrow and it is unwise to
cleave it into kingdoms, empires, and provinces.
TL-T-4

KNOWLEDGE
Learning follows various roads.
We note the start but not the end.
For Time and Fate must rule the course,
While we see not beyond the bend.

The best of knowledge is a dream
The gainer holds steadfast, uncowed
By ridicule, and moves serene,
Despised and lowly in the crowd.
P-52

L

LAW
What is Law? Who saw it coming with the sun from the
depths of heaven? What human saw the heart of God
and found its will or purpose? In what century did the

angels walk among the people and preach to them, saying, "Forbid the weak from enjoying life, and kill the
outlaws with the sharp edge of the sword, and step upon
the sinners with iron feet"?
SR-T-316

Are you a soldier compelled by the harsh law of man to
forsake wife and children, and go forth into the field of
battle for the sake of *Greed*, which your leaders mis-call
Duty?

Are you a prisoner, pent up in a dark dungeon for
some petty offense and condemned by those who seek to
reform man by corrupting him?

Are you a young woman on whom God has bestowed
beauty, but who has fallen prey to the base lust of the
rich, who deceived you and bought your body but not
your heart, and abandoned you to misery and distress?

If you are one of these, you are a martyr to man's law.
You are wretched, and your wretchedness is the fruit of
the iniquity of the strong and the injustice of the tyrant,
the brutality of the rich, and the selfishness of the lewd
and the covetous.
WM-ST-44

> Man is weak by his own hand, for he
> Has refashioned God's law into his own
> Confining manner of life, chaining
> Himself with the coarse irons of the
> Rules of society which he desired; and
> He is steadfast in refusing to be aware
> Of the great tragedy he has cast upon
> Himself and his children and their sons.
> Man has erected on this earth a prison
> Of quarrels from which he cannot now
> Escape, and misery is his voluntary lot.
> T-366

LAWS

People are saying that I am the enemy of just laws, of family ties and old tradition. Those people are telling the truth. I do not love man-made laws . . . I love the sacred and spiritual kindness which should be the source of every law upon the earth, for kindness is the shadow of God in man.
MS-V

Human society has yielded for seventy centuries to corrupted laws until it cannot understand the meaning of superior and eternal laws. . . . Spiritual disease is inherited from one generation to another until it becomes a part of the people, who look upon it, not as a disease, but as a natural gift, showered by God on Adam. If these people found someone free from the germs of this disease, they would think of him with shame and disgrace.
SP-P-31

LEARNING

Learning nourishes the seed but it gives you no seed of its own.
MS-72

Reason and learning are like body and soul. Without the body, the soul is nothing but empty wind. Without the soul, the body is but a senseless frame.

Reason without learning is like the untilled soil, or like the human body that lacks nourishment.
WM-ST-55

Learning is the only wealth tyrants cannot despoil. Only death can dim the lamp of knowledge that is within you. The true wealth of a nation lies not in its gold or silver but in its learning, wisdom, and in the uprightness of its sons.
WM-ST-61

LIARS

There are among the people murderers who have never committed murder, thieves who have never stolen and liars who have spoken nothing but the truth.
MS-72

LIBERTY

I walked lonely in the Valley of the Shadow of Life, where the past attempts to conceal itself in guilt, and the soul of the future folds and rests itself too long. There, at the edge of Blood and Tears River, which crawled like a poisonous viper and twisted like a criminal's dreams, I listened to the frightened whisper of the ghosts of slaves, and gazed at nothingness.

When midnight came and the spirits emerged from hidden places, I saw a cadaverous, dying spectre fall to her knees, gazing at the moon. I approached her, asking, "What is your name?"

"My name is Liberty," replied this ghastly shadow of a corpse.

And I inquired, "Where are your children?"

And Liberty, tearful and weak, gasped, "One died crucified, another died mad, and the third one is not yet born."

She limped away and spoke further, but the mist in my eyes and cries of my heart prevented sight or hearing.
SH-T-66

Everything on earth lives according to the law of nature, and from that law emerges the glory and joy of liberty; but man is denied this fortune, because he set for the God-given soul a limited and earthly law of his own. He made for himself strict rules. Man built a narrow and painful prison in which he secluded his affections and desires. He dug out a deep grave in which he buried his heart and its purpose. If an individual, through the dictates of his soul, declares his withdrawal from society and violates the law, his fellowmen will say he is a rebel worthy of exile, or an infamous creature worthy only of execution. Will man remain a slave of self-confinement until the end of the world? Or will he be freed by the passing of time and live in the Spirit for the Spirit? Will man insist upon staring downward and backward at the earth? Or will he turn his eyes toward the sun so he will not see the shadow of his body amongst the skulls and thorns?

SR-T-228

LIFE

Man struggles to find life outside himself, unaware that the life he is seeking is within him.

SH-T-144

Life is a woman bathing in the tears of her lovers and anointing herself with the blood of her victims. Her raiments are white days, lined with the darkness of night. She takes the human heart to lover, but denies herself in marriage.

> *Life is an enchantress*
> *Who seduces us with her beauty—*
> *But he who knows her wiles*
> *Will flee her enchantments.*
> WM-ST-85

How often I talked with Harvard professors, yet felt as if I were talking to a professor from Al-Azhar! How often I have conversed with some Bostonian ladies and heard them say things I used to hear from simple and ignorant old women in Syria! Life is one, Mikhail; it manifests itself in the villages of Lebanon as in Boston, New York, and San Francisco.

KG-P-37

LIGHT

The true light is that which emanates from within man, and reveals the secrets of the heart to the soul, making it happy and contented with life.

SR-T-255

LIMITATION

The person who is limited in heart and thought is inclined to love that which is limited in life, and the weak-sighted cannot see more than one cubit ahead upon the path he treads, nor more than one cubit of the wall upon which he rests his shoulder.

SH-T-129

LONGING

In the will of man there is a power of longing which turns the mist in ourselves into sun.

SP-ST-86

LOVE

The power to
Love is God's greatest gift to man,
For it never will be taken from the
Blessed one who loves.

SH-T-99

Love lies in the soul alone,
  Not in the body, and like wine
Should stimulate our better self
  To welcome gifts of Love Divine.

P-61

Man cannot reap love until after sad and revealing separation, and bitter patience, and desperate hardship.

TL-T-115

Yesterday I stood at the temple door interrogating the passersby about the mystery and merit of Love.

And before me passed an old man with an emaciated and melancholy face, who sighed and said:

"Love is a natural weakness bestowed upon us by the first man."

But a virile youth retorted:

"Love joins our present with the past and the future."

Then a woman with a tragic face sighed and said:

"Love is a deadly poison injected by black vipers, that crawl from the caves of hell. The poison seems fresh as dew and the thirsty soul eagerly drinks it; but after the first intoxication the drinker sickens and dies a slow death."

Then a beautiful, rosy-cheeked damsel smilingly said:

"Love is a wine served by the brides of Dawn which strengthens strong souls and enables them to ascend to the stars."

After her a black-robed, bearded man, frowning, said:

"Love is the blind ignorance with which youth begins and ends."

Another, smiling, declared:

"Love is a divine knowledge that enables men to see as much as the gods."

Then said a blind man, feeling his way with a cane:

"Love is a blinding mist that keeps the soul from discerning the secret of existence, so that the heart sees only trembling phantoms of desire among the hills, and hears only echoes of cries from voiceless valleys."

And a feeble ancient, dragging his feet like two rags, said, in quavering tones:

"Love is the rest of the body in the quiet of the grave, the tranquility of the soul in the depth of Eternity."

And a five-year-old child, after him, said laughing:

"Love is my father and mother, and no one knows Love save my father and mother."

And so, all who passed spoke of Love as the image of

their hopes and frustrations, leaving it a mystery as before.
TM-ST-88

Those whom Love has not chosen as followers do not hear when Love calls.
BW-ST-75

Love is the only flower that grows and blossoms without the aid of seasons.
BW-ST-54

Love is the only freedom in the world because it so elevates the spirit that the laws of humanity and the phenomena of nature do not alter its course.
BW-ST-35

Love passes by us, robed in meekness; but we flee from her in fear, or hide in the darkness; or else pursue her, to do evil in her name.
WM-ST-46

Love that comes between the naivete and awakening of youth satisfies itself with possessing, and grows with embraces. But Love which is born in the firmament's lap and has descended with the night's secrets is not contented with anything but Eternity and immortality; it does not stand reverently before anything except deity.
BW-ST-114

> If humanity were to
> Lead love's cavalcade to a bed of
> Faithless motive, then love there
> Would decline to abide. Love is a
> Beautiful bird, begging capture,
> But refusing injury.
> T-369

> Love,
> When sought out, is an ailment
> Between the flesh and the bone,

And only when youth has passed
Does the pain bring rich and
Sorrowful knowledge.
  T-369

Darkness may hide the trees and the flowers from the eyes but it cannot hide love from the soul.
  S

LUST

Beauty reveals itself to us as she sits on the throne of glory; but we approach her in the name of Lust, snatch off her crown of purity, and pollute her garment with our evil-doing.
  WM-ST-46

M

MADNESS

Madness is the first step towards unselfishness. Be mad and tell us what is behind the veil of "sanity." The purpose of life is to bring us closer to those secrets, and madness is the only means.
  SP-ST-62

MAIDEN

There is no affection purer and more soothing to the spirit than the one hidden in the heart of a maiden who awakens suddenly and fills her own spirit with heavenly music that makes her days like poets' dreams and her nights prophetic.
  SR-T-264

MANKIND

I love mankind and I love equally all
Three human kinds . . . the one who

Blasphemes life, the one who blesses
It, and the one who meditates upon it.
I love the first for his misery and
The second for his generosity and the
Third for his perception and peace.
SH-T-101

MARRIAGE

Marriage is the union of two divinities that a third might be born on earth. It is the union of two souls in a strong love for the abolishment of separateness. It is that higher unity which fuses the separate unities within the two spirits. It is the golden ring in a chain whose beginning is a glance, and whose ending is Eternity. It is the pure rain that falls from an unblemished sky to fructify and bless the fields of divine Nature.
WM-ST-50

MERCHANT

Are you a merchant, drawing advantage from the needs of the people, engrossing goods so as to resell them at an exorbitant price? If so, you are a reprobate; and it matters naught whether your home is a palace or a prison.

Or are you an honest man, who enables farmer and weaver to exchange their products, who mediates between buyer and seller, and through his just ways profits both himself and others?

If so, you are a righteous man; and it matters not whether you are praised or blamed.
WM-ST-34

MERCY

Do not be merciful, but be just, for mercy is bestowed upon the guilty criminal, while justice is all that an innocent man requires.
SR-T-276

MERRIMENT
>Life is not only a merriment;
>Life is desire and determination.
MS-74

MIDDLE EAST

There are in the Middle East today two challenging ideas: old and new.

The old ideas will vanish because they are weak and exhausted.

There is in the Middle East an awakening that defies slumber. This awakening will conquer because the sun is its leader and the dawn is its army. . . .

There is on the horizon of the Middle East a new awakening; it is growing and expanding; it is reaching and engulfing all sensitive, intelligent souls; it is penetrating and gaining the sympathy of noble hearts.

The Middle East, today, has two masters. One is deciding, ordering, being obeyed; but he is at the point of death.

But the other one is silent in his conformity to law and order, calmly awaiting justice; he is a powerful giant who knows his own strength, confident in his existence and a believer in his destiny.
MS-60

MIMIC

He who repeats what he does not understand is no better than an ass that is loaded with books.
WM-ST-63

MODERN GENERATION

This strange generation exists between sleeping and waking. It holds in its hands the soil of the past and the seeds of the future.
BW-ST-84

MODERN POETRY

Oh spirits of the poets, who watch over us from the heaven of Eternity, we go to the altars you have adorned with the pearls of your thoughts and the gems of your souls because we are oppressed by the clang of steel and the clamor of factories. Therefore our poems are as heavy as freight trains and as annoying as steam whistles.

And you, the real poets, forgive us. We belong in the New World where men run after worldly goods; and poetry, too, is a commodity today, and not a breath of immortality.

TM-ST-83

MODERN WOMAN

Modern civilization has made woman a little wiser, but it has increased her suffering because of man's covetousness. The woman of yesterday was a happy wife, but the woman of today is a miserable mistress. In the past she walked blindly in the light, but now she walks open-eyed in the dark. She was beautiful in her ignorance, virtuous in her simplicity, and strong in her weakness. Today she has become ugly in her ingenuity, superficial and heartless in her knowledge. Will the day come when beauty and knowledge, ingenuity and virtue, and weakness of body and strength of spirit will be united in a woman?

BW-ST-83

MODESTY

To be modest in speaking truth is hypocrisy.

TM-ST-95

MONEY

Money! The source of insincere love; the spring of false light and fortune; the well of poisoned water; the desperation of old age!

TL-T-175

Money is like a stringed instrument; he who does not know how to use it properly will hear only discordant music. Money is like love; it kills slowly and painfully the one who withholds it, and it enlivens the other who turns it upon his fellow men.

TL-T-404

MOTHER

The mother is every thing — she is our consolation in sorrow, our hope in misery, and our strength in weakness. She is the source of love, mercy, sympathy, and forgiveness. He who loses his mother loses a pure soul who blesses and guards him constantly.

Every thing in nature bespeaks the mother. The sun is the mother of the earth and gives it its nourishment of heat; it never leaves the universe at night until it has put the earth to sleep to the song of the sea and the hymn of the birds and brooks. And this earth is the mother of trees and flowers. It produces them, nurses them, and weans them. The trees and flowers become kind mothers of their great fruits and seeds. And the mother, the prototype of all existence, is the eternal spirit, full of beauty and love.

BW-ST-92

MUSIC

When God created Man, he gave him Music as a language different from all other languages. And early man sang her glory in the wilderness; and she drew the hearts of kings and moved them from their thrones.

WM-ST-58

> The moaning flute is more divine
> Than the golden cup of deep, red wine.
> T-368

God created music as a common language for all men. It inspires the poets, the composers and the architects. It

lures us to search our souls for the meaning of the mysteries described in ancient books.
   S

N

NATURE

> In the wild there is no Credo
> Nor a hideous disbelief;
> Song-birds never are assertive
> Of the Truth, the Bliss, or Grief.
> P-46

When I began to draw and paint, I did not say to
myself, "Behold Kahlil Gibran. There are ahead of you so
many ways to art: The classic, the modern, the symbolis-
tic, the impressionistic, and others. Choose for yourself
one of them." I did nothing of the sort. I simply found
my pen and brush, quite of themselves, recording sym-
bols of my thoughts, emotions, and fancies. Some think
the business of art to be a mere imitation of nature. But
Nature is far too great and too subtle to be successfully
imitated. No artist can ever reproduce even the least of
Nature's surpassing creations and miracles. Besides,
what profit is there in imitating Nature when she is so
open and so accessible to all who see and hear? The
business of art is rather to understand Nature and to
reveal her meanings to those unable to understand. It is
to convey the soul of a tree rather than to produce a
fruitful likeness of the tree. It is to reveal the conscience
of the sea, not to portray so many foaming waves or so
much blue water. The mission of art is to bring out the
unfamiliar from the most familiar.

Pity the eye that sees no more in the sun than a stove to
keep it warm and a torch to light its way between the

home and the business office. That is a blind eye, even if capable of seeing a fly a mile away. Pity the ear that hears no more than so many notes in the song of the nightingale. It is a deaf ear, even if capable of hearing the crawling of ants in their subterranean labyrinths.

KG-P-100

Nature reaches out to us with welcoming arms, and bids us enjoy her beauty; but we dread her silence and rush into the crowded cities, there to huddle like sheep fleeing from a ferocious wolf.

WM-ST-47

To Nature all are alive and all are
Free. The earthly glory of man is an
Empty dream, vanishing with the bubbles
In the rocky stream.

T-367

NATURE AND MAN

I heard the brook lamenting like a widow mourning her dead child and I asked, "Why do you weep, my pure brook?"

And the brook replied, "Because I am compelled to go to the city where Man contemns me and spurns me for stronger drinks and makes of me a scavenger for his offal, pollutes my purity, and turns my goodness to filth."

And I heard the birds grieving, and I asked, "Why do you cry, my beautiful birds?" And one of them flew near, and perched at the tip of a branch and said, "The sons of Adam will soon come into this field with their deadly weapons and make war upon us as if we were their mortal enemies. We are now taking leave of one another, for we know not which of us will escape the wrath of Man. Death follows us wherever we go."

Now the sun rose from behind the mountain peaks, and gilded the treetops with coronals. I looked upon this beauty and asked myself, "Why must Man destroy what Nature has built?"
WM-ST-83

NEIGHBOR
When you tell your trouble to your neighbor you present him with a part of your heart. If he possesses a great soul, he thanks you; if he possesses a small one, he belittles you.
MS-71

NEW YORK
He who wishes to live in New York must be a sharp sword in a sheath of honey. The sword is to repel those who are desirous of killing time, and the honey is to satisfy their hunger.
SP-ST-83

NIGHTINGALE
The nightingale does not make his nest in a cage lest slavery be the lot of its chicks.
BW-ST-122

O

OLD AGE
An old man likes to return in memory to the days of his youth like a stranger who longs to go back to his own country. He delights to tell stories of the past like a poet who takes pleasure in reciting his best poem. He lives spiritually in the past because the present passes swiftly, and the future seems to him an approach to the oblivion of the grave.
BW-ST-24

Many are the men who curse with venom the dead days of their youth; many are the women who execrate their wasted years with the fury of the lioness who has lost her cubs; and many are the youths and maidens who are using their hearts only to sheath the daggers of the bitter memories of the future, wounding themselves through ignorance with the sharp and poisoned arrows of seclusion from happiness.

Old age is the snow of the earth; it must, through light and truth, give warmth to the seeds of youth below, protecting them and fulfilling their purpose.
T-302

ONENESS

All things in this creation exist within you, and all things in you exist in creation; there is no border between you and the closest things, and there is no distance between you and the farthest things, and all things, from the lowest to the loftiest, from the smallest to the greatest, are within you as equal things. In one atom are found all the elements of the earth; in one motion of the mind are found the motions of all the laws of existence; in one drop of water are found the secrets of all the endless oceans; in one aspect of *you* are found all the aspects of *existence*.
SH-T-140

OPPORTUNITY

He who tries to seize an opportunity after it has passed him by is like one who sees it approach but will not go to meet it.
WM-ST-56

OPPRESSION

Woe to the nation that receives her conquerors beating the drums. Woe to the nation that hates oppression in

her sleep and accepts it in her awakening. Woe to the nation that raises her voice only behind a coffin and prides itself only in the cemetery. Woe to a nation that does not revolt until her neck is placed on the scaffold.
MS-99

ORIENT

The people of the Orient demand that the writer be like a bee always making honey. They are gluttonous for honey and prefer it to all other food.

The people of the Orient want their poet to burn himself as incense before their sultans. The Eastern skies have become sickly with incense yet the people of the Orient have had not enough. . . .

Numerous are the social healers in the Orient, and many are their patients who remain uncured but appear eased of their ills because they are under the effects of social narcotics. But these tranquilizers merely mask the symptoms.

Such narcotics are distilled from many sources but the chief is the Oriental philosophy of submission to Destiny (the act of God).
TM-ST-92

P

PACIFISM

Beware of the leader who says, "Love of existence obliges us to deprive the people of their rights!" I say unto you but this: protecting others' rights is the noblest and most beautiful human act; if my existence requires that I kill others, then death is more honourable to me, and if I cannot find someone to kill me for the protection of my honour, I will not hesitate to take my life by my own hands for the sake of Eternity before Eternity comes.

TL-T-8

PAIN

Pain is an unseen and powerful hand that breaks the skin of the stone in order to extract the pulp.

SP-ST-94

PAST AND FUTURE

I tell you that the children of yesteryears are walking in the funeral of the era that they created for themselves. They are pulling a rotted rope that might break soon and cause them to drop into a forgotten abyss. I say that they are living in homes with weak foundations; as the storm blows — and it is about to blow — their homes will fall upon their heads and thus become their tombs. I say that all their thoughts, their sayings, their quarrels, their compositions, their books and all their work are nothing but chains dragging them because they are too weak to pull the load.

But the children of tomorrow are the ones called by life, and they follow it with steady steps and heads high, they are the dawn of new frontiers, no smoke will veil their eyes and no jingle of chains will drown out their voices. They are few in number, but the difference is as between a grain of wheat and a stack of hay. No one knows them but they know each other. They are like the summits, which can see and hear each other — not like caves, which cannot hear or see. They are the seed dropped by the hand of God in the field, breaking through its pod and waving its sapling leaves before the face of the sun. It shall grow into a mighty tree, its root in the heart of the earth and its branches high in the sky.

MS-64-65

PATRIOT

Are you a politician who says to himself: "I will use my country for my own benefit"? If so, you are naught but a parasite living on the flesh of others. Or are you a devoted patriot, who whispers into the ear of his inner self: "I love to serve my country as a faithful servant." If so, you are an oasis in the desert, ready to quench the thirst of the wayfarer.

WM-ST-34

PATRIOTISM

What is this duty that separates the lovers, and causes the women to become widows, and the children to become orphans? What is this patriotism which provokes wars and destroys kingdoms through trifles? And what cause can be more than trifling when compared to but one life? What is this duty which invites poor villagers, who are looked upon as nothing by the strong and by the sons of the inherited nobility, to die for the glory of their oppressors? If duty destroys peace among nations, and patriotism disturbs the tranquility of man's life, then let us say, "Peace be with duty and patriotism."

SH-T-379

I have a yearning for my beautiful country, and I love its people because of their misery. But if my people rose, stimulated by plunder and motivated by what they call "patriotic spirit" to murder, and invaded my neighbour's country, then upon the committing of any human atrocity I would hate my people and my country.

TL-T-4

PEACE

Will peace be on earth while the sons of misery are slaving in the fields to feed the strong and fill the stomachs of the tyrants? Will ever peace come and save them from the clutches of destitution?

What is peace? Is it in the eyes of those infants, nursing upon the dry breasts of their hungry mothers in cold huts? Or is it in the wretched hovels of the hungry who sleep upon hard beds and crave for one bite of the food which the priests and monks feed to their fat pigs?
SH-T-82

PERPETUITY

I am saddened by the one who gazes upon the mountains and plains upon which the sun throws its rays, and who listens to the breeze singing the song of the thin branches, and who inhales the fragrance of the flowers and the jasmine, and then says within himself, "No . . . what I see and hear will pass away, and what I know and feel will vanish." This humble soul who sees and contemplates reverently the joys and sorrows about him, and then denies the perpetuity of their existence, must himself vanish like vapour in the air and disappear, for he is seeking darkness and placing his back to truth. Verily, he is a living soul denying *his* very existence, for he denies *other* of God's existing things.
SH-T-144

PERPLEXITY

Perplexity is the beginning of knowledge.
WM-ST-87

PERSECUTION

Persecution cannot harm him who stands by Truth. Did not Socrates fall proudly a victim in body? Was not Paul stoned for the sake of the Truth? It is our inner self that hurts us when we disobey and kills us when we betray.
SH-T-77

PHILOSOPHY

There is a desire deep within the soul which drives man from the seen to the unseen, to philosophy and to the divine.

MS-49

PILGRIMAGE

For every seed that autumn drops into the heart of the earth, there exists a different manner of splitting the shell from the pulp; then are created the leaves and then the flowers, and then the fruit. But regardless of the fashion in which this takes place, those plants must undertake one sole pilgrimage, and their great mission is to stand before the face of the sun.

SH-T-141

POET

Poet, you are the life of this life, and you have
Triumphed over the ages despite their severity.

Poet, you will one day rule the hearts, and
Therefore, your kingdom has no ending.

Poet, examine your crown of thorns; you will
Find concealed in it a budding wreath of laurel.

TL-T-301

Are you a poet full of noise and empty sounds? If so, you are like one of those mountebanks that make us laugh when they are weeping, and make us weep, when they laugh.

Or are you one of those gifted souls in whose hands God has placed a viola to soothe the spirit with heavenly music, and bring his fellow men close to Life and the Beauty of Life? If so, you are a torch to light us on our way, a sweet longing in our hearts, and a revelation of the divine in our dreams.

WM-ST-36

Poets are unhappy people, for, no matter how high their spirits reach, they will still be enclosed in an envelope of tears.
BW-ST-41

POETRY

Poetry, my dear friends, is a sacred incarnation of a smile. Poetry is a sigh that dries the tears. Poetry is a spirit who dwells in the soul, whose nourishment is the heart, whose wine is affection. Poetry that comes not in this form is a false messiah.
TM-ST-83

If the spirits of Homer, Virgil, Al-Maary, and Milton had known that poetry would become a lapdog of the rich, they would have forsaken a world in which this could occur.
TM-ST-82

POOR
Not all the poor are scorned;
The wealth of the world is in a loaf of bread and a cloak.
MS-75

POPULAR KNOWLEDGE
Present knowledge of the people
Is a fog above the field;
When the sun mounts the horizon
To its rays the mist will yield.
P-54

POSITION
Greatness is not in exalted position;
Greatness is for he who refuses position.
MS-74

POSSESSIVENESS

Limited love asks for possession of the beloved, but the unlimited asks only for itself.

BW-ST-114

POVERTY

My fellow poor, Poverty sets off the nobility of the spirit, while wealth discloses its evil. Sorrow softens the feelings, and Joy heals the wounded heart. Were Sorrow and Poverty abolished, the spirit of man would be like an empty tablet, with naught inscribed save the signs of selfishness and greed.

WM-ST-65

My poor friend, if you only knew that the Poverty which causes you so much wretchedness is the very thing that reveals the knowledge of Justice and the understanding of Life, you would be contented with your lot.

I say knowledge of Justice: for the rich man is too busy amassing wealth to seek this knowledge.

And I say understanding of Life: for the strong man is too eager in his pursuit of power and glory to keep to the straight path of truth.

Rejoice then, my poor friend, for you are the mouth of Justice and the book of Life. Be content, for you are the source of virtue in those who rule over you and the pillar of integrity of those who guide you.

WM-ST-64

PRAISE

My soul preached to me and said, "Do not be delighted because of praise, and do not be distressed because of blame."

Ere my soul counseled me, I doubted the worth of my work.

Now I realize that the trees blossom in Spring and bear
fruit in Summer without seeking praise; and they drop
their leaves in Autumn and become naked in Winter
without fearing blame.
TM-ST-31

PRAYER
Prayer is the song of the heart. It reaches the ear of God
even if it is mingled with the cry and the tumult of a
thousand men.
S

PREACHING
How painful is the preaching of the fortunate to the
heart of the miserable! And how severe is the strong
when he stands as advisor among the weak!
SH-T-381

PRIEST
The priest is a traitor who uses the Gospel as a threat to
ransom your money . . . a hypocrite wearing a cross and
using it as a sword to cut your veins . . . a wolf disguised
in lambskin . . . a glutton who respects the tables more
than the altars . . . a gold hungry creature who follows
the Dinar to the farthest land . . . a cheat pilfering from
widows and orphans. He is a queer being, with an
eagle's beak, a tiger's clutches, a hyena's teeth and a
viper's clothes. Take the Book away from him and tear
his raiment off and pluck his beard and do whatever you
wish unto him; then place in his hand one Dinar, and he
will forgive you smilingly.
SR-T-281

When a villager doubts the holiness of the priest, he
will be told, "Listen only to his teaching and disregard
his shortcomings and misdeeds."
TM-ST-94

PROGRESS

Progress is not merely improving the past; it is moving forward toward the future.
MS-71

PROPHET

The Prophet arrives
Veiled in the cloak of future thought,
'Mid people hid in ancient garb,
Who could not see the gift he brought.

He is a stranger to this life,
Stranger to those who praise or blame,
For he upholds the Torch of Truth,
Although devoured by the flame.
P-52

R

REASON

When Reason speaks to you, hearken to what she says, and you shall be saved. Make good use of her utterances, and you shall be as one armed. For the Lord has given you no better guide than Reason, no stronger arm than Reason. When Reason speaks to your inmost self, you are proof against Desire. For Reason is a prudent minister, a loyal guide, and a wise counsellor. Reason is light in darkness, as anger is darkness amidst light. Be wise—let Reason, not Impulse, be your guide.
WM-ST-54

REBELLION

Life without Rebellion is like seasons without Spring. And Rebellion without Right is like Spring in an arid

desert. . . . Life, Rebellion, and Right are three-in-one
who cannot be changed or separated.
TM-ST-62

Did God give us the breath of life to place it under
death's feet? Did He give us liberty to make it a shadow
for slavery? He who extinguishes his spirit's fire with his
own hands is an infidel in the eyes of Heaven, for
Heaven set the fire that burns in our spirits. He who does
not rebel against oppression is doing himself injustice.
BW-ST-112

REGRET
Be not like him who sits by his fireside and watches the
fire go out, then blows vainly upon the dead ashes. Do
not give up hope or yield to despair because of that
which is past, for to bewail the irretrievable is the worst
of human frailties.
WM-ST-68

RELIGION
If we were to do away with the various religions, we
would find ourselves united and enjoying one great faith
and religion, abounding in brotherhood.
SH-T-135

Religion is a well-tilled field,
    Planted and watered by desire
Of one who longed for Paradise,
    Or one who dreaded Hell and Fire.

Aye, were it but for reckoning
    At Resurrection, they had not
Worshipped God, nor did repent,
    Except to gain a better lot—

As though religion were a phase
    Of commerce in their daily trade;

Should they neglect it they would lose—
  Or persevering would be paid.
  P-44

Religion to man is like a field,
For it is planted with hope and
Tended by the shivering ignorant,
Fearing the fire of hell; or it is
Sowed by the strong in wealth of
Empty gold who look upon religion
As a kind of barter, ever seeking
Profit in earthly reward. But
Their hearts are lost despite
Their throbbing, and the product
Of their spiritual farming is but
The unwanted weed of the valley.
  T-364

RELIGIOUS LEADER

Are you a leader of religion, who weaves out of the simplicity of the faithful a scarlet robe for his body; and of their kindness a golden crown for his head; and while living on Satan's plenty, spews forth his hatred of Satan? If so, you are a heretic; and it matters not that you fast all day and pray all night.

Or are you the faithful one who finds in the goodness of people a groundwork for the betterment of the whole nation; and in whose soul is the ladder of perfection leading to the Holy Spirit? If you are such, you are like a lily in the garden of Truth; and it matters not if your fragrance is lost upon men, or dispersed into the air, where it will be eternally preserved.
  WM-ST-34

REPENTANCE

Paradise is not in repentance;
Paradise is in the pure heart.
  MS-74

RICHES

Riches are not in money alone;
How many wanderers were the richest of all men?
MS-75

RULER

Between the frown of the tiger and the smile of the
wolf the flock is perished; the ruler claims himself as king
of the law, and the priest as the representative of God,
and between these two, the bodies are destroyed and the
souls wither into nothing.
SR-T-269

S

SANITY

Eagles never display wonder,
Or say, " 'Tis marvel of the age."
For in nature we the children
Only hold the sane as strange.
P-64

SCIENCE

All around me are dwarves who see giants emerging;
and the dwarves croak like frogs:

"The world has returned to savagery. What science
and education have created is being destroyed by the
new primitives. We are now like the prehistoric cave
dwellers. Nothing distinguishes us from them save our
machines of destruction and our improved techniques of
slaughter."

Thus speak those who measure the world's conscience
by their own. They measure the range of all Existence by
the tiny span of their individual being. As if the sun did
not exist but for their warmth, as if the sea was created
for them to wash their feet.
TM-ST-99

SECRETS
>My heart, keep secret your love,
>   and hide the secret from those you see
>   and you will have better fortune.
>He who reveals secrets is considered a fool;
>   silence and secrecy are much better for him
>   who falls in love.
>MS-76

SEED
>The seed which
>The ripe date contains in its.
>Heart is the secret of the palm
>Tree from the beginning of all
>Creation.
>T-374

SEGREGATION
A God Who is good knows of no segregation amongst words or names, and were a God to deny His blessing to those who pursue a different path to eternity, then there is no human who should offer worship.
SH-T-142

SELF
Man is empowered by God to hope and hope fervently, until that for which he is hoping takes the cloak of oblivion from his eyes, whereupon he will at last view his real self. And he who sees his real self sees the truth of real life for himself, for all humanity, and for all things.
SH-T-140

It is vain for the wayfarer to knock upon the door of the empty house. Man is standing mutely between the non-existence within him and the reality of his surroundings. If we did not possess what we have within ourselves we could not have the things we call our environs.
SH-T-145

SELF-EXPRESSION

Is it not true, that every time we draw Beauty we approach a step nearer to Beauty? And every time we write the Truth we become one with it? Or do you propose to muzzle poets and artists? Is not self-expression a deeply seated need in the human soul?

KG-P-95

SELF-KNOWLEDGE

Know your own true worth, and you shall not perish. Reason is your light and your beacon of Truth. Reason is the source of Life. God has given you Knowledge, so that by its light you may not only worship him, but also see yourself in your weakness and strength.

WM-ST-55

SENSES

How ignorant are those who see, without question, the abstract existence with *some* of their senses, but insist upon doubting until that existence reveals itself to *all* their senses. Is not faith the sense of the heart as truly as sight is the sense of the eye? And how narrow is the one who hears the song of the blackbird and sees it hovering above the branches, but doubts that which he has seen and heard until he seizes the bird with his hands. Were not a *portion* of his senses sufficient? How strange is the one who dreams in truth of a beautiful reality, and then, when he endeavours to fashion it into form but cannot succeed, doubts the dream and blasphemes the reality and distrusts the beauty!

SH-T-148

SEX

The most highly sexed beings upon the planet are the creators, the poets, sculptors, painters, musicians . . . and so it has been from the beginning. And among them

sex is a beautiful and exalted gift. Sex is always beautiful, and is always shy.
    MS-94-95

SHADOWS

How unjust to themselves are those who turn their backs to the sun, and see naught except the shadows of their physical selves upon the earth!
    SH-T-150

SHEPHERD

In the city the best of
Man is but one of a flock, led by
The shepherd in strong voice. And he
Who follows not the command must soon
Stand before his killers.
        T-361

SIGHT

Not all of us are enabled to see with our inner eyes the great depths of life, and it is cruel to demand that the weak-sighted see the dim and the far.
    SH-T-129

SILENCE

Great truth that transcends Nature does not pass from one being to another by way of human speech. Truth chooses Silence to convey her meaning to loving souls.
    WM-ST-75

There is something greater and purer than what the mouth utters. Silence illuminates our souls, whispers to our hearts, and brings them together. Silence separates us from ourselves, makes us sail the firmament of spirit, and brings us closer to Heaven; it makes us feel that

bodies are no more than prisons and that this world is
only a place of exile.
BW-ST-48

SIN

> Perfection is not for the pure of soul;
> There may be virtue in sin.
> MS-75

SINCERITY

Many a time I have made a comparison between nobility of sacrifice and happiness of rebellion to find out
which one is nobler and more beautiful; but until now I
have distilled only one truth out of the whole matter, and
this truth is sincerity, which makes all our deeds beautiful and honorable.
BW-ST-117

SLAVERY

I accompanied the ages from the banks of the Kange to
the shores of Euphrates; from the mouth of the Nile to
the plains of Assyria; from the arenas of Athens to the
churches of Rome; from the slums of Constantinople to
the palaces of Alexandria. . . . Yet I saw slavery moving
over all, in a glorious and majestic procession of ignorance. I saw the people sacrificing the youths and
maidens at the feet of the idol, calling her the God;
pouring wine and perfume upon her feet, and calling her
the Queen; burning incense before her image, and calling her the Prophet; kneeling and worshipping before
her, and calling her the Law; fighting and dying for
her, and calling her Patriotism; submitting to her will,
and calling her the Shadow of God on earth; destroying
and demolishing homes and institutions for her sake, and

calling her Fraternity; struggling and stealing and working for her, and calling her Fortune and Happiness; killing for her, and calling her Equality.

She possesses various names, but one reality. She has many appearances, but is made of one element. In truth, she is an everlasting ailment bequeathed by each generation unto its successor.
SH-T-64

They tell me: If you see a slave sleeping, do not wake
  him lest he be dreaming of freedom.
I tell them: If you see a slave sleeping, wake him and
  explain to him freedom.
MS-72

SLEEP

Life is but a sleep disturbed
  By dreaming, prompted by the will;
The saddened soul with sadness hides
  Its secrets, and the gay, with thrill.
P-42

SOBRIETY

Few on this earth who savor life,
  And are not bored by its free gifts;
Or divert not its streams to cups
  In which their fancy floats and drifts.

Should you then find a sober soul
  Amidst this state of revelry,
Marvel how a moon did find
  In this rain cloud a canopy.
P-37

SOCIETY

Society
Is of naught but clamour and woe

And strife. She is but the web of
The spider, the tunnel of the mole.
T-376

SOLITUDE
The sorrowful spirit finds relaxation in solitude. It
abhors people, as a wounded deer deserts the herd and
lives in a cave until it is healed or dead.
BW-ST-87

Solitude has soft, silky hands, but with strong fingers
it grasps the heart and makes it ache with sorrow. Solitude is the ally of sorrow as well as a companion of
spiritual exaltation.
BW-ST-19

Your life, my brother, is a solitary habitation separated
from other men's dwellings. It is a house into whose
interior no neighbor's gaze can penetrate. If it were emp-
tied of provisions, the stores of your neighbors could not
fill it. If it stood in a desert, you could not move it into
other men's gardens, tilled and planted by other hands.
If it stood on a mountaintop, you could not bring it down
into the valley trod by other men's feet.

Your spirit's life, my brother, is encompassed by loneliness, and were it not for that loneliness and solitude,
you would not be *you*, nor would I be *I*. Were it not for
this loneliness and solitude, I would come to believe on
hearing your voice that it was my voice speaking; or
seeing your face, that it was myself looking into a mirror.
WM-ST-43

SONG

Give to me the reed and sing thou!
For the song is gracious shade,
And the plaint of reed remaineth
When illusions dim and fade.
P-39

SORROW

> Sorrow is the shadow of a God who
> Lives not in the domain of evil hearts.
> SH-T-86

> Sorrow, if able to speak, would
> Prove sweeter than the joy of song.
> SH-T-99

He who has not looked on Sorrow will never see Joy.
WM-ST-88

The sorrowful spirit finds rest when united with a similar one. They join affectionately, as a stranger is cheered when he sees another stranger in a strange land. Hearts that are united through the medium of sorrow will not be separated by the glory of happiness.
BW-ST-42

> The secret of the heart is encased
> In sorrow, and only in sorrow is
> Found our joy, while happiness serves
> But to conceal the deep mystery of life.
> T-362

SOUL

> The reason why the soul exists
> Is folded in the soul itself;
> No painting could its essence show,
> Nor manifest its real self.
> P-65

The soul does not see anything in life save that which is in the soul itself. It does not believe except in its own private event, and when it experiences something, the outcome becomes a part of it.
SP-ST-56

SOUNDS OF NATURE

When the birds sing, do they call to the flowers in the fields, or are they speaking to the trees, or are they echoing the murmur of the brooks? For Man with his understanding cannot know what the bird is saying, nor what the brook is murmuring, nor what the waves whisper when they touch the beaches slowly and gently.

Man with his understanding cannot know what the rain is saying when it falls upon the leaves of the trees or when it taps at the window panes. He cannot know what the breeze is saying to the flowers in the fields.

But the Heart of Man can feel and grasp the meaning of these sounds that play upon his feelings. Eternal Wisdom often speaks to him in a mysterious language; Soul and Nature converse together, while Man stands speechless and bewildered.

Yet has not Man wept at the sounds? And are not his tears eloquent understanding?
WM-ST-58

SPIRIT

The spirit in every being is made manifest in the eyes, the countenance, and in all bodily movements and gestures. Our appearance, our words, our actions are never greater than ourselves. For the soul is our house; our eyes its windows; and our words its messengers.
WM-ST-62

> The strength of the spirit alone is
> The power of powers, and must in time
> Crumble to powder all things opposing
> It. Do not condemn, but pity the
> Faithless and their weakness and their
> Ignorance and their nothingness.
> T-365

Through the spirit,
Not the body, love must be shown,
As it is to enliven, not to deaden,
That the wine is pressed.
T-371

You may deprive me of my possessions; you may shed my blood and burn my body, but you cannot hurt my spirit or touch my truth.
S

SPIRITS

Between the people of eternity and people of the earth there is a constant communication, and all comply with the will of that unseen power. Oftentimes an individual will perform an act, believing that it is born of his own free will, accord, and command, but in fact he is being guided and impelled with precision to do it. Many great men attained their glory by surrendering themselves in complete submission to the will of the spirit, employing no reluctance or resistance to its demands, as a violin surrenders itself to the complete will of a fine musician.

Between the spiritual world and the world of substance there is a path upon which we walk in a swoon of slumber. It reaches us and we are unaware of its strength, and when we return to ourselves we find that we are carrying with our real hands the seeds to be planted carefully in the good earth of our daily lives, bringing forth good deeds and words of beauty. Were it not for that path between our lives and the departed lives, no prophet or poet or learned man would have appeared among the people.
SH-T-146

SPIRITUAL AFFINITY

It is wrong to think that love comes from long companionship and persevering courtship. Love is the offspring

of spiritual affinity and unless that affinity is created in a moment, it will not be created in years or even generations.
BW-ST-52

SPIRITUAL AWAKENING

Spiritual awakening is the most essential thing in man's life, and it is the sole purpose of being. Is not civilization, in all its tragic forms, a supreme motive for spiritual awakening? Then how can we deny existing matter, while its very existence is unwavering proof of its conformability into the intended fitness? The present civilization may possess a vanishing purpose, but the eternal law has offered to that purpose a ladder whose steps can lead to a free substance.
SH-T-29

SPIRITUALITY

Time and place are spiritual states, and all that is seen and heard is spiritual. If you close your eyes you will perceive all things through the depths of your inner self, and you will see the world physical and ethereal, in its intended entirety, and you will acquaint yourself with its necessary laws and precautions, and you will understand the greatness that it possesses beyond its closeness.
SH-T-139

SPRING

In every winter's heart there is a quivering spring, and behind the veil of each night there is a smiling dawn.
SP-ST-57

STRENGTH

The very strength that protects the heart from injury is the strength that prevents the heart from enlarging to its intended greatness within. The song of the voice is sweet, but the song of the heart is the pure voice of heaven.

SH-T-121

SUBMISSION

Men, even if they are born free, will remain slaves of strict laws enacted by their forefathers; and the firmament, which we imagine as unchanging, is the yielding of today to the will of tomorrow and submission of yesterday to the will of today.

BW-ST-118

SWORD

Whoever reaches eternity with sword in his hand lives as long as there is justice.

MS-29

SYMPATHY

The sympathy that touches the neighbour's heart is more supreme than the hidden virtue in the unseen corners of the convent. A word of compassion to the weak criminal or prostitute is nobler than the long prayer which we repeat emptily every day in the temple.

SR-T-257

T

TALK

I am bored with gabbers and their gab; my soul abhors them. . . .

Is there in this universe a nook where I can go and live happily by myself?

Is there any place where there is no traffic in empty talk?

Is there on this earth one who does not worship himself talking?

Is there any person among all persons whose mouth is not a hiding place for the knavish Mister Gabber?
TM-ST-40-42

TEACHER

Whoever would be a teacher of men let him begin by teaching himself before teaching others; and let him teach by example before teaching by word. For he who teaches himself and rectifies his own ways is more deserving of respect and reverence than he who would teach others and rectify their ways.
KG-P-27

TEARS

He who is seared and cleansed once with his
Own tears will remain pure forevermore.
SH-T-86

The tears you shed are purer than the laughter of him that seeks to forget and sweeter than the mockery of the scoffer. These tears cleanse the heart of the blight of hatred, and teach man to share the pain of the brokenhearted. They are the tears of the Nazarene.
WM-ST-65

Love that is cleansed by tears will remain eternally pure and beautiful.
BW-ST-42

The tears of young men are the overflow of full hearts. But the tears of old men are the residue of age dropping upon their cheeks, the remains of life in weakened bodies. Tears in the eyes of young men resemble drops of dew upon a rose, but the tears of old men resemble yellow autumn leaves, blown and scattered by the wind as the winter of life approaches.
S

TEARS AND LAUGHTER

I would not exchange the laughter of my heart for the fortunes of the multitudes; nor would I be content with converting my tears, invited by my agonized self, into calm. It is my fervent hope that my whole life on this earth will ever be tears and laughter.

T-413

TEETH

In the mouth of Society are many diseased teeth, decayed to the bones of the jaws. But Society makes no efforts to have them extracted and be rid of the affliction. It contents itself with gold fillings. Many are the dentists who treat the decayed teeth of Society with glittering gold.

Numerous are those who yield to the enticements of such reformers, and pain, sickness, and death are their lot. . . .

Visit the courts and witness the acts of the crooked and corrupted purveyors of justice. *See* how they play with the thoughts and minds of the simple people as a cat plays with a mouse.

Visit the homes of the rich where conceit, falsehood, and hypocrisy reign.

But don't neglect to go through the huts of the poor as well, where dwell fear, ignorance, and cowardice.

Then visit the nimble-fingered dentists, possessors of delicate instruments, dental plasters and tranquilizers, who spend their days filling the cavities in the rotten teeth of the nation to mask the decay.

TM-ST-38

THINGS

Substantial things deaden a man without suffering; love awakens him with enlivening pains.

TL-T-3

If your knowledge teaches you not the value of things,
and frees you not from the bondage to matter, you shall
never come near the throne of Truth.
WM-ST-63

THIRST
The thirst of soul is sweeter than the wine of material
things, and the fear of spirit is dearer than the security of
the body.
BW-ST-69

THRONG
> Life amid the throngs is but brief
> And drug-laden slumber, mixed with
> Mad dreams and spectres and fears.
T-362

TIME
> This world is but a winery,
>   Its host and master Father Time,
> Who caters only to those steep'd
>   In dreams discordant, without rhyme.
>
> For people drink and race as though
>   They were the steeds of mad desire;
> Thus some are blatant when they pray,
>   And others frenzied to acquire.
P-39

> The people
> Of the city abuse the wine of Time,
> For they think upon it as a temple,
> And they drink of it with ease and
> With unthinking, and they flee,
> Scurrying into old age with deep
> But unknowing sorrow.
T-363

How strange Time is, and how queer we are! Time has really changed, and lo, it has changed us too, It walked one step forward, unveiled its face, alarmed us and then elated us.

Yesterday we complained about Time and trembled at its terrors. But today we have learned to love it and revere it, for we now understand its intents, its natural disposition, its secrets, and its mysteries.

Yesterday we crawled in fright like shuddering ghosts between the fears of the night and the menaces of the day. But today we walk joyously towards the mountain peak, the dwelling place of the raging tempest and the birthplace of thunder. . . .

Yesterday we honored false prophets and sorcerers. But today Time has changed, and lo, it has changed us too. We can now stare at the face of the sun and listen to the songs of the sea, and nothing can shake us except a cyclone.

Yesterday we tore down the temples of our souls and from their debris we built tombs for our forefathers. But today our souls have turned into sacred altars that the ghosts of the past cannot approach, that the fleshless fingers of the dead cannot touch.

We were a silent thought hidden in the corners of Oblivion. Today we are a strong voice that can make the firmament reverberate.
TM-ST-33

TORCH
The human soul is but a part of a burning torch which God separated from Himself at Creation.
WM-ST-67

TREASURE
Knowledge and understanding are life's faithful companions who will never prove untrue to you. For knowl-

edge is your crown, and understanding your staff; and when they are with you, you can possess no greater treasures.
WM-ST-62

TRUTH

Truth is like the stars; it does not appear except from behind obscurity of the night. Truth is like all beautiful things in the world; it does not disclose its desirability except to those who first feel the influence of falsehood. Truth is a deep kindness that teaches us to be content with our everyday life and share with the people the same happiness.
SR-T-255

He who would seek truth and proclaim it to mankind is bound to suffer. My sorrows have taught me to understand the sorrows of my fellow men . . . persecution . . . [has not] dimmed the vision within me.
VM-P-86

Truth calls to us, drawn by the innocent laughter of a child, or the kiss of a loved one; but we close the doors of affection in her face and deal with her as with an enemy.
WM-ST-47

U

UNAWARENESS

The human heart cries out for help; the human soul implores us for deliverance; but we do not heed their cries, for we neither hear nor understand. But the man who hears and understands we call mad, and flee from him.

Thus the nights pass, and we live in unawareness; and

the days greet us and embrace us. But we live in constant
dread of day and night.
WM-ST-47

UNSEEN
The subtlest beauties in our life are unseen and un-
heard.
SP-ST-30

The Jews, my beloved, awaited the coming of a Messiah, who had been promised them, and who was to
deliver them from bondage.

And the Great Soul of the World sensed that the worship of Jupiter and Minerva no longer availed, for the
thirsty hearts of men could not be quenched with that
wine.

In Rome men pondered the divinity of Apollo, a god
without pity, and the beauty of Venus already fallen into
decay.

For deep in their hearts, though they did not understand it, these nations hungered and thirsted for the
supreme teaching that would transcend any to be found
on the earth. They yearned for the spirit's freedom that
would teach man to rejoice with his neighbor at the light
of the sun and the wonder of living. For it is this
cherished freedom that brings man close to the Unseen,
which he can approach without fear or shame.
WM-ST-92

V

VIRGIN
There is no secret in the mystery of life stronger and
more beautiful than that attachment which converts the
silence of a virgin's spirit into a perpetual awareness that

makes a person forget the past, for it kindles fiercely in the heart the sweet and overwhelming hope of the coming future.
SR-T-264

W

WAR

You are my brother, but why are you quarreling with me? Why do you invade my country and try to subjugate me for the sake of pleasing those who are seeking glory and authority?

Why do you leave your wife and children and follow Death to the distant land for the sake of those who buy glory with your blood, and high honour with your mother's tears?

Is it an honour for a man to kill his brother man? If you deem it an honour, let it be an act of worship, and erect a temple to Cain who slew his brother Abel.
TL-T-7

Can lovers meet and exchange kisses on battlefields still acrid with bomb fumes?

Will the poet compose his songs under stars veiled in gun smoke?

Will the musician strum his lute in a night whose silence was ravished by terror?
TM-ST-98

WAY TO GOD

Perhaps we are nearer to Him each time we try to divide Him and find Him indivisible. Yet do I say that art, through drawing a line between the beautiful and the ugly, is the nearest way to God. Pure meditation is another way. But it leads to silence and to self-confinement. Silence is truer and more expressive than speech; and the hour shall come when we shall be silent. But why muzzle our tongues before that hour has struck? There is your friend Lao Tze; he became silent, but when? After he gave to the world the gist of his faith in words.

KG-P-96

WEAKNESS

That deed which in our guilt we today call weakness, will appear tomorrow as an essential link in the complete chain of Man.

WM-ST-32

WEALTH

In some countries, the parent's wealth is a source of misery for the children. The wide strong box which the father and mother together have used for the safety of their wealth becomes a narrow, dark prison for the souls of their heirs. The Almighty Dinar which the people worship becomes a demon which punishes the spirit and deadens the heart.

BW-ST-64

WILL

To Will belongs the Right. For Souls
    When strong prevail, when weak become
Subject to changes, good and bad,
    And with the wind may go and come.

Then, deny not that Will in Soul
    Is greater than the Might of Arm,
And weakling only mounts the throne
    Of those beyond the good and harm.

P-50

WINGS

God has given you a spirit with wings on which to soar into the spacious firmament of Love and Freedom. Is it not pitiful then that you cut your wings with your own hands and suffer your soul to crawl like an insect upon the earth?

WM-ST-67

WISDOM

The wise man is he who loves and reveres God. A man's merit lies in his knowledge and in his deeds, not in his color, faith, race, or descent. For remember, my friend, the son of a shepherd who possesses knowledge is of greater worth to a nation than the heir to the throne, if he be ignorant. Knowledge is your true patent of nobility, no matter who your father or what your race may be.

WM-ST-61

Keep me away from the wisdom which does not cry, the philosophy which does not laugh and the greatness which does not bow before children.

MS-72

WOMAN

A woman whom Providence has provided with beauty of spirit and body is a truth, at the same time both open and secret, which we can understand only by love, and touch only by virtue; and when we attempt to describe such a woman she disappears like a vapor.

BW-ST-39

Women opened the windows of my eyes and the doors of my spirit. Had it not been for the woman-mother, the woman-sister, and the woman-friend, I would have been sleeping among those who seek the tranquility of the world with their snoring.

SP-P-31

Writers and poets try to understand the truth about woman. But until this day they have never understood her heart because, looking upon her through the veil of desire, they see nothing except the shape of her body. Or they look upon her through a magnifying glass of spite and find nothing in her but weakness and submission.
S

WOMAN'S HEART

A woman's heart will not change with time or season; even if it dies eternally, it will never perish. A woman's heart is like a field turned into a battleground; after the trees are uprooted and the grass is burned and the rocks are reddened with blood and the earth is planted with bones and skulls, it is calm and silent as if nothing has happened; for the spring and autumn come at their intervals and resume their work.
BW-ST-71

WORDS

Wisdom is not in words;
Wisdom is meaning within words.
MS-74

WORSHIP

God does not like to be worshipped by an ignorant man who imitates someone else.
SR-T-267

WORTH

If your knowledge teaches you not to rise above human weakness and misery and lead your fellow man on the right path, you are indeed a man of little worth and will remain such till Judgment Day.
WM-ST-63

WRITER

Are you a writer who holds his head high above the crowd, while his brain is deep in the abyss of the past, that is filled with the tatters and useless cast-offs of the ages? If so, you are like a stagnant pool of water.

Or are you the keen thinker, who scrutinizes his inner self, discarding that which is useless, outworn and evil, but preserving that which is useful and good? If so, you are as manna to the hungry, and as cool, clear water to the thirsty.

WM-ST-36

Y

YOUTH

Youth is a beautiful dream, on whose brightness books shed a blinding dust. Will ever the day come when the wise link the joy of knowledge to youth's dream? Will ever the day come when Nature becomes the teacher of man, humanity his book and life his school? Youth's joyous purpose cannot be fulfilled until that day comes. Too slow is our march toward spiritual elevation, because we make so little use of youth's ardor.

TM-ST-55

Beauty belongs to youth, but the youth for whom this earth was made is naught but a dream whose sweetness is enslaved to a blindness that renders its awareness too late. Will ever the day come when the wise will band together the sweet dreams of youth and the joy of knowledge? Each is but naught when in solitary existence.

T-302

YOUTH AND AGE

Mankind divided into two long columns, one composed of the aged and bent, who support themselves on

crooked staves, and as they walk on the path of Life, they
pant as if they were climbing toward a mountaintop,
while they are actually descending into the abyss.

And the second column is composed of youth, running as with winged feet, singing as if their throats were
strung with silver strings, and climbing toward the
mountaintop as though drawn by some irresistible,
magic power.
WM-ST-36

Until when shall the people remain asleep?
Until when shall they continue to glorify those
Who attained greatness by moments of advantage?
How long shall they ignore those who enable
Them to see the beauty of their spirit,
Symbol of peace and love?
Until when shall human beings honor the dead
And forget the living, who spend their lives
Encircled in misery, and who consume themselves
Like burning candles to illuminate the way
For the ignorant and lead them into the path of light?
TL-T-300

BOOK
3

DEDICATED TO my wife, Zena, and my daughter Yasmine.

JOSEPH P. GHOUGASSIAN

Your . . . real work is beyond what in this generation or perhaps for many generations even you can realize. Only the future can show its scope. And in that day when man is calling the twentieth century an embryonic stage of himself, he will call you *like* himself. But you when that day comes will still be creating tomorrows. . . . To you now, what you write and paint expresses mere fragments of your vision. But in time the whole vision will appear in it. For man will learn to see and hear and read. And your *work* is not only books and pictures. They are but bits of it. Your work is you, not less than you, not parts of you. . . .

Your silence will be read with your writings some day, your darkness will be part of the LIGHT.

(Miss M. Haskell's prophecy of Gibran's fame.
Private Letter, Sunday, November 16, 1913.)

KAHLIL GIBRAN: WINGS OF THOUGHT

PREFACE

We FIND in many countries philosophy and the philosophers divorced from the local culture, customs, ethics and the simple *Weltanschauung* of the inhabitants. Yet, we also find in many civilizations a complete marriage between the intellectuals and the traditions of the country. One thinks, in this way, for instance, of Indian philosophy, or Mexican philosophy, or African philosophy. Gibran's trend of thoughts, also, has undergone the process of *"acculturation,"* meaning that his philosophy has assimilated the culture and beliefs of both the Western and Eastern hemispheres.

The distinction I am getting at differentiates between a people's philosopher and a philosopher's philosophy. The latter is academic, incomprehensible to the average citizen of the world, and quite abstract. The former is simple, unsystematic, yet deep in meanings which can be grasped by the reader. It is my firm conviction that Gibran is a people's philosopher as my present book will confirm till the last page.

Now it was not easy for me to expound Gibran's philosophy because he never wrote academically or logically; I had to resort to the science of *hermeneutics* in order to dig up his ideas which are scattered unsystematically in his books, and put them together following a logic that he himself expressed, but which is encumbered with emotions. Moreover, I have relied on the method of *comparative* philosophy, with the view of bringing to light the significance of Gibranism as it stands in the light of the history of philosophy. My discovery reveals that

Gibran is an *existentialist of the right wing*, though he was influenced by other mainstreams of thoughts.

Also to render Gibran relevant, I have endeavored to inform the reader about the historical events that surrounded the life and pen-ink of our author, notwithstanding the fact that I have attempted to interrelate his art, literature and philosophy with his biography.

Finally, I am greatly indebted to my wife and daughter for having had the patience to tolerate the strain of the long hours involved in the preparation which kept me away from their presence. A last expression of thanks goes to Mrs. Renate Streiter Smith for her generous help in typing the manuscript.

JOSEPH PETER GHOUGASSIAN

TABLE OF ABBREVIATIONS OF TITLES

P.	*The Prophet.*
PR.	*The Procession.*
T.L.	*Tears and Laughter.*
Th.M.	*Thoughts and Meditations.*
T.S.	*Tear and Smile.*
T.D.	*Twenty Drawings.*
M.S.	*Mirrors of the Soul.*
MM.	*The Madman.*
S.P.	*A Self Portrait.*
S.S.	*Spiritual Sayings.*
S.F.	*Sand and Foam.*
S.H.	*Secrets of the Heart.*
B.W.	*The Broken Wings.*
W.G.	*The Wisdom of Gibran.*
V.M.	*The Voice of the Master.*
N.V.	*Nymphs of the Valleys.*
E.G.	*The Earth Gods.*
FR.	*Forerunner.*
G.P.	*Garden of the Prophet.*
W.	*The Wanderer.*
J.S.M.	*Jesus the Son of Man.*
P.P.	*Prose Poem.*
S.R.	*Spirits Rebellious.*
B.P.	*Beloved Prophet. The Love Letters of Kahlil Gibran and Mary Haskell. And Her Private Journal.*

SHORT HISTORY OF LEBANON

Human "existence" is an unending "drama" so long as the individual's heart beats. It unfolds in the historical context of the person. Yet, the person's historicity is to a large extent determined, as would say Karl Marx, by the historical processes conditioned by the laws of social development. In each period these laws change, due to the fact that the social relations between individuals and countries through the intermediary of productivity constantly mutate. Human existence reflects the impact of history; and in its behaviors as well as thinking it is heavily impregnated by the Zeitgeist of the history it shares.

It is my firm belief that it is utterly impossible to understand Kahlil Gibran's philosophy and see his relevance, for instance in the fields of religion, law, and marriage, unless it be born in mind that he lived intensely the entanglements of the historical events, that have set him on his way to become the philosopher he is. Therefore, a brief survey of the history of Lebanon will shed some light on the themes that Gibran tackled and explain the "whys" of his thoughts.

History of Lebanon under the Ottoman Conquest

All historians remind us that Lebanon was originally Phoenicia, and had Tammuz and Ishtar for a religious cult. The Tammuz myth corresponds to the Greeks' Adonis and is identified with the Egyptians' god Osiris.

190

According to the Phoenician legendry, one day while Tammuz was hunting the wild boar, he was attacked by the beast and fell dead in the river of Afqah, today named Nahr Ibrahim. Following his death, life on earth began deteriorating. Then Ishtar "penetrated into the nether world" and revived him.[1] This commemorated the marriage between Tammuz and Ishtar, the goddess of love and fertility. Till the present days, poets, philosophers and painters of Lebanon like to refer to their mythological heritage. Gibran too made of Ishtar and Tammuz his muses of inspiration.

Lebanon, which means "white" in ancient Semitic language because of the eternal flakes of snow on the peaks of its mountains, has been invaded by more than ten civilizations of the world, from the Assyrian to Ottoman and Westerners, all of which brought along their culture. This explains why Lebanese immigrants feel almost at home in any foreign country and have no psychological stress in finding normal adjustments in their new environments. At any rate, every time that a new era of dominion took place, new geographical frontiers were established. Amazingly, however, Lebanon was always annexed to Syria. Either under the Assyro-Babylonian influence or the Ottoman Empire. It is only under the French Mandate after the first world war, beginning on September 1, 1920, with General Gouraud, that present day Lebanon with its geographical boundaries was proclaimed "independent."[2] And on May 23, 1926, The Greater Lebanon was made a republic. However, not until November 26, 1941, was Lebanon declared completely autonomous from the mandate and free to decide for its own course of destiny. Gibran (d. 1931) did not live to see his beloved country become sovereign master of its actions. Nevertheless, what he lived to witness was the hope of such full realization.

From 1516 until 1918 Lebanon remained under Ottoman rule, and became part of an Empire that stretched
from Hungary to the Arabian Peninsula and up to North
Africa. The illustrious conqueror of these lands was
Sulayman I (1520–1566) who became known to his subjects across the European continent as Sulayman the
Magnificent. In the words of the famous Arabian historian Philip K. Hitti,

> No such state was constructed by Moslems in mod-
> ern history. Nor did any other Moslem state prove to
> be more enduring. To his people Sulayman was
> known as Al-Qanuni (the lawgiver). . . . To outsid-
> ers he was known as the Magnificent, and magnifi-
> cent indeed he was, with a court exercising patron-
> age over art, literature, public works and inspiring
> awe in European hearts.[3]

Because of lack of space in this book we are not permit-
ted to delve into the detailed history of Gibran's homeland. Still, to quench our intellectual curiosity, I will
briefly mention a few historical data under the Ottoman
Empire, since this was the main foreign oppression
Gibran lived under.

When the Sultan Selim I defeated in 1516 the Mamluks
and established a Turkish dynasty, Lebanon was then
mostly inhabited by peasants and farmers. In the northern part, Kisrawan, the Maronite Christians were predominant while in the southern districts of Shuf, the
Druze constituted the majority. The Ottoman conquest
did not affect deeply the political structure, the language
and the way of life of the people of Lebanon. In practice
customary law was supreme, and social power was in
the hands of the feudal lords, on whom the Ottoman
governors, like their predecessors the Mamluks, mainly

relied for the security of local order and the collection of taxes.

Such being the flexibility of Ottoman politics, it was possible for the feudal dynasties of the country to pursue their factions and virtually one to vanquish the other. Thus, the greatest figure at that time was the Druze Amir Fakhr al-Din II, the head of the Ma'anids dynasty of the Shuf, who governed Lebanon throughout the sixteenth and seventeenth centuries. During his reign (1586–1635), he extended the geographical boundaries far beyond Lebanon, sometimes reaching up to the portico of Damascus and down to the Pilgrimage route that leads to the Hijaz. He was open minded toward foreign religious creeds and on several occasions encouraged European missionaries to build Christian churches. In matters of internal affairs, he cared for the prosperity, the warfare and the welfare of his country. With the aid of European architects and advisors he erected castles, developed agriculture and traded with Europe.

Captured in 1635 after a defeat by the governor of Damascus, Kuchuk Ahmad Pasha, he was sent prisoner to Istanbul where he was sentenced to death for wanting to overthrow the Ottoman Sultan. With his death followed the decline of the Ma'anids, who were succeeded in 1697 by the Chihab hegemony. This new Amirate ruled throughout the 18th century; flocks of mountaineers of the Maronite Kisrawan then migrated to the southern Shuf and mingled with the local Druzes, working unanimously for the betterment of the unified Lebanon. Of course, life was not so peaceful; from time to time there were misunderstandings between families and factions of the two traditional descendants of the Ancient Arabians of Qays and Yaman. The former were settlers of North Arabia, the latter cf South Arabia. However, when Haydar Chihab won victory against

Mahmud Pasha, head of the Yaman faction, many of the
Yamani Druzes emigrated from the metropolis of Lebanon to the hilly district of Mountain Hawran in Syria now
called *Jabal-al Druz*. For conclusion to this period the
historian Hourani writes,

> In the remainder of Syria no less than in Lebanon the
> eighteenth century was marked by conflict and un-
> rest. Finally a great part of the country fell into the
> hands of Bosnian Jazzar, Pasha of Acre, who ruled it
> ruthlessly and cruelly from 1775 until 1804. [4]

Generally speaking, the history of Lebanon during the
Ottoman Turks was principally the story of the Maronites and the Druzes. Both of these religions have
shaped the political fate of Lebanon. I may even say,
religion or "confessionalism" was the whole politics in
this part of the world. Nowadays also the political institution of Lebanon is still deeply determined by the
partitions of the various religious confessions.

The Maronites are followers of the hermit St. Maron
(d. 410), an ascetic monk who lived on a mountain in the
region of Apamea, in Syria secunda. Being persecuted by
the caliphates of Damascus and Baghdad, the Maronites
escaped the Northern Syria and began some time during
the 8th century to seek refuge from the harassments by
the Melchites, Monophysites and Muslims in the im-
penetrable mountains of Lebanon. [5] The Maronite
Church, to which Gibran belonged, still uses Syriac language in the liturgy and adheres to Catholicism. Their
first temple erected in the mountains of Lebanon was
established around 749. Ever since their settlement in
Lebanon the faithful organized a feudal system of government in the northern parts under the combined leadership of clergy and nobility, delegating the patriarch as

their feudal lord in religious and civil matters. At the time of the Ottomans the clergy feudalism exerted a fearful and ferocious influence over the poor peasants. Often, the clergy would practice "simony" and play the role of a corrupt politics. Most of Gibran's criticisms aimed at religion stem from and are directed against the feudalism of the Maronite institution.

As for the Druze religion, it entered southern Lebanon in about 1020. Such creed owes its name to Muhammad ibn-Ismail Al-Darazi (tailor in Turkish). It began in Egypt when a missionary of the Egyptian Fatimid, Al-Hakim (996–1021), while following the Ismaili doctrine of the Imam as the supreme authority and protector of Islam, proclaimed himself the incarnation of the Deity, in the same manner that Jesus Christ was for the Christians.[6] The peculiarity of the Druze religion is its utter secrecy. Their holy book is called Al-Hikma (wisdom), and is quite different from the Koran. The Syrian mountain Hawran, *Jabal Al-Druz*, bears their name because of the influx of refugees that took place at the end of the eighteenth century as a result of the victory of the Druze Qaysites, most of whom were converted to Christianity, over the Druze Yamanites.

In the nineteenth century, the Druze-Maronite relation caused two major events in Lebanon that proved to be detrimental to the security of the nation. The first important date is 1830. In that year Syria and Lebanon fell under the occupation of the Egyptian armies of Ibrahim Pasha, the son of Muhammad Ali. The Egyptians were helped by Bechir Chehab II, Emir of Mount Lebanon (1789–1840), who wanted to drive outside of his territories the jurisdiction of the Sublime Porte, i.e. Turkish dominion. He consented to the invasion of Lebanon provided he was given help by the Egyptians to strengthen his power meantime. After the conquest, Bechir II was offered by Ibrahim Pasha to rule over the entire Syria, but he declined the offer in order to care for the Lebanese alone.

The most interesting happening during the occupation is that the Maronite peasants who had travelled from the northern to southern districts of Lebanon, thus outnumbering the Druzes in their own regions, were all in favor of Ibrahim Pasha's invasion. Many times they joined the Egyptian armies to fight back the Turkish Sultan, despite the fact that the Druzes preferred the Turks. However, around 1840 the Maronites joined forces with the Druzes to expel the oppression of the Egyptians that was becoming burdensome, even to them.

Following the downfall of Ibrahim Pasha's reign, Lebanon came to be divided into two governorates. The northern mountainous areas were put under the supervision of a Maronite *qaim maqam*, or governor; while the southern was governed by a Druze *qaim maqam*. And both of them were controlled by the direct representative of the Ottoman Sultan, who presided in Beirut and Sidon. The politics of the Sublime Porte during the following forty or fifty years was the application of the old military principle of *divide et impera*, the divide and rule policy; thus the Porte would pit the two classes against each other so that he remained powerful over the weakened governors. Moreover, Turkish authorities never really intervened whenever internal upheaval and civil wars broke out between Maronites and Druzes. For instance, in 1858 the Christian farmers of Kisrawan revolted against their feudal lord, the Khazim family. The Khazim family was a system of primogeniture; they owned the lands of Kisrawan, made the peasants pay exorbitant taxes, and refused to the peasants the right to elect their own *wakils*, or representatives, as was the case in southern districts. In their insurrection against the Khazim, the peasants received moral encouragement from the Maronite clergy, and on many occasions asked assistance from the Druzes of the South.

At first, the south had decided to lend support to the beleaguered Christians. Yet, at the advice of Kourshid Pasha, the Turkish governor of Beirut, they retracted their forces and thought to protect themselves from possible peasants' revolt on their own lands. Kourshid Pasha's prediction was accurate. For around 1860, the Maronite peasants of the south, inspired by their brethren of the north, arose against their Druze overlords. Immediately, news spread that the intention of the Maronites of the south was not only meant to eliminate the feudal Druzes but also was directed against the Druze as a people. The historian Leila Meo writes about this incident:

> This class struggle soon turned into a religious war when the rank and file of the Druze, seeing the uprising as a direct threat to the continued existence of their own people, came to the assistance of their feudal chiefs. The Druze was well organized. The Maronites, although more numerous, lacked both organization and adequate arms. And so a general massacre of Maronite and other Christian villages ensued, while the local Turkish authorities made no immediate attempt to put an end to the bloodshed.[7]

Europe was not happy with the 1860's massacre, although I have to admit she was not so innocent in the whole affair. Ever since the Crusaders landed in the Levant, and due especially to the existence of the Maronite Catholics and other Eastern Christian rites, five European countries have incessantly meddled in the

Levant politics sometimes wisely, sometimes unwisely. France called itself the *protégé* of the Maronites; Russia made itself a duty to look over the interests of the Greek Orthodox; England took sides with the Druzes of Lebanon; Austria-Hungary played the mitigated role of the Catholic sects of the Eastern churches; and Prussia, more for political jealousy than other reasons, interfered in the politics of the Sublime Porte.

The immediate historical consequence following the 1860 event was the establishment on June 9, 1861, of the *Mutasarrifyya* of Mount Lebanon. This happened with the intervention of the Concert of the five European powers and the Sublime Porte. The pact concluded between these six countries stated clearly that *Mutasarrifyya* signifies that the two governorates would unify into a single government, presided over by a Christian non-Lebanese Governor General, whose duty would be to report to the Sultan in Constantinople and not any more to the Turkish Pasha of Sidon as it was before. Furthermore, the Governor General was to be elected by the Porte and confirmed by the Concert of Europe.

The first Governor General to be appointed over the new autonomous Lebanese province was Daoud Pasha, "an Armenian by birth, Roman Catholic by persuasion, director of the telegraph at Constantinople and author of a French work on Anglo-Saxon laws."[8] After him seven other Mutasarrifs followed until the outbreak of the first world War. From 1861–1914, Lebanon had calm political conditions as well as prospered economically and culturally particularly with the introduction of the Jesuit College (1875) and the presently called American University of Beirut (1866). Also, this is the period of dense emigration of Lebanese youths to the new continents of North and South America.

All of the Governor Generals ruled over a Lebanon which was geographically much smaller in superficies than the one of the Ma'anids and Chihabites Emirates. For instance, Beirut, Tripoli, Sidon, the Biqa valleys, and many more provinces were not annexed to the Mount Lebanon, but were parts of the Ottoman.

Such was the geography and history of Lebanon at the time Kahlil Gibran was born in 1883. His native village Bsherri was then located in the *Mutasarrifyya*. In over-all the Ottoman rule in Lebanon was in many respects corrupted; the rich enjoyed privileges from either the clergy or the feudal government while the poor were exploited.

LIFE OF KAHLIL GIBRAN

RARE ARE the writers who receive world recognition during their life. The factors causing the oblivion of a literator while still existing are many; the most important ones are: the life span, the economic situation, the geographical location, the educational and political activities' backgrounds of the family of the writer as well as the friends of the writer.

Did Gibran enjoy an international reputation while among men? Of course, he did not personally witness the translation in twenty languages of his masterpiece *The Prophet*, but still he did reach the Arabic readers and some American literati.[1] His fame really grew after his death, especially with the impact of his posthumous works.[2]

Gibran came from a modest socio-economic class and his presence on earth was quite brief, forty-eight years only. He was born on January 6, 1883 in the small village of Bsherri. Bsherri is geographically located in the Northern part of Lebanon, and not far from the famous Cedar forests of Biblical times, at an altitude of over 5,000 feet; it is embedded in the blue sky and pure air with the far sight of the Mediterranean Sea. The town has not much changed since the birth of Gibran, except that the population has grown in number and it has become an international spot of tourism and pilgrimage. Presently, Bsherri counts 4,000 people; it is situated as always among beautiful vineyards, apple and mulberry orchards, waterfalls and deep gorges of the Kadisha valley so much spoken of by our author. In the middle of the

village is the tomb of Gibran buried in the Chapel of the
Monastery of Mar-Sarkis,[3] and a little museum dedicated to him on the third floor of Mr. Gibran Tok's building.
The museum contains some of Gibran's watercolors and
canvases as well as several belongings of the poet.

The Gibrans belonged to the Maronite Catholic
Church.[4] The father, Khalil ben Gibran, was a shepherd
with no ambition to alter his peasant's fate. All he cared
for was playing *Taoula* (trick-trak), smoking the *Narjjile*
(water pipe), visiting friends for chit-chats, drinking occasionally a sip of native *Arrak* and strolling in the vast
field of Mount Lebanon. The father had hardly any
psychological impact on his son Kahlil. Yet, mother
Kamila played an important role in the intellectual mat-
uration of her son. She was the last child of a Maronite
priest, Estephanos Rahmi, and was born when her
mother attained the age of fifty-six. At the time Kamila
met Gibran's father, she was the widow of Hanna Abdel
Salam with whom she had emigrated to Brazil and from
whom she had a boy, Peter.

The romance between Kamila and Khalil ben Gibran
occurred after a sudden encounter when one day he
heard her singing in her father's garden. "He did not rest
until he had met her, and was immediately impressed
with her beauty and charm. And there was no peace for
him or anyone else until he had won her hand."[5]

Kamila conceived three children from her marriage
with Khalil ben Gibran. Besides our author who was
named after his father, she bore two younger daughters,
Mariana and Sultana.

Gibran received his first education at home. His
mother, a polyglot (she spoke Arabic, French and English), and endowed with artistic talents for music, was
his first tutor. We are told that she acquainted her son
with the famous Arabian old tales of Haroun-al-Rashid,

The Arabian Nights and the Hunting Songs of Abu N'Was.[6] She was also the key person who prompted him to develop his artistic sense for painting, not that she taught him to handle brushes and mix the colors, but in that she knew the rules of the game of the psychology of Behaviorism. That is, the environment in which a child comes in contact with, tends to mold somehow deterministically the capacities of the child's future personality. The situational event that caused Gibran to develop an interest for writing and drawing and to declare that "every person is potentially an artist. A child may be taught to draw a bird as easily as to write the word"[7] — goes back when at six years old he was offered a volume of Leonardo reproductions by his mother. His biographer, Barbara Young, writes:

> After turning the pages for a few moments, he burst into wild weeping and ran from the room to be alone. His passion for Leonardo possessed him from that hour, so much so indeed, that when his father rebuked him for some childish misdemeanour the boy flew into a rage and shouted, 'What have you to do with me? I am an Italian!'[8]

In 1894, Peter, the half-brother, then 18, wanting to alleviate the financial burden of his step-father and to break through the apathetic poverty of the family, decided to follow the path of many of his country friends. It came to his mind to sail to America, land of opportunity, adventure and the dollar. First the mother objected but later hearing the good news that several youth villagers had prospered in the Promised Land beyond their fathers' dreams, Kamila consented to the project of Peter with the condition that the family accompany Peter to the New World. The father refused to travel on the grounds that somebody had to take care of the small property they owned.

In the same year, Kamila, Gibran, Mariana and Sultana, under the leadership of Peter, set foot in the United States and went directly to Boston where other natives of Bsherri along with other Syrians had comprised a colony in Chinatown.

While the mother, Peter and the two sisters worked to bring money home, Gibran was forced benevolently to go to school to get the education his parents were not granted. During the two years of learning he spent in the public school of the district, Gibran recorded the highest scores from among his U.S. classmates. His teachers saw in him the precocity of his genius. Also, it was at their suggestion that he abbreviated his initial name Gibran K*h*alil Gibran into Kahlil Gibran by rotating the letter "h" of his first name.[9]

After two successful years of intense studies in American curriculum, Gibran asked permission from Peter and Kamila to return to Lebanon in order to cultivate his native language and become acquainted with Arabian erudition. His wish was met and from 1896–1901 he studied a great many subjects at the eminent *Madrasat Al-Hikmat* (School of Wisdom), today located in Ashrafiet, Beirut. Among the courses he enrolled in were international law, medicine, music and the history of religion. Also, during the period of 1898 he edited the literary and philosophical magazine *Al Hakikat* (The Truth). Finally, in 1900, motivated by admiration for the great Arabian thinkers he had studied in classes, he undertook to make drawings of these personages though no portraits of them existed. He made sketches of the early Islamic poets Al Farid, Abu N'Was, and Al Mutanabbi; of the philosophers Ibn Sina and Ibn Khaldun; and of Khansa, the great Arabic woman poet.[10] But most particularly

Gibran had one love experience which marked his life deeply. It was his first romance with Miss Hala Daher, whom he immortalized in his novel *The Broken Wings* (1912) under the name of *Selma*. He wished to marry her but was refused because she issued from a wealthy family, and was promised already as a child by her parents to the hands of someone else. This first contact with the aristocratic Lebanese family made him resent all his life the Oriental tradition of marriages that were prearranged on the grounds of social classes.

At eighteen, Gibran graduated from *Al-Hikmat* with high honors. But, still eager to acquire knowledge, he decided this time to go to Paris to learn painting. On his way from Beirut to Paris, in 1901, he visited Greece, Italy, and Spain. Gibran stayed two years in Paris, during which he wrote *Spirits Rebellious*, his famous criticism of Lebanese high official society, religious ministers, and corrupted marriage love. For this book, Gibran was excommunicated from the Maronite Church and exiled by Lebanon's Turkish Government; also both of them burned his work in the market place in Beirut.

In 1903, Gibran received a grim letter from Peter requesting him that he get back to Boston because his sister Sultana had just died from tuberculosis and his mother, Kamila, was seriously sick in bed. Shortly after his arrival Gibran had to take his mother, who was suffering from tuberculosis, to a hospital where she lay bedridden for many long months. The miseries of Gibran increased when in March of the same year Peter, the beloved half-brother who paid for his entire education, succumbed under the yoke of the same plague; three months later his mother remitted her soul into the hands of the Good Lord. The loss of Kamila was depressing to his morale for he loved her immensely. In my opinion she was his first female poetic "muse." The lines that he dedicated to motherhood in *The Broken Wings* were inspired by his mother love.

The most beautiful word on the lips of mankind is the word "Mother," and the most beautiful call is the call of "My mother." It is a word full of hope and love, a sweet and kind word coming from the depths of the heart. The mother is everything — she is our consolation in sorrow, our hope in misery, and our strength in weakness. She is the source of love, mercy, sympathy, and forgiveness. He who loses his mother loses a pure soul who blesses and guards him constantly.

Everything in nature bespeaks the mother. The sun is mother of earth and gives it its nourishment of heat, it never leaves the universe at night until it has put the earth to sleep to the song of the sea and the hymn of birds and brooks. And this earth is the mother of trees and flowers. It produces them, nurses them, and weans them. The trees and flowers become kind mothers of their great fruits and seeds. And the mother, the prototype of all existence, is the eternal spirit, full of beauty and love.[11]

Death's wretchedness left him alone with Mariana, his other sister. It goes without saying that the misfortunes of 1903 engraved deep traces of sadness on the poet's soul. Historically, I believe that if Gibran has become a philosopher of human sorrows, and a great psychologist of the finitude of human nature, it is because he immensely experienced the existential anxiety of suffering, and the facticities of human predicaments.

During the following years Gibran painted, designed book covers and wrote in Arabic many short essays as well as he revised for the second time *The Prophet* written in Arabic. By early 1904, he held an exhibition of his paintings in the studio of Fred Holland Day, a friend photographer. When the studio was opened, only a few visitors showed up. To his embarrassment no one asked the price; the audience rather criticized and laughed at his work. However, among the spectators, came one woman named Miss Mary Haskell, a principal of school, to whom Gibran's work appealed so much to her sense of beauty and mysticism that she offered him the opportunity to display his paintings in her institution: Cambridge School for Girls. From such a miraculous encounter, an everlasting tie of friendship formed between Gibran and Miss Haskell. She became his first patron and benefactress.[12] Thus, it was she who advised him to go for a second time to Paris in 1908, and financed his studies at the *Academie Julien* and at the *Ecole des Beaux Arts*. In a letter he wrote to a friend he personified Miss Haskell as heaven and a she-angel: "who is ushering me towards a splendid future and paving me the path of intellectual and financial success."[13]

It is worthwhile to pause for a moment at this point and ponder on the relationships Gibran nurtured with two women of this epoch. For one he had a Platonic love while for the other it was a Freudian love. The first was Miss Haskell, toward whom he had a spiritual and intellectual love. The second was Emile Michel, a young, beautiful and self-confident French woman, nicknamed Micheline, who taught French in Miss Haskell's school where Gibran met her. The two loves had a great effect upon him, to the point that he always spoke of women in his writings, and like John Stuart Mill he made himself a duty to promulgate Women's Liberation from the males' deceitful customs.[14]

The departure of Gibran for Paris in 1908 was not merely undertaken for the sake of learning painting, but also Gibran, as an Arab who feels grateful to those who bestow gifts upon him, wanted to forget Micheline, for he knew that this love was contrary to his sense of gratefulness toward Miss Haskell. Yet, to his surprise Micheline came unexpectedly to him in Paris. "Gibran forgot the world and he forgot Mary with the world. He opened his arms to Micheline and offered to live with her,"[15] not, however, as his wife. He asked her to be his mistress; Micheline refused because she wanted to be married to him. This was the end of a second frustrated love, the first being Hala Daher.

While in the "City of Arts" and "the Heart of the World" as he used to refer to Paris,[16] he met and made portraits of many illustrious artists, poets and writers from all over the world. Above all he tied a strong friendship with the distinguished sculptor Auguste Rodin, under whom he studied and who one day said of him that he was the William Blake of the Twentieth Century,[17] signifying by this the great resemblance in writing, painting and biography between Gibran and Blake. Also, it was in 1908, that Gibran received news from a friend in Lebanon announcing that with the replacement of the old despotic Turkish government by the Young Turks, his exile was revoked. The news made him happy but did not instigate him to sail to his homeland.

Back to Boston in 1910, Gibran began to suffer from remorses. The favors Miss Haskell poured on him had become a burden of responsibility on his shoulders. In the midst of indecision, confusion and guilt, Gibran not knowing how to repay Miss Haskell, offered to marry her, though the idea to his mind was despicable. But Miss Haskell, guessing the struggle into which his soul was plunged, made clear to him that she preferred his friendship to any burdensome tie of marrriage. Gibran felt relieved.

In exchange for the moral and pecuniary support he obtained from Miss Haskell,[18] Gibran immortalized her by dedicating to her memory many of his writings, such as *The Broken Wings*, the poem "The Beauty of Death" in *Tears and Laughter*, etc.

Around 1912, Gibran moved to New York where he took residence till the end of his life, at 51 West Tenth Street, on the third floor of the famous "Studio Building" exclusively built for painters and writers. Before and after the World War, Gibran's fame began to grow steadily ever more. He held numerous exhibitions in various galleries of the east coast. On the other hand he produced a vast literature of short essays, novels, poems, stories, aphorisms etc. . . . all of which dealt with the existential themes of the concrete life. Finally, with the publication of *The Prophet* in 1923, Gibran's reputation spread both in the Middle East and in the United States.

If today's Arabic literature feels at ease with the rules of rhyme and rhythm, it is because Gibran, along with some other literary friends, broke away from the stagnant traditional prerequisites of the Arabic verse by proposing as early as 1920 a new poetic form called "prose poem." This new idea came about, when on April 20, 1920, a new literary circle was formed after a meeting held in Gibran's studio. This was called *Arrabitah*, the Pen-Bond. Gibran was elected president among several other poets, all of them Arab immigrants in the U.S. The purpose of *Arrabitah* was to modernize Arabic literature and to promote this newly conceived idea among the Middle Eastern writers. *Arrabitah* made the name of Gibran a daily topic of discussion either among the intellectuals in the Arab countries or in the newspapers published in the Middle East.

Before concluding his biography, let me report two important incidents that occurred with two other

women. One took place in 1912 with the writer May
Ziadeh, a woman of Lebanese origin, whose family had
moved to Egypt when she was still young. May's home
was a gathering place of the Egyptian intelligentsia
where often Gibran's publications were matters of
philosophical conversation. We are told that it was May
who first introduced herself to Gibran, writing him a
letter of admiration. Touched by her candid thoughts, it
seems that Gibran fell in love at first sight with his correspondent even though he never met her in flesh and
blood. In *A Self-Portrait*, which is a collection of his letters, we read that Gibran had asked May, when his book
The Broken Wings first appeared in Arabic, to send him
her impressions about his thoughts expressed on marriage and love. Her reply on May 12, 1912, did not
totally approve of Gibran's philosophy of love. Rather
she remained in all her correspondence quite critical
of a few of Gibran's Westernized ideas. Still he had a
strong emotional attachment to Miss Ziadeh till his
death. He dreamt a lot of her and wished very much to
end his moments of life close to May. A few years before
his death he wrote her:

> I wish I were sick in Egypt or in my country so I
> might be close to the ones I love. Do you know, May,
> that every morning and every evening I find myself
> in a home in Cairo with you sitting before me read-
> ing the last article I wrote or the one you wrote
> which has not yet been published.[19]

The second of these important happenings is the meeting with his one day biographer, Miss Barbara Young. Of
her known, she tells us that it was in 1923, after listening
to the reading of an excerpt of *The Prophet* in the Church
of St. Mark's In the Bowery in New York, that she decided to let Gibran know about her admiration for him. Cor-

dially in his reply he invited her to come visiting him in his studio and "to talk about poetry and to see the pictures" he had drawn.[20] From there on Barbara kept on going regularly to the studio that was located on 51 West 10th Street. Gibran employed her sometimes as his secretary. No remuneration was paid; she was simply fascinated by this slender, mustachioed Lebanese immigrant, five feet four inches tall, with brown eyes fringed by long lashes. While Gibran was still alive, she would go to some distant city, lecturing on our author's thoughts and paintings. In her biography of Gibran she repeatedly defined her relation as "friendship," meaning probably Platonic. After Gibran's death she spread widely his fame, and even wrote a small brochure about him. Yet, in 1944, she published the now famous biography *This Man From Lebanon*, in which she recorded the personality of the Gibran she knew during his last seven years. Miss Barbara Young traveled in October 1939, to Beirut and visited the various places where Gibran lived, long before she undertook the composition of her book.

Kahlil Gibran closed his eyes peacefully on April 10, 1931, at the age of forty-eight, in St. Vincent's hospital in New York. Gibran was not buried in America but his remains were taken, to meet his wish, to Lebanon and laid down in the old deserted monastery of Mar-Sarkis in Wadi Kadisha.

The Lebanese of today, not to exempt the Arabs of the other countries, feel proud of Gibran, because with a sole hand he has elevated the dignity of the immigrants and proved to foreigners the erudition and wisdom of the Middle-East mystics. His fame can best be tested by the reader, if the latter consents to take a short trip to his nearest bookstore and witness the sale of the works of our author.

THE CONTRIBUTIONS OF THE WRITER

ONE WAY of understanding an author consists in deciphering his thoughts through his works. After all a book is a perfect self-projection of the personality, desires, ambitions and frustrations of the writer. In good philosophical language we say that there is a relation of proportionality if not identity between the "cause," the producer, and "effect," the product. Now, it is true that Gibran would sometimes refuse to be confused with his heroes, as he said, for instance, in a letter to Miss May Ziadeh concerning the personage The Madman.[1] Still, I hold the theory that the motives behind a work have to be sought in the individual contributor, in that *la raison d'être* of the product portrays the personality of the producer.

In this chapter, which I might have entitled "An Introduction to Gibran," I will depict the essential themes of Gibran's philosophy through his printed literature, in as much as I will attempt to outline the influences he bore, and the impact he left on his readers.

The Meaning of Gibran's Publications

Gibran has conveyed his thoughts through many literary forms of expression. He wrote many books ranging from poems, aphorisms, short plays, parables, to essays and novels.

The very first appearance of Gibran as a writer is that of

rebellious youth disenchanted with anything called "organization." *Spirits Rebellious* was composed in Arabic while studying in Paris in 1903. The book argues that the institutionalized laws of the church, as well as man-made social laws, are decayed, for none of them enable the individual to develop a self-identity. Rather, like Kierkegaard would say, they are "universal," and therefore, they appeal to the common mass, and mold patterned or stereotyped personalities. The book especially denounces the Maronite clergy's conduct toward the poor peasants as "simoniac," and declares human laws as unethical oppressions exercised in the name of moral justice. This work is meaningful in many respects. (1) It reveals the political and religious situations of Lebanon at the time of its publication, in that it clearly underlines that the spirit of feudalism under the Turks was detrimental to the poor for it introduced the class struggle. (2) It represents Gibran's moral philosophy.[2] Though the tone of it sounds a bit rebellious, Gibran's ethic, however, should not be identified with nowadays revolutionary radicals who abhor unconditionally whatever is called "establishment," meaning a complete rejection of rules and order in society. On the contrary, like Rousseau, Gibran is a "reformer" of the social woes caused by injustice, ineffective traditions, and the unnatural laws that hurt the innate laws of human nature. His reform asks that kindness, forgiveness and love be the guidelines of social intercourse between citizen and government. (3) Finally, the novel anticipates Gibran's later writings. In the theory-building of many philosophers, historians detect an evolution of ideas that involve contradications and ambiguities, but, Gibran really never relinquished his very first ideas and never raised paradoxes in his system.

Soon after its publication, *Spirits Rebellious* was burned

in the midst of Beirut. For punishment Gibran was ex-communicated from the Catholic Maronite Church and was exiled by the Turkish officials from Lebanon. In a letter he wrote to his first cousin, Nakhli Gibran, he expressed his melancholy for what his countrymen did to him.

> . . . I am not sure whether the Arabic-speaking world would remain as friendly to me as it has been in the past three years. I say this because the apparition of enmity has already appeared. The people in Syria are calling me heretic, and the intelligentsia in Egypt vilifies me, saying, "He is the enemy of just laws, of family ties, and of old traditions." Those writers are telling the truth, because I do not love man-made laws and I abhor the traditions that our ancestors left us. This hatred is the fruit of my love for the sacred and spiritual kindness which should be the source of every law upon the earth, for kindness is the shadow of God in man . . . Will my teaching ever be received by the Arab world, or will it die away and disappear like a shadow?[3]

However, when in 1908, the Young Turks, headed by Niyazi, overthrew the Sultan Abdul-Hamid II, the new government pardoned all the exiles including Gibran who was then in Paris studying painting with Auguste Rodin.[4]

His next novel is *The Broken Wings* (1912). Personally he writes: "This book is the best one I have ever written."[5] Best, indeed it is, yet with some reservations for *The Prophet* was not yet. In my opinion, the philosophy outlined in this book is in continuation with the philosophy of marriage stressed in *Spirits Rebellious*. Nonetheless, Gibran seems less preoccupied with

polemic than trying to describe to us the human predicament of love, which constitutes the central topic of the
whole novel. His definition of love hither is neither
Platonic nor Freudian, but between romantic and
spiritual.[6] Furthermore, he insists, after the manner of
Blaise Pascal, that love is not the work of reason but of
the heart; not the carnal or bodily sensation heart, but of
a heart that still has a logic. *La logique du coeur* is the
correct expression. What the emotions know logically,
the logic of abstract reason cannot reason about unless it
falls prey to one of Freud's defense mechanisms:
rationalization.

The story that Gibran narrates is autobiographical[7]; it
is about his first romance with Miss Hala Daher, whom
he met while studying in Lebanon. By the way, his
matrimony to Miss Daher was impeded not by the girl's
father, but rather by the town bishop, who had imposed
against the wills of the girl and her father, the decision of
a marriage with his nephew. The nephew was an irre-
sponsible man and the uncle bishop was most avid to
inherit the wealth of the Dahers. By the way, a movie has
been made about *The Broken Wings*.

A Tear and a Smile (1914) argues through poems and
prose poems that human existence oscillates between
two metaphysical predicaments, viz., joy and suffering.
These are metaphysical, because they express human
dimensions, and impregnate the core of the being of
man. Somehow, the philosophy that he expounds in this
book is neither Schopenhauerism nor Leibnizism. The
former thought that everything is evil and that our world
is the worst one that God could have ever created. To the
other extreme, Leibniz taught an exaggerated optimism,
saying that if opportunity was presented, God could not
create a better world than this one. Gibran is mid-way.
Life is both a "tear" and a "smile." The tear has an

intrinsic or extrinsic motive; the extrinsic is, however, the motive of the former. This amounts to saying, evil that surrounds us out-there in society, in politics, or in my other fellowman, is what tortures and hampers my existence, thus, affecting me from within. This being the case, we understand why Gibran has included in the book some short essays that portray the cupidities of society. Yet, Gibran does not stop at the iniquities of life, he also acknowledges the reality of happiness, joy and love. To put it bluntly, he approves of the philosophy of stoicism. The stoics bear courageously their cross; a lamentation which is not followed immediately by a pursuit of an intellectual meditation, *abases* man's intellectual capacities whose teleologic is to overcome meaningfully the pain. However, this should not make us think that Gibran's philosophy is an escape from life's frustrations through a calculative thinking process. Maybe, existentialism is the closest philosophy with which his system finds affinities. Indeed, like the existentialists, he assumes that pain and joy are complementary and interrelated. For instance, love is not without some sacrifices; there are no roses without thorns; there can be no appreciation of happiness unless the soul has first drunk of the cup of bitterness. Somehow, the book surmises that it is utopia to want a world exempted from psychological stress, in as much as it is untrue that human life knows nothing of joy, friendship, happiness. Finally, it is my personal conviction that *A Tear and a Smile* is not of a "Nietzschean inspiration," as said Andrew Dib Sherfan.[8] The overtone is similar to the British poet William Blake, whom Gibran imitated a great deal. For example, the many articles about the function of the poet in society reflect a resemblance to Blake's conception of the authentic poet: a messenger sent from Heaven to lead people on the right path of God's love.

ın 1918, at the age of thirty five, Gibran summed up his meditations in *The Procession*. The work was first written in Arabic verses. It communicates a dialogue between a youth full of vigor, an optimist, a believer in the native goodness of man, and worshipper of nature where he dwells—and an aged sage embittered by the inhabitants of the metropolis, where the rhythm of life is so mechanized and standardized that beauty, love, religion, justice, knowledge, happiness, gentleness, are veiled by false pretences. In the last page, the sage avows that if youth was granted to him, he would choose to run wild and free in nature. The poem reminds us of J. J. Rousseau's contrasts between the native goodness of human nature and the rotten constructed nature that civilizationimparts upon us through its bad stimuli. Our author had a high esteem of Rousseau. On many occasions he spoke of the latter as a liberator of mankind from tyranny and "Bastille."[9]

Gibran's first publication in English is a collection of poems and parables with the title *The Madman* (1918). Here we see Nietzsche's influence on Gibran's style. Like Nietzsche, Gibran expresses himself through parables. But also, his Madman, following the trend of Zarathustra, introduces himself to others with a *"shout."* The cry of Zarathustra was the declaration of God's death; Gibran's Madman, however, does not proclaim the diety's death but asserts a relation of cooperation between man and God concerning Creation. As we turn the pages, we are struck by the attitude of irony and sarcasm that slowly builts up till it reaches its zenith with the last parable "The Perfect World." This essay, once more, denounces the hypocritic behaviors performed in the name of a "God of lost souls."[10] The Madman is not literally mentally unbalanced; on the contrary, he is, in the language of psychosomatic medicine, perfectly healthy. His madness is only in the eyes of others, from whom he deviates in his right and just and logical doings. Gibran here agrees with the opinion held by the humanistic psychologists, namely, we tend to be what society expects from us, although these expectations could be detrimental for the development of our self-identity. Whence oftentimes we veil our true selves with masks, out of fear of being ridiculed by others. The ethics of Gibran's hero are quite simple: better be labelled madman by others, than hide my inner self with filthy social masks. The parables "The Wise King" and "The Blessed City" are significant in that they imbed, in the manner of Aesop and La Fontaine, a moral lesson from which our contemporary world could learn something about sincerity.

With *The Forerunner* (1920) Gibran becomes more mysterious and more of a mature philosopher. The title he selected is quite appropriate for the type of philosophic thoughts he conveys through the parables. In his preface he defines man as a "forerunner" meaning that we foreran what we "are" today. His logic here is not much different from the historical dialectic of Marx or Sartre. Basically, he asserts that "man invents man" (Marx); we are our own product; "I am what I am because I have made of myself what I am" (Sartre). Nobody is to be blamed for our "being" and "having," but ourselves. Psychologically speaking, this is called self-actualization. Yet, this process is Heraclitian, i.e. it never ends for the tomorrow is always stretched out-there, untouched. In other words, Gibran makes clear that we are our own destiny, and not the toy of a blind fate. Moreover, the essay makes ample reference to intersubjectivity. A man's existence does not run parallel to another's. Existence is a coexistence. For better or for worse, man is not an island; he is a social animal.

The Prophet (1923) is his masterpiece; this book has become a second Bible for the readers. Priests don't mind consulting it during mass. James Kavanaugh for instance when he was still part of the Catholic Clergy, cited during a matrimonial ceremony the lines of *The Prophet* on marriage instead of reciting the prayers of the St. Office.[11]

Now, it should be understood that Gibran had long meditated on *The Prophet* and rewrote it three times. He was just fifteen years old when he composed its first version. At the age of twenty, he revised *The Prophet* in Arabic. Then took it to his mother who was seriously ill,

> and he read to her what he had written of the young Almustafa [the hero of the play]. The mother, wise in her son's youth as she had been in his childhood, said "It is good work, Gibran. But the time is not yet. Put it away." He obeyed her to the letter. "She knew," he said, "far better than I, in my green youth."[12]

Then between 1917–1922, he rewrote the book for a third time; finally in 1923 he released it to the press.

Most particularly *The Prophet* is a direct copy of the style of Nietzsche's *Thus Spoke Zarathustra*. Yet, Almustafa does not share at all the philosophy of Zarathustra who is grim and pessimistic about the abilities of man. Here, like elsewhere, Gibran is simply fascinated by the style of Nietzsche; as to the content of Nietzsche's Zarathustra, Gibran is not the least under his spell. In my opinion the real straight forward influence on Gibran's thoughts of *The Prophet* is rather the Bible. Actually, Nietzsche himself was inspired by the figure of Jesus Christ, his speeches and style of expression, the parables. That is why we find many "numerical numbers" in Nietzsche's Zarathustra that were borrowed from the Holy Scriptures. For instance, Christ and Zarathustra both began their prophetic mission at the age of thirty.[13]

Fundamentally, all the sermons of the Prophet revolve around one dimension of human reality: the authentic social relations. Thus, Almustafa revokes all the intersubjective situations—marriage, law, children, friendship, giving, etc.—where people come in contact with each other. But also, the book teaches how these existential relations should genuinely be experienced. I know that I would not be exaggerating if for sake of comparison, I recalled to the attention of the reader that M. Heidegger, the leader of existentialism, has a somehow similar definition of the human predicament. Heidegger, following his teacher E. Husserl, characterizes man as a *Mitdasein*. That is metaphysically, man is a being-with-others, and in no instance could human nature be exempted from such a facticity; as for the case of solitude, isolation once more proves rather than disproves the "fact" of "togetherness." One may retire to his ivory tower either because he wants to reevaluate the meaning of his relations with his fellowmen, or because he has been hurt by others. But in all events we realize that the metaphysical predicament of being-with-others permeates man socially and psychologically, and not the other way around.

"Intersubjectivity" is not, however, the only kind of relation Gibran sought to express. Actually, *The Prophet* and two others, *The Garden of the Prophet* (1933) and *The Earth Gods* (1931), form a trilogy intended to outline the three-fold relational dimensions of the existential man. The corresponding technical philosophic expressions are *Mitwelt* (relation with other minds; synonymous, *Mitdasein*), *Umwelt* (relation with the world), and *Gotteswelt* (relation with God).

The Garden of the Prophet studies man's relation to nature (*Umwelt*). The emphasis is that of "ecology" and "environmentalism," not with a scientific outlook but poetic. Gibran was a worshipper of nature and wild life. Had he lived long enough to witness to what degree our scientific inventors have intoxicated the air and polluted the rivers, there is no doubt that he would have sharply deplored our tyrannical attitude toward helpless nature. It is said that our primitive ancestors fought physically and intellectually to preserve themselves from cosmic calamities; well, today the role of master-servant relation is reversed; it is man now who presents a threat to nature. At any rate, the cosmology that Gibran propounds in the book is very much anthropomorphic. He describes human emotions with concepts borrowed from nature.

As for *The Earth Gods*, it explicates God's relation to man (*Gotteswelt*). Man has the desire to be close to the Divine. In Gibran's philosophy man ascends to God "in," "through" and "with" love only. The essay is a dialogue among three gods, two of whom consider that "man is food for the gods."[14] That is, man is meat for the glory and plans of the gods, and a toy that satisfies their whims. The third god, however, is all compassion; his speech is an attempt to change the despotic attitude of the two others; he reminds them that love is the virture of the gods; finally, to win them on his side, in favor of the human, he reminds them that man is capable of practicing the very virtue of the gods: he gives them the case of the love of man for woman.

To revert back to *The Prophet*, Gibran has attained his zenith among the international scholars with "the little black book"[15], as he liked to refer to it because of its black cover. The thoughts contained in the work are so powerful and attractive that it has become one of the rare manuscripts ever to be translated in more than twenty languages. Every reader sees a bit of himself in the philosophic discourses of Almustafa. To many this "strange little book,"[16] still serves as a guide for their examination of conscience. Miss Young relates:

There was a young Russian girl named Marya, who had been climbing in the Rockies with a group of friends, other young people. She had gone aside from them and sat down on a rock to rest, and beside her she saw a black book. It was *The Prophet*, which meant nothing to her. Idly she turned the pages, then she began to read a little, then a little more. "Then," said Marya, telling us the story, "I rushed to my friend and shouted, 'Come and see—what I have all my life been waiting for—I have found it—Truth!'"

There was another man, a lawyer who sat through an hour of reading aloud from the same book in another bookshop in Philadelphia. He was a man full of years, with a benign countenance, and he listened with a quality of attention that could not fail to attract the reader's notice. When the evening was over this lawyer came to speak to me as others were doing, and he said, "I am a criminal lawyer. If I had read that chapter on *Crime and Punishment* twenty years ago I would have been a better and a happier man, and an infinitely better counsel for the defense."

I know a gentleman in New York City, the manager of a well-known real estate firm. He told me this: "My wife has three copies of *The Prophet* in our house. When we meet a new acquaintance who promises to be congenial, she lends him, or her, one of the copies. According to the person's reaction to

the book we form our opinion of his worthwhile-
ness." . . . You cannot read a page without being
moved in the depths of your consciousness, if you
are one of those "at all ready for the truth."[17]

Sand and Foam (1926) is a compilation of maxims and
aphorisms similar to those of La Rochefaucault, William
Blake, and F. Nietzche. Each of these sayings could be
used for intellectual meditation. But to consider them as
good thoughts that could be wrapped in Chinese fortune
cookies, I deem the project of bad taste.

Another major important work is *Jesus The Son of Man*
(1928). Gibran has always been attracted by the majesty
of Jesus' teachings and by the mystery of his life. He
viewed Jesus as the great human exemplar who best
fulfilled the metamorphosis of transmutation from
human nature into Godlike. As the title already implies,
the Jesus that Gibran describes is not the Jesus of theology or dogmas of whom Revelation attests as the Son
and Equal of God and the Holy Spirit in the Mystery of
Trinity. Rather, he depicts to us a Jesus made of flesh,
tormented by human passions, but who, however, has
transcended the evil limitations of lust, injustice, and
insensitiveness. At this point I remind the reader that
Gibran had no attachment for organized religion. That is
why he never meant to speak of the Jesus of the Christian, but of the Jesus of Nazareth, the man who had a
mother and a father. His real concern is to make the
image of Jesus accessible to the human. We know that
the so-called intimidated mortals consider the life and
deeds of Jesus inimitable because *a priori* they judge him
not as a human but their God. Consequently, these souls
remain unaffected by the exhortations of Jesus. Well,
Gibran's new narration of the life of Jesus purposes to
change our attitude toward this "extraordinary man,

Jesus," who after all was not made of a different stuff than us, except that he had successfully developed to its peak the divine potentialities of love and compassion that God the Creator encompasses within our nature. Gibran recounts the life of Jesus through the testimony of seventy seven persons who knew him. The last personage is "A Man From Lebanon," most probably Gibran himself. I find it difficult to conclude that our author committed the heresy of the Jacobite Monophysites, or even of the Nestorians. The point he meant to get across to us is that the supernatural is implanted within each man, and it comes to each individual to realize the divinity of his nature. "The soul is a link in the divine chain."[18] For guidance in our pursuit of being worthy of God, he recommended to follow the path of Jesus.

Finally, the remaining of the works reiterate his thoughts already elaborated in his previous books. *The Wanderer* (1932) is a posthumous collection of fifty stories; *Secrets of the Heart* (1947) is an amalgamation of short stories, among which "The Tempest" sarcastically portrays in the manner of Nietzsche the lack of spirituality in modern society; *The Nymphs of the Valley* (1948) repeats once more his polemics against the social and ecclesiastical woes; *The Voice of the Master* (1959) contains some of his correspondences with his closest friends; *Thoughts and Meditations* (1961); *Spiritual Sayings* (1962); and, *Beloved Prophet* (1972) is a collection of Gibran's letters to Haskell; also this book contains Miss Haskell's private journal about Gibran's life and personality.

In conclusion allow me to express my discontent with some of Gibran's publishers. This man from Lebanon is widely read by the scholars and the laymen, and yet I personally feel that he is little understood by either of these readers. I have spoken to many of his admirers; to my surprise I discovered that they have a vague and confusing comprehension of what he meant to convey to mankind. After much thought I believe that the cause of the symptoms of ignorance among his readers are threefold. (1) Many get acquainted with just one or a few of his works, leaving their mind blank as to what he elaborates in his other books. And yet, no scholar can be enough appreciated intellectually unless a great number of his publications are absorbed. (2) A good part of the blame for people's ignorance has to be attributed most particularly to the publisher Alfred A. Knopf, who for monetary profit has made available *The Prophet* in three different kinds of lithography: inexpensive, medium, and gift wrap format. This "little black book" has become commercial. Friends will buy it as a Christmas or anniversary gift for other companions; and if it is the big edition they are offered, the wide white cover and precious sheets, the receivers will display it along with the painting books of Da Vinci on the table in their living room, where visitors will glance at it. Still, the latest and worst subjugation of Gibran to "intellectual prostitution" is Knopf's insignificant calendar-book *Kahlil Gibran's Diary* (1971, 1972), which I am sure our author never dreamed of. (3) The last possible explanation for the reader's insufficient knowledge about Girban's message, stems from the too poetical and musical phraseology employed by Gibran. Many enjoy reading Gibran because the lecture carries them to sleep in a beautiful concert of self-complacency; thereby they cease meditating upon the deep philosophical meaning hidden beneath the sound verses.

I hope that this present manuscript will conteract successfully the epidemic of ignorance blurring the intellectual vision of the reader. This is the very reason I am endeavoring here to explicate the most basic concepts that Gibran expounded, although he presented them in a scattered way.

Gibran's Innovation in Modern Arabic Literature

In the contention of the Russian Orientalist Ignace Kratchovski, the Arab immigrants in America played an important felicitous role in the modernization of Arabic Literature.[19]

Till the turn of the nineteenth century, Arabic *belles-lettres* followed faithfully the conventional literary style laid down by the Koran and the Traditions of the Middle Ages. Thus "in poetry—notes Professor Cachia —by far the commonest form was the panegyric. . . . In all the sentiment expressed was conventional. . . . Poetic compositions were overlaid by far-fetched similes, metaphors, and allusions, with elaborate paronomasias and ambiologies. . . . [On the other hand in] fine prose . . . the narrative element became no more than a framework on which to hang verbal *tours de force*."[20] All this amounts to saying with Sir Hamilton Gibb, that "conservatism was too deeply bound up with the entire heritage of Arabic literature to allow any kind of simplification,"[21] novelty, and originality in stylistic expressions and content.

However, when Napoleon came to Egypt in 1798, and translations of eminent European thinkers were made available to Middle-East intellectuals, a sort of rejuvenation and improvement was born in Arabic literature. Yet, to a large extent, the immigrants (*Mahjar*) also concurred in emancipating modern literature from the sterile and decadent literary style of scholasticism. Most particularly, Gibran's new writing's form and content inspired his fellow country authors to adopt the "free verse" as their new stanza.

Already as early as 1913, Gibran along with other immigrant writers, Amin Rihani and Nasseeb Arida, began to publish in the New York monthly newspaper *al-Funoon*, essays, articles, poems that were drastically different from the classical metric schemes (*Sadj*). The literary style that they employed was the prose poem (*Shir manthur*).

Also, on April 20, 1920, the immigrant Arab writers, headed by Gibran as their president, formed a literary circle called "Arrabitah" (Pen-Bond), whose purpose was to update Arabic Literature "from the state of sterility and imitation to the state of beautiful originality in both meaning and style."[22] Soon "Arrabitah" impressed the Arab world. In the words of Muhammad Najm, this new school, "characterized by power, modernity and revolt against all that is traditional and rotten, is the strongest school that modern Arabic literature has known until the present day."[23]

And precisely, through the society of "Arrabitah" and the literary form of "prose poem," Gibran contributed to the innovation of Modern Arabic literature. During his time he set the example as to how to combine prose with poetry and vice-versa. In depth his writings are poetical, though the verses are proses. The strophes have rhythm and rhyme.

Of course, it is Friedrich Nietzsche, the Psalms, and the Bible filled with parables, that gave a definite literary direction to Gibran's style of expression. From Nietzsche he not only borrowed Zarathustra's form of expression which is quite similar to the Christian Gospel, but he also acquired from Nietzsche the flair for mingling emotions and thoughts, sorrow and happiness. As from the Bible he learned the old Semitic literary figure of parables, metaphors, anthropomorphism and cosmomorphism.

In summary, Gibran is hailed today by all the commentators of Modern Arabic *belles-lettres* as an innovator in Middle Eastern literature; and in my opinion, his writings can teach something to Western authors. To the Arabs he showed them how to break away from classical rhymed poetry (*Sadj*) and to feel free with the rhythm (prose-poem). To the Westerners, he is a lived example, as to how to make of philosophy a pleasant literature, and not a boring, eyes-tiring lecture of an incomprehensible language.

The Foreign Influences

No thinker can totally sever himself from the past and present ideologies. Not even the French philosopher René Descartes, who planned on breaking the ties with traditional philosophy, did succeed in keeping his system virgin from foreign influences. Well, Gibran too bore some influences in his art work, poetry and philosophy. It is not possible for us to estimate accurately all the influences that shaped his art and thoughts. Nor is it possible for us to draw chronologically the evolution of influences on Gibran. Nevertheless, we do in fact detect a few major currents that attracted him as an artist and a writer.

Thus, Gibran's *paintings* reflect the impact of the Paris schools, *Academic Julien* and *Ecoles des Beaux Arts*, and most especially, that of his teacher Auguste Rodin under whom he studied in 1908 in France. But also as the critic of his *Twenty Drawings*, Miss Alice Raphael noted: "In painting he is a classicist and his work owes more to the findings of Da Vinci than it does to any modern insurgent."[24] Gibran's interest in Da Vinci dates back to when at six years old he was given by his mother a volume of Leonardo's reproductions.

On the other hand, in his *literature*, Gibran was impressed by the early-Islamic poet Mutanabbi,[25] and the notorious Persian Ibn al-Muqaffa, who is best known for his translations of Pahlavi works into Arabic. Ibn al-

Muqaffa employed a lavish rhetorical style for recounting fables which encompassed a moral lesson.[26] Gibran in his turn, used the style of fables in order to communicate to his reader a moral teaching. Also, Amin Rihani, Mikhail Naimy, Nasseeb Arida, the Egyptian woman author May Ziadeh, and many other Arab literati left deep imprints on Gibran's expressionistic literature.

Yet, it seems that his exposure to European culture refined by far his prose-poetry and provided him with philosophic ideas. Lest I repeat the names of those who influenced him in both his literary form and philosophical content, let's outline in brief the main Eastern and Western ideological movements that gave a special orientation to his philosophy and style of expression.

FRIEDRICH NIETZSCHE

This German philosopher (1844–1900) has probably next to the Bible the most influenced Gibran's thoughts and style of expression. Miss Haskell reports that Gibran had read Nietzsche since "he was twelve or thirteen."[27] Gibran had a high respect for Nietzsche. He would call him: "the loneliest man of the nineteenth century and surely the greatest."[28] On other occasions Gibran depicted him as "a sober Dionysus—a superman who lives in forests and fields—a mighty being who loves music and dancing and all joy."[29]

Essentially, Nietzsche's philosophy denounces society for the despiritualization and demoralization in the world. He blames Christianity and the social institutions for the dehumanization of the individual, and the occurrence of "slave morality."

Of all the works of Nietzsche, Gibran liked most *Thus Spoke Zarathustra*. His books, *The Madman,The Forerun-*

ner, *The Prophet* and *The Tempest* were written with a Nietzschean inspiration. From Nietzsche Gibran learned how to convey his ideas in a messianic overtone, while at the same time using an inflammatory style for criticizing organized religion and the social establishment.

Now, to be precise, I call your attention to the fact that although Gibran was attracted by Nietzsche, he was not, however, in complete agreement with his teacher's philosophy. For one, Nietzsche was a pessimist and an atheist. His Zarathustra declared the death of God, and denied the immortality of man.[30] But Gibran's Almustafa is theocentric and believes that Good will prevail over Evil. Of his own, Gibran confesses: "His [Nietzsche's] form [style] always was soothing to me. But I thought his philosophy was terrible and all wrong. I was a worshipper of beauty—and beauty was to me the loveliness of things."[31] In the text, I will, when needed, further elaborate on the similarities and dissimilarities between the two.

THE BIBLE

When I visited the private library of Gibran located in the Museum in Bsherri, I noticed many editions of the Bible and in different languages, among his few other readings. This indicates, in contrast to Nietzsche's *The Antichrist*, that Gibran is a firm believer in the teachings of the Gospel. And indeed, his philosophy of love recapitulates in its fullest details Christ's sermons on "Agape." Actually, it is my understanding that Gibran's hermeneutics of life is his personal paraphrasing in a simple and highly emotional language, of the Holy Book. Besides the parabolical figure of speech that he borrows from Jesus and the anthropomorphism of the Gospel's metaphors, I find it interesting that he makes ample use of the biblical numbers 3, 7, 12 and 30, whenever he wants to convey a messianic or prophetic numerology of events. About these numbers, he once attempted to explain them in the following way: "7 is probably from the five planets the ancients knew, and the sun and the moon. And 12 was sacred too, from the months of the year, and 4 from the four seasons and the four points of compass. And 3 we can never get away from."[32]

BUDDHISM

In *The Poet From Baalbek*, *The Nymphs of the Valley*, and "The Farewell" of *The Prophet*, in as much as in many other passages, Gibran speaks of the reincarnation of the soul and Nirvana. Undoubtedly, through reading his predecessors the Middle-Age philosophers Avicenna, Al Farid and Al Ghazali on whom he wrote articles[33], he got acquainted with the doctrine of transmigration.

A brief expose of reincarnation as propounded by Buddhism will help us to understand the spirit of Gibran.

The term used in Buddhism for transmigration or rebirth is *samsara*, that is, moving about continuously or coming again and again to rebirth. The term refers to the notion of going through one life after another. The endlessness and inevitability of *samsara* are described in *Samyutta - Nikaya*, II. (A portion of the Buddhist scriptures.)

The idea of rebirth in Buddhism receives its most essential meaning from the Buddhist truth of the *dukkha* or suffering entailed in all existence. To understand suffering, it is not enough to consider one single lifetime, wherein *dukkha* may or may not be immediately evident; one must have in view the whole unending chain of rebirth and the sum of misery entailed in this whole seemingly endless process.

One of the great affirmations of Buddhism is that human consciousness cannot be transformed in a single lifetime. The first conviction of Gautama was the conviction that became known as first of the Four Holy Truths, namely: "now this, monks, is the noble truth of pain; birth is painful, old age is painful, sickness is painful, death is painful, sorrow, lamentation, dejection, and despair are painful. Contact with unpleasant things is painful, not getting what one wishes is painful." Suffering or *dukkha* means more than just physical pain; it is the pain of heart and mind. Conflict, alienation, estrangement is at the very root of man's existence. It is claimed by Buddha that to appreciate properly the truth of *dukkha* entailed in all existence one must keep in mind this whole frightful chain of rebirth.

But *samsara* refers not only to round after round of rebirth in human forms. The whole range of sentient beings is included from the tiniest insect to the noblest man. This range forms an unbroken continuum.

The good news of Buddhism, however, is that the continuum can be broken and has been broken. At the stage of human existence *samsara* can be transcended and released and Nirvana (or the Pali word, Nibbana) be attained. Nirvana was the final peace, the eternal state of being. But how to describe for his followers the state in which all identification with a man's historical finite self is obliterated while experience itself remains and is magnified beyond all imagination did not occupy the mind of the Buddha. When he was asked by a wandering monk if it was possible to illustrate by a simile the place called Nirvana, the Buddha replied:

If a fire were blazing in front of you, would you know that it was?

Yes, good Gautama.
And would you know if it were to be put out?
Yes, good Gautama.
And on its being put out, would you know the di-
rection the fire had gone out to from here—east,
west, north, south?
This question does not apply, good Gautama.

The Buddha then closed the discussion by pointing
out that the question the ascetic has asked about existence after death was not rightly put either.
"Feelings, perceptions, those impulses, that consciousness" by which one defines a human being have passed
away from him who has attained Nirvana. "He is deep,
immeasurable, unfathomable, as is the great ocean."
(*Sammyutta-Nikaya*).[34]
Later on, I will come back to this issue.

WILLIAM BLAKE

Among the Anglo-Saxon authors, Blake (1757–1827)
played a special role in Gibran's life. Most particularly
Gibran agreed with Blake's *apocalyptic vision* of the world
as the latter expressed it in his poetry and art. Also,
Gibran followed the path of Blake in becoming a "poet of
the Bible." Blake who was deeply touched by the life and
teachings of Jesus, believed that in this world we could
perceive the direct manifestation of the Divine presence,
if we took away the scales of our eyes. Accordingly,
the Divine is incarnated in everything. And the material
world of our sense perceptions corresponds to the
spiritual world. This correspondence is not a Platonic
copy of a shadow to its light, but real for Blake, as it
became for Gibran. The reason we lack this vision or

enlightenment for seeing the unity between the material and the spiritual, is because, concluded Blake, as Gibran would later say, the vision of modern civilization is encrusting; symbolically speaking, we are caught up in the old Jerusalem and fail to see the new Jerusalem.[35] The man of the world creates polarities, social class differences, moral disparities, and speaks in a double language logic. Blake stresses this point in his two well-known metaphysical poems "The Little Black Boy," and "The Tyger."[36] But to the man of vision the polarities come together in the unity of God, who indwells in the tiniest matter as in the superior intelligences. Jesus, for Blake and Gibran, is a live exemplar who realized the Christian enlightenment, by perfecting through self-discipline and inner struggle his human and divine nature. But also, the poet—considered Blake and Gibran—is a man who has an apocalyptic vision of the world, seeks the correspondence between the transcendence and immanence of God, and who has a messianic mission in leading the people back to Truth.

No wonder that Gibran spoke favorably of Blake. "Blake is the God-man," he wrote. "His drawings are so far the profoundest things done in English—and his vision, putting aside his drawings and poems, is the most godly."[37] On the other hand, I find it true what Miss Haskell wrote in January 25, 1918 to Gibran: "Blake is mighty. The voice of God and the finger of God are in what he does. . . . He really feels closer to you, Kahlil, than all the rest."[38] This closeness in thinking and painting even Auguste Rodin noticed; that is why he called Gibran "The twentieth century Blake."

Finally, let me add, that Nietzsche, the Bible, Buddhism, and Blake were not the only foreign influences on Gibran. I think that Rousseau, Hugo, Lamartine, Voltaire, Bergson, Freud and many others have provided Gibran with some insights. Since the scope of my research is to bring to light both the meaning of Gibranism and its place in history, I will then, when needed, compare our author's idea with those who influenced his trend of thought. However, it is important to keep in mind, that an influence is always partial and temporary. Gibranism is a *Weltanschauung* of its own.

GIBRAN'S PHILOSOPHY OF AESTHETICS

As a poet and an artist Gibran experienced psychologically the metaphysics of aesthetics, and like William Blake he successfully achieved an art oriented toward the disclosure of the meaning of aesthetics in the life economy of the individual. The following two sections, "The Essence of Poetry" and "The Essence of Art," discuss the concept of the beautiful in Gibran's philosophy.

The Essence of Poetry

TRUTH, THE GOAL OF POETRY

In the history of high learning, poetry has become part of the "liberal arts" and especially of rational philosophy ever since Aristotle included it in logic. Poetry is not a vain work of imagination, but an intellectual art; and though the weakest form of argumentation, poetry by its essence aims at disclosing truth and leading the reader to truth. As Heidegger says, poetic thinking is "the foundation of truth" (*Stiftung der Wahrheit*).[1] This is also the objective of Gibran the poet. The poet in the writings of our author appears as a conscientious mind who knows that he has a mission to accomplish among his fellowman. His duty is to teach "truth" which "is the will and purpose of God in man."[2]

In what way does poetry convey truth? According to

the traditional answer given by Aristotle, the poet presents his truth in terms of images, metaphors and similes, for men naturally delight in images.[3] Gibran too as a writer uses the means of representation, imitations and parables in such a pleasing manner that he leads one to agree with his philosophical judgments. Yet, the images he uses are not empty entities. Rather, I should say, Gibran describes poetically the *historic* events of reality in view to induce the reader to perform an action. As such, though the style of Gibran belongs to the movement of romanticism, the content of his stories reminds us of the "realist." Like Kafka, Sartre, Camus . . . Gibran's heroes live in a concrete situation and at a certain period of the Twentieth Century. They are committed and engaged in the political, religious and social ideologies of the contemporary world. It is important to bear this in mind for it proves that literature according to Gibran ceases to be mere fiction intended to embellish romantically life situations. The difference between romanticism and realism lies in their difference of approach to the existential world of man. The former uses a style, form and content heavily imbued with self-obsession. The romantic poet simply writes about his egoistic inner struggles and sufferances with almost no heed of what goes on outside of him. On the other hand, the realist hardly speaks of life in the first person; his literature is an impartial description of life endured by concrete individuals in as many idiosyncratic ways. Such approach makes literature committed (*engagée*, would say Sartre) in helping mankind in its present predicament.

Also Gibran's poetry fulfills the second principle of poetry stated by Aristotle. That is, poetry has the obligation to represent good human action as good and bad human action as bad. Aristotle writes:

The objects the imitator represents are actions, with agents who are necessarily either good men or bad —the diversities of human character being nearly always derivative from this primary distinction, since the line between virtue and vice is one dividing the whole of mankind.[4]

Gibran, too, in his attempt to represent human action presents a judgment bearing on the morality of these acts. These judgments are universal in their applications, even though the story concentrates on the action of one particular individual living in a set of situations. For example, Gibran induces us to accept the universal judgment that marriages contracted by force or tradition lead to the downfall of genuine love, by giving us a particular representation of this in the person and action of Rose Hanne in *The Spirits Rebellious*. It should be kept in mind, however, that Gibran does not "moralize" poetry in the sense of imposing morality upon art, but as a poet, he observes faithfully human actions in view to qualify some deeds as good and others as bad. It comes to the philosopher of jurisprudence only to formulate and promulgate behaviors of morality, and anticipate the moral worth of conduct. Meanwhile, *the ethics of the poet is truth*. Gibran once said: "I shall follow the path to wherever my destiny and my mission for Truth shall take me."[5] Still, however, the poet's truth is not a matter of opinion as much as a constant search for the apodictic. The teleology of the poem is to "portray" phenomenologically the meaning of genuine reality in the way reality manifests itself. Hence Gibran writes: "Poetry is not an opinion expressed. It is a song that arises from a bleeding wound or a smiling mouth."[6]

INSPIRATION, THE MODE OF POETIC THINKING

Is the truth communicated through poetry a matter of logical syllogism? In other words, should poetry be reduced to the games and rules of logic? Basically, Gibran considers poetry the work of the spontaneous "thought feelings." Like the existentialists he does not give priority to abstract thinking. "Poetry is a flame in the heart, but rhetoric is flakes of snow. How can flame and snow be joined together?"[7] And again,

> Poets are two kinds; an intellectual with acquired personality, and an inspired one who was a self before his human training began. But the difference between intelligence and inspiration in poetry is like the difference between sharp fingernails that mangle the skin and ethereal lips that kiss and heal the body's sores.[8]

Gibran distinguishes sharply between "abstract thinking" and "inspiration" because he personally feels that abstract thinking fails to comprehend the *Gestalt* of reality. To quote Henri Bergson, who held a similar discrimination between these two thinking processes, I would say that the "here and now" falls outside the realm of abstraction but lies within the range of intuition which is a sympathetic mode of conversing with reality in its personality. After all, abstraction, etymologically as well as operationally, comprehends bits of reality; it is a focus of the mind upon one aspect omitting the other correspondent portions that comprise the unity of a concrete existence. While abstract disciplines, for instance, sciences, proceed by dissecting a whole into its parts, e.g. water is composed of hydrogen and oxygen, "poetry is the understanding of the whole."[9]

Now the thinking that poetry exercises is *inspiration*. It is a type of knowing other than the work of "reason." Inspiration is the thinking of the "heart." For Gibran as for Pascal, the heart has a way of reflecting upon the world which is quite different form that of reason. Pascal writes: "The heart has its reason that reason itself does not know."[10]

The emotions involve the whole of the person, mind and body, and render the individual aware of the inter-subjective relation which is experienced in the given moment. Were man by his metaphysical nature asocial, there would be no emotions. Feeling signifies to experience a psychic surge in front of something or someone. Even in the case of solitude the one-to-many relation is realized; for ideas are atoms animated by emotions. The latter are the ones that vivify ideas with powers and invest upon them the energy for actions. All this amounts to saying that the thinking process of poetry is a thought that "feels" with the heart the Beauty, Love, Sorrow and Truth encompassed in Life. Gibranism may well be labelled "irrationalism," a tag by which the existentialists are today referred; yet, irrationalism is not synonymous to antireason; it merely suggests that one does not sever "reason" from "feeling." Bluntly put, irrationalism is rather combative against rationalism, that famous philosophical movement begun by Descartes who stressed the separation between subject and object, and divorced man from his world, this world the individual dwells in and depends upon psychologically and physically. Really, Gibranism and existential irrationalism blend "reason" and "feeling" in the human. Witness how Gibran unites the two:

Poetry is wisdom that enchants the heart.
Wisdom is poetry that sings in the mind

... enchant man's heart and at the same
time sing in his mind. ... .[11]

One way of distinguishing between poetic thinking, *la
logique du coeur*, and abstract scientific thinking, *la logique
de la raison*, consists in that the latter makes use of "explanation" and "proofs" to convey its truth to his audience; yet, the truth of inspiration lies beyond proof.
When Gibran writes "Inspiration will always sing; inspiration will never explain,"[12] he has in mind his own
sayings that state: "The truth that needs proof is only
half true,"[13] and again, "Truth is the daughter of Inspiration, analysis and debate keep the people away from
Truth."[14]

If we ponder seriously on the meaning of these words,
we see how much sense they make. The truth of poetic
thinking is metaphysical in contrast to being epis-
temological, in that it depicts existence *qua* existence and
not *qua* in the mind. The Middle Ages philosophers used
to say, *ens verumque convertuntur*. Existence and truth are
correlated. Now, poetry, being a faithful representation
of reality itself, does not need to prove the truth of
reality, for what exists "is" what it is. We don't demonstrate existence for nothing is prior to "existence." Still
however, instead of aspiring to becoming rigorous and
metempirical, poetry lives by the heart, the senses and
singing. Poetic thinking understands life better than abstract thinking. In his parable *The Scholar and the Poet*,[15]
Gibran emphasizes the superiority of the poet's knowledge and stresses the fact that inspiration is both a
thinking and a feeling about the "is." In Heidegger's
own words, poetic thinking and philosophy transcend
scientific thinking because the former are able to represent the whole meaning of a given individual existence:
"Poetry . . . has so much world space to spare that

each thing—a tree, a mountain, a house, the cry of a bird—loses all indifference and common-placeness."[16] With these words, Heidegger, who incidentally possesses a philosophy of literature much similar to that of Gibran, discriminates between scientific knowledge and philosophical or poetic knowledge, on the basis that only poetry and philosophy encounter each reality in its entirety, while the empirical sciences with their methods aim at discovering the universal, the eternal and the immutable. As we know, each specific science approaches reality from one angle and after repeated experiments enunciates laws that prove to apply unconditionally to any member of a given class group. In Gibran's and Heidegger's opinion such attitude makes the individual reality lose it unique traits that separate it from the rest of the mass. And far from disclosing the "meaning" of that reality, science rather shatters it. Take for instance the smile: in scientific terminology a smile signifies the contraction of the jaw muscles, period. Yet, for philosophical and poetic thinking, a smile is more than a physiological activity; it expresses "joy," "happiness" or maybe "irony," depending on the "meaning" projected by the individual smiler.

In brief, the inspiration of poetry is something divine and in essence, naturalistic, for it is accessible to anyone who leads the life of Truth, Beauty and Love.

THE FUNCTION OF THE POET

Who is the poet? What is his role in modern society? To answer to these questions we have first to distinguish between the authentic and inauthentic poet. The latter is typically motivated by ambition. His verses lack truth and moral directiveness for the people. His poems are

"full of noise and empty sounds."[17] Sincerity is shattered by the spirit of profit. In this respect, Gibran complains about modern poetry because it has become "a
lapdog of the rich," a means to acquire "worldly goods,"
"a commodity"[18] and a "mere arrangement of words."[19]
When Jean-Paul Sartre writes in *What is Literature?*
"Poetry is the loser . . . the poet is the man who commits
himself to losing,"[20] he has in mind contemporary
poetry. And like Gibran, he attributes this to the poet
who has become utterly wordly.

The authentic poet, on the other hand, feels that he
has a messianic mission among his brethren. He is, in the
opinion of Gibran, a prophet sent to "enlighten"[21] the
people about the will of God, Truth, Love and Beauty.
The poet is not for himself but for *others*. In *A Poet's Voice*
Gibran writes:

> Heaven fills my lamp with oil and I place it at my
> window to direct the Stranger through the dark. I do
> all these things because I live in them; and if destiny
> should tie my hands and prevent me from so doing,
> then death would be my only desire. For I am a poet,
> and if I cannot give, I shall refuse to receive.[22]

It is interesting to know that also J. P. Sartre conceives
the function of the writer to be the "voice of the people."
Note the similarity between this quote from Sartre and
that of Gibran cited above:

> It is not true that one writes for oneself. That
> would be the worst frustration. . . . The operation
> of writing implies that of reading as its dialectical
> correlative and these two connected acts necessitate
> two distinct agents. . . .
> There is no art except for and by others.[23]

Now for Gibran, the messianic mission of the poet does not stop at the national boundaries of his native country but extends to all mankind. "The universe is my country and the human family is my tribe."[24]

If the poet by profession identifies himself with the whole of mankind, irrespective of the color of skin, political ideologies and ethnological boundaries, it is because as William Blake would say, the poet fulfills the same role as the priest, namely, he mediates between the Gods and people. Such definition of the poet's function is also found in Heidegger, for whom the poet is the mediator between the gods and the humans, and Heidegger calls this: "In-between" (Zwischen). The poet shows the openness (offene) of this "In between" between the divine and the human.[25] Furthermore, the poet is the shepherd of "language" as much of the being of truth.[26] Similar ideas are found in the writing of Gibran too.

> The means of reviving a language lie in the heart of the poet and upon his lips and between the creative power and the people. He is the wire that transmits the news of the world of spirit to the world of research. The poet is the father and mother of the language, which goes wherever he goes. When he dies, it remains prostrate over his grave, weeping and forlorn, until another poet comes to uplift it.[27]

It is clear from this passage that poetizing is that which makes language possible. Every poet is in close relation with the language of a historical people. And so long as history continues, poets will be present to guide their listeners. Consequently, Gibran sees the poet as the custodian of language. "The poet is the father and mother of language." Also, the poet employs three means for unveiling the essence of language: (1) through "feelings," for he alone has noble sentiments, (2) through speech; and (3) through the activity of writing. "The means of reviving a language lie in the heart of the poet and upon his lips and between his fingers." If Gibran ascribes to the poet the responsibility for protecting language it is because he sees, as Heidegger would say, *"Sprache ist das Haus des Seins"* ("Language is Being's House"). Only through language does the Gibranian poet communicate the saying of the gods.

It is noteworthy to elaborate a bit more on the relation between "language" and "being." Today people have almost lost touch with the meaning of the words of language. We learn and practice it unconsciously, somehow believing the fallacy committed by the Middle Age philosopher Abelard who said, language is but a *"flatus vocis"* (i.e., empty sounds). And yet, according to Gibran language reveals "reality"; it states explicitly "the what is," no matter whether it is a "real," "fictitious" or "rational" being. If we had to rely only on our sense perceptions for deriving epistemologically the nature of "being" (*Sein*), then our acquaintance with the real would be quite limited, since our senses have a narrow reach. For instance, we cannot perceive with our naked eyes what lies five miles away, nor can we hear beyond a certain distance. Nevertheless, it is a fact that we claim acquaintance, let us say, with the "reality" of South America, although we might have never travelled across the boundaries of our parochial cities. How is this possible? Here it is either the spoken or written language that disclosed the "reality" of South America; spoken, if we heard some friends recounting to us their journeys to such land; written, if we read some geographical books about it. At any rate, it is always language that discloses to us there being a South America. It is equally true, furthermore, that "language" more than "thinking" is the guarantor of "being." Along with Gibran we do not deny the temporal priority of thinking, for we think before we speak; but this is not the point. Had we been incapable to utter verbally and expressively our thoughts, it would have followed that the "realities" known by thinking would have remained imprisoned in the luggage of thinking as a dead log, ineffective and solipsistic. Each one of us would have been locked up in himself with his small baggage of knowledge of "being." But fortunately, language fulfills brilliantly the means of "communication," in breaking down the barrier of isolation between the humans. One of the major differences between the animal kingdom and the human sphere consists in that the latter has devised "language" which in its turn resulted in the formation of society, the advent of scientific progress and the welfare of mankind. Once more, let us say with Gibran that thanks to "language," the "beings" in the thoughts of the many human mortals are transmittable in the extramental world where each individual is presented with the opportunity of discovering a bit more about the facets of "being" that others have grasped. Language is a *dialogue*. This is how the "reality" of the past is treasured and known about. If we have now understood why "Language is Being's House," then it is apparent also why the poet, according to Gibran, is *par excellence* the guardian of "language"; poetry is the written or spoken "language" of "being" and of the *Zeitgeist* in which the poet participates.

From whom does the poet get his authority to lead the people and protect language? He is "sent by the Goddess,"[28] replies our author. And his duty is to "preach the Deity's Gospel."[29] The major and unique theme of God's gospel is "Love"[30] with its twofold expressions of "Truth" and "Beauty." At this pont I have to add that Gibran's consideration of the poet is different from that of Nietzsche. On one hand, Nietzsche calls the poet liar; on the other hand, he does not believe that poets hold their inspiration from the gods. Nietzsche rather ridicules the gods. ". . . All gods are . . . poets' prevarications."[31] While Nietzsche adopts the atheistic standpoint, Gibran in the manner of W. Blake moves to name the poet "an angel"[32] and the "holy."[33] The poet is human like his mortal fellowmen, yet, he has a divine vocation. In the words of Victor Hugo, whom our author venerated passionately, the poet is the messenger of Heaven amidst men. And contrary to Kierkegaard's logical fallacy, not all the poets are attracted to describing Beauty in a sensuous Epicurean fashion; the authentic poet sees that God's Gospel is transmitted adequately to His people. By way of comparative philosophy, I remind the reader that Gibran's philosophy of poetry corresponds to the third stage of life, called faith, of which the Danish philosopher Soren Kierkegaard spoke, and not to the aesthetic stage. It was Kierkegaard's contention that there are three ways of leading life. One is the aesthetic; this is the life of sense-experience typified by Don Juan. The second stage is the ethical, wherein the individual adjusts his existence according to some universal principles of morality. Socrates is the hero. Finally, the third stage was known to Kierkegaard as faith. The individual is totally related to God. Abraham is the exemplar. It is interesting to see the resemblance in thinking between Gibran and the founder of existentialism, Kierkegaard. In the next section, the concept of God will be once more underlined in reference to Beauty and the role of the artist. Gibran was deeply religious like Kierkegaard.

THE FATE OF THE POET IN SOCIETY

One would presume that poets are appraised by their people because of their divine messages, yet, retorts Gibran, this is not the case. People's incredulity and persistent ignorance have made of the poets solitary figures. In *The Broken Wings* we read: "Poets are unhappy people, for, no matter how high their spirits reach, they will still be enclosed in an envelope of tears."[34] The poet sheds tears because people close their heart and mind to the teaching of God's gospel. In consequence, the poet is a perfect stranger in this world, among his people and to himself. His soul yearns to depart from his body and to rejoin the after life, since "there is no one in the Universe who understands the language"[35] of the angels that he speaks. *The Poet's Death is his Life* argues that death is the deliverance of the poet from the bondage of human company. On earth, the poet is as good as dead for no one of the mob enables him to realize his sacred duty, namely, allows him to teach truth. What kills the poet, the precursor of humanity, is "man's ignorance."[36] This is indeed what has afflicted nearly all the prophets. Their body extinguished because of the psychological frustrations they suffered from their surroundings.

It is said that Gibran believed that poets commit sin only when they deny their own nature[37] which is God-like. Actually, none of Gibran's heroes committed such a sin, in that none would compromise the divine teaching imparted to him with the worldly pleasures and man-made social laws, even if this disaccord cost him his life.[38] And incidentally, all the poets of Gibran seem to disagree with the precepts of their politicians. They break the rules fabricated by the government or religious ministers. In simple words, the poets of Gibran are revolutionary ones. In depth, style, form and content, the literature of our author is rebellious. In his own words, ". . . I like in literature, rebellion. . . . And the three things I hate in it are imitation, distortion, and conformity."[39]

The Essence of Art

GIBRAN'S ART

Gibran the artist and Gibran the poet philosopher are not two different persons; what Gibran conveys through his metaphysical poems, he succeeds in representing through his art. In his art work and writings he is a mystic with a special evangelic message. And as he imitates the biblical style in his prose, so he imitates the biblical approach in his paintings. According to Anni Salem Otto, Gibran employs the parabolical method in both his art and his paintings. Now, it is understood that the parable is characteristic of the Holy Scriptures. It is important to keep in mind that the Bible has always been for Gibran, as it was for William Blake, a source of prophetic inspiration that presented a visionary narrative of the life of man between creation and apocalypse.

Far from being a mere collection of pencil drawings or papers brushed with some water colors, Gibran's art encompasses a message; in depth, line, shapes, shades, shadows and forms his paintings describe concrete human situations. They recount a story and hide a moral lesson. Typically, his art portrays only human forms. Gibran never painted an apple, a prairie or the sun down, but people. Even in the rare cases where the symbol of the drawing stands for a "rock" or the "earth" Gibran draws human bodies in such a way that they figurate the meaning of the material object.[40] Yet, on the other side, our author in his prose poems will borrow ample metaphors from nature to represent a human feeling or thought. Here are some expressions: "The tree of my heart is heavy with fruit," "My heart overflows with the wine of the ages," etc. . . .[41] His art and poetry confirm what I said previously about his anthropomorphic *Weltanschauung*. As a mystic of a school different from Plato or the ascetics, he does not regard matter as inferior to volatile spirituality. Nature has human shapes, and *vice versa* man has the shape of nature. *The Garden of the Prophet* abounds with this anthropomorphic view of reality.

You and the stone are one. There is only a difference in heart-beats. Your heart beats a little faster, does it my friend? Ay, but it is not so tranquil.[42]

At this stage, we ought to remember that W. Blake held a similar philosophy of art and philosophy of poetry. Northrop Frye, in his lengthy introduction on Blake, repeatedly insists that Blake's "art is the attempt of the trained and disciplined human mind to present this concrete, simple, and outrageously anthropomorphic view of reality."[43] Now, the real motives for Gibran's anthropomorphic art are to be found in his cosmological ecology and environmentalism, much like what is happening today. His love for nature, and belief that both nature and man are the creation of God, explain why he portrayed in his art and depicted in his poems

the man-nature coexistence. Ecologists and environmen-
talists may estimate the essay *Nature and Man* of great
importance. Here are some excerpts:

> One of the flowers raised her gentle head and whis-
> pered, "We weep because Man will come and cut us
> down, and offer us for sale in the markets of the
> city." . . .
> And I heard the brook lamenting like a widow
> mourning her dead child and I asked, "Why do you
> weep, my pure brook?"
> And the brook replied, "Because I am compelled to
> go to the city where Man contemns me and spurns
> me for stronger drinks and makes of me a scavenger
> for his offal, pollutes my purity, and turns my good-
> ness to filth."
> And I heard the birds grieving, and I asked, "Why
> do you cry, my beautiful birds?" And one of them
> flew near, and perched at the tip of a branch and
> said, "The sons of Adam will soon come into this
> field with their deadly weapons and make war upon
> us as if we were their mortal enemies . . .
> . . . "Why must Man destroy what Nature has
> built?"[44]

Besides the portraits he made of many eminent figures,
Gibran painted a lot of human naked bodies. He never
drew a body clothed. When Miss Haskell asked him why
he painted bodies naked, Gibran answered,

> Because life is naked. A nude body is the truest and
> noblest symbol of life. If I draw a mountain as a heap

of human forms or paint a waterfall in the shape of
tumbling human bodies, it is because I see in the
mountain a heap of living things, and in the waterfall a precipitate current of life.[45]

What the German existentialist Karl Jaspers said of art:
"The fine arts make our visible world speak to
us"—applies quite well to Gibran's art. The mission of
authentic art, according to our author, is not to be for the
sake of the artist's satisfaction, but expresses cultural,
historical and education ambitions. For one, the artist
"is" and "lives" in a historical context; his art records and
projects the "climate of the age" which he shares; secondly, by profession the artist's work purposes to influence the thoughts of the viewers and to contribute along
with the politicians and businessmen to the making of
history. That is, artists influence fashions, styles and to a
certain extent the behaviors of a people. For instance,
movies, fashion designers, music composers, painters
and architects do have an impact on people's conduct.
Art is *creative* of something new which never existed.
Gibran writes,

If you think more deeply on the subject, you will
find that arts reflect and influence customs, styles,
religious and social traditions—every aspect of our
life.[46]

Elsewhere Gibran states explicitly that art is not to be
imitative, otherwise creativity fades away. To copy is to
repeat what exists already, but creativity means originality.

Art arises when the secret vision of the artist and the manifestation of nature agree to find new shapes.[47]

The artist's secret vision reaches not the phenomenal appearances of the shell of reality but peeps into the noumenal of nature. For every phenotype level, there is the genotype; to every surface there must be a bottom; beyond every phenomenal manifestation there is the noumenal revelation. Art penetrates into the immanence of nature in order to unveil what our bare eyes cannot see. This is called the *meaning* of existence.

Furthermore, the purpose of art is to transport the audience toward the discovering of God the creator. Art portrays the beauty of humanity and reality with the intention of revealing the presence of the Maker of Beauty, although sometimes the artist's intention may be different. It takes courage and faith to experience through art the existence of the metempirical. Gibran writes:

Art is a step from nature toward the Infinite.[48]

and again

Art is a step in the Known toward the unkown.[49]

Finally, when Gibran published in 1919 *Twenty Drawings*, Miss Alice Raphael wrote an introduction in which she acknowledged that Gibran's art is an attempt to unify the East and West, in that he engages in the struggle of reconciling the old and the new, the past and the present fashions, traditions and novelties. Also, in Miss Raphael's opinion our artist's work "owes more to the findings of Da Vinci than it does to any of our modern insurgents."[50] However, this does not limit his scope in search for new themes and in their realizations. If we had to classify him in a school of art, he would be at the "dividing line of East and West, of the symbolist and the ideationist."[51] Indeed, as a symbolist, he is an intuitive artist who follows his instinctive flair for truth and while his art is concerned with the life of the inner-self, it projects a moral lesson; but as an ideationist or pre-Raphaelite, he goes into the minute details of the situation in which the human in question is entangled with a spirit of sincerity, and delicacy of finish. Here is the long text of Miss Raphael:

> The quality of the East and West are blended in him with a singular felicity of expression, so that while he is the symbolist in the true sense of the word, he is not affixed to traditional expression, as he would be if he were creating in the manner of the East, and though he narrates a story as definitely as any pre-Raphaelites, it is without any fanfare of historical circumstances or any of the accompaniment of symbolic accessories. In his art there is no conflict whether emotion shall sway the thought, because both are so equally established that we are not conscious of one or the other as dominant. They co-exist in harmony and the result is an expression of sheer beauty in which thought and feeling are equally blended. In this fusion of two opposing tendencies the art of Gibran transcends the conflicts of school and is beyond the fixed conceptions of the classic or romantic tradition.[52]

THE MANIFOLDNESS OF BEAUTY

In all of Gibran's portraits, as well as in his writing, *Beauty* is the incentive force and the final arbiter of his productions. What is the aesthetics and metaphysical import of the beautiful in his mind? Gibran gives many and varied definitions of Beauty. He defines it as "truth," "a timeless language," "solve the problem of human existence," "the visible, manifest and perfect handiwork of God," etc. . . . These definitions of Beauty, however, escape any etymological or nominal definitions of the logical textbooks. Frankly speaking, Gibran does not think that the essence of Beauty could be comprehended by means of the logical method of definition. Only the process of phenomenological description can unveil the meaning of Beauty. Applying Husserl's phenomenological method, I have found in the texts of Gibran many approaches to the problem of Beauty. At least three major methodological conceptions are elaborated. On one hand, Gibran speaks of Beauty in terms of psychology; on the other hand, he undertakes the analysis from the standpoint of theodicy; finally, he tackles the issue with a metaphysical outlook.

Psychologically speaking, Beauty is a matter of sensation, feeling and experience. Beauty speaks to the heart and the spirit without using the language of proof or analysis.

Only our spirits can understand beauty, or live and grow with it. It puzzles our minds; we are unable to describe it in words; it is a sensation that our eyes cannot see . . .[53]

Moreover, the aesthetic experience in Gibran's philosophy of art is not a privilege of artists solely; every mortal is liable to enjoy it. "Beauty . . . is a timeless language, common to all humanity."[54] Each one of us is at some time an artist in his own way. The professional artists are merely those who experience Beauty longer than the average men and are able to project in paintings, music or architecture the forms of Beauty.

As a psychological experience, Beauty could either be the result of joy or originate out of sorrow. Happy movies as well as sad movies always move us deeply emotionally. This is why for Gibran Beauty is found in both a tear and a smile combined. "Beauty is that harmony between joy and sorrow which begins in our holy of holies and ends beyond the scope of our imagination."[55]

Unlike Leibniz, Gibran does not profess an exaggerated optimism in that our world is the best, and unlike Schopenhauer he does not teach pessimism in that our world is the worst one. Gibran's philosophy is realistic. He knows that life is a mingle of happiness and suffering. But these two are not contradictory to each other, rather complementary. Hence, Beauty, the expression of life, is

a magnificence combined of sorrow and joy, it is the Unseen which you see, and the Vague which you understand, and the Mute which you hear—it is the Holy of Holies that begins in yourself and ends vastly beyond earthly imagination.[56]

As a general rule, Gibran consents with the

philosophers of aesthetics that the aesthetic value is *subjective*. Hence Beauty is interpreted and defined in different ways and manners according to each individual's conception. In *The Prophet*, Gibran attributes these variations of experience to the pragmatic interests each individual has in life. Beauty at this point becomes an emotional drive for "needs unsatisfied."[57] In other words, psychologically, the value discovered in the object, event or person is an unconscious projection of the inner-self. "The appearance of things changes according to the emotions and thus we see magic and beauty in them while the magic and beauty are really in ourselves."[58] This means that ugliness too is a subjective quality. As the old adage says, Beauty and ugliness are in the eyes of the beholder. "Beauty is not in the face; Beauty is in the heart."[59] What is commonly termed ugly is a sentiment in the heart totally enslaved by prejudices, pride and selfishness.

It is not that which you have never striven to reach, into whose heart you never desired to enter, that you deem ugliness?

If ugliness is aught, indeed, it is but the scales upon our eyes, and the wax filling our ears.
Call nothing ugly, my friend, save the fear of a soul in the presence of its own memories.[60]

Finally, in essence, the aesthetic experience for Gibran, in addition to bringing immediate pleasure and satisfaction by revealing certain experiential aspects of reality, it can also fortify us in various ways to meet the

practical demands of life. Beauty is *therapeutic*. It stimu-
lates or soothes us; it changes the rate of the heart beat,
renews our spirits, exciting us and giving us courage to
overcome the existential vacuum that dashes upon us at
the time of despair. In *The Broken Wings* Gibran tells us
that after his friend gave him some information about the
misfortunes that Selma Karamy had to encounter in her
life, Gibran's friend "turned his head toward the window as if he were trying to solve the problems of human
existence by concentrating on the beauty of the
universe."[61]

From the *metaphysical standpoint*, Gibran holds, like the
scholastic philosophers, the thesis which asserts that
Beauty is a transcendental predicament of being. "When
you reach the heart of life you shall find beauty in all
things, even in the eyes that are blind of beauty."[62] This
amounts to saying that what is called ugly is but a
psychological subjective emotion aroused either in the
presence of a deformed physiology or due to some personal indispositions; yet, existence *qua* existence is "pul-
chritude." In other words, real Beauty is not essentially
what we experience through sense perceptions, for these
may well be defective and thus yield false information
about reality, as for example, blindness, color blindness
or deafness. This point is most vital, for Gibran's
philosophy concentrates more on delineating the
metaphysical meaning of Beauty than on its psychological effect. In the parable titled "Faces" he writes:

I know faces, because I look through the fabric my
own eyes weave, and hold the reality beneath.[63]

Somewhere else he explains that Beauty is in being in as

much as being is Beauty. He also distinguishes between the physical Beauty and ontological Beauty, rating the latter superior to the former. As I already said, Beauty defined only in terms of sense appreciations leaves room for possible error, since the senses are arbitrary and very subjective. Actually, rather than enlarging our horizon of the understanding, Beauty captured by the senses may eventually enslave us and later on torture us. For instance, this is the unfortunate happening of those who define love in terms of physical prettiness; in Ronsard's poetic words, physical Beauty is momentary, the rose is not rose forever, it will fade someday, whence arise disappointments, frustrations and infidelity. In Kierkegaard's vernacular sensitive Beauty belongs to the aesthetic stage. On the other hand, however, Beauty experienced through the spectacles of metaphysics is a resigning attitude of the mind in accepting existence for what it "is"; such Beauty frees us from the spells of the domination of the physical contours of Beauty. Here it is the heart, namely the spontaneous thought-feeling in contrast to the calculative thinking and the senses, that is involved.

> Great beauty captures me, but a beauty still greater frees me even from itself.

> Beauty shines brighter in the heart of him who longs for it than in the eyes of him who sees it.[64]

Another way to show the transcendental relation between being and Beauty consists in correlating Beauty with truth. In the essay *Nature and Man*, we read: "Is Truth Beauty? Is Beauty Truth?"[65] Here Gibran is not so much questioning doubtfully the relation between

Beauty and truth. For in his mind, to use Aristotle's terminology, the relation is not predicamental but transcendental. A predicamental term signifies that the term is restricted in its application to a certain "kind" of things; while the transcendental applies to "all" existences unconditionally, and is interchangeable with existence (being). Although Gibran does not make use of such technical language, he does nevertheless convey this meaning when in the poem *Song of Beauty* he writes: "I [Beauty] am a Truth, O people, yea, a Truth,"[66] And again in the essay *Before the Throne of Beauty*, Gibran emphasizes that Beauty leads the investigator to truth. "A beauty . . . is a stepping-stone for the wise to the throne of living truth."[67]

It is worthwhile to ponder seriously on the meaning of these words in order to bring to light the depth of Gibran's philosophy. The metaphysics of truth in contrast to those of falsity entail that the mind asserts reality in the way reality is. For what exists is what it is itself, and not other than itself. Being is harmonious and congruent with itself. To acknowledge reality for what it is, is to know truthfully reality. Now, what is truthfully itself does not involve contradiction nor inconsistency with itself, but is well ordered and harmoniousy structured in its very being. Hence, it is Beautiful, for Beauty "is" harmony, order and truthfulness. Such is the backbone of Gibran's logic which claims that metaphysically, "ugliness" is a subjective psychological emotional uptightness and never a possible characteristic of existence. Objective Beauty is not of the province of the sense perceptions.

Beauty . . . is not the image you would see nor the song you would hear, but rather an image you see

though you close your eyes and a song you hear
though you shut your ears. It is . . . a garden for *ever*
in bloom and a flock of angels for *ever* in flight.[68]

Finally, Gibran's third approach to Beauty is from the
standpoint of theodicy. It is obvious to Gibran's mysticism
as it was for Plato, that Beauty found in nature is the
handiwork of God. In his short essay *Creation*, Gibran
explains the mystery of Creation as a divine act of
Beauty. "The God separated a spirit from Himself and
fashioned it into Beauty"[69] Beauty on earth is the
reminder of God the Invisible. If someone wants a proof
of God's existence, Gibran retorts, let him see Beauty. In
case now, he still doubts of the veracity of God, let him
then take Beauty, answers Gibran, as his new religion.
To worship Beauty is to worship God.

Are you troubled by the many faiths that Mankind
professes? Are you lost in the valley of conflicting
beliefs? Do you think that freedom of heresy is less
burdensome than the yoke of submission, and the
liberty of dissent safer than the stronghold of acquiescence?
If such be the case, then make Beauty your religion,
and worship her as your godhead; for she is the
visible, and manifest and perfect handiwork of God.
Cast off those who have toyed with godliness as if it
were a show joining together greed and arrogance,
but believe instead in the divinity of Beauty that is at
once the beginning of your worship of Life, and the
source of your hunger for Happiness.[70]

I remind the reader that this quotation does not advocate a Rousseauian naturalistic religion; rather like Pascal

Gibran is proposing a proof of God by playing the game of "Wage." It is better at least to worship Beauty in nature than to be an arrogant atheist, who may lose everything if after death God should exist. Also, this quote suggests a proof of God reminiscent of the early Greek philosophers who believed in the Divine because of their amazement and admiration in the face of the harmony and Beauty found among the celestial and terrestrial systems. The intention of Gibran being an attempt to unravel the presence of God, we understand now why in all his art work and literature he pursues Beauty. Beauty is the acid test of God's existence.

For MOST contemporary poets, and not for Sartre alone, literature ought to become "committed"—*Une littérature engagée*. Literature which is not committed is not literature at all. As an "engaged" writer, Gibran has composed many poetries and parables that are social in depth.

He mainly developed a hermeneutics of law, wherein he portrays the pathos of present day society. Methodologically speaking, however, Gibran likes to introduce us to his study of legalism through the narration of concrete life-events.

But also, Gibran had a historical and nationalistic motive for tackling the issue of "justice" as practiced within the field of the legislative branch of government. With his lucid analysis of legality he aimed at attacking the types of decayed laws that the Ottoman Turks were enforcing in Lebanon, his native land.

To insure a good presentation of Gibran's thought, I proceed to divide this chapter into three sections. (1) Humanistic Social Contract; (2) The Issue of Law; (3) Parables on Authority.

Humanistic Social Contract

THE ZEITGEIST OF MODERN SOCIETY

Like J. J. Rousseau, in *Social Contract*, Gibran did not extoll our social ways of behaving. To do this would be easy for him. The mission of the critic is not to praise virtues already acquired but to exhort people as to what should be done in order that imperfections be removed.

Gibran, the social philosopher, instead of concentrating his polemic around the evils of technology as do most existential thinkers, e.g., Heidegger, Jaspers, Marcel and Erich Fromm, prefers to attack people's social ways of behaving. Yet he agrees with the existentialists that technology is being misused to the point that nowadays the machine is no more a mere means for higher ends, but has become the supreme value, and man, the inventor, is the slave of his own invention. Definitely, Gibran is not suggesting that we should close down the factories, as if the technical were evil in itself or progress at the technological level were the very reason for all types of social inequalities, and sins against clean Mother Nature. On the contrary, to pretend that this were the solution for solving the present crisis mounting up in the human and environmental spheres, would be to relapse into the superstitious ways of our ancestors. The real blame comes to man alone who abuses intentionally of the merits of technology for the satisfaction of his egoistic desires. Thus, the spirit of technocracy affects psychologically the technocrat's *Weltanschauung*. In his relation with others, he treats them as subordinates, less valuable economically than his industrial plant. In his relation with his Creator, he wishes to occupy God's place, to repeat His deeds, to reorganize a man-made cosmos according to man-made laws of reason, efficiency and foresight — this is the ambition of the twentieth century technocrat that Gibran denounced vehemently when he wrote

When man invents a machine, he runs it; then the machines begin to run him, and he becomes the slave of his slave.[1]

One mischief that he attributed to the misuse of technological invention is the manufacture of technological weapons. He immensely deplored their discovery and considered them an indication of a step backward into primitiveness; killing one another is no sign of progress, civilization or education, but a direct manifestation of regression to the barbaric stage.

> The world has returned to savagery. What science and education have created is being destroyed by the new primitives. We are now like the prehistoric cave dwellers. Nothing distinguishes us from them save our machines of destruction and our improved techniques of slaughter.[2]

For Gibran, a Christian philosopher, the world of the technocrat has rejected theocentrism and replaced it with anthropocentrism. For example, what religion teaches about "procreation," the technocrat preaches as "fabrication." In contemporary vernaculars, "idolatry," "pantechnism," "autolatry," "technolatry," and "technomia" are all rubrics that describe the *behaviors* of the technocrat.

But besides the technocrat's wrongdoings, Gibran elaborates on the lack of spirituality in modern society. In a short essay, *The Tempest*, we read the story of a man called Yussif El Fakhri who at thirty years of age withdrew from the tumult of society and took residence in a hermitage away from the town. The name of Yussif was a subject of conversation among the citizens of the city, especially since Yussif never left his solitude. One day a young man hearing the tales advanced by the gossips of the town decided to go and visit Yussif. While he was on his way, a tempest of rain, wind and thunder arose. Instead of being discouraged, the lad thought that the storm was a good excuse for him to ask refuge at Yussif's house. When he reached the hermitage, he knocked at the door and pleaded to be received inside the house until the tempest calmed down. Once accepted inside, in a cold way by Yussif, the adolescent asked the man what made him flee society. Yussif's reply was straight and explicit. Yussif first denied that he retreated to the mountains in order to meditate on religion or God. God can be worshipped anywhere, even in the midst of the turmoils of the city. By such token, Yussif, who personifies Gibran, refused to call himself a *misanthrope*. (It is capital to keep this in mind, for none of Gibran's heroes are haters of human company. At this point Gibran agrees with the Danish philosopher Soren Kierkegaard in that "It is dangerous to isolate oneself too much, to evade the bonds of society.")[3]

Yet, the reasons Yussif enumerated to his unexpected visitor reflected the same reasons that have irritated today's European existentialists, most particularly Kierkegaard, Dostoyevski, Tolstoy, Gabriel Marcel and Franz Kafka—namely, it is the lack of spirituality, human understanding and responsibility on the part of the people. Thus, Yussif exclaimed,

> I left civilization because I found it to be an old corrupt tree, strong and terrible, whose roots are locked into the obscurity of the earth and whose branches are reaching beyond the cloud; but its blossoms are of greed and evil and crime, and its fruit is of woe and misery and fear. . . .
>
> . . . . No, my brother, I did not seek solitude for religious purposes, but solely to avoid the people and their laws, their teachings and their traditions, their ideas and their clamour and their wailing.

I sought solitude in order to keep from seeing faces of men who sell themselves and buy with the same price that which is lower than they are, spiritually and materially.

. . . . I deserted the world and sought solitude because I became tired of rendering courtesy to those multitudes who believe that humility is a sort of weakness, and mercy a kind of cowardice, and snobbery a form of strength.

. . . . I ran from the office-seekers who shatter the earthly fate of the people while throwing into their eyes the golden dust and filling their ears with sounds of meaningless talk.

I departed from the ministers who do not live according to their sermons, and who demand of the people that which they do not solicit of themselves.

. . . . I came to this far corner of God's domain for I hungered to learn the secrets of the Universe, and approach close to the throne of God.[4]

This lucid litany of societal woes acclaimed by Gibran is so relevant in itself, because it portrays the misconducts of our culture and echoes the cry of our youth. To limit myself to one geographical spot, I see, for instance, great similarities between Gibranism and today's American youth who are totally dissatisfied with the traditional sets of values of their forefathers. The U.S. youngsters are searching for spiritual values, in contrast to the material aspirations of the previous generations, at the cost of trespassing the social laws established for centuries, and severing, if needed, their parental ties.

Wouldn't you admit that many of those sincere hippies resemble Yussif?

In another story, *Khalil the Heretic*, we are told that a youth abandoned the convent life, because of his discontentment with "this age of falsehood, hypocrisy and corruption"[5] practiced by the very priests, supposedly the emissaries of God. Gibran calls his present society "sick."[6] And elsewhere he labels figuratively society with all its inventions and masks: "decayed teeth."[7] Gibran's terrible indictment of society finds ground among many philosophers; thus, Buber, a contemporary philosopher, recognizes that the trouble with our society consists in the phenomena of "lie," which modern man has invented and "introduced into nature"[8] as synonymous to truth.

NATURE VS. ARTIFICIALITY

So far I have compared Gibran's social analysis to the existentialists' mode of thinking about our technological world.However, from the historical standpoint, Gibran is closer to Rousseau than to any other philosopher when it comes to his hermeunetics of the *Zeitgeist* of present society. I may even say without fear of historical error that Gibran was immensely inspired by Rousseau when he undertook his criticism of society. Actually, many of the contemporaries were themselves influenced by Rousseau's social philosophy. For instance Leo Tolstoy and Fyodor Dostoyevski, to whom I have alluded in the previous pages, were in the words of the Russian historian V. V. Zenkovski, followers and worshippers of Rousseau.[9] Gibran, too, often expressed in his letters[10] his admiration for Rousseau. And every time he dreamed of returning for a second time to Paris, he related his desire to be "enlightened by the social studies . . . in the capital of capitals of the world where Rousseau . . . lived."[11] Rousseau's inspiration can best be seen in *The Procession*. This work of his reminds us of Rousseau's two well known manuscripts *Discourse on the Origin and Foundation of Inequality among Man* (1758) and *Social Contract* (1762). It is worthwhile at this point to give a brief explanation of this French author of the Enlightenment period and draw a parallelism between Gibranism and Rousseauism.

In 1749 the Academy of Dijon announced that it was giving a prize for the best article on the question whether the sciences and arts had contributed to the advancement of, or rather introduced corruption in, morality. Jean-Jacques Rousseau then submitted his *Discourse on the Arts and Sciences* which won the prize. Instead of praising the progress of sciences and arts, Rousseau oriented his pen toward an attack on the so-called civilized society, naming it "artificial social life." In such society human nature is not fundamentally better than it was during the primeval. Now, he writes, "we no longer dare to seem what we really are, but lie under a perpetual restraint."[12] This "perpetual restraint" is the masks that artificial society fabricates under the assumption of conventionality, and forces upon us as a second nature intended to replace our native nature. Prior to artificial civilization man was *l'homme de la nature*, "satisfying his hunger at the first oak and slaking his thirst at the first brook; finding his bed at the foot of the tree which afforded him a repast; and, with that, all his wants supplied."[13] Such a primitive man wandered up and down the forest, without home, without industry, and was an equal stranger to war and violence. His native nature was goodness. Evil came later with the establishment and development of cultures. In the eyes of Rousseau, the transition from the state of nature to the state of civilization lies in the phenomenon of "private property." "Private property" is the removal of equality and the cause of inequality among men. And, with the advent of the insecurity and other evils that "private property" introduced in life, and moved by the desire to preserve their liberty, Rousseau contends that man created governments, states, and political institutions. Yet, adds Rousseau, political institutions "bound new fetters on the poor and gave new powers to the rich; irretrievably destroyed natural liberty, fixed eternally the law of property and inequality, converted clever usurpation into unalterable right, and for the advantage of a few ambitious individuals, subjected all mankind to perpetual labor, slavery and wretchedness."[14]

Two centuries later, Gibran attacked with the same vigor the institutionalized society, and developed his logic of the evils of civilization on the same lines as Rousseau. For instance, he too does contrast the two types of nature called "native" and "artificial." This is best revealed in the youth and the sage, reported in *The Procession*, where the youth constantly emphasizes the life "in the wild" as being void of illusions, confusions, disbelief, injustices, slavery, unhappiness, despair and death; "in the forest" there is only love, eternity, fertility, hope and freedom. On the other side, the sage complains about the evil social ways that civilization introduced in the behavior of the people in the cities. The primordial law of existence "in the wood" is the belief in the native goodness of "Nature," whereas the philosophy of culture reiterates the British Thomas Hobbes' axiom of *Homo homini lupus*, i.e., each man is to another as a wolf. Most suggestive is the epilogue of the old sage who expresses the wish to rejoin the youth in his freedom in the wilderness.

Had I the days in hand to string,
   Only in forest they'd be strewn,
But circumstances drive us on
   In narrow paths by Kismet hewn.

For Fate has ways we cannot change,
   While weakness preys upon our Will;
We bolster with excuse the self,
   And help that Fate ourselves to kill.[15]

At this point I remind the reader that the concepts "forest" and "society" that Gibran contrasts should not be defined according to their strict nominal definitions, as if our author is advocating a return to peasant life or sublimating the attitude of misanthropy. Gibran is aware of the corruption nurtured in society, but he is not implying a total renunciation of society or a retreat to a hermitage in the forest. On the contrary, as he wrote on April 15, 1914, to his benefactress Miss Haskell,

Personally, I can get along with the two extreme links of the human chain, the primitive man and the highly civilized man. The primitive is always elemental and the highly civilized is always sensitive.
                                        (B.P., pp. 182-183)

Human nature by its very ontological structure discloses the *a priori* of "sociability." Men are bound to live together. As I will show later when I will tackle the issue of intersubjectivity in the Chapter on Love, Gibran did emphatically stress the idea that no individual could fulfill his personality all by himself, for the other part of the self is found in the other fellowman. Hence, it is not "togetherness" that Gibran discredited. He was rather antagonistic against false communal life. And this is the very reason he uses the concept "forest" *symbolically* as an indication of simple, innocent, pure, free, uncorrupted, unprejudiced, ethical existence. Conversely, the notion "society" with its "culture" and "civilization" denotes symbolically the inauthentic existential conducts that conventionality, traditions, customs and man-made laws introduce in the life economy of the individual person. Human existence oscillates between two diametrically opposed existential behaviors. One is the authentic that embalms a freshness, purity and naturality similar to the fragrance that Mother Nature proliferates. The other, the inauthentic, is not in accordance with the natural inclinations of goodness but a deviation from nature. In an essay titled *Your Lebanon and Mine* Gibran parallels phenomenologically the *Geist* of these two types of behavior.

> . . . Your Lebanon is two men—one who pays taxes
> and the other who collects them.
> My Lebanon is one who leans his head upon
> his arm in the shadow of the Holy Cedars, oblivious
> to all save God and the light of the sun.
> . . . Your Lebanon is appointees, employers, and
> directors,
> My Lebanon is the growth of youth, the resolution of maturity, and the wisdom of age.
> . . . Your Lebanon is disguises and borrowed ideas
> and deceit,
> My Lebanon is simple and naked truth.
> Your Lebanon is laws, rules, documents, and
> diplomatic paper,
> Mine is in touch with the secret of life
> which she knows without conscious
> knowledge. . . .

Your Lebanon is a frowning old man, stroking
his beard and thinking only of himself,
My Lebanon is youth erect like a tower, smiling
like dawn and thinking of others as he thinks of
himself.
. . . But who are the sons of your Lebanon?
. . . They are free and ardent reformers, but only
in the newspapers and on the platform.
. . . They know no hunger unless they feel it in
their pockets. When they meet with one whose
hunger
is spiritual, they ridicule him and shun
him saying, "He is not but a ghost walking in a
world of phantoms" . . .
. . . Now let me show you the sons of my Lebanon:
They are peasants who turn the stony land into
orchards and gardens.
. . . The sons of my Lebanon are the vinedressers
who
press the grapes and make good wine.
The fathers who raise mulberry trees and the
others who spin the silk.
The husbands who harvest the wheat and the
wives who gather the sheaves. . . .
. . . They walk with sturdy feet toward truth,
beauty and perfection.[16]

Lebanon in this context is not necessarily the geographic
and ethnographic spot, but represents symbolically the
ways of authentic and inauthentic *communal* behaviors.

Now Gibran's social philosophy is not as detailed as
that of Rousseau, nonetheless, like his predecessor he
knows how to tap down the real cause of all social
trauma. In his eyes, the superego of civilization disturbs
the natural equilibrium of the psyche because it conflicts

with the native aspirations of goodness. If for Rousseau "private property" begets inequalities, and if Nietzsche attributes the reality of despiritualization to the will-to-power, Gibran sums up in one word all the evil pathos of cultural superego: *hypocrisy*. This was the one human vice that he could not tolerate. He blamed society, culture and civilization for having created hypocrisy. Hypocrisy is at the root of inequality, injustices, class struggles, materialism, irreligiosity, selfishness, restraint of freedom, etc. . . . Hypocrisy disguises itself under the garments of man-made laws, customs and corrupted traditions.

From the literary, psychoanalytical and socio-cultural standpoints, it is interesting to note that Gibran associated all the rich with the spirit of hypocrisy, although, he admitted that the poor were also capable of concealing their corrupted disguised intentions behind gentle smilings, soft words and loving gestures. In all his novels, essays and poems he depicted the rich as self-centered persons, unsatisfied with the wealth they stole from the poor. After all, it is true that money breeds the worst social conducts. However, there was ony one wealthy personage of whom he spoke with compassion: the father of Selma, Farris Effandi, who was not affected by the disease of hypocrisy.

> I do not know any other man in Beirut whose wealth has made him kind and whose kindness has made him wealthy. He is one of the few who comes to this world and leaves it without harming anyone, but people of that kind are usually miserable and oppressed because they are not clever enough to save themselves from the crookedness of others.[17]

In short, Gibran condemned like Rousseau the

Pharisaic social philosophy. And in the words of his
biographer Barbara Young,

> He had intolerance only for hypocrites. All other
> forms of wrongdoings or misdoings he accepted
> either as explainable or stupid. And of all these he
> said, "Leave them be." But against hypocrisy he
> raged.[18]

It is said of Rousseau that at one time he was so
disgusted with the decadence of social life that he gave
up everything he had received as clothes from society
and retreated to the mountains. Some of Rousseau's
followers, likewise discovering the evil of societies, decided to live like hermits. For example, Tolstoy refused
to eat and drink, and dedicated himself to meditations in
the desert. Gibran too experienced the same feeling of
uneasiness. True, he spent the rest of his years in the
busy city of New York. Yet, there, he would seclude
himself for days and nights in his studio. And in 1922, he
wrote confidentially to his friend the philosopher
Mikhail Naimy, who was then living in a hermitage on
Mount Sanin, in Lebanon,

> Your thoughts on "repudiating" the world are
> exactly like mine. For a long time I have been dream-
> ing of a hermitage, a small garden, and a spring
> water. Do you recall Youssif El-Fakhri? Do you recall
> his obscure thoughts and his glowing awakening?
> Do you remember his opinion on civilization? I say,
> Meesha [nickname for Mikhail], that the future
> shall place us in a hermitage on the edge of one of
> the Lebanese valleys. This false civilization has
> tightened the strings of our spirits to the breaking
> point. We must leave before they break. But we

must remain patient until the day of departure. We must be tolerent, Meesha.[19]

SPIRITUAL AWAKENING, A REMEDY

In Gibran's opinion, modern man lives in shadows and not in genuine reality. What man holds to be true is nothing but a shadow and a projection of his ill-desires. Modern man believes that he is awake and acts consciously in each concrete situation, but this is a delusion; like the man of Plato, modern man is found at the very bottom of the "cave" where only shadows of the True Light reach him. He lives his life, not to its fullness or genuineness. Hypocrisy masks and hinders the natural course of his social growth. Though, now, our author is aware of the present plight of society, he does *not*, however, assume a *nihilistic attitude*. There is a remedy for society; it will redeem itself if it reawakens from the slumber and semideath that false civilization plunged it into. The nature of such awakening is the revival of the belief in the spiritual. What distinguishes man in his very existential structure from the kingdom of organism is not biology but the spirit. Therefore, to be oneself one must accept his ontological existence as it is structured and live up to the ways nature has fathomed man. That is, man's existence and behaviors ought to focus on the spiritual. "The spiritual awakening is the most essential thing in man's life, and it is the sole purpose of being."[20] This spiritual awakening of which Gibran speaks is something that cannot be attained through the five senses. It is a type of awareness, not logical or mathematical, but of communion. It is *"love,"* Agape, the golden rule *versus Eros*. And here he gives us a personal experience as to how love, the spiritual awakening, works,

Man finds . . . pleasure . . . through the five
senses. But Gibran's soul has already grown beyond
that to a plane of higher enjoyment which does not
require the mediation of the five senses. His soul
sees, hears, and feels, but not through the medium
of eyes, ears, and fingers. His soul roams the whole
world and returns without the use of feet, ears, and
ships. I see . . . far near and I perceive everything
around . . . as the soul regards many other invisible
and voiceless objects. The subtlest beauties in our
life are unseen and unheard.[21]

It is not blood-shedding revolutions nor communistic
control of the inequalities among man that will save
mankind, but this spiritual consciousness, called love,
when it becomes general and practiced by all societies.
To discover "love," we need not search for it with the
most sophisticated technological instruments; for really
such spiritual awakening is not of the realm of scientific
or philosophic reasoning. It lies in the province of feeling
with the whole body and mind. The success of this
feeling consists in returning back to Nature, where goodness resides. And the goodness of Nature awakes itself
in love. Love, understanding among people and respect
for each other, is what Gibran proposes as medicinal for
curing the shortcomings of modern society. Historically,
Gibran is not the first philosopher to make of "love" the
unshakable foundation for erecting authentic societies.
From time immemorial philosophers, religious men,
poets and politicians have preached or defended with
wit the forcefulness of the power of love.

Here, Gibran's hermeneutics of society finds plenty of
support from the part of many leading international figures. For example, I was personally fascinated to notice
the great resemblance between his Social Contract and
the social theory of the Mexican philosopher Antonio

Caso (1883-1946), who was, incidentally, born the same year (and most probably acquainted with our author). Caso's philosophy distinguishes two types of existences much as Gibran's does; viz., *La existencia como economía* (existence as economy), and *La existencia como caridad* (existence as charity). In the former situation, the individual relates to others with the intentions of using them as means for the attainment of his personal interests. Furthermore, he does nothing without previously calculating and prerating the revenue of his actions. Simply worded, he is an economist. In Caso's vernacular, people who lead such a life are "primitive" even though they happen to inhabit a highly conglomerate technological environment. For after all, to think always in terms of "maximum gain with minimum of effort"[22] is to revert back to the primitive law of seeking preservation of the biological principle of homeostasis by avoiding pain. What is catastrophic in a society of *existencia como economía* is that the human relations degenerate to pure egoism.

On the other hand, *la existencia como caridad* is typical of the disinterested existence. In such situation the individual transcends his limited biological spatio-temporal egoism in order to encounter in a sympathetic attitude the other selves. He is like an artist, because "art is not an economic activity,"[23] but an innate disinterestedness expressed in sympathetic intuitions unto the nature and essence of the other, and from the other standpoint. The society of *La existencia como caridad* breeds a spiritual human society composed of persons wherein each one treats one another with respect, and follows the precept of "maximum of effort with minimum of [personal] gain";[24] its motto of life ascribes to the following:

. . . *The table of human values is this: the more you sacrifice merely animal life to disinterested ends, and the more difficult it becomes to make the sacrifice, until you arrive, from esthetic contemplation and simple good deeds, to heroic action, the more noble you are.*[25]

The conclusion we arrive at reiterates what we have been stating all through these pages about the internationality and ingenuity of Gibranism. Gibran like many other humanists is a *problem-center* thinker very much concerned with the welfare of society. Not only is he critical of the wrongdoings, but also explains what has to be done to counteract the mischiefs. Fortunately, the solution he proposes is the very same that Christ, the right wing of existentialism, Antonio Caso and a host of other humanists have taught about "love," the spiritual awakening. In the next chapter, I will dwell more explicitly on the phenomenon of love, thereby reinstating the social message of Gibranism.

HISTORICAL IMPLICATIONS

None of Gibran's writings have fairytale inspirations, especially the stories found in his philosophical essays. He belonged to the movement of "committed literature"—*la litterature engagée*. This is mostly manifest in his articles on social ideas. To put it bluntly, our author developed his Social Contract because of some contemporary historical events that afflicted his society.

In the previous pages I have delved abstractly on the meaning of authentic and inauthentic society; it is time to narrow the concept to his native country and dig up all the historical facts that led him to pronounce his terrible indictment against the corruption of modern age culture.

Researching about this topic has not been easy, for Gibran appears here and there with different personalities, confused and confusing the reader. Joseph

Sheban has made an accurate estimate when he called Gibran a "dual personality."[26] Instead of defining this accusation, let us show how the dual Gibran has enacted passionately toward the Middle East societies.

OTTOMAN CORRUPTION
AND FRENCH EXPEDITION

Readers should not forget that Gibran was an Arab, knew perfectly his mother tongue, and was always kept informed of the political developments in the Middle East. Now, the situation in the Middle East was quite different from existence in America. The Turks had conquered the Arab lands from the fifteenth century and remained sole rulers till the first World War. The invasion of the Ottomans had never been favorable to the Arabs, either militarily, intellectually, economically, geographically, socially or in matters of legality. The one time glory of the Arab Empire, Arab wisdom, Arab knowledge in the fields of mathematics, astronomy, philosophy, medicine and architecture that enlightened Europe from its dark ages, was jeopardized and eclipsed with the advent of the big bulk of ignorance, illiteracy and savagery of the Turks. For five centuries the Arab world suffered the Turkish heavy yoke of injustices, usurpations, ignorances and slavery. Fate was slightly changed when a Turk-revolted Pasha, Muhammad Ali, sent to Egypt (1799) to appease the natives' insurrections, turned later on against his own government. Muhammad Ali is today acclaimed the liberator of Egypt. However, Lebanon, Syria and many other Arab countries were not so successful in resisting the burden of the Turks as Egypt, who by the way was not so completely free.

The coming of Napoleon in 1798 to Egypt was a break for the Egyptians and the surroundings lands. The expedition was a happy event. The European knowledge which was at one time carved on Arabian erudition was brought back to the people with a far richer treasure of literacy, philosophical and scientific insights. Also, the first Arabic printing that Napoleon seized from the Collegio Propaganda in Rome now enabled translations from French into Arabic. Europe *awakened* the Middle East from its slumber. Yet, such awakening aroused different reactions from the few thinkers there were.

1. To the *ulema* (educated) conservatives, it merely awoke in them a "response of reaction," i.e. the feeling that Islam is higher than any other culture because it alone possesses the Koran, which is Truth incarnate. These traditionalists set themselves to revive early Islamic thinking as a shield against the intrusion of Western new ideas. Politically they remained obedient to the Turkish Sultan.

2. To the *ulema* reformists, the French on the scene instigated them to revise their traditional thoughts along with a spirit of reformation. They rejected the stagnant thinking (*taqlid*) of the conservatives and propelled the *ijtihad* or independent judgment. The champions of this movement were the leaders Jamal ad-Din al Afghani (1839-1897), Muhamad Ábdu (1849-1905), Muhammad Rashid Rida (1865-1935), and, Abd al-Qadir al-Mughrabi (1867-1956). The West provided them with many ideas about social reforms, and above all made them conscious to fight against the decayed politics of the Ottoman whom they judged was the cause of the degradation of Muslim faith. Because of their political dissension, the reformists were many times exiled like Gibran himself. Their

main emphasis was put on the reform of spirituality *versus* the cultural materialism of the Ottoman and Europe (somehow like Gibran except that Gibran was Christian). Al-Afghani writes on this matter: "Every Muslim is sick and his only remedy is in the Koran."—"Muslim backwardness was not caused by Islam but rather by the Muslim's ignorance of its truth."[27] The new political system they sought was the reunification of all Islamic states under the standard of Pan-Islamism.

3. To a third group of Muslim *ulema*, Europe awoke in them a stronghold for secularist intellectualism. Reason was proclaimed the sole agent for truth. And in contrast to the Muslim reformists, the secularists were not religiously oriented. They appealed to secular values and norms, especially with regard to politics. Political liberty consisted not in seeking advice from religion but in fighting tyranny and oppression with enlightenment and education. Knowledge dissipates political fear. One of the secularist axioms for cultural reform was economic balance and equitable distribution of the goods between poor and rich. Also, they violently opposed ill-traditions. (Note the similarity with Gibran Social Contract.) Qasim Amin (1863-1908), the pioneer, writes: "Among the causes of our suffering is the fact that we base our life on traditions which we no longer understand, which we preserve only because they have been handed down to us . . ."[28]

4. To the Arab Christians, the West made them become totally free thinkers. Most of the Christians were then educated in the Universities of Paris and The Propaganda (the Maronite school) in Rome. At home they

were a source of inspiration to the Muslim secularists. In their political stand, they were anti-Ottoman corruption. Here, the study of Gibran's Social Contract is appropriate for twofold reasons: on one hand, he informs us quite well about the Arab societies; on the other hand, he expresses more or less the same feelings that other Arab Christians nurtured toward the Middle East of the early twentieth century.

DECAYED TEETH

Gibran has much in common with the *ulema* reformists and secularists. With the former he agreed that Arab nations were "sick" for accepting benevolently the oppressions with no attempt at changing their fate or cultivating the spiritual richness of their forefathers. His political polemic *Decayed Teeth* denounces the slumber which the Syrian (*N.B.* Lebanon and Syria were one then) people lived in. The essay portrays the injustices, hypocrisies, and wrongdoings of the Syrians under the Ottoman Government. Ironically, he calls his country "rotten, black, and dirty teeth that fester and stink."[29] And then he gives some instances where most of the deterioration is experienced.

If you wish to take a look at the decayed teeth of Syria, visit its schools where the sons and daughters of today are preparing to become the men and women of tomorrow.

Visit the courts and witness the acts of the crooked and corrupted purveyors of justice. See how they play with the thoughts and minds of the simple people as a cat plays with a mouse.

Visit the homes of the rich where conceit, falsehood, and hypocrisy reign. But don't neglect to go
through the huts of the poor as well, where dwell
fear, ignorance, and cowardice.

Then   visit   the   nimble-fingered   dentists
[metaphorically the leaders], possessors of delicate
instruments, dental plasters and tranquilizers, who
spend their days filling the cavities in the rotten
teeth of the nation to mask the decay.[30]

What mostly irritated Gibran was that the Syrians
were contented with the filth in which they lived. Instead of extracting completely the "decayed teeth," they
rather preferred to conceal the teeth with gold fillings. In
other words, the Syrians concealed their inner-self with
the garment of "hypocrisy."

And if you suggest extraction to them, they will
laugh at you because you have not yet learned the
noble art of dentistry that conceals disease.[31]

In another essay, *Narcotics and Dissecting Knives*, once
more Gibran takes the offensive position against the
weaknesses of the Orient in the manner of Muslim
reformers and secularists. He sees the greatest threat
to the downfall of the Arab nation in the so called
Arab leaders who instead of trying to improve their
destiny, went along with the oppressors in administer-
ing "narcotics" (metaphorically speaking), so that
the Orient remains in its slumber.

The Orient is ill, but it has become so
inured to its infirmities that it has

come to see them as natural and even
noble qualities that distinguish them
above others. . . .

Numerous are the social leaders in the Orient,
but many are their parents who remain uncured
but appear eased of their ills because they
are under the effects of social narcotics.
But these tranquilizers merely mask the
symptoms.[32]

The leaders whom he blames are the native politicians
and the religious. He recognizes that the former begin
well when they incipiently revolt against their Turkish
superiors. But, he also acknowledges that many of them
later on prostitute their ideals with the silence of money
or official promotions offered by their enemy. (This
event was current in the whole Middle East.)

A group or party revolts against a despotic government and advocates political reforms . . .
But a month later, we hear that the government has
. . . silenced him [the leader] by giving him an
important position. And nothing more is heard.[33]

On the other hand, the religious leaders of the Middle
East were not spared from his criticism. Gibran often
held them responsible for the ignorance, exorbitant
taxes and legal injustices to which their faithful were
subjected. Historically, the clergy at that time enjoyed
many privileges from the Ottomans.

From what has been said up to now, it is clear that
Gibran was calling for drastic changes; also, the tone of
the appeal was not gentle but that of an exasperated
social engineer. Indeed temper was his personality.[34] In

his political essays we see him *raging against his country-men* for being afraid of changing their sour existence. The poem *My Countrymen* was written in great angriness against his own people.

> I have cried over your humiliation and submission; and my tears streamed like crystalline, but could not sear away your stagnant weakness; . . .
>
> My tears have never reached your petrified hearts, but they cleansed the darkness from inner self. . . .
>
> Your souls are freezing in the clutches of the priests and Sorcerers, and your bodies tremble between the paws of the despots and the shedders of Blood, and your country quakes under the marching feet of the conquering enemy; . . .
>
> Hypocrisy is your religion, and Falsehood is your life, and Nothingness is your ending; . . .
>
> I hate you, My Countrymen, because you hate glory and greatness. . . .[35]

Despite all this, Gibran still was a real *Habbibi* (kind); he felt sorry for the treacherous wretchedness that plagued his beloved countrymen. Getting simultaneously angry and affable is one indication of his dual personality. At any rate, he showed deep sympathy for his people, when early in the winter of 1916 famine stared the population in the face, and the entire land became a paradise for disease germs as a result of World War One, and the Turks exporting the material goods of the nation leaving the natives starving to death. Gibran, then in the U.S., formed with other immigrants a Relief

Committee, and was elected its secretary. This Committee was to send to the people of Mount Lebanon food and material goods; however, when the Turkish government forbade such enterprise, Gibran with the others appealed to Washington to intervene; finally on December 17, 1916, with the help of the United States Navy and the American Red Cross Society the boat *Caesar* sailed with foodstuffs estimated at a value of $750,000.00. Of this experience, Gibran writes:

> It is a great responsibility but I must shoulder it. Great tragedies enlarge the heart. I have never been given the chance to serve my people in a work of this sort. I am glad I can serve a little and I feel that God will help me.[36]

In the same year Gibran wrote the famous poem *Dead Are My People* in which he lamented the miseries, the famines, the diseases and the death of his countrymen. He felt remorse that he was spared from the famine. Guilt pushed him to wish in delirium that he were an "ear of corn," a "ripe fruit" or a "bird flying" so that he could satiate the hunger of some:

> Gone are my people, but I exist yet, . . .
> The Knolls of my country are submerged by tears and blood, for my people and my beloved are gone, and I am here . . .
>
> My people died from hunger, and he who did not perish from starvation was butchered with the sword; and I am here in this distant land, . . .
> . . .
> My people died a painful and shameful death and here am I living in plenty and in peace. . . .[37]

GIBRAN'S PHILOSOPHY OF LAW AND SOCIETY 287

The amazing thing about Gibran as a concerned social engineer—and here I am getting deeper to the dual personality—is that even during his moments of sympathy toward his suffering people, he would burst momentarily with anger against them wishing that they had died like rebels with the sword in their hands fighting courageously their oppressors.[38]

In general, one of the direct implications Gibran was trying to achieve with his social writings was to awake his countrymen from slumber to rebellion. I am not too wrong in suggesting that he was looking for a bloodshedding revolution. Actually, he himself often used the word "revolution." For instance, in 1913 Gibran was asked by some Syrians of New York to be their representative at a Paris International European Conference, where the New Home Rule for Syria and Lebanon was to be discussed. Gibran turned down the assignment because he was asked to be patient, gentle and diplomatic in his speeches about the Turkish regime; personally he wanted revolution and war at all cost. This idea of revolution motivated him to think organizing in New York "a July Conference between some of the men from Paris and the leading Syrians in this country," during which they would plan a military maneuver against Turkey; supposedly, the troops were to be commanded by "Damascene Eresi (or some such name)" and by his good friend the General Giuseppe Garibaldi, the grandson of the Italian hero. Of course, such a political gathering never took place. (*B.F.*, p. 127-129).

But most of all the kind of revolution he was preaching was a social *reform*. Like his neighbors, the Egyptian Muslim secularists, he wanted to inculcate in the attitude of the Orientals, an open mindedness toward the West.[39] For that he undertook a strong criticism of the class inequalities, asking for a reform in economy. After all, there is nothing that the rich could claim to be his own.

The product is never the complete work of the owner; the employees assisted in the production.[40] But also, like the Muslim reformers and secularists, Gibran submitted all the Oriental traditions and customs to a revision of scrutiny, rejecting those that he deemed too old-fashioned. For instance, marriage contracted for sake of fame, social appearances or on the basis of parents' consent only, no matter whether the partners love each other or how aged is one in regard to the other. Gibran called such marriages adultery, irreligious and immoral, even if the engagement was concluded in the church.

In simple words, Gibran condemned what his teacher Nietzsche labelled "slave ethics" or "herd morality," because such morality breeds passive citizens, masses of ignorant sheep depersonalized and dehumanized, and who happen to be toys at the mercy of potent masters. Here is the famous Nietzschean inspiration on Gibran:

I found the blind slavery, which ties the people's present with their parents' past, and urges them to yield to their traditions and customs, placing ancient spirits in the new bodies.

I found the must slavery, which binds the life of a man to a wife whom he abhors, and places the woman's body in the bed of a hated husband, deadening both lives spiritually.

I found the deaf slavery, which stifles the soul and the heart, rendering man but an empty echo of a voice, and a pitiful shadow of a body.

I found the lame slavery, which places man's neck under the domination of the tyrant and submits strong bodies and weak minds to the sons of Greed for use as instruments to their power.

I found the ugly slavery, which descends with the infants' spirits from the spacious firmament into the home of Misery, where Need lives by Ignorance, and Humiliation resides beside Despair. And the children grow as miserables, and live as criminals, and die as despised and rejected non-existents.

I found the subtle slavery, which entitles things with other than their names—calling slyness an intelligence and emptiness a knowledge, and weakness a tenderness, and cowardice a strong refusal.

I found the twisted slavery, which causes the tongues of the weak to move with fear, and speak outside of their feelings, and they feign to be meditating their plight, but they become as empty sacks, which even a child can fold or hang.

I found the bent slavery, which prevails upon one nation to comply with the laws and rules of another nation, and the bending is greater with each day.

I found the perpetual slavery, which crowns the sons of monarchs as kings, and offers no regard to merit.

I found the black slavery, which brands with shame and disgrace forever the innocent sons of the criminals.

Contemplating slavery, it is found to possess the vicious powers of continuation and contagion.[41]

Once his fellow Arabs besought him earnestly to return to Lebanon in order to become a political leader, to which Gibran exclaimed: "I am not a politician, and I would not be a politician. No. I cannot fulfill their desire."[42] Oftentimes, however, they reacted negatively against his harsh criticisms of the Orientals. And during his youth (1903), both the government officials and the Maronite Church issued a joint *communiqué* proclaiming his exile and excommunication. Gibran suffered from being rejected by his homeland. Analyzing his own social philosophy, he laments:

> . . . If men and women were to follow Gibran's counsels on marriage, family ties would break, society would perish, and the world would become an inferno peopled by demons and devils. . . .

> Such is what people say of me and they are right, for I am indeed a fanatic and I am inclined toward destruction as well as construction. There is hatred in my heart for that which my detractors sanctify, and love for that which they reject. And if I could uproot certain customs, beliefs, and traditions of the people, I would do so without hesitation. . . .[43]

Let us, now, revert back to the "decayed teeth" and "sick society" and ask Gibran how does the law behave morally in relation to the individual citizen? Hence, we come to our next section.

The Issue of Law

SCEPTICISM TOWARD MAN-MADE LAWS

From what will be said about Gibran-and-the-established-laws, we should not the least suspect that our author was a belligerent personality nor that his philosophy is anarchist. Actually, many are the contemporary writers who railed vehemently against the ineffectiveness of man-made laws. Take for instance, the German novelist Franz Kafka, who after graduating in law and practicing for some time in an insurance firm, abandoned his profession on the account that it is utterly corrupted. Now Kafka's philosophy of law is much similar to that of Gibran. A brief presentation of Kafka will disclose what I mean.

Kafka's writings have for central theme the problematic of *authority*. In the novel *The Trial*, Kafka illustrates with a good understanding of the legal procedures, what really occurs inside and outside courtrooms, and how most of the time legal authority inflicts on man more damages that it does to protect him. *The Trial* has been written simply to show the absurdity of legal authority. Also, in his parable "Before the Law," Kafka demonstrates the ignorance and the injustices done by all institutionalized authority. The parable portrays the case of a man who one day came to the Law to seek advice. Reaching to the domicile of the Law, he found a doorkeeper. The man asked the doorkeeper permission to enter through the door that leads to the Law; the doorkeeper insisted, in return, that the man could not be admitted at the moment. Then, the man, on reflection, inquired if he could see the Law later. The doorkeeper's reply was affirmative. Following such conversation, the man asked if he could wait in front of the door. The doorkeeper offered him a stool to sit on until the moment came for him to enter inside. To the man's surprise, however, days, weeks, months and years passed, and he was still waiting to be received by the Law. Finally, Kafka concludes,

his eyes grow dim and he does not know whether
the world is really darkening around him or whether

his eyes are only deceiving him. But in the darkness he can now perceive a radiance that streams immortaly from the door of the Law. Now his life is drawing to a close. Before he dies, all that he has experienced during the whole time of his sojourn condenses in his mind into one question, which he has never yet put to the doorkeeper. He beckons the doorkeeper, since he can no longer raise his stiffening body. The doorkeeper has to bend far down to hear him for the difference in size between them has increased very much to the man's disadvantage. 'What do you want to know now?' asks the doorkeeper, 'You are insatiable.' 'Everyone strives to attain the Law,' answers the man, 'how does it come about, then, that in all these years no one has come seeking admittance but me?' The doorkeeper perceives that the man is at the end of his strength and that his hearing is failing, so he bellows in his ear: 'No one but you could gain admittance through this door, since this door was intended only for you. I am now going to shut it.'[44]

The factual implication of this parable suggests that men who seek justice from the man-made laws die before obtaining their rights. The doorkeeper represents the lawyers and the codified written laws, both of whom claim that authority has been invested upon them from the Almighty Law whom none has seen. Kafka at this point asks what guarantees us that man-made laws spring from the Law since no one has yet heard of him? The doorkeeper never received immediately and directly his job from the Law; only another doorkeeper from inside the courtroom had secured him the appointment. What Kafka resents most is that man-made justice treats the individual in an impersonal way. Kafka, himself a lawyer, knows that the laws are for the rich.

. . . The laws were made to the advantage
of the nobles from the very beginning,
they themselves stand above the laws,
and that seems to be why the laws were
entrusted exclusively into their hands.[45]

In my opinion, Kafka's harsh criticism of human
codes explains why all his personages are in search of
their self-identity in a society geared by stereotyped
laws.

Now Gibran was not a professional lawyer like Kafka,
yet, he has denounced in an identical manner the absurdity of man-made laws.

In *The Cry of the Graves*, Gibran tells us the story of
three different individuals who are sentenced to death
by a human authority for the good deeds they have
fulfilled. *The first case* is that of a chevaleresque soul who
killed in self-defense one of the Emir's officers who was
trying to take advantage of a young girl of a poor family.
The second case concerns a young woman accused by her
aged husband of adultery, merely because she met unin-
tentionally one day her true beloved person and talked to
him. *The third case* is the story of an old man who grew old
and sick after dedicating many years of hard work in a
religious convent. One day he begged from the priests
some bread for his youngsters, but was repelled. To
satisfy the natural hunger of his children he resolved to
steal the food from the convent. Unfortunately he was
caught; the priest who trapped him accused him in front
of the judge of burgling the sacred vase.

In all these three stories Gibran revolts against the
Emir who condemned innocent people without giving
fair trial to each one. The reason for declining a plea of
self-defense is due to the fact that the accusers are all
nobles and the defendants come from a low social
economical class. And yet, as Kafka has said it, "The Law

is whatever the nobles do."[46] In Gibran's opinion the prosecutors are far more criminal than the criminals. Hence, like Kafka, Gibran retorts sceptically to himself,

What is Law? Who saw it coming with the sun
from the depths of heaven? What human saw the
the heart of God and found its will or purpose?
In what century did the angels walk among
the people and preach to them, saying,
'Forbid the weak from enjoying life, and
kill the outlaws with the sharp edge of the
sword, and step upon the sinners with iron feet'?[47]

ABSURDITY OF THE LAWS' SANCTIONS

The ethics of punishment is altogether wrong and above all self-contradictory for the law meets evil with evil, and sanctions the criminals by becoming itself criminal. "Shall we meet evil with evil and say this is the law? Shall we fight corruption with greater corruption and say this is the rule? Shall we conquer crimes with more crimes and say this is justice?"[48]

If even a man is guilty, society has no right to bring a harsh sentence against him. Man is not man because of his deeds, but because he was born man. Personhood is an intrinsic value and characterizes essentially and existentially the nature of man. The value of personhood is not quantitative in that it may increase or decrease. Also, it is not true that one person "is" more valuable than another. Would you say that a moron is less of a human than the normal one? Or poor less than rich? Personhood, to reiterate Nicolai Hartmans and Max Weber, is in itself a value and the highest in the scale. This is the idea we read in *Kahlil the Heretic*, where Rachel and Miriam rescue in the midst of the night a man in the snow. Miriam begins fearing that he might be a criminal. But Rachel replying to Miriam says: "It makes no difference whether he is a monk or criminal; dry his feet well my daughter."[49]

At this stage, I have to say that Gibran's ethics does not permit the sanction of capital punishment. For him no law has the right to take premeditatively and willingly the life of someone else. As for the lay murderers, they need mental and social rehabilitation. The logic behind such assertions is threefold. (1) Each man is a unique mystery in himself; to really bring a judgment against the accused, requires on the part of the outsider a complete knowledge of him and the circumstances that made him — "And you who understand justice, how shall you unless you look upon all deeds in the fullness of light?"[50] —which is utopia for no mind can have full understanding of another person's idiosyncrasies; hence, writes Gibran: "You cannot judge any man beyond your knowledge of him, and how small is your knowledge."[51] (2) Secondly, when a good judge begins to scrutinize carefully all the circumstances that surround the deed of the criminal he will discover that these circumstances "forced" and "conditioned" the accused to perform his action. Furthermore, the analysis will disclose that the defendant is not alone responsible for the crime, but somehow, society with its righteous people bears part of the blame. No man is an island. If it is true that one's success owes to the contribution of others, it is equally true that crimes are the work of participation of others. The Prophet says:

The murdered is not unaccountable
for his own murder,

And the robbed is not blameless in
being robbed.

The righteous is not innocent of
the deeds of the wicked, . . .

So the wrong-doer cannot do wrong
without the hidden will of you all.[52]

(3) Finally, the value "personhood" admits but one external criterion; this is God, the creator of the person. As
for the authority of man-made laws, Gibran is sceptical
since earthly laws see differences in the value of personhood; and yet, "The life of one man is as weighty in the
scales of God as the life of another."[53]

Therefore, all sorts of legal punishments are injust.
Here, Gibran is relying more on the Evangelic ethics than
on speculated philosophical arguments. Somehow, he is
repeating Christ, who once said to an angry crowd raging against the adultress Magdalene: "whoever thinks he
is pure of heart, let him cast the first stone"—to which
the people dispersed for they were all sinners. Well, this
is the same message he allots in the parable *The Saint*. A
brigand came one day to a Saint and sought absolutions
for the "countless crimes" he committed. To his surprise
the Saint refused to be his judge before God, and replied:

I too have committed crimes without
number. . . . Then the brigand stood
up and . . . went skipping down the hill. . . .
At that moment we heard the brigand singing
in the distance, and the echo of his song filled
the valley with gladness.[54]

The thief was happy because he found that even Saints

sin at least seven times a day. Also, the lesson of this parable implies that no human is an angel. As Blaise Pascal, the French philosopher, used to say: "who wants to play the angel, mimics it badly like a beast";[55] so too, Gibran defines man a microcosm, limited in perfection; there is not shame in not being Perfection, otherwise we should be ashamed of being human. The poem *Perfection* emphasizes that man reaches to perfection when he accepts willingly his weaknesses, instead of boasting for what he is not.[56]

MAN-MADE LAWS AND THE PLEA OF UNIQUENESS

I believe without fear of contradiction that Gibran's heroes rebel against the institutionalized stereotyped norms of conduct simply because they feel that these laws hinder to the growth of their individuality. However, none of them would follow the ideological path of an Abbie Hoffman or an Angela Davis. They are not anarchists; and Gibran himself was not a social rebel. Once he said to his fellow Lebanese of American birth that they ought to become good citizens and loyal to America, despite their being descendants of Lebanese. "I believe that it is in you to be good citizens. . . . You should be proud of being an American. . . ."[57]

The heroes of our author argue for a personality freedom, and their dispute is based on the same philosophical premises that Tolstoy, Kafka, Dostoyevski and Blake insisted on in their writings.

In short, according to Gibran, man-made laws afflict great injuries on the individual by imposing fixed patterns of conduct and in seeing that these ways of thinking and doing be realized literally. After all it is true that human laws aim to have a wide range of application without consideration of the idiographic situation in which the person lived at the time he performed his deed. The so used expression by the police, politicians, lawyers, or bureaucratic administrators: "IT IS THE LAW," exemplifies how absurd man-made laws are when the accused seeks to justify his actions.

The psychological feeling that originates in a man who feels his personality oppressed and burdened by the institutionalized codes advanced either by society or the Church is that of "statistics" or being "a number among other numbers." Gibran is aware that the spirit of statistics is predominant in our technological society; people are becoming increasingly deindividualized. As for our education it does its best to mold us in conformism and totalitarianism. And yet, for Gibran the purpose of education is to enable each one to develop his innate endowments, thereby one's self-identity. "Education sows not seeds in you, but makes *your seeds grow*."[58]

Gibran blames two categories of oppressors for robbing the subjectivity of the individuals. These oppressors have in common the privilege of being rich and of making laws to which the poor have to conform, while they themselves are exempted. As for their differences, one wears a cassock and is called priest and his norms are religious; the other is a layman who lives in palaces built with the tears and money of the poor and his laws are societal. Now, in Gibran's vernacular of words, priests are like ivies that climb high in the skies while their roots plunge in the ignorant kindness of the poor stealing from them in the name of God their individuality and finances. "I beheld priests, sly like foxes; and false messiahs dealing in trickery with the people".[59]

The consequences of man-made laws are detrimental to the uniqueness and dignity of man. Like his friend the Swiss psychoanalist Carl Jung, whose portrait he painted, Gibran acknowledges that in a world where the feeling of statistics prevails, morality tends to decrease. Jung writes,

> The individual is increasingly deprived of the moral decision as to how he should live his own life, and instead is ruled, fed, clothed and educated as a social unit, accommodated in the appropriate housing unit, and amused in accordance with the standards that give pleasure and satisfaction to the masses.[60]

Similarly, Gibran reckons the downfall of morality as a result of "institutionalized morality." For instance he pokes at the Superego's morality of present-day politics. "Organized political duty" is false morality since it norms the good and the evil on criteria invented by the politicians. The example is patriotism for whose sake people tear each other apart in war. I remind the reader at this point, that Gibran is not equating patriotism "with love of the native land."[61] In his opinion, patriotism at the expense of human life is a "construct" with no concrete foundations; it is an invented sentiment of attachment to the land; it is a rumor fabricated by politicians. Yet, "love of the native land" has no ethnological, social, juridical, geographical, political or religious connotations. My native land is the planet earth where humans survive, and eventually, the whole universe in which I am born as part of it. "Love of the native land" is a natural inclination, which, however, does not surpass the "love for/of others" which stands higher in the scale of values.

> Beware, my brother, of the leader who says, 'Love of existence obliges us to deprive the people of their rights!' I say unto you but this: protecting others'

rights is the noblest and most beautiful human act; if
my existence requires that I kill others, then death is
more honorable to me, and . . . I will not hesitate to
take my life by my own hands for the sake of Eternity before Eternity comes.[62]

And again,

If duty exiles peace from among nations, and patriotism makes havoc of man's tranquility, then away
with duty and patriotism![63]

Now, moraltiy is shattered because the individual,
pressed by the codified conducts, gives up his exisential
freedom to assume a generic social and religious responsibility. "I beheld . . . true freedom walking alone in the
street, seeking shelter before doors and rejected by the
people."[64] In the final analysis, if there is someone to
blame for the deterioration of the inner-self and freedom,
this someone is man alone who

set for the God-given soul a limited and earthly law
of his own. He made for himself strict rules. Man
built a narrow and painful prison in which he secluded his affections and desires. He dug out a deep
grave in which he buried his heart and its purpose.[65]

NATURAL LAWS VS. MAN-MADE LAWS

From the preceding pages one would think that
Gibran is an anarchist. Yet, to an alert philosopher, he
really appears as a guarantor of laws. This is manifest
not only in his work but also in his life. Gibran was
never put in jail for violation of a social code nor has he

ever participated in a demonstration rally. When he attacks man-made laws he does so not so much out of caprice as much as out of concern for his fellowman. He merely objects to man-made laws because he feels that these norms hinder the individual's search for the "spiritual awakening" that leads to happiness. After all he accepts the absoluteness of the "eternal law"[66] and its corollary, the natural law. A brief comment on these laws will disclose the thoughts of Gibran.

The distinction Gibran makes between the eternal law, natural law and man-made law is something commonly accepted by most moralists, especially the Thomists. Concerning the eternal law, many are the passages where Gibran mentions it.[67] The eternal law is the rule of divine wisdom, which is eternal, ordering all things to their end, man included. In Thomas Aquinas' own words to quote an outsider,

. . . Granted that the world is governed by divine providence . . . the whole community of the universe is governed by the divine reason. Therefore the very motion of the government of things in God, the ruler of the universe, has the nature of a law. And since the divine reason's conception of things is not subject to time, but is eternal . . . this kind of law must be called eternal.[68]

For Gibran too, the rule of divine wisdom whereby God provides for creatures from eternity is called eternal law. The existence of such law is founded on the divine attribute of wisdom in God. God directs creatures to Himself, who is the Highest Good of all. Moreover, this eternal law is universally knowable by man, and therefore, is not a prerogative of priests or educated man.

Whoever lives on the paths of Love, Beauty and Truth fulfills the eternal law.

As for the natural law this is the participation of the eternal law in both the rational nature and non-rational nature through the natural inclinations. In man, furthermore, the natural law participates in the eternal law through the first principles of practical reason. The light of reason is a natural inclination, proper to man. Man's nature is rational and he alone discovers the natural law by the light of natural reason in drawing conclusions about his nature. According to Gibran God promulgates the natural law to man through the endowment of the rational nature. It is written so to speak in our very beings. The laws of the universe are a replica of the eternal law. "Even the laws of Life obey Life's laws."[69] And the primordial precept of nature is "Love," along with those virtues that "Love" entails, such as compassion, forgiveness, forebearance. Justice is a type of kindness.

What about man-made law? In Gibran's terminology this refers to the law that the religious or political legislative government decreed. But, in his opinion these laws are neither deduced from the natural law nor dictated by the eternal law. Contrasting the natural law to man-made law, Gibran exclaims, "The only authority I obey is the knowledge of guarding acquiescing in the Natural Law of Justice."[70]

His motive for considering the organized laws as contradictory to the natural or eternal law square with the fact that there is a discrepancy between human laws and "justice." Quite lucidly he is aware that these two are not interdependent in present society, not even among the professional guarantors of law enforcement. Lawyers will try to be successful with their client's case not so much for justice' sake as much as for personal social ambitions or professional duty. I myself often heard that lawyers have a professional duty toward their clients regardless of the worth of their deeds, and the interest of justice. This unbridgeable gap is best delineated in Gibran's satirical prose-poem *The Procession* (sometimes translated as *The Cortége*), a long dialogue between an old sage and a youth concerning the differences between the earthy authority and the natural law. The sage represents a man who spent his entire life span in the turmoils of the city, and toward his society he feels bitter because of the corruptions, defamations, desecrations, injustices and hypocrisies that human laws have brought in the lives of the citizens. The youth, on the other hand, symbolizes innocence unspoiled by any of the amoral tricks of the social laws. The only law in which the youth abides is that of nature.

SAGE

Justice on earth would cause the Jinn
To cry at misuse of the word,
And were the dead to witness it,
They'd mock at fairness in this world.

Yes, death and prison we mete out
To small offenders of laws,
While honor, wealth, and full respect
On greater pirates we bestow. . . .

YOUTH

In Nature there is no justice
Nor is there a punishment.
When the willows cast their shadow
O'er the ground without consent,
No one hears the cypress saying,

'This act is versus law and right!'
Like the snow, our Human Justice
Melts from shame in warm sunlight![71]

To condense what we have been saying, let us repeat that our author takes a harsh stand against man-made laws simply because these directives for living are inflexible, established on vicious customs, corrupted practices, conflict with the idiosyncrasies of the individual and breed masses of depersonalized individualities. In a letter he wrote to his first cousin in 1908 after the incident of the burning of his *Spirits Rebellious* in the market place of Beirut, Gibran confessed,

People are saying that I am the enemy of
just laws, of family ties, and old traditions.
Those people are telling the truth. I do not
love man-made laws and I abhor the traditions
that our ancestors left us.[72]

A life-situation that grows on man-made law and which Gibran mostly criticized is the case of marriages in the Orient. As a matter of fact at the time of Gibran, but less now, marriages in the Mediterranean countries were conjugated almost for material reasons without there being any genuine love between the conjoints. Either the parents would promise the hand of their daughter, while still a young girl, or one of the partners would consent to the other because of his riches. Now, according to the Church-made law, once the two were consecrated in front of a priest, there could be no divorce and the two would be *legally* married. Here, Gibran's ethics replies, could love be bought? Is love a mere paper formality? What is the difference between the prostitute and the person who has intercourse the same night after signing some official documents, that he or she thought would be beneficial?[73] This is one way of showing the absurdity of institutionalized codes.

At this stage I would like to introduce an idea of mine which reflects the intentions of Gibran. The purpose of any type of law is to help the individual to develop to its peak his personality. The success of the law resides in its understanding of all the concrete events that make the concrete situation of a unique individual. The law should never become bureaucratic. But as Gibran says, "Kindness should be the source of every law upon the earth, for Kindness is the shadow of God in man."[74] Otherwise, the law will become a mere dead written letter found in books on the shelves of a library. This is the idea that Almuhtada conveys in his sermons on *Of the Martyrs to Man's Law*.[75]

In conclusion, it is obvious to our author that he who abides in the eternal law and natural law has attained moral happiness and a freedom similar to that of the birds. The bird symbolizes freedom.

> The bird has an honor that man does not have. Man lives in the traps of his fabricated laws and traditions; but the birds live according to the natural law of God, who causes the earth to turn around the sun.[76]

Parables on Political Authority

The purpose of this present section is twofold. On one hand, it serves as a *conclusion* for this chapter; on the other hand, it delves into the various forms of "political authority."

Accordingly, Gibran distinguishes three types of government. These are (i) weakened rulers; (ii) wicked rulers; (iii) co-operative rulers. Also Gibran employs the parabolical style of expression in order to convey in a pleasant and direct way to his readers the moral lesson encompassed in the stories.

WEAK GOVERNMENT

The parable "The Wise King," in *The Madman*, portrays a king who ruled over the city of Wirani with wisdom and might. The king and his subjects lived in mutual understanding until one night a witch came into the city and dropped seven drops of a strange liquid in the sole well which provided water to the entire populace, and cast a spell: "From this hour he who drinks this water shall become mad."[77]

On the next day, the inhabitants drew their water supply from the well and drank of it. Suddenly, they became mad, as the witch had predicted. However, the king and his lord chamberlain were not affected, because they had not touched to the water. Their behavior was the same.

What was peace, before, now turned to uprising. For during the course of the day, the citizens gathered in small groups and murmured to each other: "Our King and his lord chamberlain have lost their reason. Surely we cannot be ruled by a mad King. We must dethrone him."[78] They knew of the madness of the monarch, because the latter did not behave as usual, according to their expectations.

Having heard of the rumor to overthrow him, the King, afraid of losing his crown and power, commanded his soldiers to bring him in a golden goblet some water from the well. He drank the water and gave a portion to his lord chamberlain. From then on, concludes the parable, "there was great rejoicing in that distant city of Wirani, because the King and its lord chamberlain had regained their reason."[79]

Now, as we ponder seriously on the meaning of this fairytale, we understand that the King who was both "wise" and "powerful" decided at the end to sell his wisdom in order to retain his authority. He consented to become mad like all his citizens, instead of finding a cure for healing the madness of the city. In other words, there are many political rulers—Gibran surmises—whose acts, thinking and decision-making are foolish, degrading, uncivilized, uneducated, backward, caught up with traditions but which nevertheless reflect the general consent of their citizens. These governments let themselves be ruled by their "mad" people instead of enlightening and guiding them according to the rules of contemporary social, cultural and educational progress. Might, power, authority are their preference over "wisdom." I believe that there exist among the underdeveloped countries some governments who resemble Gibran's "Wise King of Wirani."

WICKED GOVERNMENT

In the parable "The Lion's Daughter," Gibran depicts another version of authority, known as autocratic, tyrannical, despotic and dictatorial.

The story revolves around four slaves fanning their old queen sleeping on her throne, and a cat sitting on the lap of the monarch. While the queen is sound asleep, each slave ridicules the queen's old age, ugliness, and complains about his destitution. The cat, on the other side, attempts to awake the slaves from their state of servitude and slumber. The dialogue between the slaves and the cat reaches its heights, when the queen nodded her head in her sleep and "her crown fell to the floor."[80] At this moment one of the slaves exclaimed, "That is a bad omen."[81] And the others unanimously agreed with the first slave. However, here, the cat purred: "The bad omen of one is the good omen of the other."[82]·Meaning, that if the slaves wanted, they could now revolt against their queen, who is also made of flesh and blood. The crown which symbolizes "authority" is not a quality, a privilege, or a right with which she alone could be identified. For as a matter of fact, the crown, that is her authority, was fragile and could be dislocated from her. It fell on the ground.

Surprisingly enough, the slaves consented together to put back the crown on the head of the queen. They expressed fear that should the queen wake up and find the crown besides her feet, she might punish them, believing that they threw away her sceptre. To the slaves, the cat purred: "Only a slave restores a crown that has fallen."[83]

In brief, Gibran contends that in the political situation of despotism, it is not the dictator who should be blamed for exercising tyranny, but the people themselves who allow that their wicked government go into existence. The people's failure to revolt in order to change their fate is to be condemned. Actually, it is understood that no political revolution could be successful unless a few shed blood. Well, for Gibran it is better "Dying for freedom . . . than living in the shadow of weak submission."[84]

PEOPLE'S GOVERNMENT

Gibranian political philosophy discredits the two previous forms of government as ineffective and contrary to the welfare of the people. In his opinion only a government that cares for, is elected by, and functions directly with the *people* deserves to continue in existence. Reading his parable *"The King"* one gets the impression that Gibran wrote it under the inspiration of President Abraham Lincoln's Gettysburg address, November 19, 1863. As Lincoln was a firm believer in a government "of the people, by the people, for the people," so too was Gibran. This point is well stressed in his story of the monarch who ruled over the Kingdom of Sadik.

One day, the people of the city approached the palace, and with one voice shouted down to the King of Sadik. His majesty promptly showed up on the scene, and hailed the people in a friendly manner; after which he yielded with no resistance his crown and sceptre to his audience, saying: "My friends, who are no longer my subjects, . . . I will be one of you . . . I would work together with you [in] the fields and vineyards. . . . All of you now are King."[85]

Yet—the story continues—the Kingdom of Sadik did not find peace and justice once the King abdicated. Rather, the people's discontent increased every day, because they were now cheated by their masters the rich. And so, as the people had dethroned the monarch, later it became their wish to restore the King by conferring upon him all the rights to govern them. "Now rule us," they told him, "with might and justice."[86] The King replied: "With might, I can, for any man is capable of this ambition. Yet with justice, it is difficult; for justice is a Divine quality and a gift of Heaven."

During the following days, the people voiced their complaints to the King about three masters. (Note carefully the monarch's dialogue and sense of justice.) The first person whom the plebeians brought to trial was a baron; their grudge against the defendant was that he treated them as serfs and not as human beings.

Straightway the King prounounced against the baron: "The life of one man is as weighty in the scales of God as the life of another. And because you know not how to weight the lives of those who work in your fields,"[87] you are hereby exiled from our Kingdom. Next, the people reported the cruelty of a countess. Instantly, the King ordered her to be brought to trial. Again, he banished her from the city, laying down the reason: "Those who till our fields and care for our vineyards are nobler than we who eat the bread they prepare and drink the wine of their winepress."[88] Finally, the people denounced their bishop as inhuman and greedy for he made them build a cathedral without remunerating them for their hours of labor. To this the King called the bishop, and angrily admonished the prelate, saying: "That cross you wear upon your bosom should mean giving life. But you have taken life from life and you have given none. Therefore you shall leave this Kingdom never to return."[89]

From that day on—the parable adds—the people lived happily, because their ruler was always on their side.

In conclusion to this whole chapter, I believe that Gibran's social contract, legal philosophy and political system do not advocate the ideology of democracy; for as I see it, democracy is a utopia, while in practical life it breeds capitalism and the class struggle. It is my contention that Gibran leans rather towards socialism; however, not the communistic type but towards a humanistic one; since communism proliferates atheism, and secretly practices the inequality between the governor and the governed. Only within the framework of *authentic socialism*, do the human laws conform to the Divine precepts. One indication of this correspondence between the human laws and the Divine Will consists in the perennial proposition to which Gibran wholeheartedly ascribes, namely, *"vox populi vox Dei"* ("the voice of the people is the voice of God"). Actually Gibran emphasizes this humanistic-socialistic-Divine argument in the conclusion of his parable *"The King,"* of which we spoke a while ago. In the words of the monarch, the hero of the story, the people themselves are the genuine rulers: "You yourselves are King." As for him, he is "but a thought in the mind of" all of them, and he exists not save in their actions. "There is no such person as governor. *Only the governed exist to govern themselves."*[90]

LOVE, THE QUINTESSENCE OF HUMAN EXISTENCE

$\mathbf{A}$ GREAT system of thought pivots around one basic fundamental notion. With this key notion, its author tries to explain existence and all the facets of life. In the mind of the author the fundamental idea becomes a threefold thesis: (1) a *metaphysical* description of existence; (2) an *ethical* categorical imperative for living morally; and (3) finally, a *psychological* counsel for developing a mature personality.

In Gibranian philosophy, *love* occupies the most important place. Already in the previous pages we show the relevancy of "love" both in reference to the mission of the poet, and for the establishment of an authentic society. Now, it remains to lay down the foundation of Gibran's theory-building, and construct his entire system of thought as it actually erects from the dynamics of love. Essentially, therefore, his doctrine consists of this: The meaning of human existence is the conscious and progressive manifestation of that principle or source of everything, the manifestation of which in us is signified by love; thus love is the core of human life and the divine supreme law that should guide us and sustain natural law.

Nowadays, when international and national conflicts seem so easily to shatter our human relations, much is being spoken of love as the effective remedy for lessening the misunderstanding between nations, and individuals. However, because of the so many versions proposed by the myriad of the professional theologians, philosophers, psychiatrists, sociologists, magazine editors and literary minds—the true meaning of love is no longer apparent to us. Hence, the hope of this chapter is to reinstate and to reeducate us in genuine love. On this issue, Gibran is a Grand Master, and his interpretation deserves attention.

Basically Gibran distinguishes two forms of love, which correspond to the two regions of human existence, namely, the body and the mind. I personally denominate them by the familiar Greek names of *Eros* and *Agape*. For the sake of clarity, let me here mention that these two are not in Gibran's view contradictory; yet, he holds the possibility that Eros can be misused; only then will one form of love conflict with the other. Henceforth, for methodological reasons I divide this chapter into two sections: (1) Eros, and (2) Agape.

Eros

CRITIQUE OF THE PREVAILING MISCONCEPTIONS

Following the trend of thought of Gibran, I am not defining the concept Eros in a Freudian sense; broadly speaking, it signifies "sensuous love." Accordingly, the person derives his pleasure from bodily sensations, and sex is the prototype expression. However, concerning Eros, Gibran speaks of acceptable and perverted acts. A few words will show the position of our author.

About the carnal love, I have the feeling that Gibran elaborated his theory because of his dissatisfaction with the previous philosophies of Eros. He cast his role as a judge of the prevailing two extreme schools that history has recorded, and while engaged in argumentation his position of "acceptable Eros" developed. These extremes teach either an extravagant "mortification" of the senses, or an extravagant "gratification" of the flesh. Yet, Gibran holds a midway position. His understanding of Eros involves an understanding of the correlated issues of "mind-body," "pleasure" and "pain." How? I believe the best way to grasp his position is to draw respectively the differences between his ideas on Eros and the two historical approaches just stated.

1. Indeed, many ascetics of Platonic mysticism judge the sex-eros taboo, and despise the body which they consider to be the prison where the soul dwells enslaved by the physiological drives. One recalls for instance the famous words of Plato:

> Every seeker after wisdom knows that . . .
> his soul is a helpless prisoner, chained
> hand and foot in the body, compelled to
> view reality not directly but only through
> its prison bars, and wallowing in utter
> ignorance.[1]

Historically, Plato's mysticism appealed to the early fathers of the Church, who, fearing that their bodily-inclinations would drag them to seeking terrestrial happiness, "they shun all pleasures, lest they neglect the spirit or offend against it."[2] This was the period of the hermits, monks, and religious cloisters. Till today we find, however, the ascetics mortifying their senses, and flagellating their bodies, as still do some Christian monks, notably the Trappists. Yet Gibran's common sense of reality sees no evil in the biological functions of the body. After all, human existence is not a pure spirit like the angels nor solely flesh like the animals. Man's being is psychosomatic. Furthermore, nothing that God has created is scandalous, not even sex; "God made our bodies temples for our souls."[3]

Moreover, Gibran, who was well acquainted with

Freud's psychoanalysis[4] and Jung's psychology, often times said that man could not successfully eliminate, suffocate or self-deny his bodily drives without becoming neurotic. He knew that an excessive rejection of a bodily desire would not nullify the wish but "repress it in the unconscious, until someday the desire would burst out at the surface, causing damages to the psyche of the individual. In *The Prophet* we read this psychoanalytic note:

> Often times in denying yourself pleasure you
> do but store the desire in the recesses of
> your being.
> Who knows but that which seems omitted today,
> waits for tomorrow?
> Even your body knows its heritage and its rightful
> need and will not be deceived.
> And your body is the harp of your soul.
> And it is yours to bring forth sweet music from it
> or confused sounds.[5]

The real problem is, those who deem sex to be taboo, err in their hypothetical thinking that the body and mind are two separate entities. Gibran disagrees with such exaggerated spiritualism—which personally I attribute partly to our heritage of Manichaeism that believed in the co-eternality of the principles Good and Evil. Supposedly the body is the evil principle, and the spirit the good principle, one fighting against the other. Gibran lucidly points out:

> There is no struggle of soul and
> body save in the minds of those
> whose souls are asleep and whose
> bodies are out of tune.[6]

Allow me at this point to interject a comment of mine. Despite that personally Gibran has not used the very same expressions of the existentialists about the meaning of the human body and its functions, we nevertheless get the impression that he conveyes their same basic ideas. That is, the relation man has to his body is not of a "possessive" kind nor of "having," but is a relation of "being." "I am my body" is a much better linguistic expression that does justice to Gibran's philosophy. However, it should be kept in mind that the statement "I am my body" should not be interpreted as if my existence equals solely my body, otherwise we would err in materialism that sees no other human features beyond the bones, blood and physiological activities. To be faithful to Gibran's trend of thought, the expression "I am my body" merely signifies that my body is the embodiment of my self-consciousness, and conversely the self informs, permeates, and pervades the body, thus constituting a psychosomatic unity.

To repeat then, against the dualistic philosophy, man by his metaphysical existence "is" a sexual being; and from the very biological fact that an individual is identified as either a male or a female, it is clear that sex is a reality diffused through all man's being and not to some part, though organically it is localized in some definite regions of the organism. Yet, as an energy, it pervades over the whole man. This is the meaning Gibran conveys when he says:

Of Love, Understanding is necessary. . . . To love I must understand—even understand with the *body*, too. When for instance I see a beautiful flower, my *body* understands its beauty, is drawn to it.[7]

And one day, when he was harassed by an impertinent inquisitive lady who kept on asking him, "But have you never been in love?" Gibran unashamed answered:

I will tell you a thing you may not know.
The most highly sexed beings upon the planet
are the creators, the poets, sculptors,
painters, musicians—and so it has been
from the beginning. And among them sex is
always beautiful, *and it is always shy*.[8]

Although now, Gibran affirms the bond between the physiological drives and intellectual activities, and justifies the innate biological need of sex, he nevertheless warns us against the perverted abuse of carnal-love. Here, he directs his critics against the "playboy" who practices the opposite exorbitances of the spiritualists. Also, he seems more bitter against this extreme extravagance than he is toward the ascetic mystics.

2. Historically, the early Greek philosopher Aristippus of Cyrene (*ca*. 435-355 B.C.) was the first to advocate that the purpose of life consists in the complete gratifications of the bodily inclinations. His theory of hedonism held three principles which are still professed by the sex oriented minds: *One*, that happiness is identical to seeking pleasure and suffering the least possible pain; *secondly*, that pleasure is quantitative and not qualitative; *thirdly*, that a man should never let go the opportunity of satisfying his biological urges, especially the enjoyment of sex, no matter what are the resulting consequences. Now, judged from the standpoint of Gibran's ethics, metaphysics and psychology, the Aristippus playboy's threefold principles are existentially erroneous.

Thus, concerning the *first principle*, Gibranism recognizes that pleasure is an essential part of life, but not to the point of confusing it with the goal, happiness. Definitely it is God's desire that man searches for happiness.[9] Yet happiness is not synonymous to pleasure nor contradictory to suffering. Quite the contrary, happiness necessitates pain and pleasure.[10]

The Aristippus men "who seek pleasure as if it were all,"[11] as *The Prophet* surmises, are really hoping for a utopia. Because any attempt to find a psychological adjustment in the principle of tension-reduction which is their guiding motive for absolute pleasure, is doomed to failure and doomed rather to increasing the tension. This psychological statement of Gibran is shared by many humanistic counselors. Thus, the founder of the third Viennese School of Psychotherapy Viktor Frankl writes:

I consider it a dangerous misconception of mental hygiene to assume that what man needs in the first place is . . . a tensionless state. What man actually needs is not a tensionless state but rather the striving and struggling for some goal worthy of him.[12]

Realistically speaking, then, man cannot evade the advent of pain in his life. And far from trying to minimize or to escape neurotically the striking of suffering, man should do better in accepting and finding the true meaning encompassed in suffering. Anxiety, failures, and frustrations are existential predicaments of human essence which when humbly accepted enrich one's life with genuine experiences. Joy and pain are complementary to each other. Hence, Gibran writes:

I would not exchange the laughter of
my heart for the fortunes of the

multitudes; nor would I be content
with converting my tears, invited by
my agonized self, into calm. It is my
fervent hope that my whole life on this
earth will ever be tears and laughter.[13]

Furthermore, Gibran estimates that pleasure is only at
best a by-product or a means-project, because itself it
lacks the depth and the height of a concrete goal. In *The
Prophet* we read:

Pleasure is a freedom-song
But it is not freedom. . . .
It is a depth calling unto a height,
But it is not the deep nor the high.
It is the caged taking wing,
But it is not space-encompassed.[14]

As for the *second principle* of the Aristippus man,
Gibran provides us with countless lucid life examples
that disprove its feasibility. Indeed, it would be impru-
dent on our part to jump on the first coming occasion for
gratifying our sexual urges. Quality is far better than
quantity. Actually, it is when sex becomes an end in-
itself, and the sexual act is always practiced, that the
greatest disappointments in life occur. For instance,
some psychological studies show that people who have
had plenty of physical relations end up by hardly feeling
any climax in intercourse. We also know that the failure
of many marriages stems from an original misintention
that the conjoints had about love. They got married
simply in order to experience sex, since outside of marriage their religion and superego forbade them to have
intercourse. Gibran too in the story of *Madame Rose Hanie*
recounts the disappointments of a man who, having at

first believed that his happiness lied in bodily enjoy-
ments, later on abandoned in frustration such a goal, and
dedicated himself like a miser to amassing wealth. Quality and moderation in sex are virtues of a healthy carnal
eros.

Finally, about the *third leitmotive* of the Aristippus
which insists on unconditional sex, Gibran retorts that
such principle yields a false picture of human existence.
While the mortifiers of the flesh had a philosophy that
defined the essence of man as *"res cogitans,"* i.e., a
spiritual substance, the playboy's approach is
materialistic, since he extols the body over the mind. In
Gibran's opinion, whoever thinks that the meaning of
life resides in the total enjoyment of his senses, regardless of the harm he might cause to his fellowman, has
degraded human nature, become an animal, and not
fulfilled his manhood. Our author pronounces terrible
indictments, somehow similar to those of Soren Kierkegaard who in *The Banquet* describes pejoratively the
behaviors of the Don Juan. Gibran calls the perverted
sex-eros "the animal that is concealed in a human
being."[15] If sex was all there is to man, then what difference would there be between the human and the beast?
A dog is capable of having sexual intercourse! And animal species seek always to gratify their physiological
needs; their existence is regulated by the biological law of
homeostasis! Then what is there so unique to man? . . .

Above all Gibran rejects Aristippus' third principle of
life, because unethically this principle allows the individual to place his interests over those of the other man.
This is known as "egotistic hedonism." Yet, lust always
infringes on the freedom of the other fellowman, and
defames the Beauty present in the human body. "Beauty
reveals herself to us. . . . ; but we approach her in the
name of Lust, snatch off her crown of purity, and pollute
her garmet with our evil-doings."[16]

It is interesting to notice at this point, that Gibran blames the social nobility and the rich people for the recurrence of sexual perversions. He conjectures that among the wealthy persons, we find the great majority of Don Juans. A classic example of everyday sex vice is the story of Martha. One day a young nobleman was trotting in the forests, and saw a beautiful girl gazing at the flowers and trees. He stopped and "in a manner no man had ever used before" chatted with Martha, who was very much impressed by the wealth and kindness of the charming prince. The latter went so far as to promise Martha to make her his wife. Unfortunately, after having taken advantage of the poor orphan, he let her down and departed. Martha, pregnant, became later a prostitute in the City of Lebanon, simply in order to provide housing and food to her child Fouad. Commenting on the story Gibran says:

All this did he do, smiling, and
behind soft words and loving gestures
did he conceal his lust and animal desire.[17]

In connection to the foregoing I have found some texts where Gibran sounds a bit like the Platonists whom I discussed above. It is my personal conviction that Gibran wrote those lines not in contradiction to what he held at one time against the ascetic Platonist, but simply to counsel us contrary to the Aristippus man not to give way unrestrictedly to all the whims of the flesh; otherwise these erotic inclinations could run wild in our life, making us slave of our reinforced carnal habits. If this had to happen, we would twice hurt ourselves and hurt those whom we encounter as the story *Martha* shows. Thus, in his poem *Have Mercy, My Soul*, Gibran figures that a body grown strong in its desire is a prison for the spirit grown weak.

You, O soul, are rich in your wisdom;
this body is poor in its understanding.
You deal not with leniency
And it follows you not.
This, my soul, is the sum of wretchedness.[18]

And elsewhere he writes: ". . . my mind . . . fled from
the prison of matter to the realm of imagining, . . ."[19]

I repeat, these passages do not make of Gibran a
philosopher who severs the body from the mind; they
merely remind us, contrary to the Aristippus
philosophy, of Gibran's advice to keep control over our
bodily desires, and to be moderate in our sexual life. Man
should regard his sex-eros not as an end in itself, but as a
mode of expression for his disinterested love. At this
moment Eros fuses into Agape, and becomes a version of
genuine love. That is to say, sex is justified as soon as it
becomes a vehicle of love-agape. It is vital to understand
at this point, for it is in this way only that Gibran sanc-
tifies sex.

Speaking of Eros-Sex-Agape, let me add that I discovered in Gibran some prerequisite conditions that render
the physical intercourse acceptable. These are
"shyness,"[20] "honesty, reality,"[21] "honor and cleanness
and decency,"[22] and above all, love for one another
should be the motive for the sexual act. If one partner
feels no real attachment for the other, then the act is
prostitution. This is the logic Gibran develops about
those marriages that have been contracted for other
reasons than love-agape. In his opinion, the signing of
marriage papers does not give permission to the conjoints to sleep together, if in the first place there was no
love between them. Love is not a matter of legality of
law. Nor is sexual love restricted to marriage situations.

Gibran is permissive about premarital sex so long the two "care" for each other. Haskell reports:

> He has no code about sex except honesty, reality. 'Should you say,' asked I, 'that if a man or woman loved seven and lived sexually with seven it was all right?' 'If the seven were all willing, yes,' said he.[23]

In conclusion, let us sum up the misconceptions of the disguised love. Love is not synonymous with sex, notwithstanding that sex when properly defined becomes a way of expressing the experience of that ultimate togetherness called love. Gibranism does not inhibit Eros, he simply subordinates it to Agape. Also, authentic love is not a love that "reckons" and "sorts out" for personal interests, such as financial purposes, social prestige.[24] On the contrary Gibran has all reasons to believe that a calculative love is a self-love that neurotically has never transcended the Freudian primary narcissistic stage of a masochist child.

GIBRAN'S SEXUAL LIFE

Was Gibran sincere and consistent in his daily actions with what he preached philosophically to others about the sanctified sex?

Many biographers have discussed Gibran's sexual life. In my opinion most of what they wrote lacks biographical verification. I consider some of their sayings either speculative or incomplete, because really they were acquainted with out author only for a short time. Therefore I see the justification to raise anew the theme "Gibran's sexual life."

The last book that Knopf pubished *The Love Letters of*

Kahlil Gibran and Mary Haskell, and Her Private Journal
(1972) brings new revelations to the scholars on Gibran.
And although Miss Mary Haskell could not have recorded in her journal all the minute details of Gibran's
private life, since she lived in Boston and he was in New
York, still her biography contains the clue to our question.

In reading Haskell's diary and the correspondence the
two sent to each other, I get the picture that Gibran was
definitely not an impotent sexual man. Rather like most
of the great minds he seems to have believed that success
in artistic and literary creativity somehow demands the
presence of a woman. And indeed, Gibran had rapports
with many women. It is not possible for us biographers
to estimate accurately how many women entered his
private life. Nevertheless, I count among them a French
girl nicknamed Micheline who followed him to Paris in
1908 from Boston; the American biographer Barbara
Young who remained with him from 1923 to 1931; an
"older woman" in Paris who kept him in her home
"because he had no money, because a woman was
likelier than a man to supply money, and because such
things weren't done without pay,"[25] and of course, his
benefactress Miss Mary Haskell; and a host of female
models who would pose nude during his painting.

Was then Gibran sexual-minded? Not at all! Haskell
testifies that "Kahlil is not sexual-minded, but absorbed
in bigger things." He was "physically shy,"[26] and sometimes ignorant about sex. In a letter he wrote to Haskell
in 1917 in reply for the gifts and a book on sex that the
latter had sent him, he confessed being naive about
sexuality.

Thank you for the sugar and the books. I shall consume both with much care! Somehow I have never

been able to enjoy fully reading a book on sex. Perhaps I have not been curious enough, or perhaps I have been mentally timid. But I now want to know all things under the sun, and the moon, too. For all things are beautiful in themselves, and become more beautiful when known to man. . . .[27]

Instead of spending his sex-energy in intercourse, Haskell reaffirms that Gibran transformed the libidinal power into art-production.[28] All this comes to confirm what Freud said of artists, namely, they "sublimate" and "cathect" their sexual warmth into creativity.[29] I find it interesting that Gibran made statements in 1912 and 1914 similar to those of Freud concerning the sex-economy among the artists. Thus, he used to speak to Haskell: "And I too, have great warmth sexually. I think a great deal of sex power goes transformed into my work."[30]

Actually, his dedication to drawing and writing was the very reason why he refused to get married, notwithstanding that the idea of marrying Haskell haunted him from 1910 to 1912.[31]

Discussing marriage one afternoon in the studio, after he had read the piece on *marriage* from *The Prophet*, one of the several guests said smilingly, 'Tell us, why have you never married?' Smiling also he replied 'Well . . . you see it is like this. If I had a wife, and if I were painting or making poems, I should simply forget her existence for days at a time. And you know well that no loving woman would put up with such a husband very long.'[32]

We are also told by Haskell that Gibran would sometimes abstain from physical intercourse, because he feared the possible "misfortune consequences"[33] of such a liaison, viz., "pregnancy" of the woman. Another reason for which he would keep his "sex emotion down"[34] was for sake of respect and love-agape he held towards the woman. "Love—the greater love—is extremely careful about intercourse and is bodily shy."[35] I am not trying to prove with these quotations that Gibran always sublimated his sexual urges. Nor am I trying to convey to the reader the impression that Gibran had little sexual relations. Whoever peruses the private journal of Miss Haskell would rather see how intensely moved he was by the idea of sex.

He had said, there are three centers in everybody— head, heart, sex. One or another or two of them lead, in each person—not in the same equilibrium at different times perhaps in a given person. 'With me,' he said, 'head and heart led until a few years ago. And then sex' . . .[36]

Let us take, as an example, his rapport with Haskell. At no time has Haskell bluntly reported that she slept with Gibran. But she avowed that they kissed and freely touched each other.[37] She even one day undressed herself in his studio, and Gibran put his arms round her neck and kissed her on the breasts, as they stood.[38] Personally, I believe Gibran had a sexual relation with Haskell, as with many others who visited him frequently in his studio. Nevertheless, I also believe that he was not a sex maniac as some have pretended. From the very fact that we know he never hurt somebody, but was considerate of others, Gibran had sanctified sex in his life and converted it into Agape. A man acts as to what personality he is. The next section testifies that Gibran lived the precepts of Agape over and above the erotic impulses.

Agape

Originally, "Agape" was coined by the Greeks to describe the early Christians' "brotherly love" in connection with the Lord's Supper. With time the word came to signify the Evangelic-love in contrast to the Erotic-love or concupiscence. In Gibran, Agape stands for spiritual love, but not necessarily the Christian, although he is deeply influenced by Christ's sermons on Love. Gibranism extrapolates the philosophy of Agape illustrated in the New Testament, and makes it a natural, universal phenomenon pertaining to all creeds. Therefore, you don't need to be a Christian to practice Agape; such love is primarily a metaphysical datum and its directives apply unconditionally to any one who wants to live morally worthy, in as much as it is a psychological rule for developing a healthy personality.

To insure a clear exposition to the reader, I propose to elaborate step by step Gibran's phenomenology of Agape, and in the long run integrate the eclectic elements that our author develops in reference to love.

LOVE, THE ESSENCE OF EXISTENCE

Every profound thinker has for a major concern the search for an answer to Shakespeare's question: "To be, or not to be," i.e., why is there being instead of non-being? In technical language we call metaphysics or ontology the discipline that searches for the meaning of existence. Up to the present day, the history of thought abounds with the many proposed metaphysics. Gibran, too, discussed existence, yet his theory is not as abstract and theoretical as the philosophies of the scholar academicians. Gibranism is a people's philosophy, something quite different from a philosopher's philosophy. Nonetheless, his system makes much sense.

In his opinion, then, the true essence of existence is "love." In the essay *The Victors* we read the exclamation: love, "You are my very being."[39] Also, the novel *The Broken Wings*, calls love "the law of nature,"[40] i.e., the *"raison d'être"* of existence. And in his poem *Song of Love*, he states that love is the very essence of nature, man, and the historical events. The world is guided by the principle of love. Love generates, produces, even sometimes destroys life, yet it always sustains the world in its eternity.

> . . . I smiled at Helena and she destroyed Tarwada; yet I crowned Cleopatra and peace dominated The Valley of the Nile. I am like the ages—building today and destroying tomorrow. . . .[41]

To understand why Gibran makes of love the ontological necessity of existence, we must recall that for him existence entails an act of "creation" and not of "fabrication" or "generation." His metaphysics is that of a believer in God. God creates existence. "The God separated a spirit from himself and fashioned it into beauty."[42] Now, God creates out of an act of love. Furthermore, Gibran holds the same metaphysical idea of the scholastic philosophers, when he reasons that between the effects and the cause, there is a degree of proportionality in existence. Thus his logic maintains that if "God is love"[43]—because "The Infinite keeps naught save Love, for it is in its own likeness,"[44]—so will the products of God "be" made of love.

Gibran's philosophy of existence is *monistic*, in that he believes in the reality of the One principle that causes life. That source of everything is love. ". . . Everything bespeaks love."[45] Hence, Gibran answers to the Shakespearian interrogation; "If existence had not been better than non-being, there would have been no being."[46] The adverb "better" in this state of affairs stands synonymous to "love"; love, then, is the quintessence of existence, and "no thing shall prevail against it."[47] As for the second *"nous"* (in Greek, spirit) of the Manichaeians and Platonists, which is the Evil, Gibran disqualifies its autonomous reality. He assumes that if evil exists it is only present in man's actions, and it is never an independent principle, that governs the world as an equal to love.

At this stage, I remind the readers that our author is not the only thinker who philosophizes that love is the ontological core of existence. Our contemporary existentialists of the right wing, the theists, share Gibran's thesis. For instance, Kierkegaard, Marcel, Buber and Jaspers have concluded that the essence of being is love. They also teach, much like Gibran, that the self cannot genuinely encounter reality unless man assumes the existential attitude of love. In such attitude the individual does not differentiate what he is from what he finds in front of him. Because in the final analysis, the being of the individual man is not different from the other beings, since in the first place both the person and the rest of the universe have issued from the same source, namely, the Love of God. Nurturing such a metaphysical attitude one finds himself on the right path to discovering truth, and living in peace with the world. Gibran would ascribe to Marcel's statement *"esse"* is *"co-esse,"* to be is to be-with-the-rest-of-the-world. Gibran illustrates this metaphysical inseparability in the following way:

> Everything in creation exists within you, and everything in you exists in creation. You are in borderless touch with the closest things, and, what is more,

distance is not sufficient to separate you from things far away. All things from the lowest to the loftiest, from the smallest to the greatest, exist within you as equal things.[48]

Between the self and the rest of reality there is an intimate bond, which is explainable from the fact that the two come into being from an identical focus point: the love of God. Marcel, too, considers love the best ontological attitude for communicating and entering into the sphere of existence:

Love, insofar as distinct from desire or as opposed to desire, love treated as the subordination of the self to a superior reality, a reality at my deepest and more *truly me* than I am myself—love as the breaking of the tension between the self and the other, appears to me to be what one might call the *essential ontological* datum.[49]

If existence is fashioned of love, then what should man *do* in order to live up to the expectations of love? How does a man animated by Agape behave *morally* worthily? Which are the *criteria* and *norms* of genuine love? The following headings attempt to provide a sincere solution to these queries.

LOVE IS DISINTERESTEDNESS

One of the signs of Agape is that it doesn't "reckon" nor is "self-centered." Agape is vivified by the spirit of "giving" without calculation of receiving in return. Here, the self generously gives to others not with the pretence of what they need most for themselves; rather the self gives to the point of depriving itself of what it personally needs most. The kind of "giving" Gibran advocates is other than the material goods. Almustafa, the prophet, preaches that the giving of *oneself* is a far more superior type than the giving of possessions. "You give but little when you give of your possessions. It is when you give of yourself that you truly give."[50] To illustrate the deep meaning encompassed in the statement, I will cite the case of a lady whom I once heard responding to a call received from the Saint Vincent De Paul organization: "Well, I really don't mind to help the unfortunates. I will send you every month a check, but please don't ask me to volunteer of my time for visiting the poor and the sick in the hospital. . . ." In the prophet's opinion, this lady did not practice the noblest act of giving, because she refused to give of herself. It is easy to give of one's overabundant wealth, yet, the truly meritorious act is that of making oneself available to others.

> Generosity is not in giving me that which I need more than you do, but it is in giving me that which you need more than I do.[51]

True love, then, makes sacrifices for the happiness of the beloved. It is unselfish. Leibniz, the philosopher of the eighteenth century, used to say: *Amare est gaudere felicitate alterius.* (To love is to seek the felicity of the beloved.) The novel *The Broken Wings* provides us with an instance of this thinking of disinterestedness. In the chapter "The Sacrifice," we read that Gibran asked Selma, who knew that she had to marry the nephew of the bishop, to flee with him to another country despite a possible indictment from the prelate. But, Selma turned down the offer of Gibran on the ground that her beloved might someday be looked upon by the native villagers as an adulterer and a homebreaker. She was thinking in the interests of Gibran, notwithstanding that the proposal would have saved her from the fate of marrying a man she never loved. Witness how she expresses her unselfish feelings.

Love only taught me to protect you even from myself. It is love, purified with fire, that stops me from following you to the farthest land. Love kills my desires so that you may live freely and virtuously. Limited love asks for possession of the beloved, but the unlimited asks only for itself.[52]

LOVE KNOWS NO TIME AND NO SPACE

To many minds, the adage "out of sight out of mind" seems to hold. Yet, retorts Gibran, should oblivion of the beloved result as a consequence of an abscence or a lack of physical encounter, then, it should be assumed that in the first place genuine love had not planted its deep roots in the hearts of the lovers. It is much safer to presume that their love was "romanticism." Paradoxically, the prophet teaches that spatial distance and the lapse of time increase love. By being far away from the beloved, the lover learns more to appreciate his partner, and ceases to take him or her for granted. "Love knows not its own depth until the hour of separation."[53]

In time of separation, love becomes a "longing" and a "hope" that inspires the anticipation of unification in the near future. When Almustafa returned after twelve years to his homeland, a woman named Karima who assisted at the death of the prophet's mother, complained that he remained too long hidden from the people's face. But, the prophet Almustafa replied:

Twelve years? Said you twelve years, Karima? I measured not my longing with the starry rod, nor did I sound the depth there of. For love when love is homesick exhausts time's measurements and time's soundings.[54]

For a person to know if he really is in love, he should try for a while the acid test of separation. Today many counselors are beginning to recommend a trial separation for a couple whose marriage is on the verge of crumbling. The idea is that one sees best the situation when one is aloof. Love too needs distance. In a letter Gibran wrote in 1911 to Haskell, he stated: "To understand the world one must be far, far away from the world. . . . One must be at a little distance from great things in order to see them well."[55]

The person who surges stronger during the moments of separation, experiences that his love transcends the spatial and temporal frontiers. And indeed, it is the mark of Agape to be boundless. The prophet speaks wisely with the words:

Who among you does not feel that his power to love is boundless? . . . And is not time even as love is, undivided and spaceless?[56]

LOVE IS STRONGER THAN DEATH

In connection with the idea that love is timeless and spaceless, Gibran develops his theory of love for the departed souls. He maintains that death does not separate the lover from the beloved. Death is not the end of a love affair. Love *per se* involves a relation of communication, of intimacy, which can never be destroyed, not even by death. Had love a life span, then it would be futile and existence as such would be absurd because there would be no guarantee for the value of the love-deed. Forgetfulness is an indication of a love-desire, but not of a love-deed. Gibran points out:

> Verily the vastest distance is that which lies between
> . . . that which is but a deed and that which is a
> desire . . . For in remembrance there are no dis-
> tances; and only in oblivion is there a gulf that
> Neither your voice nor your eye can bridge.[57]

Here we are at the peak of Agape. In relation to the dead, Agape assumes the attitudes of "hope," "faithful-ness" and complete "availability" towards the deceased. First *hope*, because such longing strengthens the will in time of despair and sorrow. The lover convinces himself that the beloved has not disappeared. The presence of the beloved accompanies the lover everywhere. Hence, hope at this stage of love becomes creative *fidelity*. Between the survivor and the dead arises a relationship in which the self surpasses his awareness of a solitary ego; he sees himself bound to the memories and the resolutions he took while the beloved was alive. In other words, the self experiences a deep *availability* of dedica-tion to the loved one. He remains faithful to the image of the dead not only on Sunday or for a few hours every morning but till the end of his life.

For Gibran love proves philosophically the *immortality of the soul*. But the very fact that I still love my beloved even after his death is not a hallucination nor a psychotic phase. My love is a reality. My beloved probably waits for me someplace, where we will unite again. Love out-lives the biological death. In the *Nymphs of the Valley* we are told that two lovers met each other after two thousand years in the temple of Astar, and finally realized their wish, which was to be together, a desire that was forbidden them by the priests.

Astarte bring back to this life the souls of lovers who have gone to the infinite before they have tasted of the delights of love and the joys of youth. . . . We shall meet again, Nathan, and together drink of the morning dew from the cups of the narcissus and rejoice in the sun with the birds of the fields.[58]

All those who have believed in love have emphasized the role *God* plays in keeping the tie between the partners. Love is stronger than death because love is a gift from God.[59] And God himself is eternal. After vowing to each other faithfulness and spiritual love, despite the fact that Selma was to be married legally to Mansour Bey, Gibran finds consolation in love and retorts to Selma: "Love, my beloved Selma, will stay with me to the end of my life, and after death the hand of God will unite us again."[60]

To understand Gibran on this point, we must be Gibran. It is difficult for a scientific and technocratic mind to comprehend the meaning of that feeling. It is a personal experience felt by the self. In Max Weber's and Nicolai Hartman's words: neither intelligence nor the senses will ever make us discover a real value. The simple definition of love will not teach very much to him who has not loved. It is certain that this value appears to us concretely insofar as we *live it*, and insofar as we sense it penetrating our life of feeling, volition, intellection, freedom, etc. . . . in one word, we have to feel its presence enveloping us entirely.

Yet, Gibran is not alone for proposing love as a proof

for the veridicality of immortality. The theistic existentialists have advanced a similar argument. A character in
one of Marcel's plays says that to love is to affirm "Thou,
at least, Thou shall not die." Also, in a lecture titled *Death
and Immortality*, Marcel alluding to the death of his wife
exclaimed: "You cannot simply have disappeared; if I
believed that I would be a traitor."[61] I purposely quote
from academic philosophers, in order to establish the
relevancy of Gibran's simply worded philosophy.

LOVE COMMANDS UNIVERSALITY

A closely related issue to the limitlessness of the feeling of love, is the meaning that love *per se* prescribes no
national, cultural or political frontiers. Or to put it
bluntly, love ought to be *universal*. Often times our author depicts love as an inexhaustible "power."[62] By this
token he conveys that the human heart has the *natural
capacity* to engulf the whole of humanity; Agape motivates man to enter in communion with the entire creation. "Who among you does not feel that his power to
love is boundless?[63] In Gibran's opinion, the cultural,
religious and political values are largely responsible for
the restrictions put on the power of love. For example,
we know that politics indoctrinates the self to care for
only those who are born in the same geographical milieu.
Politics inculcates in the minds of its citizens attitudes of
discrimination, segregation and prejudices towards the
humans of other nations. Politics narrows the range of
expansion of the love-energy. Actually, all the so-called
extrinsic social values represent a hindrance to the
growth of the spirit of humanism in the individual. That
is why Gibran reacts harshly against the partition of the
earth into government countries, and places humanism
over patriotism.

Humans are divided into different clans and tribes, and belong to countries and towns. But [for] . . . myself . . . the universe is my country and the human family is my tribe. . . .

. . . If my people rose, stimulated by plunder and motivated by what they call "patriotic spirit" to murder, and invaded my neighbor's country, then upon the committing of any human atrocity I would hate my people and my country. . . .

Humanity is the spirit of the Supreme Being on earth and that Supreme Being preaches love and good-will.[64]

Occasionally, Gibran maintained that love makes us develop a "universal consciousness,"[65] which is a sense of feeling meaningfully linked to humanity through the sacred ties of existence. Love at this moment becomes a categorical universal imperative that guides our conscience in her moral conducts. To illustrate the point, let me refer to another great philosopher, Immanuel Kant, who somehow preceded Gibran on this maxim. To Kant's contention, an action is morally worthy if one can will that it becomes a universal rule which all should imitate; otherwise it is wrong. That is, the acid test of the moral rightness of an action lies in whether one could allow that his action set an example which everyone should follow. If one cannot "will" this, then the conduct is evil. This is why lying is not morally justifiable under any circumstances; for we cannot will that lying becomes a universal practice which individuals ought to use.[66] Kant's ethical formulation repeats in different words Christ's golden rule that Gibran himself has adopted, namely, "Do unto others as you would have them do unto you." Of course, the only available standard we have to judge the pros and cons of the deed is the law of love. Love, therefore, originates in us a "universal consciousness," because its precepts command us at least to respect all humans regardless of their race, religion and socio-economic class.

With this same trend of thought, Gibran adds that the practice of universal love develops in us what he calls "the Greater Self."[67] Accordingly, there are two "me's" in constant civil war against each other.[68] The small self is egotistic, and its scope of "human concern" is confined to parochialism; the greater self, on the other hand, is motivated by spiritual love, and aspires to a cosmic union with the universe. Humanists, visionaries, mystics and philanthropists have experienced the presence of "the larger and better self." Miss Haskell, in one of the entries in her private journals, provides us with a good description as to how the greater self of Gibran would behave and feel.

> 'Did you ever look upon the present through the eyes of the future?' said Kahlil at night. 'I have become familiar with the human mind today—in many parts of the world—its attitude toward things, its reactions, its tendencies, its modes of working and I know how it will look upon things a hundred years from now.' . . .
> I have come to a sense of a larger I. . . . My Buddha, I call that larger, longer-living self; and now I pray to lend itself to the Larger's purpose. . . .
> There is, in Kahlil, a being longing simply to be allowed to love, to lavish itself, to speak its innermost, to be closer than inner souls can conceive—an unspeakable sensitiveness.[69]

LOVE, HATE, FORGIVENESS

How does Gibran reconcile the situation of enmity with the precept of universal love? I confess that I find

Gibran's ethics of love quite realistic on the topic of "hate." He is not full of optimism like Leibniz, nor is he impressed by the pessimism of Hobbes. He knows that there exist sadistic men who enjoy hurting others. Still, he holds that Agape transcends the sclerosis of hate. *"Forgiveness," "tolerance"* and *"pity"* constitute the secret strength of a love harassed by hostilities. And rather than weakening the dynamics of love, the enmity of others is a beneficiary source for cleansing the heart, for renewing our humanism, and above all a blessed occasion for practising the universal love. If there were no outside negative interferences, then the course of love would be a matter of mechanical routine, a conditioned habit and a monotony. Fortunately, life gives us the opportunity to prove to ourselves our ability to love, even our opponents.

> It is only when you are pursued that you
> become swift.[70]
> The truly good is he who is one with all
> those who are deemed bad.[71]
> Love which is not always springing is always
> dying.[72]

The person "metamotivated" by *Agape*—to borrow a concept from A. Maslow's psychology—lucidly understands that he simply cannot always succeed in having his neighbors return his love. He has to live on his own with his enemies. Towards his adversaries he assumes the attitudes of "forgiveness" and "kindness" which is "the shadow of God in man."[73] Now, it is this "universal love," i.e., the sense of feelings related unrestrictedly to the whole of Being, that binds the individual to accept with *resignation* the sufferings, ridicules and rejections that his enemies inflict upon him. After all, love is not rosy, its ways "are hard and steep."[74] "For even as love crowns you so shall he crucify you. Even as he is for your growth so he is for your pruning."[75] Of course, Gibran does not advise us to go after our enemies and seek that they hurt us so that we keep on testing ourselves on the precepts of love. This would be masochism rather than heroism.

What happens to "hate" in the metaphysics of Gibran? Could hate be given a status of independent existence? The metaphysics of hate is a crucial one. To grasp its place in Gibran's system helps us explain two theses: (1) Why he has insisted that love is all there is to existence, and that, therefore, love by its very essence is absolute, timeless and spaceless; and (2) why he thought of love as the sole existential attitude for meeting reality and gaining perfect knowledge of reality.[76]

To Gibran's contention, human existence, and all existences, could not have been fashioned by hate; only Love and Life are identical.[77] Yet, the old Persian philosophers would have us believe in the equal principles of Good and Evil. Gibran discards the Evil principle, on the ground that Life is Harmony, Beauty, Truth. Had the Evil principle prevailed we would have experienced confusion, contradiction and disorder in the face of existence. Gibran goes even so far as to deny that there is any evil *per se* in human actions, or that man is capable of evil for evil. In other words, man cannot aim at evil as an end. Evil is never apprehended for, in and through itself. What is called evil, the individual perceives as a good, whose fulfillment it is believed will realize a desired goal. For example, a thief does not steal for the purpose of doing evil; rather he judges the act of robbing to be a desirable means for procuring himself good. The scholastic philosophers used to say that evil is a transformed good. Similarly Gibran maintains that evil is but a desire invested with the features of good.

Of the good in you I can speak, but not of
the evil.
For what is evil but good tortured by its own
hunger and thirst? . . .
You are good in countless ways, and you are
not evil when you are not good, you are only
loitering and sluggard.[78]

Whenever Gibran speaks of hate, he does so from the psychological standpoint. I found three psychological statements concerning hate. (1) Hate is an *"emotion"* whose power is proportional to the energy of love. Chronologically, one must have loved first so that he may hate afterwards. Hence, hate is but love to hatred turned. Or also, as Mikhail Naimy, a close friend to our author, put it: "And what is Hate but love repressed, or Love withheld?"[79] Gibran illustrates the transformation of love into hate in the parable *The Love Song*. Once upon a time a poet composed a beautiful song on love and sent a copy to all his acquaintances, including a lady he had just met. Some time later, a messenger came inviting the poet to visit the parents of the lady, in order to talk about the preparations for the "betrothal." But the poet replied: "My friend, it was but a song of love . . . sung . . . to every woman." Immediately the lady got aggressive, and exclaimed: "From this day unto my coffin-day I shall hate all poets for your sake."[80]

(2) From another psychological viewpoint, only the weak personalities employ the technique of hate as a protective strategy in order to guard their self-esteem. Hate becomes a Freudian *mechanism of ego-defense* against circumventive discomforts and anxieties. This is common to personalities whose Agape has not become universal. They react violently towards the external obstructions with the shield of hate. Now, the students of Freud

will remember that the use of defense mechanisms is an indication of neurosis. Gibran writes: "Often times I have hated in self-defense; but if I were strong I would not have used such a weapon."[81]

(3) Finally, Gibran dissuades us from practicing hate for mental health purposes. Hate destroys our mental hygiene; it weakens our faculties of thinking, feeling and volition; it raises our blood pressure and in the long run may accelerate the moment of *death*. Note that Freud too attributed our biological death to the hyperaggressiveness withheld inwardly. In our context aggressiveness is identical to hate. Gibran in his turn equates hate with death. "Hate is a dead thing. Who of you would be a tomb?"[82]

The conclusion we reach emphasizes that in love, forgiveness and kindness, the self preserves its health and self-actualizes its personality, because the self then learns to cope realistically with but not *escape* from the advent of frustrations and sorrows.

LOVE GIVES DELICIOUS PAIN

Following what has been said in the preceding section, it is clear that human history unfolds itself in situations of joy and sorrow. No man can be exempted from experiencing desolation. However, not everybody seems to accept with resignation this fate of human destiny. The pessimists advocate that because suffering is unavoidable then existence is *absurd* and God is our executioner. And many atheists have become unbelievers for failing to reconcile intellectually the recurrence of pain, either the physical, moral or psychological, with the idea of an Omnipotent, *Summum Bonum Deity*.[83] Yet in the opinion of Gibran, there is a way to justify human miseries. His argument is not scientific, but one of "common sense." Whoever adheres to it, I believe will find both the fulfillment of his humanism and eventually his faith in the Divine. Gibran's argument runs, therefore, as follows: rather than hindering the growth of self-identity, anxieties procure self-knowledge. The French poet Alfred de Musset once wrote: *"Nul ne se connait tant qu'il n'a point souffert."* Translated in Gibran's vernacular, Musset's statement signifies that "perplexity is the beginning of knowledge"[84] Life would be quite dull, and the person a pantomime, if there were no situations of tragedy to awaken us from the slumber of routine. The self gets more conscious, more involved when he faces afflictions. Similarly, concerning the positive life-events such as happiness, joy, contentment— the self could not *appreciate* them enough, if from time to time he were not tested by sufferings, pains and discomforts. "Who has not seen sorrow cannot see joy."[85] Hence, instead of complaining and blaming God, Gibran sees goodness even in the worst.

Actually, it is the spirit of Agape that counts for Gibran's attitude of resignation in front of vexations. Around 1903 when our author lost consecutively his mother, sister, and half-brother, he grew to visualize that pain and sufferings were necessary conditions that ought to be mixed with Agape, so that the foundations of the latter become unshakable in the heart of the individual. A love that has to shed tears in order to prove its love is a true love. "Love that is cleansed by tears will remain eternally pure and beautiful."[86]

The adage says, there are no beautiful and scented roses without thorns. So too it goes for love. To love is to be willing to undergo self-sacrifices. And indeed, when you love, you assume the beloved's misfortunes, shortcomings and sorrows. The *responsibility* that accompanies love will sometimes cause you headaches. Verily, love is one with tears. Yet, they are tears of "painful joy."[87] "The pain that accompanies love . . . and responsibility also gives delight."[88] Once again, the prophet Almustafa preaches:

When love beckons you, follow him,
Though his ways are hard and steep.
And when his wings enfold you yield
to him,
Though the sword hidden among his
pinions may wound you.
And when he speaks to you believe in
him,
Though his voice may shatter your dreams
as the north wind lays waste the garden.[89]

In brief, Gibran teaches that love is a *"molar behavior."* He compares it to an atom with its sub-atomic particles. "The chemist who can extract from his heart's elements compassion, respect, longing, patience, regret, surprise and forgiveness and compound them into one can create that atom which is called LOVE."[90] And in *The Broken Wings* he states lucidly that love is pervasive over the whole self. Also, he enumerates the three states of presence of the beloved: in the mind, the heart, and at nights in the dreams. "She [Selma] became a supreme thought, a beautiful dream, and an overpowering emotion living in my spirit."[91]

LOVE DEVELOPS GENUINE BONDS OF INTERSUBJECTIVITY

The human being could not survive at all if he had to depend on his own instincts and abilities alone. Biologically and psychologically, the person needs the help of other minds in order to grow healthy and self-realize his birth potentials. In the words of our contemporary European philosophers, man is a *relational being* by the very nature of his existence. This simple truth was actually discovered and expressed more than twenty centuries ago by the Stagirite, Aristotle, in his famous dictum "Man is a social animal." Gibran too has reiterated that man is a *communal* creature. No man is an island. Frankly, the self owes to others what he possesses and how he behaves existentially; "In truth . . . you owe all to all men."[92] The self can at no time and place divorce his existence from the presence of other minds; the self is somehow doomed (pardon me for the expression) to live his life always and everywhere, even during solitude, in relation to other selves.

Your most radiant garment is of the other
person's weaving;
Your most savory meal is that which you eat
at the other person's table;
Your most comfortable bed is in the other
person's house.
Now tell me, how can you separate yourself
from the other person?[93]

Being-together is a law of existence; for that, Gibran advises us to nurture good interpersonal relations instead of the negative social attitudes. In a healthy intersubjectivity the self gains everything, while in the opposite the self loses everything, including his psychological well-being, as we showed previously about "hate." Here, Gibran has in mind the principle of brotherhood and love as the solution for establishing authentic interpersonal contacts. Once more the prophet Almustafa teaches:

We live upon one another according to
the law, ancient and timeless. Let us
live thus in loving-kindness. We seek one
another in our aloneness, and we walk the
road when we have no hearth to sit beside.
My friends and my brothers, the wider road
is your fellow-man.[94]

If we ruminate seriously on the last quotes, we should
come to agreement with Gibran that at birth we are
simply *"one-half"* of our self. The other half is outside of
us and can be discovered just and only through the
love-encounter with the other. Gibran illustrates this
point in the short tale *The Victors*. A poor fellah fell in love
at the sight of a pretty girl. But he was not allowed to
marry her because the girl belonged to a high social rank;
she was the daughter of the Emir. While pensive in
melancholy, the princess appeared to him and in a loving
voice exclaimed: "You appeared in my dreams of sadness, and your image ended my loneliness. You are the
compassion of my lost soul, and you are my *other half*
from which I was torn when I came to this world."[95] The
story ends saying that the two flee together to another
village.
    Gibran is not at all wrong when he maintains that true
love develops one's personality. In practical life, there is
no discovery of the self, no self-realization and no self-
knowledge, until the individual consents to share life
with another "self." And it is precisely the appeal of the
other self which helps me to break loose from my self-
centeredness, and liberate myself from myself. In my
daily interpersonal dealings, the other's appeal reveals
to me an entirely new, perhaps wholly unsuspected
dimension of my being. In relation to him I find the
answers to the Socratic question: Who am I? Am I a

patient or impatient personality? Am I capable of faithfulness in married life? Have I been socially conditioned
to hate Negroes, Jews, communists, etc?

The idea that human nature is a paradox, as many
thinkers have stated, seems to hold true. Our topic at
hand proves the veridicality of the paradox. Indeed, *on
one hand*, we know that the individual man is a subject, a
being who exists for himself, a presence to himself, a
self-regulating being. Man is a self-hood. Yet, *on the other
hand*, life shows that man is a selfhood only in being
fused with the non-I. This enigmatic aspect of human
existence is put even in sharper relief by love. Love, as I
pointed out previously in the section "love toward the
dead," is the ready availability (*disponibilité* would say
Marcel) of my being, its belonging to the subject which
the other is. By giving and surrendering myself, it is
manifested to me what my selfhood really is. Gibran
conveys well this truth. "They say if one understands
himself, he understands all people. But I say to you,
when one *loves people*, he learns something about
himself."[96]

From the preceding quotation it is clear that self-
knowledge and self-realization (Who am I?) depends on
the acceptance of the existence of others and not vice-
versa. The other, as discovered through love and not the
sense perceptions, is the prerequisite condition for establishing my self. As for adverse relationships such as hate,
enmity, jealousy, etc., these seem often to hinder the
maturity of self-identity. True self-knowledge comes
only through amicable relationships. In the essay *The
Philosophy of Logic*, Gibran ironically describes the case of
a self-knowledge not acquired through love. One day
Salem Effandi Daybiss, moved by the desire to find a
personal answer to Socrates' dictum "Know thyself,"
went in front of a mirror and glanced at himself. But the

only reflection he could see in the mirror was the shape of his body. And so he began to compare his nose to that of Voltaire and George Washington, his stature to that of Napoleon, his eyes to those of Paul the Apostle and Nietzsche, his neck to that of Mark Antony. At the end Salem Effandi resumed his thoughts shouting: "This is myself — this is my reality. I possess all the qualities of great men from the beginning of history to the present. A youth with such qualities is destined to great achievements."[97] Yet, as he came to decide the kind of achievement with which he should start, he found himself confused, not knowing "what great deed" he should begin with. And thus, he went to sleep "in his untidy clothes upon his filthy bed," as he always did. The lesson of the story concludes that Salem did not learn the real meaning of his existence; his self-knowledge narrowed down to knowledge of his physiognomy, because he sought to know himself through the use of the method of comparison and not through the love-encounter.

To sum up, Gibranism advocates that love, the "in-between," is the best human achievement for realizing our self-identity, in contrast to the inauthentic intersubjectivity professed by Jean-Paul Sartre and Simone de Beauvoir. The latter philosophers deny the ontological root of the need for interpersonal relationships. They assert that "the other person is my hell," "the other person is my downfall," "the other person kills my potentialities and robs me of my subjectivity." But Gibran rests content with the theistic existentialists that the individual establishes his selfhood in so far as he really believes "in the existence of others and allows this belief to influence his conduct."[98] For this very reason Gibran insists on calling the other my "half-self," and elsewhere my "other self."[99] "In truth the other person is your most sensitive self given another body."[100]

One day in his studio, Gibran told Barbara Young:

"We shall never understand one another until we reduce the language to seven words."[101] After a pause he asked Miss Young to guess which were these seven magic words. The latter was hesitant. Then Gibran slowly and almost breathlessly spoke. "These are my seven words: You, I, take, God, love, beauty, Earth,"[102] And combining them together he made this poem:

Love, take me.
Take me, Beauty.
Take me, Earth.
I take you,
Love, Earth, Beauty.
I take
God.[103]

LOVE GUARANTEES FREEDOM

An interpersonal relation that grows only on knowledge of the other person without love, such a relationship may eventually rob the other of his individuality and limit his *freedom*. In Jean-Paul Sartre's existential psychoanalytical words, such a meeting is grounded on *"the stare,"* whereby the person stared at becomes a being-for-the-sake-of-the-looker.[104] Gibran agrees with Sartre on this point. On July 8, 1914, Gibran confided to Haskell:

I have always held, with my *Madman*, that those who understand us (without love) enslave something in us. It is not so with you. Your understanding of me is the most peaceful freedom I have known.[105]

It is when love does not accompany the knowledge one might have of another's personality, that the privacy of the person is endangered, in that at any time his personality weaknesses, intentions, projects, past life may be unveiled and ridiculed. "Blackmail" is an instance of a knowledge lacking the sense of Agape. Love then is the safeguard of freedom and subjectivity. And vice-versa, to Gibran's contention, there can be no real freedom unless love animates human relationships. *The Broken Wings* emphasizes: "Love is the only freedom in the world because it so elevates the spirit that the laws of humanity and the phenomena of nature do not alter its course."[106] And in the *Spirits Rebellious*, Madame Rose Hanie recognizes that "the spiritual law of Love and Affection" gave her the courage to abandon the life of adultery she was leading with her husband, Rashid Bey Naam, an old man who married her with her parents' consent but not hers.

> I was a sinner in the eyes of God and myself
> when I ate his bread and offered him my body
> —in reward for his generosity. Now I am pure and
> clean because the law of Love has freed man and
> made me honorable and faithful.[107]

Yet, paradoxical as it seems, the freedom engendered through love is not a freedom of absolutism that would preserve the individual from any stringent forces nor of libertinage, in that he could do anything he pleases; rather it is a freedom that imposes limitations on the instincts, impulses and self-interests. It prescribes norms and conditions for conduct. Freedom is not easy; it is hard; it is a heavy "burden" for it weighs on the individual's sense of *responsibility*. A man who has attained a high level of freedom knows that he has to weigh consciously and conscientiously his acts before the execution of the decisions. For he knows that his decisions will have tremendous repercussions on his environs and those whom he loves.

Definitely, it is Agape that enchains and handcuffs freedom; love implies reponsibility, or as *The Prophet* puts it, love signifies "to care"[108] for the beloved. "The truly free man"—writes Gibran—"is he who bears the load of the bond slave patiently."[109] Elsewhere, we find once more the concepts "slave," "love" and "freedom" interconnected:

You are free before the sun of the day
and free before the stars of the night; . . .
. . . You are even free when you close your
eyes upon all there is.
But you are a slave to him whom you love
because you love him,
And a slave to him who loves you because
he loves you.[110]

Nevertheless, the servitude caused by love and responsibility is a "pleasant" one, and therefore should not be confused with the kind of slavery imposed by political despots or the blind coercions of the environment. The difference between the love-slavery and coercive-slavery consists in that the latter is imposed by an outside-will while in the former case the self seems to be his own conditioner.[111] The lover choses of his own a matrix of obligations and duties which he promises to be faithful to. And whenever he transgresses one of his principles, he feels remorse and blames himself for having failed to cope with the ideal conduct he had obligated himself with. In this respect, Gibran says that love alleviates the yoke of freedom and responsibility. He even sees love giving more freedom than limiting the self."
And thus your freedom when it loses its fetters becomes

itself the fetter of a greater freedom."[112] At this point, however, it should be kept in mind that Gibran is not advocating an absolute freedom of doing; quite the contrary, he knows that man is extremely limited in his physical actions; the only type of freedom he accepts is in thinking. In the region of thinking, man's privacy is safeguarded from the intrusion of any outside coercion. "You may chain my hands and shackle my feet; you may even throw me into a dark prison, but you shall not enslave my thinking, because it is free."[113] And precisely, it is in the thinking of the lover that the beloved occupies his existential place. The essential of love is not to fulfill materially all the wishes of the beloved, but to let him know that the lover wishes intentionally (i.e., in his thinking) that the beloved's desires be someday realized. So as it seems, love does increase the freedom of the two partners to the point of letting each one establish his own *subjectivity* and develop his own *personality*. The following section explains what I mean.

LOVE AND THE PLEA OF UNIQUENESS

The law of creation proclaims that there was never in the *past* as there is not *now* and there will never be in the *future* two identical human existences. Each one of us is an unrepeatable historical event in the history of thought and is called upon to fulfill his idiosyncrasies.

Gibran has no scientific proofs to substantiate his firm belief in the uniqueness of man. Yet, his observation is accurate; today the humanistic biologists, psychologists and biochemists have established scientifically the truth of human uniqueness. The greatness of Gibran consists in having formulated poetically, philosophically and mystically many truths that science had to discover through painful investigations. In his vocabulary the words "lonely," "loneliness" or "solitary" are meant to express the predicament of "idiosyncrasy." Thus, one of the favorite themes the disciple Almuhtada liked to preach to the people after the death of his Master was the issue that life-loneliness is a metaphysical consequence of our individuality.

Your spirit's life, my brother, is encompassed by loneliness, and were it not for that loneliness and solitude, you would not be *You*, nor would I be *I*. Were it not for this loneliness and solitude, I would come to believe on hearing your voice that it was my voice speaking; or seeing your face, that it was myself looking into a mirror.[114]

Oftentimes Gibran contended that the world would be too small if there just existed two identical human beings. "If there were two men alike, the world would not be big enough to contain them."[115] The reader who is acquainted with existentialism should remember that this school is precisely called such because its adherents speculate from the standpoint of the individual. The person is not a Platonic universal idea, nor a Hegelian logical species, but a concrete, unique reality whose life's meaning is caught in the whirls of the historical moments he happens to participate in. In my opinion, Gibran is a fullfledged existentialist, despite that he never used the label nor knew about its founder.[116] Future historians of Arabic philosophy should keep in mind my estimation, lest they commit a grotesque error of historiography. And now in order to sustain my belief about Gibran's existentialism I will quote freely from some leading Western existentialists the passages that emphasize the uniqueness of man. Thus Soren

Kierkegaard, the father of existentialism, often stated: "My listeners, do you at present live in such a way that you are yourself clearly and eternally conscious of being an individual."[117] The Spanish José Ortega y Gasset also wrote: "There is no abstract living. Life means the inexorable necessity of realizing the design for an existence which each one of us is. . . . We are indelibly that single programmatic personage who must be realized."[118] Along the same line, Martin Buber also held: · "Every person born into this world represents something new, something that never existed before, something original and unique. It is the duty of every person to know . . . that there has never been anyone like him in the world, for if there had been someone like him, there would have been no need for him to be in the world. Every single man is a new thing in the world and is called upon to fulfill his particularity in this world."[119]

Although Gibran insisted emphatically in the manner of the European existentialists that man should develop his idiosyncrasies, he warned us, however, that the conditions in which modern society lived constituted a real threat to the growth of the individual. Most particularly he denounced the spirits of "conformism" and "totalitarianism" as detrimental social patterns that yield groups of "crowd" and impersonal statistical entities. It is interesting to note at this stage that Gibran considered all his heroes to be "*Madmen.*" They were made not because of some mental derangement of psychosomatic illness but because they all refused to identify themselves with and behave like the rest of the crowd. So in the eyes of the big bulk, they were abnormal and mad since they departed away from the norms of traditions, customs and the "mass." In *The Wanderer* we are told that a youth wilfully escaped from the presence of his parents and teachers and came to live in a madhouse.

When asked why, the youth candidly replied: My father wanted me to be a reproduction of himself; while my mother wished that I follow the path of my grandfather; still on the other hand my sister always reminded me of the perfect example of her husband; in his turn my brother thought that I should be like him, a fine athlete. As for my teachers, they were all determined to have me a reflection of their own personalities. "Therefore I came to this place. I find it more sane here. At least, I can be myself."[120]

The plea for uniqueness is in constant danger; our political ideologies, educational systems, religious institutions, social laws, family environments, yes, even our friendly relationships, tend all of them to rob us of our subjectivity, suffocate our freedom to realize a self-identity. The only way to remedy such a situation is to lead the life of *Agape*. For genuine love is disinterested, not despotic, not egoistic, and does not interfere in the other person's freedom of "to-be", "to-do" and "to-belong." Quite the contrary, authentic love establishes interpersonal relationships which guarantee freedom of subjectivity. Here Gibran illustrates with some examples how love works in the intimate relationships of marriage, parenthood and friendship.

(1) In the case of marriage he asks that none of the two spouses attempt to copy the personality of the other. The statements that describe marriage as the union of two bodies with one soul, or two souls in one body, are statements of fantasies, romanticism and not of realistic love. Actually, it is when the partners in love begin to imagine that they should each become the other, that failure of this realization causes psychological exasperation and eventually the divorce. The success of a good marriage lies in the practice of mutual respect and in the ability of each to help the other actualize his idiosyncra-

sies. I remember Shakespeare once said: "Variety makes beauty." And now let us hear the prophet on the subject of matrimony:

> Love one another, but make not a bond
> of love:
> Let it rather be a moving sea between
> the shores of your souls.
> Fill each other's cup but drink not from
> one cup. . . .
> Sing and dance together and be joyous,
> but let each one of you be alone,
> Even as the strings of a lute are alone
> though they quiver with the same music.
>   . . .
> And stand together yet not too near
> together:
> For the pillars of the temple stand apart,
> And the oak tree and the cypress grow
> not in each other's shadow.[121]

(2) Many parents believe, with good intentions, that they have a legal and an ethical right to make their children conform to their ways of thinking and doing. But, this is the very reason for parent-child *gap*. In present day psychoanalysis it is acknowledged that *extreme possessiveness* and *overprotection* on the part of the parents will cause the child either to develop a weak and neurotic personality,[122] or to revolt and abandon his parents' mansion. Hence, Gibran here too exhorts the parents to express their love in self-sacrifice, and not to be oppressive.

> You may give them your love but not
> your thoughts.

For they have their own thoughts.
You may house their bodies but not
their souls.
For their souls dwell in the house of tomorrow, which you cannot visit, not even
in your dreams.
You may strive to be like them, but seek
not to make them like you.
For life goes not backward nor tarries
with yesterday. . . .[123]

(3) Finally, on friendship, Gibranism seems to repeat
the Holy Book which says: "When you have found a
friend, you have found an inexhaustible treasure." A
true friend is one to whom you may go when you are sad,
in joy or in need, knowing that you will be accepted and
comforted without preconditions to repay him back.

Your friend is your needs answered.
He is your field which you sow with love
and reap with thanksgiving.
. . . you come to him with your hunger,
and you seek him for peace.
And let there be no purpose in friendship
save the deepening of the spirit.

Gibranism is a Metaphysics of Love. It is in itself the
expression of the spiritual meaning of being. It is a mystical attitude oriented toward the value of being. Furthermore, Gibranism teaches that though the love-
experience is expressed in countless ways, the characteristics of genuine love remain identical in all the interpersonal relationships. "Beloved, the fires of Love de-
scend from heaven in many shapes and forms, but their
impress on the world is one."[124]

Also, it is understood for Gibran that love is not gener-
ated after long courtship and repeated dates. Love is not
something that you have to fall in love with. Love is an
internal spiritual condition that permeates our whole
being.

It is wrong to think that love comes from
long companionship and perservering courtship.
Love is the offspring of spiritual affinity and
unless that affinity is created in a moment, it
will not be created in years or even generations.[125]

Finally, the dialogue between the lover and the beloved needs not to be expressed in "words." Once
Gibran said to Miss Barbara Young: "Silence is one of the
mysteries of love."[126] In *The Broken Wings* too we find the
dialogue of silence animating the conversation of the
lovers.

We were both silent, each waiting for the
other to speak, but speech is not the only
means of understanding between two souls.
It is not the syllables that come from the
lips and tongues that bring hearts together.

There is something greater and purer than
what the mouth utters.
Silence illuminates our souls, whispers
to our hearts, and brings them together.[127]

GIBRAN'S PHILOSOPHY OF RELIGION

ONE OF THE strong appeals of Gibranian philosophy felt by his readers is the in-depth emphasis it puts on spirituality. Gibran is called a *Prophet* by his followers, because in this technocratic twentieth century his teachings still play the same effective social role in educating the minds in spirituality, as did the earlier prophets during their times. His prophetic message can be described as (a) an impassioned utterance; (b) poetical; (c) intensely preoccupied with God and moral issues; (d) forcefully compulsive to declaring the will of God, even sometimes with a tone of anger against the hypocrites.

Essentially, Gibranism holds that the goal of social life and the aim of personal life should consist in the perfect realization of the spirit of Agape which definitely culminates in the triumphant realization of the Kingdom of God both on earth and in the heart of the individual. In such a project, the practice of religion attests to a psycho-spiritual manifestation of the presence of God. However, as we know religion has not always been interpreted by the establishment of organized creeds, as a *natural* inclination of the soul towards his Creator. And here is where we find our author rebelling against the institutionalized beliefs, while on the other hand stressing the indispensability of religious faith in human existence.

In order to bring out the real position of our author on the issue of religion and God, I propose to divide this crucial chapter into three parts: (1) Critics of Organized Religion; (2) Nature of Authentic Religion; (3) Some Comments on *Jesus The Son of Man*.

Critics of Organized Religion

Any knowledgeable person in the history of thought knows that institutionalized creeds have often times been attacked by great religious men themselves. In the eyes of the latter it was observed that organized religions were at the bottom the cause of moral degeneration, social injustices, political corruption and the decrease of faith. Thus, instead of promoting peace, love and understanding among people and among nations, often each institutionalized religion, with the help of its specific codes, rigid ritualistic ceremonies and guilt oriented consciences, would install in the heart of its own faithful the sentiment of hate, prejudice and bigotry toward the faithful of other Churches.

Without delving into the past, let me at least mention a few well known God-lovers who denounced the evils of organized religions on the ground that they perpetuate the spirit of "Machiavellianism," the unscrupulous scheme of practicing duplicity in statecraft and religion. For example, Leo Tolstoy blamed the State Church for the violence found in the world: "If only the men of our world were freed from this lie — from the perversion of Christian doctrine by Church faith and from the vindication and even the exaltation of the State which is advanced on the basis of faith, but which is incompatible with Christianity and is based on violence—then of itself there would be eliminated from the souls of all men, Christian and non-Christian, the chief obstacle to the religious recognition of the supreme law of love that tolerates no exceptions or violence."[1] S. Kierkegaard too was bitter against his own Protestant Church: "That religious conditions are wretched, and that people in respect of their religion are in a wretched condition, nothing is more certain."[2]

These very same feelings are also shared by Kahlil Gibran who revolted everytime that "truth," "human freedom," and "the will of God" were in danger. When alive he was called by his countrymen "heretic," and was excommunicated in 1904 from his Maronite Church precisely for having declared war against the organized religions. Actually, in all his controversial essays on religion his polemic centers around the *"clergy" (Khouri)*. He holds the priests responsible for the many social and individual miseries encountered today in the world. *Khalil the Heretic* is in my opinion the best essay that expresses explicitly the real position of Gibran toward "ecclesiastical religion." A deep analysis of it will outline Gibran's main arguments.

The story is about an adolescent who entered the monastery in order to prepare himself for priesthood, yet after a brief period the youth was expelled by his superiors as unfitted for clerical life. The motive we are told for passing such a judgment is that Khalil dared one morning to preach to the monks about the true meaning of religion, while criticizing them also for fooling the poor with their pharisaic teachings. The essay calls Khalil a *reformer*. Why a reformer? I found four reasons in the article for which Khalil, the protagonist of Gibran, was anticlerical: simony, despotism, Machiavellianism, and treacherousness. Now, these reasons are not fairytales nor incidental but historically true, for they portray the role the clergymen played in Lebanon at the time of Gibran. A few words will explain the intent of these four epithets.

SIMONY

Historically the term simony is taken from Simon Magnus, the magician of Samaria who begged the Apostles to impart upon him the power of conferring the gifts of the Holy Ghost in exchange for a big sum of money (Acts 8.18-24). Essentially then simony is the buying or selling of the spiritual or something spiritual for a temporal or material price. The practice of simony spread calamitously over Europe, especially from the 9th to 11th centuries. Not only the lower clergy and convents committed this sacrilege but even among the high officials of the Catholic Curia the traffic of exchange between the material and spiritual was common. Thus Pope Gregory VI (1045-1046) was accused of simony. Supposedly, during these periods, you could buy a piece of land in Heaven or bargain your way out of penances by buying indulgences that would shorten your stay in purgatory.[3]

Well, for one Khalil condemned the clergy for committing the sin of simony. Twice he tells us that the priests of Deir Kizhaya in Northern Lebanon used to trade their prayers for money; and that they would punish those who refused to buy financially their blessings. "What teachings allow the clergymen to sell their prayers for pieces of gold and silver?"[4] Elsewhere we read: "He [the pastor] sells his prayers, and he who does not buy is an infidel, excommunicated from Paradise."[5]

DESPOTISM

On other occasions, Khalil reports that the monks were despots and tyrannical; that they would revert to physical violence, if crossed in words by a secular man, with the pretext of the in-the-name-of-God.[6] They also oppressed the poor villagers and voluntarily kept them in utter ignorance of the Scriptural knowledge and knowledge of nature. In the essay *John the Madman*, Gibran goes so far as to describe his hero John as being persecuted by the priests because the latter caught John reading the Gospel, the forbidden Book. "The priests objected to the reading of the Good Book, and . . . warned the simple-hearted people against its use, and threatened them with excommunication from the church if discovered possessing it."[7]

The idea that Gibran is here trying to bring to light is that the messengers of God did not want their fellahins to be educated so that they remain in power and therefore instill fear among the simple minded people. Ignorance is the strongest weapon in the hands of despots for ruling over their slaves.[8]

Yet, contends Gibran, there could be no happiness and no true understanding of religion unless ignorance "be removed."[9] After all, "God does not like to be worshipped by an ignorant man who imitates someone else."[10]

MACHIAVELLIANISM

Again historically the word "Machiavellian" is derived from Niccolò Machiavelli (1469-1527), the famous Florentine statesman, author of *The Prince*, who argued that every means is legitimate to secure the desired end, which was considered to be always political; he even conceived that politics could use religion and morality as *instrumentum regni*, i.e., instruments.

Now, in Gibran's opinion, the established Churches are nothing else than institutions hungry for power, either political, economical, or in social prestige. They employ the pretense of religion to reinforce their will and wishes among the faithful. Throughout both writings, *Khalil the Heretic* and *John the Madman*, we see the church officials occupying themselves with politics, exerting political pressures on the Sultan governors of the regions, investing themselves with governmental privileges, and amassing tremendous wealth.

To really appreciate the value of Gibran's critics, it is worthy to trace the history of the then Lebanese clergy. As you recall, Lebanon was ruled by the Ottoman Empire which had embraced the Islamic faith. On the other hand, the members of the Maronite Church were for the great majority poor farmers. In order that Christianity became important in the Porte's politics it was necessary for her to become feudal. The Christian seculars themselves participated in making their Church feudal by gifting lands and properties to the clergy. However, as the Church grew in her possessions, she became extremely greedy, always demanding more from her faithful who were employed to cultivate the lands and had to pay her sometimes exorbitant taxes. It was the strong economy of the Church that won her the political power of the Turkish Sultans. Often a Turkish governor had to yield to the will of the priests, if indeed he wanted to remain in power. And unfortunately there were times when the fathers would dictate to the Ottoman representatives the political decisions to be taken, though they proved to be detrimental to individual villagers. Thus, in the story of Khalil it is Father Elias who suggested to Sheik Abbas to punish Khalil for absolutely no real offense.

The political corruption of the Church is even more apparent in the short essay *John the Madman*, where we are told that John was twice the target of the priests. During the first time he was imprisoned because his oxen had devastated the plantations of the convent and consequently was forced by the priests to repay the damage, following which, however, John called the clergymen mercenaries, hypocrites and irreligious. As for the second time, John's father was asked by the Governor, who wanted to please the pastors, to disseminate the rumor that his son was "mad." This happened after that one day John, in the square of the town Bsherri, stretching his hands towards the sky invoked Jesus to come to restore religion that the prelates had dishonored.

Now both Khalil and John were ridiculed by the Reverends for having discovered the true teaching of Christ, revolted against the unorthodox teachings of the priests, and used direct quotation from the New Testament to excoriate the clergy's behavior. Gibran tells us explicitly that Khalil and John were persecuted for their knowledge of the Scriptures. Also the two personages appear as reformers. Their reform, however, is not the advocation of a new creed; it is merely a return to the primary source of Christian belief, namely the Gospel. Like Martin Luther, therefore, Gibran heralds the Holy Book as the true teaching of Christ. The Jesus of Khalil and John is the God of love, forgiveness, kindness, and compassion, and detached from every political favouritism.

SPIRITUAL DISTORTION

Finally, Gibran reacts with indignation toward organized religion because it falsifies the true meaning of the Scriptures, and spreads errors. In his opinion these Scriptural mistakes stem from the twin ignorances: the literal uneducation of the clergy itself,[11] and its ignorant interpretation of the literal sense of the Holy Texts. In regard to the last argument, Gibran makes his point through the parable *The Blessed City.*

A youth was once told of the existence of a "blessed city" where inhabitants lived happily according to the Scriptures. Moved by curiosity, adventure and a desire to lead a perfect life in a perfect environment, the young man went searching for this city. After forty days he discovered a town where each person had but one eye and one hand. Approaching some people he asked them to indicate to him the way to the "blessed city." Their answers were that this was it. Amazed by the physical appearance of the individuals, he further inquired what had happened to them. In reply they took him to the temple and showed him "a heap of hands and eyes." Still astonished the youth exclaimed: "Alas! what conqueror has committed this cruelty upon you? . . . And one of the elders stood forth and said, 'This doing is of ourselves. God has made us conquerors over the evil that was in us.' " Then all pointing to an inscription engraved over the altar, the youth read the famous passage where it is written: If an eye has offended thee, cast it away, for it is better to enter the Eden with one eye than to be damned in the Gehenna. And if a hand has committed sin, cut it off, for it is better to be admitted in Heaven with one hand instead of going to Hell on the account of the evildoing of this hand.

The youth, more astonished than before, turned toward the crowd and cried: Is there any one among you who possesses two eyes or two hands? And they replied: None among the grown, except the infants who can't yet read nor understand the Scripture. Upon listening to these words, our visitor nodded his head with disappointment and straightway left that "blessed city."

The parable terminates with irony, sarcasm and a moral lesson all of which are encompassed in the final words of the youth: "When we had come out of the temple, I straightway left that Blessed City; for I was not too young, and I could read the scripture."[12]

INTRINSIC VS. EXTRINSIC RELIGION

We would be wrong to suspect for one moment that Gibran's anticlericalism was an expression of irreligiosity. Actually, to put it bluntly, Gibran was a deeply religious person. He simply objected to the manner of the "use" of religion by the State Church; he observed that religion put in the hands of the clergy-agency becomes something to "use" but not to "live." This is what we call "extrinsic religion"; in such a context faith surfaces at the outskirts of good intentions, but never implants profound roots in the soul. The logic of extrinsic religion is always utilitarian in orientation. Also, religion gets to be practiced not as an end in itself, but as a motive that serves other motives, e.g., need for security, political power, ambition for social prestige, or pecuniary greed. On the other hand, continues Gibran's criticism, the extrinsic religion of the organized church promotes racial and ethnic bigotry, religious prejudice, and leads its faithful to discrimination, segregation and denials of others' rights. Extrinsic religion commits all these wrong-doings under the standard of the will of God, love of God and teachings of Christ. For example, till not long ago, the Catholic Church in which Gibran was baptized professed that there was no salvation and redemption of mortal sin outside of its own faith.[13]

No wonder that Gibran wrote: "The truly religious man does not embrace a religion; and he who embraces one has no religion."[14] If a person affiliates with a particular church, and shares its morality and legality, then frankly, conjectures Gibran, this person has not discovered the "intrinsic" nature of religion. For religion is not a book of codes or a lawyer's manual; nor is God a privilege entrusted only to the clergy.

In my opinion, Gibran is harsh on established religion because he sees a similarity between society as an institution built on fabricated laws and the church, another social institution resting on man-made laws promulgated by a self-appointed hierarchy of clergymen. Essentially, a sectarian church exists so long as it prescribes laws of conduct that differ markedly from those of other organized creeds. And a believer is Protestant, Catholic, Jewish, Orthodox or Muslim, if, and only if, he claims to follow the precepts of his own church, which most of the time, by the way, conflict with the precepts of other churches. God here ceases to be a Deity and the Creator of humanity; rather he gets reduced to a puppet or a glamorous object for which each partisan religion fights the other sects in order to be the first to claim possession. History attests to this fact; remember, for instance, the Holy war of the early Muhammadans (*jihad*) or the Catholics' *Inquisition* period, or the Jews' exasperating Hope of the coming of *Christ conqueror* of the lands of the world, etc. . . .

Gibran, like all great mystics, was intensely religious and therefore had no preference for any "formulated" religion. He believed in the "communion of spirits"[15] and in "ecumenism" that makes all men "brothers before the face of heaven."[16]

Your thought advocates Judaism, Brahmanism, Buddhism, Christianity, and Islam.

In my thoughts there is only one universal religion whose varied paths are but the fingers of the loving hand of the Supreme Being.[17]

This "one universal religion" is what we call *intrinsic religion*. Accordingly, the person motivated by the interiorized total creed of his faith intends more on serving religion than on making it serve his interests. In this respect religion is nothing else than a natural *élan* of the soul, a gift given to all human mortals; it has no political, no ethnic, no acquired, no formal baptismal origin. Its manifestation is in the practice of Agape, the only real divine law. Of course Gibran knows that it is possible for the individual man to suffocate this intrinsic spiritual impulse of loving everything created. Nevertheless, the point that he is bringing to light stresses that religion and the presence of God are immanent, and therefore, they ought to be searched from within the soul. "God has placed *in each soul* an apostle to lead us upon the illumined path. Yet, many seek life from *without*, unaware that it is *within* them."[18]

Under the following heading, let us ponder in a detailed manner on the issue of intrinsic religion.

Nature of Authentic Religion

"HOMO EST NATURALITER ANIMAL RELIGIOSUM"

Since its birth, mankind has shown an attachment for the "sacral." Driven by superstitions and educated in mythology, the primitive clans already exercised ritual ceremonies. Preanimism, Totemism, Fetishism, Idolatry and many more were the early forms of worship. With the progress of tools and the expansion of the group, however, our ancestors' polytheism decreased in number. Then slowly with the advent of the positive sciences, agnosticism and atheism have become fashionable forms of beliefs.

This brief introduction raises the question of whether

man "is" by his very being a "religious" creature. Gibran answers positively. And on the same line of thought, Gibran maintains that religion has no cultural origin; only the "manner" of worshipping is cultural. Actually, to be faithful to Gibran's hermeneutics of religion, I should rather state that if there are various prescribed liturgical ceremonies practiced around the world, this is possible because in the first place religion is a *metaphysical* dimension of human reality, and consequently there is a primordial "manner" of worshipping, natural to the soul. Praying, bowing, repenting are natural impulses. It was only when churches established Canon laws and enforced rigid commands for the "manner" of worshipping, that the alienation between "religion" and "practice" occurred. Now organized religions put heavy emphasis on "practice"; repentance for instance is no longer a natural inclination of the soul asking forgiveness from the Compassionate God, but an asking of forgiveness from an institution for having transgressed an invented prohibition. Here Gibran replies: "Inhibitions and religious prohibitions do more harm than anarchy"[19]—for as we know, they ride the psyche with guilt complexes, thus causing neuroses.

Religion, therefore, is eternally inscribed in the very core of human existence and is not the privilege of some institution. In a letter he sent to a friend, Gibran wrote about *John the Madman*: "I found that earlier writers, in attacking the tyranny of some of the clergy, attacked the practice of religion. They were wrong because religion is *a belief natural to man*."[20]

It is interesting for us who are dissecting Gibran's thoughts and examining him in the light of history to find that many great philosophers have similarly held that "man is a religious animal." For example, St. Augustine's cry conveys the same idea as Gibran's:

"Thou hast made us for Thyself, and our heart will not find rest until it rest in Thee."[21] St. Thomas Aquinas too made of religion a natural desire in man: "Man has a natural inclination to know the truth about God."[22] The contemporary existential theologian philosopher Paul Tillich shares also the same thesis: "When we say that religion is an aspect of the human spirit, we are saying that if we look at the human spirit from a special point of view, it presents itself to us as religious. . . . You cannot reject religion with ultimate seriousness, because ultimate seriousness, or the state of being ultimately concerned, is itself religion."[23] Amazingly, even the atheists and agnostics of today are beginning to claim that they too are *religious*, though their object of worshipping is different from the theists'. For instance, Jean-Paul Sartre, the leading atheist existentialist, avows in his autobiography that he is religious while the Christian believers are irreligious. "An atheist was a . . . fanatic encumbered with taboos who refused the right to kneel in church, . . . who took upon himself to prove the truth of his doctrine by the purity of his morals, . . . a God-obsessed crank . . . ; in short, a gentleman who had religious convictions. The believer had none."[24] In the USA the atheist philosopher Ernest Nagel maintains that "atheism is not necessarily an irreligious concept. . . . The denial of theism is logically compatible with a religious outlook upon life. . . . Atheism is not to be identified with sheer unbelief."[25]

In conclusion, there seems to be a common consent among Gibran, the theist philosophers, and the atheists, that religion arises from the basic structure of human nature. However, lest I confuse my readers, let me add that for our author in contrast to the atheist, religion is not merely a natural inclination, or a matter of forming convictions, or having faith, but above all religion elevates the soul towards a beatifying union with *God* as the *Creator of the universe*. In the following section I will show that Gibran never ascribed to Nietzsche's theology of the death of God, which has, nevertheless, become the leitmotive of contemporary atheism.

IS THERE SUCH A THING AS AN ABSOLUTE GOD?

Among modern speculative theories of religion, we find three major schools of thought that argue our issue with different presuppositions. *For one*, the atheists profess to be religious, citizens of good moral standards and anti-theist. Their religious faith, however, is *anthropocentic* and *humanistic*. As for God, they teach that this is a fiction of our subconscious wishing protection from the crushing superior forces of nature. In other words, God is a projection of the self or father image authority, or if one prefers, "man is fundamentally desire to be God." It is interesting to know at this stage that all the leading atheists, Nietzsche, Marx, Freud, Sartre, have notwithstanding recognized that the religious belief in God must have helped civilization at one time to get rid of the many supersititions inherited from the primates. But now, they say science can take care of man's needs. Faith in and love of man alone constitute their religion. Echoing Nietzsche's cry of the death of God[26], Sartre, to give an example, writes:

> God is dead. Let us not understand by this
> that he does not exist or even that he
> no longer exists. He is dead.
> He spoke to us and is silent. We no longer
> have anything but his cadaver. Perhaps he
> slipped out of the world, somewhere else,

like the soul of a dead man. Perhaps he was
only a dream . . . God is dead.[27]

From the point of view of literature I was fascinated to
find some of Gibran's essays that favour an anthropocen-
tric religion. As a literary piece, only, *The Grave Digger*
has much ressemblance to Nietzsche's *Zarathustra* in
style, form and content of ideas. The article ridicules the
belief in the supernatural on the basis that "Man has
worshipped his own self since the beginning calling that
self by appropriate titles, until now, when he employs
the word 'God' to mean that same self."[28]
As I said, such an essay should not confuse our understanding of the real position of Gibran. We should rather
study such essays from the standpoint of the value of
comparative literature, but never with the assumption
that the ideas herein are those of Gibran, the
philosopher. Because, actually, Gibran has publicly rejected Nietzsche's pessimistic philosophy. His religion is
theocentric.

His [Nietzsche's] form [style] always was soothing
to me. But I thought his philosophy
was terrible and all wrong. I was a worshipper
of beauty . . . [of God].[29]

At the opposite of atheism, many theist intellectuals
advance the theory that it is possible to prove God's
existence by means of philosophical thinking. This
second school makes of religion something rationalized
and discovered logically. The history of philosophy
abounds with many logical proposals: Augustine, An-
selm, Aquinas, Descartes, Liebniz, etc.
The *third* approach to religion denies that God's exis-

tence could be proved rationally; yet nevertheless, its partisans claim to be theocentric for reasons other than the logical investigations. Gibran, Kierkegaard, William James, Marcel, Buber represent this school.

Against the atheists Gibran and the others of this movement spurn Nietzsche's theology of the death-of-God on the ground that the soul has a natural "hunger for that which is beyond itself," and because "the soul seeks God as heat seeks height, or water seeks the sea. The power to seek and the desire to seek [God] are the inherent properties of the soul."[30]

But also against the theist logicians, Gibran and the tenets of the third school of religion resent making of God a game for the gifted mathematical-type-thinking minds, or an idea that fits a compartment of our finite intellect. In Gibran's opinion, it is easier for the human mind to talk *to* God but not *about* Him, for "we cannot understand the nature of God because we are not God."[31] The human intellect is limited, imperfect, and consequently impotent to comprehend God directly, the Infinite and the most Perfect. Often times Gibran confided to Miss Haskell: "It is not because I don't want to, but because I just can't talk about God."[32]

I have the feeling that somehow, Gibran abhorred any type of intellectual explanation of God, because he was afraid to commit the sin of intellectual pride so common among the antitheists and some Christian philosophers. Yet, on the other hand, his refusal of a philosophical proof of God, on the ground of the finitude of our reasoning ability, reminds us of Kant, who asserted that human understanding was so constituted in itself that it lost itself in contradictions when it ventured to reason from any factual data or any necessary features of experience, to conclusions about things in themselves and the existence or the nature of God. However, if we compare closely Kant's reasons to Gibran's, a sharp line of demarcation is seen to separate the two. Kant's position was a matter of skepticism that he inherited from the empiricist David Hume and which expressed itself as a mental doubt towards anything metaphysical. Gibran, on the other side, does not completely eliminate the possibility of knowing God through sense-experience. He calls the data of "the sense-experience" the "visible expressions of God."[33] The world attests to God's presence, as the effects to their Cause.

Nevertheless, this understanding of God through creation is not a philosophical understanding *"about"* God, but is a natural inclination which psychologically motivates our mind and body "to" speak religiously "to" God in the practice of prayer, repentance, bowing. As He is in Himself, God is incomprehensible; yet he can be known in the bond of mutual relationship. Here Martin Buber agrees with Gibran that religion is theocentric, and not founded on a noetical act. "It is not necessary to know something about God in order really to believe in Him: many true believers know how to talk *to* God but not *about* Him."[34]

FAITH

Gibran's religious worship of God is a matter of "faith." In that respect he is very close to Kierkegaard and the existentialists of the right wing. Faith for both Gibran and Kierkegaard is not the object of a scientific investigation. Hence, the two distinguish between "faith" and "knowledge." The latter represents the state of affairs that are liable of being either empirically or logically demonstrated; faith, however, is a spiritual disposition to accepting propositions which are *not* known, are extremely *unreasonable*, but which are believed to be *true*. Witness how Gibran and Kierkegaard are very much alike on the topic of religious faith. Kierkegaard writes:

> Suppose a man who wishes to acquire faith; let the comedy begin. He wishes to have faith, but he wishes also to safeguard himself by means of an objective inquiry. . . . What happens? . . . Now he is ready to believe, . . . and he ventures to claim for himself that he does not believe as shoemakers and tailors and simple folk believe, but only after long deliberation. Now he is ready to believe [i.e., to accept on faith]; and so now it has become precisely impossible to believe it. . . . For the absurd is the object of faith, and the only object that can be believed.[35]

In this passage Kierkegaard explicitly affirms that faith is the "absurd," a "paradox," and startles the mind of the philosophers and scientists. By the way even St. Paul in his Epistle to the Corinthians acknowledged the fact that it was an insult to man's intelligence and foolishness to accept something on faith.[36]

Well, Gibran feels the same way towards man's faith in God. For sake of precision, let us quote and paraphrase our author's basic conception of faith. I have personally numbered the words which I propose to expound.

> Faith is (1) an oasis (2) in the heart (3) which will never be reached by the caravan of thinking.[37]

(1) This citation makes clear that faith like the oasis defies the physical and mental eyes of man. Like the oasis it is not something which you could lay your hands upon, or detect through a microscope or telescope; to the

scientific world it is a hallucination, a fiction. Yet to the hallucinator himself, the hallucination is something real, and he believes in it. As J. Dewey used to say, "Illusions are illusions, but the occurrence of illusions is not an illusion, but a genuine reality." Faith from the standpoint of systematic thinking is the *absurd*; as from the standpoint of the individual affected by it, faith is real and like the oasis it points to a lack, a craving that the soul has for it. Translated in Gibran's technical terminology, this lack signifies that the soul has an "inherent desire to reach God," which is indeed apprehended as a "hunger."[38]

(2) Here the use of the term "heart" stand opposite to "thinking." Henceforth the oasis or faith is directly related to and real for the heart alone. All this amounts to saying that faith in God can only be attained when the individual consents with resignation not to attempt to reduce the Supreme Being to an object that the mind could dissect into its properties and elements.

Like most of the contemporary humanistic philosophers, Gibran draws a sharp dichotomy between *"la logique du coeur"* and *"la logique de la raison."* In his opinion, the "heart" has better and more efficient ways of grasping truth than the slow pace and the indecisiveness of discursive reasoning. Note that William James, a fellow contemporary—of whom Gibran, I believe, must have heard—has with the same vigor defended the thesis that faith makes sense to a soul animated only by "passions" and scarcely interested in proving scientifically its worth.[39]

In some other entries of his works, Gibran details the motives for confining faith to the region of the heart. He writes: "Faith is a knowledge within the heart, beyond the reach of proof."[40] Hereby, he acknowledges that faith is not a blind, mechanical or habitual ignorance.

Quite the contrary, faith in itself is a source of knowledge which is unknown to scientific thinking. Such knowledge is of God, immortality, human destiny, human origin, etc. . . . Man's passions or feelings perceive the truth of these facts without the believer suffering from any hang ups. "Faith perceives Truth sooner than Experience [i.e., scientific experiments] can."[41] Actually, it would be a weakness on the part of faith if it had to "explain" or "prove" its truth; because to desire just for an instance, that faith probed its premises, this would be an indication of incredulity, the mental attitude which is incompatible to faith. Hence, Gibran states: "The necessity for explanation is a sign of weakness,"[42] and "The truth that needs proof is only half true."[43] After all, the purpose of faith is to stir the will-to-believe of the person. Also the essence of faith is to remain incomprehensible to logic and science.[44]

(3) Finally, we should bear in mind that for Gibran faith is superior to science. And though "the caravan of thinking" may ridicule faith as an impossibility (oasis), so in its turn faith defies thinking as incapable of comprehending it. Again, if thinking treats faith as a pathological syndrome, ironically so to speak, faith in its turn treats thinking as "impotent" epistemologically to pierce the realm of the "beyond-the reach-of proof" (i.e., faith).

From what preceded, it is clear now why Gibran never provided us with a philosophical argument on behalf of the nature and the existence of God. He never raised the Middle-Age methodological questionings of "An sit?" (Is there a God?) and "Quid sit?" (What is the essence of God?). He was primarily concerned with stressing the double relations: the importance of God for the man in faith, and the relation of God to man. Hence, we come to our next section.

IMMANENCE OF GOD

How does man relate to God? How should man express his faith towards God? Where should man search for God? These questions are crucial in Gibran's 'Weltanschauung. We may sum up their answers in one affirmation: God, faith, and religion are "intrinsic" to man. The error of organized religions consists in having extrapolated and alienated God from man, confined God to the priests, and restricted the visit of man to the Divine in the Church on Sunday, the Mosque on Friday, the Synagogue on Saturday. But, Gibran replies: "The Church is within us. You yourself are your priests."[45]

Gibran's theory of the immanence of God establishes three implications.

(1) Such a belief assists the individual's CONSCIENCE to become PERSONALISTIC. The individual is motivated to search out God in his own unqiue way, for the interior presence of the Supreme Being appears differently to different persons. Also, it affirms that none of the formulated creeds possess the whole truth about God. On the contrary, as the Hindu Wisdom teaches: "Truth is one but men call it by many names." So too Gibran professes his ecumenism by saying: "God made Truth with many doors to welcome every believer who knocks on them."[46] Furthermore, the idea of immanence makes of the human body the genuine and primordial tabernacle that hosts the Creator.[47] Accordingly man should seek God in himself, in his neighbours or in nature. God's presence is felt everywhere and not in one fixed geographical sanctuary. Moreover, in order that the person expresses his faith towards God, he simply needs to love, respect and care for

others. In the authentic human relation of I-Thou, the individual "I" successfully encounters, sees and addresses God clothed under the shape of the human "Thou."

Let us speak no more now of God the Father.
Let us speak rather of the gods, your neighbours, and of your brothers, . . .
Again I bid you to speak not so freely of God, who is your All, but speak rather and understand one another, neighbour unto neighbour, a god unto a God. [48]

(2) Another implication of this Divine immanency entails that *MAN* is *GODLIKE*. As the last quotation explicates, however, we should bear in mind that when Gibran concedes "we are God,"[49] he is not at all repeating Nietzsche's view that the human is the maker of everything and beyond whom there is no superior Reality. To put it in simple terminology, Gibran entertains the thought that because God indwells in us, we in our turn are rendered divine. Actually, Gibran is not the first to hold the Godliness of man. It is a common belief among the mystics of the Orient (the Sufis, Naimy, Rihani, Iqbal, the Hasidists) to regard man as a "microtheos." Gibran and the Middle-Eastern mystics demonstrate the "microgod" of man through the spiritual assumption that between God-nature-man there is an indispensable interrelation of "mutual emergence." In philosophical language, we call this emergence: "evolution." Accordingly, existence is not made up of static atoms or chunks of matter. Life is dynamic, and always in the making. Referring to Darwin's theory of Evolution, Gibran finds it incomplete; for

the author of the *Origin of Species* limited his perception to organic life; spoke of evolution in terms of
"accidental" variations; never succeeded in answering the question why evolution has so far followed
the course which it has in fact taken; and above all
omitted God from the process.[50] Yet, in the vision of
our author, the evolution that started aeons ago
must have involved the dialectical movement of
God-nature-man.

At this point, let me express an apparent difficulty
I am encountering in interpreting and paralleling
with history the obscure passages where Gibran
deals with the topic of evolution. As I read his
private metaphysical journal of January 6, 1916 to
March 1, 1916, and April 18, 1920, I get the impression at first sight that Gibran is leaning towards a
"disguised materialism"; in a way similar to the
theories of DeVries, Lamark and Spencer, who
speculated that matter was at the beginning animated by an internal powerful energy that erupted
into cosmic development. Thus, for example, Gibran
states that "Reality is Transmutation of Matter: Everything is matter,"[51] and "God is not the creator of
man. God is not the creator of the earth. God is not
the ruler of man nor of earth."[52] But on a second
thought, I figure that it would be a historical mistake
on our part if we had to read the literal sense of such
statements, without an attempt to disclose the mysticism or allegory or metaphor of the whole text. If
these articles were to be submitted to a microscopic
analysis through the spectacles of history, I believe
that a much clearer understanding of Gibran's position could be reached, and which would prove that
our author was a firm theocentric thinker. Let us try
to shed some light on these texts.

Gibran's theory of evolution maintains that God is *Desire*[53] and as Desire He evolved into earth and man. Ever since then, "desire" has become the creative force that "changes all things. It is the law of all matter and all life."[54] Now, this emergence of the universe was caused by "love," which is the never extinguishing energy, but, always increasing impetus. God desired that "man and earth . . . become like Him";[55] He desired that man and earth share His happiness. And to see that He becomes the gravitational center, He installed in man's soul and the world an innate "hunger" to rise to and seek Him. Gibran writes: "God is growing through His desire, and man and earth, and all there is upon the earth rise toward God by the power of desire."[56] Note that Gibran does not equate God with man and earth. He considers the world and human beings as *"a"* part of God,[57] thereby implying that the Supreme Being is greater in divine perfection than the created.

Speaking of the concept creation, Gibran believes in it and often refers to it;[58] yet, occasionally he prefers to interchange the use of this concept for a more biological, scientific and philosophical notion, namely, "evolution," or "emergence." Hence when he contests: "God is not the creator of man. God is not the creator of the earth"[59]—this double negation is less indicative of a skepticism than a linguistic matter of choice of words. Why does Gibran refuse to employ the term "creation"? What could this word convey symbolically to make our author exchange it for the label "evolution"? The answer is the following: the notion "creation" *could* suggest functionally the same meaning as "production"; i.e., the producer, once he manufactures his product, stands *outside* his artifact, and *transcends* his invention

in the sense of both being a non-provider and exhib-
iting a dissimilarity in existence.[60]

But this in the opinion of Gibran is wrong. Because
the creatures are not made of a different stuff than
their Creator; nor is creation a random calculation, or
a performance on an outside pre-existing reality, nor
an extrinsic act performed at one time in the past and
now alienated from the Creator. Again, the Creator
is not seen by Gibran as an Aristotelian Prime Mover
unrelated and unconcerned with His creation. Quite
the contrary, creation is still outgoing today in the
world; and between the Creator and His creature
there is a great resemblance in type of existence. No
estrangement between God and His work! God reveals himself in matter-nature and in man; He indwells in every part of the Cosmos; *on one side* He
emerges as "walking in the cloud, outstretching His
arms in the lightning and descending in
rain. . . . [And] smiling in flowers, then rising and
waving His hands in trees";[61] *on the other side*, He
evolves as a "microtheos" in human spirits.

In her private journal of April 18, 1920, Miss Haskell reports that Gibran once told her: "Some believe
God made the world. To me it seems more likely that
God has grown from the world because he is the
furthest form of Life. Of course the possibility of God
was present before God himself."[62] If such statements are taken in their literal sense, then the reader
might conclude Gibran was a materialist. But, if they
are understood allegorically, and read very carefully
in conjunction with the statements: God is Desire,
and desire-love is the inherent mighty power and
mighty law that changes all matter and all life—then
a threefold conclusion follows:

(i) the world is not something made after the manner

in which an industrialist makes soaps, but as Gibran says, the world has "emerged" from the growing desire which God had to process "the earth to become like Him, and a part of Him."[63] (ii) The world did not exist physically before God; rather the converse is true. The divinity of the flower, clouds, rain, trees, etc., evolved because God was present as possibility before these divine objects evolved in fact. In other words, Gibran suggests that in a primordial state God-nature-man constituted a single nebula. In the evolution process, however, God separated himself from the world and the upshot was a process of separation analogous to the theory of Empedocles in which under the influence of Love the four elements became separated. That God grows from the world, means to Gibran that God receives the perfection of the world unto himself and preserves it; He takes the world up into himself and reenacts the perfection of the world. And *vice-versa* when Gibran claims that the world emerges from God, he means that God supplies the potential for the Becoming of the world. (iii) Finally, nature is not merely composed of chunks of atomic matter, for "all matter—affirms Gibran— seeks a form." This seeking is the result of the law of desire. The form is the "meaning" or "the signification" of the being of matter. Each object means something specific, stands for a concrete purpose distinct from that of other things. An apple tree, for instance, means what it is because such is the form "appleness" which characterizes it in its being of matter. In simple words, there is a *mysticism of reality*, an interior spiritual aspect in each matter; it is God inhabiting matter, but who is not identified with it.[64]

To keep on this subject, it is apparent in the writings of Gibran that the Divine emergence and the

Divine immanence is best perceived in the birth of the human form. Accordingly, the human spirit evolves twice as divine, if I may say so. How? Why? Man, answers Gibran, is both a *"microtheos"* and a *"microcosm."* And in each of these states of existence, man exudes his godliness.

It is worthwhile to recall that the vision Gibran holds of the world, man and God resembles very much Blake's *apocalyptic vision*. Blake outlined the correspondence between the material and the spiritual; Gibran likewise describes the unity of existence, as a coming together of polarities. Specifically in the genesis of man we see manifestly the phenomenon of unity in multiplicity (*e pluribus unum*), and that of multiplicity in units (*unitas multiplex*).

To understand this point, let us first expound on the *"microgod"* of man. Under the influence of the Bible, Gibran portrays the birth of man as an emergence from God through a process of separation: "And the God of gods separated a Spirit from Himself and created"[65] man. Elsewhere in his metaphysical journal, he depicts this process of separation as a Hegelian process of conceptual clarification which God undergoes, in order to emerge at the end as the maker of human consciousness which begins to seek, and becomes fully aware of, Him. Thus, Gibran recounts:

When I sleep something in me keeps awake to follow it and to receive more from it and through it. My very eyes seem to retain that slowly developing picture of the birth of God. I see him rising like the mist from the seas and the mountains and plains. Half-born, half-conscious. He rose. He himself did not know himself *fully* then. Millions of years passed before he moved with His own will, and sought more of Himself and his own power and through His own desire. And man came. He sought man even as man and the soul of man were seeking Him. Man sought him first without consciousness and without knowledge. Then man sought Him with consciousness but without knowledge. .[66]

Now it was Gibran's understanding that human consciousness was the last to develop in the chain of the Divine evolution.[67] For this very reason, he entertained the thought that the unity of human existence embodies the greatest multiplicity. In his words, "We are more than we think. We are more than we know."[68] What he really means is that man, besides being fashioned in the image of God, also represents in his being the totality of created nature. He is a *"microcosm,"* a whole universe though in miniature. The article *The Spirit* describes the genesis of man after the manner of the philosophers Empedocles and Hippocrates, who believed that the person as a microcosm reflected in his own make-up the four elements—fire, water, air, earth—of nature as microcosm. Gibran writes:

And the God took *Fire* from Wrath's furnace,
and a *Wind* from the desert of Ignorance,
and Sand from the *seashore* of Selfishness,
and *Earth* from beneath the feet of the ages,
and He created man.[69]

Comparatively speaking, Aristotle's rational psychology and the Scholastics' metaphysics hold a similar view. Their axiom says: *Anima humana est quodammodo omnia*,[70] i.e., the human soul reflects in itself everything that exists. This thesis Gibran explains in the following way:

> Everything in creation exists within you,
> and everything in you exists in creation.
> You are in bordeless touch with the closest
> things, and, what is more, distance is not
> sufficient to separate you from things far
> away. All things from the lowest to the loftiest,
> from the smallest to the greatest, exist within
> you as equal things.[71]

The culminative idea that Gibran reaches — as he philosophizes about the immanence of God in man, about the issue "microtheos," and about the composition of man the "microcosm" as made of everything in the world—maintains that human existence is the intersecting point between two infinites, two ends, two extremities, viz, the infinity of the Supreme Being (Macrotheos), the infinity of the Cosmos (Macrocosm). This apocalyptic vision of Gibran which goes beyond the sense perception, is the very reason why, a while ago, I called man twice divine; the person possesses the divinity of nature plus he possesses another form of divinity which is not granted to the world-matter, namely, a spirit which is directly as God's idea, as the image of God. "We ourselves are the infinitely small [in comparison to the Macrotheos and the Macrocosm] and the infinitely great [in comparison to the macrocosm because of our spirituality]; and we are the path between the two."[72]

(3) At last but not the least, Gibran includes in his philosophy of the "Immanence of God," the mystery of the Divine *OMNIPRESENCE*. The attribute signifies that God is everywhere present: in the leaf, in the river, in the sun, in the atom, in myself, and in my neighbours.[73] The whole creation attests to the living presence of God the Creator. This is one of the reasons why Gibran rejected the teaching of theological rationalism as propounded by the established religions, and instead professed his belief in the natural and non-dogmatic religion.

However, speaking of God's presence in man and in nature, Gibran draws a line of demarcation between the divinity of the person and the divinity of matter. God is not present within both of us in an identical manner, and this for a twofold reason. *First*, man is an axiological, an evaluatory, category; yet matter has no ethical life. And furthermore, the existential purpose of man in this world is to find genuine happiness. Here Gibran reminds us of the dual attitude Christianity has assumed towards the person. For example, on the one hand, the neo-Platonist fathers of the Church seemed to demean man in recognizing him as corrupted, sinful, called to humility and blind obedience. And this Gibran finds unforgiveable on the part of the priests. But on the other hand, Gibran acknowledges that the Christianity of the Gospel exalts man, recognizing him as the image and the likeness of God. Thus, one of Gibran's heroes exclaims:

> Vain are the beliefs and teachings that make man miserable, and false is the goodness that leads him into sorrow and despair, for it is man's purpose to be happy on this earth and lead the

way to felicity and preach its gospel wherever he goes. . . . We came not into this life by exile, but we came as innocent creatures of God, to worship the holy and eternal spirit and seek the hidden secrets within ourselves from the beauty of life. This is the truth which I have learned from the teaching of the Nazarene.[74]

And another of his heroes proclaims:

God does not want me to lead a miserable life, for He placed in the depth of my heart a desire for happiness; His glory rests in the happiness of my heart.[75]

Secondly, the divinity of man differs from that of matter, on the basis of the mystery of *immortality* which characterizes man alone, while the divinity of matter is fugacious and temporary.

I propose to return to the topic of immortality immediately after having explained this coming section.

TRANSCENDENCE OF GOD AND GOD'S RELATION TO MAN

We should beware not to infer from the preceding section of "Immanence" the conclusion that Gibran committed the heresy of *Pantheism*, which is a philosophical and theological doctrine that God is everything and everything is God. It is true that Gibran delved into the dialectic God-nature-man in such a manner that his theory seems to remind us of Hegel (1770-1831), the famous post-Kantian philosopher whose dialectic of the

Spirit precisely terminated in pantheism. Hegel believed that there was only one Reality, which he called the Absolute Spirit, a synonym for God. He also explained that the Absolute Spirit underwent a never ending cycle through the stages of thesis, antithesis, and synthesis. At the thesis stage, the Spirit did not know fully Himself. For this, He would alienate and exteriorize Himself in many forms and shapes; and in this antithesis stage, Hegel saw the creation of man and nature, he considered each individual person and every atom to be nothing else but historical moments in the evolution of God Himself. Finally, Hegel conjectured that in the synthesis stage, the Absolute Spirit would know Himself as to what He "is" and could "do." But because the Absolute Being is infinite, Hegel induced that once the Spirit reached the synthesis period, He would revert back to the thesis level and repeat indefinitely the cycle.[76] All in all Hegel did not make the distinction between the Creator and His creatures. He taught that creation was the very presence and existence of the Creator. God, he thought, was pure immanence.

Now, the process philosophy that Gibran advocates, and which I have outlined in the previous pages, hardly professes the Hegelian pantheism. As a matter of fact, our author strongly believed in the transcendence of God, and the autonomy of man, and the individuality of the world. For him, *"desire"* is the law of creation in as much as it is the law that keeps God-man-nature interdependent, but not in the sense of identical. Together God, man and nature form a perfect *union* in existence, though one is not the other. The inherent property of the soul is "the desire to seek" God; nature too moves upward towards God; in his turn the Divine receives unto Himself both the perfections of man and the perfections of the world and preserves them. All this amounts to saying that Gibran conceives of man as a co-creator with God. The perfection of the world was not *ab initio* formally accomplished; rather, God wanted that man contributes to the perfection of the world.

Philosophically speaking, the metaphysical system of Gibran is not pantheistic but *panentheistic*. Accordingly, the godly in the world must be brought through man's action to ever greater and purer perfection. The human being has a role in creation which enables him to be a co-worker with the Divine in the perfection of the world. Hence, the emphasis of Gibranism is on the actual realization of the life of faith — the inward experience of the presence of God and the actualization of that presence in all our conduct. In this sense Gibran as a process philosopher has great similarities with Bergson,[77] Mikhail Naimy his friend the Lebanese philosopher,[78] Ameen Rihani his compatriot a Sufi,[79] the Russian existentialist Berdjaev[80] and even with Teilhard de Chardin, the remarkable Jesuit Scientist.[81] To prove my point about the significance of Gibran's vision concerning God's immanence and transcendence, let me compare it with the theory of Teilhard de Chardin (1881-1955). In his posthumous book *The Phenomenon of Man*, Teilhard pictures creation as a continuous upward process toward ever higher and better things; today we are at the stage of the "noosphere," at which human consciousness has appeared. Optimistically, Teilhard saw the whole movement of revolution tending toward an ultimate stage, the "omega" (God), which will be the climax of the development of the "noosphere." Furthermore, Teilhard considered that although infinite and transcendent is the "omega," God will still remain in immanent continuity with the ongoing process of nature, and man.

Similarly, Gibran describes the transcendence of God by saying that the seeking of man and of nature is an upward seeking toward the Supreme Being. Now this power of seeking and desiring does not vanish, for instance, when the soul reaches God; quite the contrary, the soul retains its individuality, in that in God, it keeps on seeking more of itself *ad infinitum;* because it then becomes conscious of being *in* God the absolute, the infinite who cannot be encompassed all together by a "finite" being. Gibran writes:

> The soul never loses its inherent properties when it reaches God. Salt does not lose its saltness in the sea; its properties are inherent and eternal. The soul will retain consciousness, the hunger for more of itself and the desire for that which is beyond itself.
> The soul will retain those properties through all eternity, and like other elements in nature it will remain absolute. The absolute seeks more absoluteness, more crystallization.[82]

Therefore as a transcendent Being, God relates to man, however, not after the manner a master relates to his slaves; but, as man is in need of God, God is also in search of man. Here Gibran reiterates what the contemporary Christian philosophers and the right wing of existentialism have taught about God's relation to man, namely, the human is not a means for God, and he was not created for the Glory of God. Otherwise, we would imply that God is imperfect and lacks something which only man could supply Him. Actually such a doctrine demeans both man and God; for any doctrine that demeans man demeans God as well, since the person is a divine-human being.

The best way to describe the relation of God to man is to acknowledge first that each is a *per se* existence, yet mutually interrelated and in search of each other.

When the soul reaches God it will be
conscious that it is in God, and that
it is seeking more of itself in being in
God, and that God too is growing and
seeking and crystallizing.[83]

To be precise, Gibran always portrayed God with the
features and the personality of a sensitive *woman*. Why?
In his opinion, as it was for Kierkegaard, the female sex is
far from being inferior to man, she is rather more
perfect.[84] Also the qualities of compassion, providence
and love suit better the female than the masculine gender. Consequently, speaking of God's relation to man,
Gibran understands that relation to be qualitatively similar to that of a woman, and specially of a *"mother."*

Most religions speak of God in the masculine gender. To me He is as much a Mother as He is a Father.
He is both the father and mother in one; and Woman
is the God-Mother. The God-Father may be reached
through the mind or the imagination But the God-
Mother can be reached through the heart only—
through love.[85]

As we see, Gibran defends the transcendence of God
with the argument that the Super Being establishes living relations with the humans through the bond of
LOVE. Incidentally for this very reason Gibran undertook to rewrite the New Testament with his book *Jesus
The Son of Man*. Supposedly one of the motives for which
Jesus descended upon the earth was to change the images of His Father as depicted in the Old Testament. The
God of Moses was a god of vengeance, punishment;
while the God of Jesus is "a God too vast to be unlike the

soul of any man, too knowing to punish, too loving to remember the sins of His creatures."[86]

Also, within the context of God's love for man, Gibran outlines a theology of *eschatology*. It runs as follows: God is absolute kindness, love, forgiveness. What man calls *evil*, is something which he personally denominates but not God—"God does not work evil."[87] And when man begins to fear the *devil*, this dreadful experience frightens his heart and mind as a result of lack of confidence and trust in God—"Fear of the devil is one way of doubting God."[88] Furthermore, what we know of the reality of *hell* is not a matter-of-fact, as if there existed a physical fire in another world; our personal fear of hell constitutes hell itself, and our damnation is a self-blame which occurs in moments of despair and at the time we refuse to accept the absolution from God's bounty—"The fear of hell is hell itself, and the longing of paradise is paradise itself."[89]

The following sections on immortality, reincarnation, and death represent further developments of Gibran's doctrine of eschatology.

DEATH AND IMMORTALITY

Gibran strongly believes in the immortality of the soul. Yet he does not offer us a philosophical or a logical syllogism to support his argument; his belief is a simple matter of conviction on the grounds of *faith* which teaches him that the eternal divinity of man will never perish. And he does not care whether or not the astute scientific minds agree with his personal faith. Thus, he would tell Miss Haskell: "I'm probably one of the surest of people, and stubborn when I'm sure. If all the other inhabitants of the earth, for instance, believed that the individual soul perished with death it would move me not an atom to agree with them, because I know my soul won't perish."[90] Incidentally this attitude in thinking has become a universal fashion among the humanists and the existential philosophers; nowadays, the humanists hold that there are many human events that lie beyond man's ability to comprehend them either logically or scientifically. One of those metaphysical mysteries is the phenomenon of death and immortality.

Gibran consents to the fact that the physical appearance of man upon this earth is not everlasting. Death strikes man in his innermost personality. However, this death can only be biological, never spiritual. The phenomenon of biological death is the result of a physical clash between the organic elements of man and the chemical elements in nature. Nature is an enormous mass of forces which easily crush the smallness of man and destroy him. In *The Voice of the Master*, Almuhtad instructs the people that the earth with its geological cataclysms and cosmic eruptions overpowers the forces of man; and besides damaging whatever man erects on the fact of the earth as castles, towers, temples—nature also wrecks man in his biological make-up.[91]

Almuhtad's sermon "Of the Divinity of Man" reflects the influence that Gibran bore from the French philosopher B. Pascal who once stated: "Man is but a reed, weakest in nature, but a reed which thinks. It needs not that the whole Universe should arm to crush him. A vapour, a drop of water is enough to kill him. But were the Universe to crush him, man would still be more noble than that which has slain him, because he knows that he dies and that the Universe has the better of him. The Universe knows nothing of this."[92]

In a like style and content Gibran demonstrates the

greatness of man over nature through the fact that the person remains godly even after he dies.

But man in his Divinity I saw standing like
a giant in the midst of Wrath and Destruction,
mocking the anger of the earth and the raging
of the elements.

Like a pillar of light Man stood amidst the ruins
of Babylon, Nineveh, Palmyra and Pompeii, and as
he stood he sang the song of Immortality:

Let the Earth take
That which is hers,
For I, Man, have no ending.[93]

His convictions concerning the immortality of the soul explain why he never looked at the phenomenon of death from a pessimistic angle. On the contrary he exalts the coming of death, "and entitle(s) it with Sweet names, and praise(s) it with Loving words, secretly and to the Throngs of taunting listeners."[94] This attitude makes Gibran an Epicurist. Because for Gibran and Epicurus life and death are but one and the same thing. Epicurus teaches: "You should accustom yourself to believing that death means nothing to us, since . . . living well and dying well are one and the same thing."[95] Note the similarity with Gibran: "For life and death are one, even as the river and the sea are one."[96]

It is possible to compare Gibran's eschatalogy to Epicurus's philosophy of death as long as the reader remembers that there is still a difference between the two. Actually, Epicurus implores us not to dread the idea of death in order to avoid the pains that such reminiscence could cause in our being. Now Gibran does not advocate such an extreme hedonism, although his philosophy leaves room for a certain type of hedonism. Speaking in the strict sense of history, Gibran's exposition on death is meta-religious and precedes the existentialists' conception. For example, Gibran and Heidegger conceive death as the culminative stage of perfection in human exitence. Man is being unto death (*Sein zum Tode*). To die means to fulfill the purpose of human reality. For to be human (*Dasein*) implies to be born, to suffer, love, work, feel guilts, *and die*. Death is an existential situation which no human mortal can escape; it is the very last predicament of man. Furthermore, Gibran, like the Christian existentialist, looks at death as the deliverance of the spirit from the body-matter. Death gives freedom to the spirit.

> For what is it to die but to stand naked
> in wind and to melt into the sun?
>   And what is it to cease breathing, but to
> free the breath from its restless tides, that
> it may rise and expand and seek God
> unencumbered?"[97]

REINCARNATION

From the preceding lines, it becomes obvious that Gibran's philosophy of religion is anti-Nietzschean; as we know the hero of Nietzsche, Zarathustra, denied the immortality of the soul:

> "By my honor, friend—answered Zarathustra—all that of which you speak does not exist: there is no devil and no hell. Your soul will be dead even before your body: fear nothing further."[98]

Gibran left innumerable texts which proclaim the ever-lasting existence of man. The real difficulty, however, that I experience with these articles is the issue of the rebirth of the soul, which is included in his theory of eschatology. As mentioned previously, Gibran got acquainted with the doctrine of the transmigration of the soul through his reading of the Middle Age Islamic philosophers, who were influenced on one hand directly by Indian religion, and on the other hand by Neo-Platonism.[99] According to both doctrines, the Veda and Platonism, the soul after death undergoes a continual process of rebirth and purification until it is completely purified, and then returns to its god. Now how far has the theory of Nirvana and the transmigration of the soul influenced the thinking of Gibran? For one, there is plenty of evidence that shows that our author believed in the return of the soul to the life on earth. For example, in The Poet From Baalbek, Gibran conveys his belief in rein-carnation in the following words:

And the Emir inquired, saying: "Tell us,
O sage . . . will my spirit become
incarnated in the body of a great King's
son, and will the poet's soul transmigrate
into the body of another genius? . . .
And the sage answered the Emir, saying,
"Whatever the soul longs for, will be
attained by the spirit. Remember, O
great Prince, that the sacred Law
which restores the sublimity of Spring
after the passing of Winter will reinstate
you a prince and him a genius poet."[100]

Similar words are also found in The Prophet:

Fare you well, people of Orphalese.
This day has ended. . . .
Forget not that I shall come back to you
dust and foam for another body.
A little while, and my longing shall gather
A little while, a moment of rest upon the
wind, and another woman shall bear me.[101]

Again in *The Garden of the Prophet* we read the same
prophecy about the return of Almustafa:

O Mist, my sister, my sister Mist,
I am one with you now.
No longer am I a self.
The walls have fallen,
And the chains have broken;
I rise to you, a mist,
And together we shall float upon the sea
    until life's second day,
When dawn shall lay you, dewdrops in
    a garden,
And me a babe upon the breast of a
    woman.[102]

Should we conclude from all these passages that
Gibran was a direct follower of Buddhism, or even of
Platonism? Contrary to the error of Miss Barbara Young,
his biographer, it seems to me that Gibran has accepted
the doctrine of "rebirth," and has definitely used the
technical expression of "reincarnation" in order to convey his convictions in the transmigration of the soul.[103]
Yet, as I think deeper on the meaning that Gibran ascribes to the concept of "rebirth" and compare his theory

with that of Buddhism and Platonism, I notice some differences between them. For instance, unlike the Veda philosophers Gibran does not hold the theories of purification and Nirvana. "To me," he states, "all reality is movement. Repose is the harmony of motion. But Nirvana is motionless."[104] But also, unlike Plato, he does not suggest that the status of living of the reborn soul depends on the ethical conduct that the soul had practiced during her previous life on earth.[105] In all simplicity, Gibran maintained that a soul will always come back and will retake the same social status of action in order to continue from there where she left during her last death. And now if you ask him why should the soul come back? —His answer is that "*Love*," either the positive one or the negative one, is the very motive that keeps the continuity of the cycle of life going endlessly. However, it appears that Gibran excluded the souls contaminated by the spirit of indifference, from being reborn anew. His biographer, Barbara Young, reports:

It was his profound certainty that
the life that is the human spirit
has lived and shall live timelessly,
that the bonds of love, devotion and
friendship shall bring together these
endlessly reborn beings, and that
animosity, evil communications, and
hatred have the same effect of reassembling
groups of entities from one cycle to
another. Indifference acts as a separating
influence. Those souls who neither love
nor hate but remain entirely self-contained
as regards one another, meet but once
in the pattern of ages.[106]

Let us comment in brief on the above quote.

To Gibran's contention what we call hate is nothing else but "love turned into hate." Therefore, it is really love that accounts for reincarnation, since even hate is a former love changed into negative, with the exact same quantitative and qualitative aspect of positive love. As by "indifference," we understand those souls who are "useless" because they have no inclination for the either/or conducts. Consequently, why should they come back, when they have accomplished nothing in their previous life that deserves to be continued, nor have they undone something that now necessitates to be done for the best? It is clear to Gibran's logic that if creation is the work of love, then life on earth should pivot around the axis of love; and hence, there is a need in the world for those souls, who have practiced authentic love, that they return; in as much as another chance in a future life should be granted to those souls who have practiced inauthentic love in order that in their new rebirth they retransform their negative destructive love into positive constructive power. These were Gibran's beliefs—"this was his faith—changeless as day and night, and as forthright."[107]

Some Comments on Jesus the Son of Man

Gibran was a great admirer of Jesus and His philosophy of life. In most of his religious essays, Gibran describes his heroes as strong believers in the teachings of Christ. Thus, in *Khalil the Heretic* and *John the Madman* we find the protagonists of the story holding in their hand the New Testament at the time they were caught by their enemies, the clergy (*Khouri*). As Miss Barbara Young has well testified, Gibran perfected his conception of Jesus in the evening of November 12, 1926, when, following a moving mystical vision, he wrote down the

402   KAHLIL GIBRAN: WINGS OF THOUGHT

very first words of what later had to become his monu-
mental book *Jesus the Son of Man*.[108]

It is my firm conviction that Gibran undertook to re-
compose the history of Jesus in order to complement the
one-sidedness that has prevailed among the scholar
theologians concerning the nature of Christ. While the
Church has put too much emphasis on the *divine* aspect
of Christ, the primary motive of Gibran has rather consisted in portraying the *human* nature of Christ. All this
concurs with what I said in the previous pages, namely,
that Gibran has humanized religion and has given it
human characteristics which radiate the immanence of
God in man. Also, to put it bluntly, Gibran has stressed
the human features of the personality of Christ, precisely
in order to remind us that religion and God are not some
kind of a privilege restricted to the rich or the clergy.
Actually, as Gibran saw it, the mission of Jesus never
consisted in establishing an organized institution with
rules, codes, sanctions, and a hierarchy of minds. Furthermore, Jesus never meant to erect a specific geographical location where God his Father would and
should be physically present.

> Jesus came not from the heart of the circle
> of Light to destroy the homes and build
> upon their ruins the convents and monasteries.
> He did not persuade the strong man to become
> a monk or a priest. . . . Jesus was not sent
> here to teach the people to build magnificent
> churches and temples amidst the cold wretched
> huts and dismal hovels.
> . . . He came to make the human heart a temple,
> and the soul an altar, and the mind a priest.[109]

The beauty of the book *Jesus the Son of Man* lies in the
lavishly poetic phraseology and in the creative imagina-

tion that Gibran expresses through the thoughts and deeds of Jesus. As I compare Gibran's Jesus to the work of the four evangelists, it follows that there are some truth and some discrepancies in the writing of Gibran. The discrepancies stem from the fact that many of the personages that Gibran included in the dyadic relation of Christ are simply fictitious persons who never existed. For example, the men Georgus of Beirut, Barca the merchant of Tyre, Sarkis called the madman, and many more are the creation of Gibran. Yet, it is my personal opinion that the exegesis, the thinking, and the deeds of his Jesus correspond to the personality of the evangelists' Jesus. As a matter of fact Gibran describes the Nazarene as possessed with *ambivalent* emotions: kindness towards the sinners, and simultaneously raging against the merchants in the temple.[110] Gibran stressed the antinomies of emotions for the simple reason that his conception of Jesus as a man was closely similar to the nature of the man in the street. That is, it is human to have emotions of kinship, compassion, along with the opposite emotions, rage, rebellion, revolt. Gibran goes even so far as outlining the physical beauty of Jesus, and shows how such a body beauty moved the heart of the female listeners.[111]

Now does Gibran commit the old theological heresy of the Jacobites Monophysites, or of the Nestorians? It is hard to give a clear cut theological answer. I know that he believed in the divinity of Jesus, who came on this earth in order to redeem mankind from its downfall, original sin—"Have mercy, O Jesus, on these multitudes joined together as one by Thy name on the day of the resurrection. Have compassion on their weakness."[112] Yet, on the other hand, it is apparent that he overemphasizes the human nature of Jesus to the point of giving the impression that he denied the divinity of Christ. Passages like the following ones are misleading:

Once every hundred years Jesus of Nazareth
meets Jesus of the Christian in a garden among
the hills of Lebanon. And they talk long; and each
time Jesus of Nazareth goes away saying to Jesus
of the Christian, "My friend, I fear we shall never,
never agree."[113]

And elsewhere he states

There are three miracles of our Brother
Jesus not yet recorded in the Book:
the first that He was a man like you and me;
the second that He had a sense of humor;
and the third that He knew He was a conqueror
though conquered.[114]

Also his *Jesus the Son of Man* put the accent on the
expression "He was a man."[115]

Now, it is my personal conclusion that Gibran did not
so much reject the divinity of Christ in as much as he
intended to replace the old conception of Jesus who
stands above the human, with a more humanly accessible image of the Nazarene. He assumed that in delving in
depth into the human aspect of our Saviour he could (1)
motivate man to follow the examplar path of Jesus—
another son of man—and (2) could inspire man to develop his higher self, in the manner in which Jesus
realized his godly nature.

Jesus the Son of Man has its charm, and it can be read by
anybody including the unbeliever, without that the latter
feels any imposition to embrace the faith of Christianity.
Of course the book does not seek a legal confirmation on
the part of the Church for its authenticity, although
Gibran has repeatedly confessed that he saw and talked

to Jesus himself on a number of occasions.[116] I highly recommend it to the reader. Finally, in the words of its reviewer, Mr. P. W. Wilson,

> . . . In the endeavor to explain or at least to suggest the significance of Jesus in the universe, Mr. Gibran has to resort to imagery, which evidently, is an endeavor by means of line and shadow to express the inexpressible. Like William Blake himself, he is striving to define the unseen in the forms which are visible to the eyes.[117]

EVALUATION OF GIBRANISM

In the foregoing writing I have tried in many ways to bring to light the essentials of Gibran's philosophy. It is time now to come to a *subjective* critique of the foremost fundamental themes that characterize Gibranian trend of thought. To be concise yet precise, I propose to present in a systematic way my negative reaction and my positive evaluation of our author's *Weltanschauung*.

Weaknesses in Gibran

As I ponder on the history of philosophy, I find that no serious thinker has ever come too close to the perfection of truth. Man is not only finite in his existence, but also limited in his knowledge. It is human to err. To come to the point, I have personally experienced dissatisfactions with the ways Gibran has treated some philosophical problems. In my eyes, his system commits three logical fallacies and one methodological mistake. These are: the fallacies of overgeneralization, oversimplification and incompleteness, and the methodological lack of systematization in his presentation. A few words will explain what I mean.

The fallacy of *overgeneralization*, or as the manuals of logic call it *"secundum quid,"* is the most predominant error in his system. The fallacy consists in drawing absolute conclusions from the occurrence of a few particular instances. This attitude in thinking we find in Gibran.

For example, he tends to be harsh against the social laws, the institutionalized marriage, and the established religion, on the basis that he has personally witnessed in a limited number of situations, the injustice, corruption and immorality that man-made laws, traditional marriage and the clergy have unfortunately sometimes exhibited. Again, his conception of the rich as evil and degenerate leaves no room for someone to be virtuous and rich at the same time. Now, this either-or type of logic is incorrect, because it offends against the great variety of human situations.

To make myself clear, let us expound on his fallacy of *oversimplification* which is closely tied up with the above sophistry. Gibran commits this error in the fields of legal philosophy and theodicy. About the former, Gibran, with almost no background in law, dares to condemn all man-made laws, as if some of these were not actually logically derived, directly or indirectly, from the natural laws. And yet, in the opinion of the professional ethicists, many of the man-made laws are norms of moral conduct established on the natural or divine laws; and their purpose is to safeguard the practice of the two other laws. This idea Gibran has missed. But also concerning the fact of the formulated creed, Gibran is oversimplifying the matter. He is shortsighted for having failed to see that the social agency of the clergy is something that God himself has instituted for communal ends. It is rightly said that if God had sent his angels as his priests, instead of choosing his messengers among the weak human mortals, we would have then complained that the preaching of the angels surpasses our human finiteness. I think that Gibran expects more than the human priests can accomplish. He forgets that priests are human, and therefore, liable to mistakes.

As for the third fallacy, *incompleteness*, his system

raises so many pertinent questions: natural laws, reincarnation, marriage, etc. —and yet falls short in answering them in full details. For example, he was not in favor of legal marriage and yet he never solved the perplexing questions of divorce, of who is to take care of children, of alimony, of polygamy, etc.

Finally, in terms of *methodology*, his system lacks coherence, systematization, and logical procedure. Being too poetical and spontaneous, his ideas are dispersed, here and there, in many unrelated books or articles. This accounts—in my opinion—for his being widely read but little understood by his own followers.

Relevancy of Gibranism

All throughout the manuscript I have tried many times and in many ways to praise Gibran, and relate his concepts to our everyday existential situations. Lest I repeat myself here, I would like to state briefly a few of the merits of his thinking.

Despite the fact that Gibran never thought nor wrote in the manner of an Aristotelian philosopher, and never dreamed to create a new "ISM," it is still my belief that the system he developed deserves the title of philosophical. Actually, the term philosopher is too difficult to define, because it is not a reality that can be touched by our senses; rather it is a state of mind and emotion experienced in relation to life. I would call a mind a philosopher if he manifests the desire to pursue some fundamental questions which concern human reality. Now, Gibran fits this definition of mine, for he has pondered on the predicament of human existence. For a too long time, Gibran was not accepted as a genuine thinker who should occupy a chapter in the history of either Arabic or

Western philosophy. This prejudice on the part of the academicians is the result of their ignorance in the wide spectrum of philosophy in as much as it is due to their little knowledge of Gibran. My whole purpose for delving into *comparative* philosophy was to locate the exact place where Gibran's philosophy squares with traditional schools. My conclusions lead me to assert that Gibran is an *existentialist* of equal caliber as some of the right wing of existentialism. Gibran is closer to Kierkegaard, Marcel, Buber, Berdjaev, Ortega y Gasset, Unamuno—than he is to Heidegger, Sartre, Merleau-Ponty, Simone de Beauvoir . . .

Though an Arabian existentialist, he stresses the idea of "perspectivism" which emphasizes the individual point of view. That is to say, his philosophy does not entangle with abstract thinking, but centers around concrete existential moments of life. His heroes live the anxieties and sublimations of the historical, economical, and geographical situations that comprise their actions. This confirms the fact that his literature is *engagée*—committed. He does not write poetries and prose poems simply for literary and artistic reasons, but also, his literature is his style for conveying his philosophical ideas.

As for his being unsystematic, as I critized a while ago, well, it is a trade-mark of many right wing existentialists —Kierkegaard, Marcel, Buber, Berdjaev— to write impulsively, and purposely without a methodology. Their motive is the following: priority should be given to emotions, in counter-reaction against the rigid rationalism of Descarte and the stereotyped idealism of Hegel.

Speaking of existentialism, we should bear in mind that this contemporary "ism," which is more of a label than an actual philosophical ideology, allows that its tenets diverge from one another. What are then the essential features of Gibran's existentialism? For one,

Gibran is unique for combining Hindu, Middle-Eastern and Western ideas. Also, one of his advantages is that he relates intimately with his American readers and points directly to the pressing issues which confront the U.S., such as ecology, environmentalism, spiritual revival in Jesus (remember "Jesus Christ Super Star"). Another trait of his philosophy is simplicity, freshness and humanism. Finally, his existentialism is mystical, as it is the case with most of the right wing. Gibran is a mystic because he explores the spiritual aspect of reality. Nothing is purely material. Molecules, things, events, deeds encompass a "meaning"; they stand for "something," a "purpose."

These and other points which I outlined in the chapters form the bulk of Gibran-*ism*. I was happy to read that Professor St. Elmo Nauman has recently included our author in his scholarly history of American philosophy as a contemporary influential figure (*Dictionary of American Philosophy*, Philosophical Library, 1973). At last, let me quote the definition that Mr. Claude Bragdon gave for Gibranism:

The character and depth of his influence upon the entire Arabic world may be inferred from the fact that it gave rise to a new word, *Gibranism*. Just what this word means English readers will have no difficulty in divining: mystical vision, metrical beauty, a simple and fresh approach to the 'problem' of life . . . extraordinary dramatic power, deep erudition, lightning like intuition, lyrical life, metrical mastery, and Beauty which permeates the entire pattern in everything he touches [quoted in Barbara Young, p. 37].

NOTES AND REFERENCES

Short History of Lebanon

1. Hitti, P. K., *Lebanon in History*, New York: Macmillan Co., Ltd., 1957, p. 130. According to some texts of mythology, the marriage of Tammuz (or Dumuzi) was rather with Inanna, the fertility of nature. Also, Tammuz (or Dumuzi) was a shepherd-god appointed by Enki who in his turn was asked by Anu and Enlil to organize the economic life of Mesopotamia, by instituting different social functions in the different parts of the country. Now, the yearly marriage of the goddess Inanna to the god Tammuz (or Dumuzi) commemorates the revival of "the creative powers of spring." (H. and H. A. Frankfort, and J. Wilson, and Th. Jacobsen, *Before Philosophy: Adventure of Ancient Man*, Baltimore, Maryland: Penguin Books, 1971, p. 175; pp. 214-215).
2. Meo, Leila, M. T., *Lebanon: Improbable Nation. A Study in Political Development*, Indiana University Press, 1965, pp. 40-64.
3. Hitti, P. K., *op. cit.* p. 364.
4. Hourani, A. H., *Syria and Lebanon*, London: Oxford University Press, 1946, p. 25. *See also* P. M. Holt, *Egypt and the Fertile Crescent 1516-1922*, Cornell University Press, 1966, pp. 112-123.
5. Hitti, P. K., *op. cit.*, pp. 247-252.
6. *ibidem*, pp. 257-265.
7. Meo, Leila, M. T., *op. cit.*, p. 30.
8. Hitti, P. K., *op. cit.*, 443.

Life of Kahlil Gibran

1. Naimy, Mikhail, "A Strange Little Book", *Aramco World*, XV, 6, 1964, p. 12.
2. In reading some of Gibran's commentators we get the impression that Gibran attained the peak of his fame while alive. Unfortunately, these historians wrapped in the emotion of pride, fail to stress bluntly the distinction between the "before" and "after". (See for instance: Andrew Dib Sherfan, *Kahlil Gibran: The Nature of Love*, New York: Philosophical Library, 1970, pp. 29 – 31; and Habib Massoud, *Joubran Hayyan wa Mayyitan*, Beirut: The Rihani House, 1966, p. 21 sq.). Yet, in the opinion of others, such as Suheil Bushrui and John

Munro, Gibran hardly received recognition from academic modern American literature; and when his books were printed none of the leading Journals in the West ever reviewed his books. (*Kahlil Gibran: Essays and Introduction*, eds., by Suheil Bushrui and John Munro, Beirut: The Rihani House, 1970, p. 1 sq.). This amounts to saying that he truly became world famous after his death only.

3. The Monastery of Mar-Sarkis was the playground of Gibran and his refuge for meditation whenever things did not work out at his home. The young Gibran always had hoped to buy someday the deserted cloister. Incidentally, we are told by his best friend Mikhail Naimy, that "he had begun negotiations to buy the monastery" prior to 1923. But really, he did not succeed paying the full amount requested by the real estate because he became bankrupt after trying unsuccessfully to collect his due from some old lady to whom he had rented a building he had bought in Boston during the depression time." (Mikhail Naimy, "A Strange Little Book," *Aramco World*, XV, 6, 1964, p. 15; *see also* by the same author, *Kahlil Gibran, His Life and His Work*, Beirut: Khayats, 1964, p. 197).

4. The Maronites accept the infallibility of the Pope. And in contrast to the Latin priests, the Maronite priests may contract marriage legally. However, today more and more the idea of marriage among the clergy is fading away. Historically, it was in 1736 that the Maronite Church joined affiliation with the Roman Church. The precursor is Mar-Maron. *See below* p. 17.

5. Young, Barbara, *This Man From Lebanon*, New York: A. Knopf, 1970, p. 144.

6. Otto, Annie Salem, *The Parables of Kahlil Gibran*, New York: The Citadel Press, 1963, p. 16.

7. Young, Barbara, *op. cit.*, p. 10.

8. *ibid*, p.7.

9. *PR.*, p. 13. It is unfortunate that some writers keep on spelling Gibran's family name differently from the way he himself used to sign in Roman alphabets. For example, to name only two, the French orientalist, Jean Lecerf, spells our author's name as "Djbran Khalil Djbran", (*Orient*, magazine, 3, 1957, pp. 7-14); and the illustrious Harvard professor, Sir Hamilton Gibb refers to him as "Jibran Khalil Jibran," (*Studies on the Civilization of Islam*, Boston: Beacon Press, 1968, p. 272). In my opinion these false orthographies are due to the fact that some of his commentators still prefer to write foreign nouns as they sound to their ears, even though their correspondent Roman inscriptions already exist.

10. Miss Young (*op. cit.*, p. 184) and Miss Otto (*op. cit.*, p. 20), commit a grotesque historical error when they call Avicinna, a pre-islamic poet and Ibn-Sinna, a philosopher. Actually, those two names, are of the same person. The former is spelled (improperly) in Latin (it should be Avicenna) and the latter in Arabic. Furthermore,

Ibn-Sina (980-1037) lived after Mohammed. He is considered as one of the greatest Moslem philosophers of the medieval eastern group. For a good presentation of his philosophy consult Majid Fakhry, *A History of Islamic Philosophy*, Columbia University Press, 1970, pp. 147-183.

11. *BW.*, pp. 82-83.

12. Young, Barbara, *op. cit.*, p. 185.

13. *SP.*, p. 8.

14. "The Bride's Bed" essay condemns the rotten customs of marriage, in favor of women's freedom. (*TL.*, pp. 87-94). I believe that if Gibran had lived to witness the new movement called "Women's Liberation Front," he would have lent them full support with his sharp pen. He had a profound understanding of the psychology of women. He also avowed that he was indebted for everything that he possessed to the intervention of the women in his life: "I am indebted for all that I call 'I' to women, ever since I was an infant. Women opened the windows of my eyes and the doors of my spirit. Had it not been for the woman-mother, the woman-sister, and the woman-friend, I would have been sleeping among those who seek the tranquility of the world with their snoring." (*SP.*, p. 96). Indeed, his "philosophy of woman" finds some similarities with Simone de Beauvoir's book: *The Second Sex*, and with the Dutch psychologist F. Buytendijk's book: *Woman. A Contemporary View.* His sharp critic is advanced unconditionally against anybody who degrades the function of the female in society. Definitely the nowadays abundantly printed pornography finds no room for justification in his ethics. Finally, he writes: "Writers and poets try to understand the truth about woman. But until this day they have never understood her heart because, looking upon her through the veil of desire, they see nothing except the shape of her body. Or they look upon her through a magnifying glass of spite and find nothing in her but weakness and submission." (*WG.*, 81).

15. *The Prophet*, translated by Sarwat Okasha, Cairo: Dar al Maarf, 1959, "Introduction", p. 14.

16. *SP.*, p. 4.

17. Massoud, Habib, *Joubran, Hayyan wa Mayyatan*, Beirut: The Rihani House, 1966, p. 20.

18. According to Joseph Sheban, there is rumor that the true benefactress of Gibran was a wealthy Lebanese lady named Mary Khoury. Up to date, however, there is no evidence that shows whether Mary Khoury did really give financial aid to our author. Nevertheless, it seems that a lady by such a name did exist. As to what was her genuine relation with Gibran, it is unknown yet. (*MS.*, pp. 88-89).

19. *SP.*, p. 97.

20. Young, Barbara, *op. cit.*, IX.

The Contributions of the Writer

1. *S.P.*, p. 34.
2. *See* "Chapter Five".
3. *S.P.*, p. 14.
4. Barbara Young, *This Man From Lebanon*, New York: A. Knopf, 1970, p. 186.
5. *S.P.*, p. 20.
6. I am in complete disagreement with Andrew Dib Sherfan who considers that the kind of love Gibran displays in this narration is Freudian. (Kahlil Gibran: *The Nature of Love*, New York: Philosophical Library, 1971, p. 26). Freudian love is a far more intricate and unconscious type than the love Gibran describes in *The Broken Wings*. Sublimation, cathexis, and sex are the unconscious processes that underline Freudian love; a love which by the way substitutes the pleasure principle with the reality principle. Whatever were the carnal desires of Gibran in *The Broken Wings*—and they are not non-existent—express merely romanticism, youth and idealism, but hardly Freudism. In Chapter Six I will come back on this issue.
7. Accordingly, Gibran once confessed to Miss Haskell that the experiences and the personages reported in *The Broken Wings* were not his own. (*B.P.*, pp. 50-51) Now, to us historians, Miss Haskell's information sheds confusion on the biographical credibility of the novel. Whom should we believe? Miss Haskell who was told by Gibran? or the gossip folks of Bsherri who till today vaunt with pride that the great philosopher Gibran fell in love with one of their daughters, Miss Hala Daher whose family is still alive? As a biographer, this is my answer: there is plenty of doubt about Miss Haskell's knowledge of Gibran's early personal life; for one, whenever Gibran spoke to Haskell of his family, he overexaggerated with lies the story. For example, he did tell her the lie, that his father was wealthy and a tax collector in the Lebanese Government who unfortunately was trialed one day and found guilty of "embezzlement of taxes", but was then granted pardon, exiled etc. . . . (*B.P.*, pp. 20-21). Another reason why Haskell was misled about the real autobiographical value of *The Broken Wings*, has to do with the fact that Gibran never revealed to Haskell the names of his early love affairs, though he spoke freely about their adventures. (*B.P.*, pp. 68-69). Most probably, I believe Gibran denied in front of Haskell the autobiography of the novel, in order that he makes the dedication of the book to Haskell more genuine. Yet, in conclusion, I do concur with the biographers J. Sheban, A. Dib Sherfan, A. Otto, the natives of Bsherri, etc., that *The Broken Wings* is an autobiography of Gibran's first romance with the Lebanese girl, Hala Daher.
8. Andrew Dib Sherfan, Kahlil Gibran: *The Nature of Love*, New

York: Philosophical Library, 1971, p. 26. Also, it should be noted that Gibran titled his book *Tears and Laughter*, but H. Nahmad when he translated it from Arabic he preferred for sake of phonetic the word "Smile" instead of "Laughter". In *A Self-Portrait* Gibran refers to it twice. (*S.P.*, p. 7 and p. 35).

9. *S.P.*, p. 4.

10. *MM*. pp. 69-71.

11. *The National Catholic Reporter*, July 21, 1968.

12. Barbara Young, *This Man From Lebanon*, New York: A. Knopf, 1970, p. 56.

13. Cf. *The Portable Nietzsche*, ed. by Walter Kaufman, (New York: The Viking Press, 1968), p. 121; and *The Gospel of Luke*, Ch. 3, verse 23. In *The Voice of the Master* the hero prophet is 30 years old. (*V.M.*, p. 7).

14. *E.G.*, p. 11. About the complete trilogy of the prophet the third book that Gibran planned to publish along the same lines of *The Prophet* and *The Garden of the Prophet*, was *The Death of the Prophet* —whose content was to be about man's relation to God. Unfortunately, this book did not appear. (Cf. Barbara Young, *op. cit.*, p. 119). Fortunately, however, Gibran did ponder occasionally on the theme of man's relation to God. In the text I have taken the liberty of calling *The Earth Gods* a work that deals with man and God, with the exception that this time it is God's relation to man which is under speculation.

15. Barbara Young, *This Man From Lebanon*, New York: A. Knopf, 1970, p. 13.

16. Mikhail Naimy, Kahlil Gibran, *His Life and His Work*, Beirut: Khayats, 1964, p. 194.

17. Barbara Young, *This Man From Lebanon*, New York: A. Knopf, 1970, p. 64; pp. 16-17; and p. 65.

18. *N.V.*, p. 19.

19. Ignace Kratchovski, *Monde Oriental*, Tome XXI, Fasc. 1-3.

20. P.J.E. Cachia, "Modern Arabic Literature" in *The Islamic Near East*, ed. by D. Grant, Toronto: University of Toronto Press, 1960, p. 284.

21. Sir Hamilton Gibb, *Studies on the Civilization of Islam*, Boston: Beacon Press, 1968, p. 261.

22. Quoted in Nadeem Naimy, *Mikhail Naimy. An Introduction*, Beirut: American University Press, 1970, p. 121.

23. *ibidem*, p. 123.

24. Gibran, *Twenty Drawings*, with an Introduction by Alice Raphael, New York: A. Knopf, 1970, p. 3.

25. R. A. Nicholson, *A Literary History of the Arabs*, Cambridge, England: Cambridge University Press, 1969, pp. 304-313.

26. A. J. Arberry, *Aspects of Islamic Civilization*, Michigan: The University of Michigan Press, 1967, pp. 73-118.

27. *B.P.*, p. 83.

28. *ibidem*, p. 93.
29. *ibidem*, p. 36.
30. "Thus Spoke Zarathustra", in *The Portable Nietzsche*, ed. by W. Kaufman, (New York: The Viking Press, 1968), "Prologue", pp. 121-137.
31. *B.P.*, p. 83.
32. *ibidem*, p. 344.
33. *M.S.*, pp. 46-50.
34. *The Wisdom of Buddhism*, ed. by Christmas Humphreys, New York: Random House, 1961. See also, *The Teachings of the Compassionate Buddha*, ed. by E. A. Burett, New York: The New American Library, 1955.
35. *Selected Poetry and Prose of William Blake*, ed. by Northrop Frye, New York: The Modern Library, 1953, pp. 264-316.
36. *ibidem*, p. 25, and p. 43.
37. *B.P.*, p. 260.
38. *ibidem*, p. 296.

Gibran's Philosophy of Aesthetics

1. Heidegger, M., *Holzwee*, Frankfurt am Main: Klosterman, 1957, p. 62.
2. *S.S.* p. 59.
3. Aristotle, *Poetica*, 1448b 4-24.
4. *ibidem*, 1448a 1-5.
5. *S.S.*, p. 59.
6. *S.F.* p. 21.
7. *S.S.*, p.15. Elsewhere he writes: "Thinking is always the stumbling stone to poetry." (*S.S.*, p. 24).
8. *S.S.*, p. 33. From this passage it is apparent that Gibran would never classify poetry among the treatises of logic as Aristotle did.
9. *S.S.*, p. 15.
10. Blaise Pascal, *Pensée*, Paris: Librairie Generale Francaise, 1962, p. 236, No. 477. "Le coeur a ses raisons, que la raison ne connait point." (Engl. transl. by the author).
11. *S.F.* p. 23. That Gibranism is not anti-intellectualism can best be seen in the essay "Of Reason and Knowledge", which stresses the importance of reason in our life. If a man lets himself be governed by "impulses" and "passions" alone, then his existence becomes animalistic and impetuous. Hence he writes: "Reason is a prudent minister, a loyal guide, and a wise counsellor . . . Be wise—let Reason, not impulse, be your guide." (*V.M.* p. 53).
12. *S.F.*, p. 23.

13. *S.S.*, p. 18.
14. *S.S.*, p. 7.
15. *F.R.*, pp. 47-49.
16. Heidegger, M., *Introduction to Metaphysics*, Garden City, New York: Doubleday & Co., Inc., 1961, p. 22. The reason I make ample references to outside writers, is simply to show the relevance and depth of Gibranism.
17. *V.M.*, p. 31.
18. *Th.M.*, pp. 72-73.
19. *S.S.*, p. 29.
20. Robert D. Cumming (ed.) *The Philosophy of Jean-Paul Sartre*, New York: Random House, Inc. 1966, p. 370.
21. *S.S.*, p. 29.
22. *T.L.*, p. 81.
23. Robert D. Cumming (ed.), *The Philosophy of Jean-Paul Sartre*, New York: Random House, Inc., 1966, p. 375.
24. *T.L.*, p. 81.
25. Heidegger, M., "Holderlin" in *Qu'est-ce-que la Metaphysique?* Paris: Gallimard, 1951, p. 250.
26. *ibiden*, pp. 243-244.
27. *S.S.*, pp. 51-52.
28. *T.L.*, p. 28; p. 44.
29. *ibiden*, p. 44. See also *V.M.*, p. 31. For Heidegger the poet and the thinker (*penseur*) have some commonesses, but, are not identical. "Only poetry stands in the same order as philosophy and its thinking, though poetry and thought are not the sense thing." (*An Introduction to Metaphysics*, Garden City, New York: Doubleday & Co., Inc., 1961, p. 21). Gibran too makes this distinction, however, for him poetic thinking surpasses philosophic thinking. According to Gibran, philosophy is metempirical (*S.S.*, p. 13), is an "intellectual prostitute" (*S.F.*, p. 64). finally, but not the least, an intellectual perusal of "man's mind, his deeds and his desires" (*S.F.*, p. 65).
30. See "A poet's voice" in *T.S.*, pp. 167-174.
31. Nietzsche, F., "Thus Spoke Zarathustra," in *The Portable Nietzsche*, ed. by Walter Kaufman, New York: The Viking Press, 1969, Part II, sec. 17, p. 240.
32. *T.L.*, p. 44.
33. *T.S.*, Introduction by Robert Hillyer, p. V.
34. Quoted in *The Wisdom of Gibran*, ed. by Joseph Sheban, New York: Philosophical Library, 1966, p. 59.
35. *S.H.*, p. 47.
36. *T.L.*, p. 29.
37. *T.S.*, Introduction by Robert Hillyer, p. V.
38. In his short play "Assilban" we are told how a poet may commit the sin of renegation against his divine vocation. The follow-

ing passage enumerates the possible ways of derogation: "There are
. . . many poets . . . They all sell their voices, their thoughts and their
conscience for a coin, for a meal, for a bottle of wine. . . . They are like
talking machines of sorrow and joy. If the occasion does not call for
then, these machines will be set aside like used utensils. . . . I blame
them for not scorning the pretty and trifling. I blame them for not
preferring *death to humiliation.*" (*S.S.*, pp. 89-90. The italics are mine).

39. *S.S.*, p. 8.
40. See the paintings in *The Parables of Kahlil Gibran* (by A. Salem
Otto, New York: The Citadel Press, 1963), p. 108 and p. 142.
41. *V.M.*, p. 22.
42. *G.P.*, p. 36.
43. Frye, N., (ed.), *Selected Poetry and Prose of Blake*, New York:
Random House, Inc. 1953, Intr. xxviii.
44. *V.M.*, pp. 86-87.
45. Naimy, Mikhail, *Kahlil Gibran. His Life and His Work*, Beirut:
Khayats, p. 59.
46. *S.S.*, p. 78.
47. *S.S.*, p. 24.
48. *S.F.*, p. 83.
49. *S.S.*, p. 20.
50. *T.D.*, Introduction by Miss Alice Raphael, p. 6.
51. *ibidem*, p. 9.
52. *ibidem*, p. 9.
53. *B.W.*, p. 24.
54. *ibidem*, p. 23.
55. *T.L.*, p. 69.
56. *ibidem*, p. 69.
57. *P.*, p. 75
58. *B.W.*, p. 41.
59. *M.S.*, p. 75.
60. *G.P.*, pp. 26-28.
61. *B.W.*, p. 16. In the poem "Song of Beauty," Gibran once more
recognizes the psychotherapeutic effect of Beauty on a soul filled with
anguish. "Youth beholds me, his toil is forgotten, and his life becomes a stage for sweet dreams." (*T.S.*, p. 161). Many times it is
enough to glance at a field of beautiful roses or listen to a beautiful
music in order to distract the mind from an idea that causes anxiety.
62. *S.F.*, p. 26.
63. *M.M.*, p. 52.
64. *S.F.*, p. 67.
65. *V.M.*, p. 85.
66. *T.S.*, p. 161.
67. *ibidem*, p. 52.
68. *P.*, p. 76 I have underlined the words "ever" for it emphasizes
that Beauty like being are unchangeable, universal and eternal. Since

Gibran is a poet he uses the term "nature" to mean "being," the concept of the metaphysicians. Here is the passage where he explicates the transcendental relation between "nature and Beauty:" My life [it is the Nymph who speaks] is sustained by the world of Beauty which you will see, wherever you rest your eyes, and this Beauty is Nature itself" . . . (*T.L.*, p. 68).

69. *T.L.*, p. 15.
70. *V.M.*, pp. 27-28.

Gibran's Philosophy of Law and Society

1. *S.S.*, p. 39. Gibran always condemned the ecological and environmental calamities of pollution. And on other occasions he favored a halt in technological progress, because he predicted that such advancements would endanger the peace among nations. Miss Young tells us, for instance, that Gibran was against the early productions of airplanes. He believed that air supremacy during wartime would cause grave disasters. Gibran once uttered: "If I could I would destroy every airplane upon the Earth, and every remembrance of that flying evil from men's mind" (B. Young, *op. cit.*, p. 26). This quote should not make us think that Gibran was against scientific or technical *Knowledge qua* such. It simply expresses Gibran's concern for his fellowmen who were someday to be slaughtered from the air. Remember the aircraft that carried the atomic bomb to Hiroshima, or the destruction from the air of the city of Hamburg, or the billions of tons of napalm dropped from the air over Vietnam and elsewhere.

2. *Th.M.*, p. 89.
3. Soren Kierkegaard, "Journals:. quoted in *A Dictionary of Existentialism* edited by Ralph B. Winn, New York: Philosophical Library, 1960, p. 98.
4. *S.H.*, pp. 17-19.
5. *S.R.*, p. 58.
6. *S.H.*, p. 19.
7. *Th.M.*, pp. 27-29.
8. Martin Buber, *Good and Evil*, New York: Scribner's Sons, 1953, p. 9.—It would seem odd to many intellectuals that I quote a Jewish scholar in a treatise dedicated to an Arab. But I have my reasons which are not political and aim at no politics. My intention is to draw the similarities between Gibran's thought and the classic thinkers acknowledged by the world.
9. Zenkovsky, V. V., *A History of Russian Philosophy*, New York: Columbia University Press, vol. I, 1967, p. 391.
10. *S.P.*, p. 4; p. 9.
11. *ibidem*, p 9

12. Jean-Jacques Rousseau, *Discourse on the Arts and Sciences*, London: J. M. Dent and Sons Ltd, 1947, p. 122.

13. Jean-Jacques Rousseau, *Discourse on the Origin of Inequality*, London: J. M. Dent and Sons Ltd, 1947, p. 163.

14. *ibidem*, p. 205. Gibran's social philosophy is much closer to Rousseau's than to Nietzsche's. True, Nietzsche denounced the despiritualization and slave-morality that predominate in contemporary culture; however, it is equally true that he entertained some grim ideas about the basic nature of man, which he considered to be ontologically evil. Nietzsche was pessimistic in his thoughts, much like Schopenhauer. He always depicted man as "merciless, greedy, insatiable, murderous," who hangs "upon the back of a tiger." ("On Truth and Lie," in *The Portable Nietzsche*, ed. by W. Kaufman, New York: The Viking Press, 1968, p. 44). This last statement is a good proof in itself, that shows the discrepancy between Nietzsche and Gibran who emphatically kept faith in the *goodness* of human nature unspoiled by the superego of culture. Of course, I am not implying that Gibran was not, somehow, inspired by Nietzsche's theory of the "superman." Quite the contrary, I have good reasons to suspect that Nietzsche enlightened Gibran about the "slave-morality" and the despiritualization prevailing in our contemporary society.

15. *The Procession*, p. 74.

16. *S.S.*, pp. 96-101. Although Gibran never asked us to flee from urban life in order to reestablish the now dying rural form of society, he does seem, nevertheless, attracted to peasant existence. I partially attribute this inclination to his boyhood period, when he lived in Bsherri with his father who was himself a shepherd, farmer and a man of nature. Still, Gibran had philosophical and psychological reasons for doubting of the benefits of the cultural superego upon the psyche of the individual. The following passage contrasts nature versus culture: "We who live amid the excitements of the city know nothing of the life of the mountain villagers. We are swept into the current of urban existence, until we forget the peaceful rhythms of simple country life, which smiles in the spring, toils in summer, reaps in autumn, rests in winter, imitating nature in all her cycles. We are wealthier than the villagers in silver or gold, but they are richer in spirit. What we sow we reap not; they reap what they sow. We are slaves of gain, and they the children of contentment. Our draught from the cup of life is mixed with bitterness and despair, fear weariness; but they drink the pure nectar of life's fulfillment. (*Th.M.*, p. 44).

17. B. W., p. 15. When it comes to psychoanalyzing the psychic of the rich, Gibran is a master. Accordingly, riches (1) grow from greed, (2) lead to miserliness, and (3) despair. His best essay on this subject is *Today and Yesterday*. The article speaks of a man who was poor "yesterday" but happy; "today" the same man has become rich, yet he is

unhappy. Witness the differences in behaviors among the socio-economical clssses: "Yesterday was I granted life and nature's beauty; today I am plundered of them: yesterday was I rich in joy; today I have become poor in my riches. Yesterday I was with my flock as a merciful ruler among his subjects; today I stand before gold as a cringing slave before a tyrannous master. I knew not that riches would efface the very essence of my spirit, nor did I know that wealth would lead it to the dark caves of ignorance. And I reckoned not that what people call glory is naught except torment and the pit." (*T.S.*, pp. 39–40).

18. Barbara Young, *This Man from Lebanon*, New York; Alfred A. Knopf, 1970, p. 128.

19. *S.P.*, pp. 74–75. Yussif El-Fakri is the same person of whom we spoke early in this chapter. (Cf. above p. 89 sq.)

20. *S.H.*, p. 24.

21. *S.P.*, pp. 16-17.

22. Antonio Caso, *La existencia como economía, como interés y como caridad*, 3rd ed., Mexico: Secretaría de Educación Pública, 1943, p. 43 (Translation by the author).

23. *ibidem*, p. 102. (Translation by the author). Note that Gibran too considers art not as an economic activity but spiritual. "Art is a bird that soars freely in the sky or roams happily on the ground. No one can change its behavior. Art is a spirit that cannot be bought or sold." (*S.S.*, p. 91.)

24. *ibidem*, p. 178. (Translation by the author).

25. *ibidem*, p. 178. (Translation by the author).

26. *M.S.*, p. 24.

27. Al-Afghani, quoted in Muhammed al-Makhzumi, *Khatirat Jamal al-Din al-Afghani al Husaymi*, Beirut, 1931, p. 88; p. 218. (Translation by the author).

28. Qasim Amin, *Tahrir al-Marah*, Cairo: Dar al maaref 1899, p. 154. (Translation by the author). It should be kept in mind that though the secularists identified themselves with European secularism, they never became, however, atheists nor doubted of the validity of Koranic Dogmas. In case of a conflict between religious truth and scientific truth, they would side rank with the *ulema* reformists.

29. *Th.M.*, p. 28.

30. *ibidem*, pp. 28-29.

31. *ibidem*, p. 29.

32. *ibidem*, p. 83.

33. *ibidem*, p. 84.

34. Barbara Young, *This Man from Lebanon*, New York; Alfred A. Knopf, 1970, p. 126.

35. *S.H.*, pp. 71-73.

36. *B.P.*, p. 274; pp. 276-278. *See also*, Philip Hitti, *Lebanon in History*, New York: St. Martin's Press, 1957, p. 484.

37. *S.H.*, pp. 92-93. *In the Dark Night* is another poem composed during the famine in Syria and Lebanon. (Cf. *Th.M.*, pp. 35-37).

38. *S.H.*, p. 94. Gibran writes:
". . . And if my
People had attacked the despots
And oppressors and died as rebels
I would have said, "Dying for
Freedom is nobler than living in
The shadow of weak submission, for
He who embraces death with the sword
Of Truth in his hand will eternalize
With the Eternity of Truth, for Life
Is weaker than Death and Death is
Weaker than Truth." (*S.M.*, p. 94).

39. The essay *The Fex and the Independence* is full or ironies. It denounces the narrow mindedness and obstinacy of the Orientals. The Orientals manifest paradoxical behaviors; on one hand, they criticize the Occidentals; yet on the other hand, they keep on imitating the Europeans' life-style and using their products. (Cf. *S.S.*, pp. 73-75).

40. The following is the way the rich should socially dialogue with the poor: "Take now, my brother, and return on the morrow with your companions and take you all of what is yours? (*T.S.*, p. 41). For a complete list of the reforms Gibran was seeking to introduce in the Middle-East, read the essay "Your Thought and Mine," in *S.S.*, pp. 109-114.

41. *S.H.*, pp. 26-27. *See also* F. Nietzsche, *Genealogy of Morals* Transl, by F. Golffing, (Garden City, New York: Doubleday, 1956), pp. 170-172.

42. Barbara Young, *This Man From Lebanon*, New York: Alfred A. Knopf, 1970, p. 125.

43. *Th.M.*, pp. 81-82.

44. Franz Kafka, *The Trial*, New York: Vintage Books, p. 269.

45. Franz Kafka, *Parables and Paradoxes*, New York: Schoken Books, 1961, p. 155.

46. *ibidem*, p. 157.

47. *S.R.*, pp. 36-37.

48. *ibidem*, p. 36.

49. ibidem, p. 56.

50. *P.*, p. 43.

51. *S.F.*, p. 49.

52. *P.*, pp. 40-41.

53. *W.*, p. 24.

54. *FR.*, p. 28.

55. Pascal, *Pensées*, Paris: Librairie Générale Française, 1962, p. 151, No. 329, (Translation by the author).

56. *Th.M.*, pp. 103-104. Elsewhere Gibran writes: "He who vaunts his scorn of the sinful vaunts his disdain of all humanity." (*Th. M.*, p. 111). Note that this was the same thesis of Pascal. (*See* Pascal, *op. cit.*, ch. III).

57. *M.S.*, pp. 34-35.

58. *S.S.*, p. 21. The italics are mine.

59. *T.S.*, p. 35.

60. Carl Jung, *The Undiscovered Self*, New York: A Mentor Book, 1958, p. 22. (Cf. *B.P.* p. 120).

61. *T.S.*, p. 20.

62. *T.L.*, p. 84.

63. *T.S.*, p. 19.

64. *ibidem*, p. 36.

65. *S.R.*, p. 28.

66. *T.S.*, p. 129.

67. *S.H.*, p. 15; *B. W.*, pp. 95-96.

68. Thomas Aquinas, *Summa Theologica*, P. I-II, p. 91, a.1.

69. *S.S.*, p. 46.

70. *T.L.*, p. 85.

71. *P.R.*, pp. 47-48.

72. *S.P.*, p. 14.

73. Fortunately today the Catholic Church has mitigated her position toward marriages contracted in coercion. However, it is also a known fact that only rich people get their marriage annulled, whereas few are the poor who are successful with this matter. My last remark is a rebuke against Fr. Andrew Dib Sherfan who seems to disregard the right comments of Gibran about the church and forced marriages. (Cf. Sherfan, *Kahlil Gibran: The Nature of Love*, New York: Philosophical Library, 1971, pp. 94–95).

74. *S.P.*, p. 14.

75. *V.M.*, pp. 41-42. *See also*, *P.*, pp. 44-46.

76. *S.S.*, p. 53.

77. *MM.*, p. 27.

78. *ibidem*, p. 28.

79. *ibidem*, p. 28.

80. *FR.*, p. 23.

81. *ibidem*, p. 23.

82. *ibidem*, p. 23.

83. *ibidem*, p. 24.

84. *S.H.*, p. 94.

85. *W.*, p. 22.

86. *ibidem*, p. 23.

87. *ibidem*, p. 24.

88. *ibidem*, p. 24.

89. *ibidem*, p. 25.

90. *ibidem*, p. 26. The italics are mine.

Love the Quintessence of Human Existence

1. Plato,, *Phaedo*, 82e.
2. *P*. p. 71.
3. *S.S.*, p. 54.
4. *B.P.*, p. 278.
5. *P.*, p. 72.
6. *S.F.*, p. 26.
7. *B.P.*, p. 113. (The italics are mine).
8. Barbara Young, *This Man From Lebanon*, New York: Alfred A. Knopf, 1970, p. 129.
9. *S.R.*, p. 23. I remind the reader that Gibran has never spoken of Aristippus. I am solely responsible for introducing Aristippus' philosophy. I am doing so, simply in order to clarify Gibran's position in respect to the playboy who seems to recapitulate Aristippus' *Weltanschauung*.
10. *B.P.*, p. 67.
11. *P.*, p. 70.
12. Victor Frankl, *Man's Search For Meaning*, Washington Square Press, 1963, p. 166.
13. *W.G.*, p. 74.
14. *P.*, p. 70.
15. *N.V.*, p. 20.
16. *W.C.*, p. 48.
17. *N.V.*, p. 21.
18. *T.S.*, p. 44.
19. *ibidem*, p. 51.
20. Barbara Young, *This Man From Lebanon*, New York: Alfred A. Knopf, 1970, p. 129.
21. *B.P.*, p. 113.
22. *ibidem*, p. 69. On the other hand, the sexual attitudes of the Casanova are exhibitionism, hypocrisy, fake, dishonorable, unesthetic and indecent.
23. *ibidem*, p. 113.
24. *S.R.*, pp. 17-20.
25. *B.P.*, pp 136-137.
26. *ibidem*, p. 113.
27. *ibidem*, p. 292.
28. *ibidem*, p. 113.
29. Sigmund Freud, *On Creativity And The Unconscious*, New York: Harper & Row Publishers.
30. *B.P.*, p. 113 and p. 169. It is clear from these passages that Gibran must have read something of or about Freud. Also, the Reader should remember that Freud came to America in 1909 at the invitation

of Professor Stanley Hall, President of Clark University, Worcester, Mass.
31. *ibidem*, p. 22; p. 24; p. 29; p. 72.
32. Barbara Young, *This Man From Lebanon*, p. 129; *see also B. P.*, p. 70.
33. *B.P.*, p. 223.
35. *ibidem*, p. 224.
36. *ibidem*, p. 194.
37. *ibidem*, p. 185.
38. *ibidem*, p. 220.
39. *T.L.*, p. 56.
40. *B.W.*, p. 43.
41. *T.L.*, p. 59.
42. *ibidem*, p. 15.
43. *T.S.*, p. 24.
44. *ibidem*, p. 32.
45. *T.L.*, p. 55.
46. *S.S.*, p. 32.
47. *T.S.*, p. 32.
48. *S.S.*, p. 48.
49. Gabriel Marcel, *Being and Having*, New York: Harper & Row, Publishers, 1965, p. 167. (The italics are mine).
50. *P.*, p. 19.
51. *S.F.*, p. 34.
52. *B.W.*, p. 106.
53. *P.*, p. 8.
54. *G.P.*, p. 8.
55. *B.P.*, p. 49.
56. *P.*, pp. 62-63.
57. *G.P.*, p. 22.
58. *N.V.*, p. 31. sq.
59. "Love is a precious treasure, it is God's gift to sensitive and great spirits." (*B.W.*, pp. 104-105).
60. *B.W.*, p. 64.
61. Gabriel Marcel, *Searchings*, New York: Newman Press, 1967, p. 64. *See also, Presence and Immortality*, Pittsburgh, Pa.: Duquesne University Press, 1967.
62. *S.R.*, p. 11.
63. *P.*, p. 62.
64. *T.L.*, pp. 81-82.
65. *B.P.*, p. 335.
66. *Kant Selections*, ed. by T. M. Greene, New York: Scribner's, 1929, p. 302.
67. *FR.*, p. 30 sq.
68. *B.P.*, p. 118.
69. *ibidem*, pp. 102-103.

70. *S.F.*, p. 39.
71. *ibidem*, p. 44.
72. *ibidem*, p. 76.
73. *S.F.*, p. 14.
74. *P.*, p. 11.
75. *ibidem*, p. 11.
76. In a letter to Haskell he wrote: "Yes, beloved Mary, we know without knowing that we know, and we unconsciously live according to something in our depth which our surfaces do not understand. The real thing in us is in the presence of all that is real outside of us," namely, love, (*B.P.*, p. 291).
77. *S.S.*, p. 32.
78. *P.*, pp. 64-66.
79. Mikhail Naimy, *The Book of Mirdad*, London: Stuart & Watkins, 1962, p. 62.
80. *W.*, p. 9.
81. *S.F.*, p. 41.
82. *ibidem*, p. 47.
83. M. J. Cotereau, secretary of the Federation of French Free-thinkers, avowed during the course of a discussion on secular versus religious morality held in Brussels in February 1960: "I do not believe in God because if he existed, he would be Evil. I had rather deny him than make him responsible for evil."
84. *T.S.*, p. 33.
85. *ibidem*, p. 33.
86. *B.W.*, p. 32.
87. *B.P.*, p. 67.
88. *S.S.*, p. 36.
89. *P.*, p. 11.
90. *S.S.*, pp. 36-37.
91. *B.W.*, p. 42.
92. *S.F.*, p. 66.
93. *ibidem*, p. 30.
94. *G.P.*, p. 30.
95. *T.L.*, p. 58 (The italics are mine). In contrast, S. Kierkegaard ridicules the expression of "half" in love. "In considering a person, one naturally supposes him to be an entity, and so one does believe till it becomes apparent that, under the obsession of love, he is but half which runs about looking for its complement. . . . In fact, the more one thinks about the matter the more ridiculous it seems." (*Selections from the Writings of Kierkegaard*, transl. by Lee M. Hollander, Garden City, New York: Doubleday & Co., Inc., 1960, p. 65). But on the other hand Plato in his *Symposium* develops an allegory of love in which the yearning between the two sexes is explained in terms of an original union which was split in two by the power of the Gods. As a result of this division the two sexes arouse; ever since they have been

seeking one another as complementary halves. (Plato, *Symposium*, 189d-191d).

96. *S.S.*, p. 37. (The italics are mine).

97. *ibidem*, p. 66.

98. Gabriel Marcel, *Homo Viator*, New York: Harper & Row, Publishers, 1962, p. 22. Similarly, Karl Jaspers, another existentialist, writes: "The individual cannot become human by himself. Self-being is only real in communication with another self-being." ("On My Philosophy," Felix Kaufmann, transl., in *Existentialism: From Dostoyevsky to Sartre*, Walter Kaufmann, ed., Cleveland: Meridian Books, 1956, p. 145). Martin Buber too shares the same idea: "There is no *I* taken in itself, but only the *I* of the primary word *I-Thou* and the *I* of the primary word *I - it*." (*I and Thou*, New York: Charles Scribner's Sons, 1958, p. 4).

99. *T.L.*, p. 74.

100. *S.F.*, p. 46.

101. *ibidem*, p. 30.

102. Barbara Young, *This Man From Lebanon*, New York: Alfred A. Knopf, 1970, p. 91.

103. *ibidem*, p. 92.

104. Jean-Paul Sartre, *Being and Nothingness*, transl. by Hazel E. Barnes, New York: Philosophical Library, Inc., 1956, Part III, Ch. IV.

105. *B.P.*, p. 198. (The words within the brackets are mine).

106. *B.W.*, p. 25.

107. *S.R.*, p. 16.

108. *P.*, 47.

109. *S.F.*, p. 50.

110. *ibidem*, p. 32; See also *PR.*, p. 55.

111. *P.*, p. 49.

112. *ibidem*, p. 49.

113. *W.G.*, p. 29.

114. *V.M.*, pp. 39-40.

115. *S.S.*, p. 5.

116. Actually, Kierkegaard never used the label existentialism, though historians consider him to be the father of this movement of thought. The Italian philosophers Nicola Abbagnano, Luigi Pareyson, Annibale Pastore, were first to popularize the new "ism" for "existentz."

117. Soren Kierkegaard, *Purity of the Heart*, New York: Harper & Row, Publishers, 1956, p. 184.

118. José Ortega Y Gasset, "Pidiendo un Goethe desde dentro", in *Obras Completas De José Ortega Y Gasset*, Madrid: Revista De Occidente, S.A., 1966, Vol. IV, p. 400. (Translation by the Author).

119. Martin Buber, *Hasidism and Modern Man*, New York: Horizon Press, Inc., 1958, p. 139.

120. *W.*, pp. 42-43, (The italics are mine).

121. *P.*, pp. 15-16.

122. Anna Freud, "The Role of Bodily Illness in the Mental Life of Children," *Psychoanalytic Study of the Child*, Vol. 7. New York: International University Press, 1952, p. 78.

123. *P.*, p. 17.

124. *V.M.*, p. 97.

125. *B.W.*, p. 42. sq.

126. Barbara Young, *This Man From Lebanon*, New York: Alfred A. Knopf, 1970, p. 130.

127. *B.W.*, p. 38.

Gibran's Philosophy of Religion

1. Leo Tolstoy, "The Law of Violence and the Law of Love," in *A History of Russian Philosophy*, ed. by Kline, New York: Columbia University Press, Vol. II, 1967, pp. 225 sq.

2. S. Kierkegaard, *Selections from the Writings of Kierkegaard*, transl. by Lee Hollander, Garden City, New York: Doubleday and Co., Inc., 1960, p. 226.

3. Cf. "Simony" in *New Catholic Encyclopedia*, New York: McGraw Hill Book Co., 1967, vol. 13.

4. *S.R.*, p. 97.

5. *ibidem*, p. 101.

6. *ibidem*, p. 70 sq.

7. *S.H.*, p. 74.

8. *S.R.*, p. 87.

9. *ibidem*, p. 81.

10. *ibidem*, p. 80.

11. "In the opinion of the head priest, a man cannot become a monk unless he is blind and ignorant, senseless and dumb" (*S.R.*, p. 59).

12. *MM*, pp. 42-44.

13. Barbara Young, *This Man From Lebanon*, New York: A. Knopf, 1970, p. 41. See also, *W.*, p. 15.

14. *S.S.*, p. 46.

15. *T.S.*, p. 136 sq.

16. *S.R.*, p. 93. Elsewhere he writes: "If we were to do away with the various religions, we would find ourselves united and enjoying one great faith and religion, abounding in brotherhood." (*W.G.*, p. 63).

17. *S.S.*, p. 112.

18. *S.S.*, p. 49. (The italics are mine).

19. *ibidem*, p. 41.

20. *M.S.*, p. 57. (The italics are mine).

21. St. Augustine, *Confessions*, BK I, C. 1.
22. St. Thomas Aquinas, *Summa Theologica*, I - II, p. 94. a.2.
23. Paul Tillich, *Theology of Culture*, New York: Oxford University Press, 1959, pp. 5-9.
24. J. P. Sartre, *The Words*, Greenwich, Conn.: Fawcett World Library, 1966, p. 62.
25. From *Basic Beliefs: The Religious Philosophies of Mankind*, ed. by J. E. Fairchild, (New York: Sheridan House, Inc., 1959), p. 167. In Europe it is becoming fashionable to title books as *La Foi d'un Paien* (transl. "The Faith of a Pagan", Jean-Claude Barreau, Paris: Editions du Seuil, 1967); also, Francis Jeansen, a follower of Sartre, published recently a book, *La Foi d'un Incroyant* (transl. "The Faith of an Unbeliever," Paris: Editions du Seuil, 1963). All this confirms what Gibran stated about religion as "a natural belief to man."
26. F. Nietzsche, *Zarathustra*, "Prologue."
27. J.-P. Sartre, *Situations I*, Paris, 1947, p. 153.
28. *S.H.*, p. 109.
29. *B.P.*, p. 83.
30. *ibidem*, p. 267.
31. *ibidem*, p. 264.
32. *ibidem*, p. 121.
33. *ibidem*, p. 264.
34. Martin Buber, *Eclipse of God*, New York: Harper and Row, Publishers, 1965, p. 28. Note the similarity between Buber and Gibran when both parallel the expressions "talk to God" and "about God."
35. S. Kierkegaard, "Concluding Unscientific Postscript," in *A Kierkegaard Anthology*, ed. by Robert Bretall (Princeton: Princeton University Press, 1947), pp. 220-221.
36. St. Paul, *I Corinthians*, Ch 1, V. 17-23.
37. *S.F.*, p. 71.
38. *B.P.*, p. 267.
39. W. James, *The Will to Believe and Other Essays in Popular Philosophy*, New York: Longmans, Green and Co., Ltd., 1896, pp. 1-30.
40. *S.S.*, p. 27.
41. *ibidem*, p. 41.
42. *ibidem*, p. 27.
43. *ibidem*, p. 18.
44. *ibidem*, p. 32.
45. B. Young, *This Man From Lebanon*, Alfred A. Knopf, 1970, p. 38.
46. *S.S.*, p. 13.
47. *S.H.*, p. 18.
48. *G.P.*, pp. 39-40.
49. *ibidem*, p. 41.
50. *B.P.*, p. 265.
51 *ibidem*, p. 265.

52. *ibidem*, p. 266.
53. *ibidem*, p. 266.
54. *ibidem*, p. 266.
55. *ibidem*, p. 266.
56. *ibidem*, p. 266.
57. *ibidem*, p. 266.
58. *T.S.*, pp. 21-22.
59. *B.P.*, p. 266.
60. I am sure Gibran would not argue with the scholastic philosophers about the difference in meaning between the concepts "creation" and "production." Yet his decision for giving up the word creation is less a matter of philosophical dispute, in as much as for poetical, mystical and practical reasons. Not everybody can understand the abstract philosophical definition of creation as found in the scholastic's metaphysics.
61. *P.*, p. 79.
62. *B.P.*, p. 329.
63. *ibidem*, p. 266.
64. *G.P.*, p. 41, also see *P.*, p. 79.
65. *T.S.*, p. 21.
66. *B.P.*, p. 266.
67. *ibidem*, p. 267.
68. *ibidem*, p. 268.
69. *T.S.*, p. 21 sq. (The italics are mine).
70. Aristotle, *De Anima*.
71. *S.S.*, p. 48.
72. *W.*, pp. 80 - 81.
73. *P.*, pp. 78 - 79; *G.P.*, p. 41.
74. *S.R.*, p. 64.
75. *ibidem*, pp. 22 - 23.
76. Hegel, "Logic," in *The Philosophy of Hegel*, ed. by Carl J. Friedrich, New York: The Modern Library, 1954, pp. 203 - 217.
77. Henri Bergson, *Creative Evolution*, New York: Henry Holt, 1911.
78. Mikhail Naimy, *The Book of Mirdad*, London: Stuart and Watkins, 1962, Ch. 34.
79. Ameen Rihani, *The Path of Vision*, Beirut: The Rihani House, 1970.
80. Nicolai Berdjaev, *Solitude and Society*, transl. by G. Reavey, London: Geoffrey Bles, 1947.
81. Teilhard de Chardin, *Phenomenon of Man*, New York: Harper and Row Publishers, 1965.
82. *B.P.*, p. 267.
83. *ibidem*, p. 267. See also, *M.M.*, pp. 9 - 10.
84. Note the similarity between Kierkegaard and Gibran on the issue woman: "it is my joy that, far from being less perfect than man, the female sex is, on the contrary, the more perfect," (S. Kierkegaard,

Selections From the Writings of Kierkegaard, transl. by Lee Hollander, Garden City, N.Y.: Doubleday, Co., 1960, p. 103). Gibran likewise writes: "Women are better than man. They are kinder, more sensitive, more stable, and have a finer sense about much of life." (*B.P.*, p. 286.

85. *W.G.*, p. 30.
86. *J.S.M.*, p. 32.
87. *V.M.*, p. 56.
88. *S.S.*, p. 23.
89. *ibidem*, p. 8.
90. *B.P.*, p. 342.
91. *V.M.*, pp. 49 - 52.
92. Blaise Pascal, *Pensee*, Paris: Librairie Generale Francaise, 1962, p. 130, No. 264. (Translation by the author). Note the fact that Gibran too used the word "reed" in connection to death and immortality. (*P.R.*, p. 71).
93. *V.M.*, p. 51 - 52.
94. *S.H.*, p. 136.
95. Epicurus, *The Philosophy of Epicurus*, ed. by G. K. Stirodach, Evanston: Ill.: North-western University Press, 1963, p. 180.
96. *P.*, p. 80.
97. *P.*, p. 89. Also in a letter to Haskell, May 16, 1916, he writes: "No, Mary, death does not change us. It only frees that which is real in us—our consciousness—and the *social* memories that lie in our consciousness. . . . Human consciousness is the print of the infinite past. The infinite future will make it ripe but it will never change its properties." (*B.P.*, p. 274).
98. F. Nietzsche, "Zarathustra," in *The Portable Nietzsche*, ed. by W. Kaufman, New York: The Viking Press, 1968, p. 132.
99. M. Fakhry, *A History of Islamic Philosophy*, Columbia University Press, 1970, p. 47.
100. *Th.M.*, pp. 5-6.
101. *P.*, pp. 94 - 95.
102. *G.P.*, pp. 66 - 67. See also, *B. P.*, p. 427.
103. Miss Young erroneously tells us that Gibran "never used the word" reincarnation. Yet, I found the word written in some of his articles. (See for instance *Th.M.*, pp. 1 - 8. Compare with B. Young, *This Man From Lebanon*, New York: A Knopf, 1970, p. 84).
104. *B.P.*, p. 335.
105. Plato, *Phaedo*, 80e - 81 d. In Plato's opinion, only the philosopher never returns back to this life; yet, a soul which returns will receive a certain shape of a body which corresponds to the type of acts she performed during her previous existence on earth.
106. B. Young, *This Man From Lebanon*, New York: A. Knopf, 1970, p. 94.
107. *ibidem*, p. 94.

108. *ibidem*, p. 99.
109. *S.H.*, p. 103.
110. *J.S.M.*, p. 89.
111. *J.S.M.*, p. 12 - 15.
112. *N.V.*, p. 74.
113. *S.F.*, p. 77.
114. *S.F.*, p. 84.
115. *J.S. M.*, p. 107.
116. *B.P.*, pp. 167-168. *Also* in Barbara Young, *This Man From Lebanon*, New York: A. Knopf, 1970, pp. 99-111.
117. P. W. Wilson in "Jesus Was the Supreme Poet," *The New York Times Book Review*, December 23, 1928, reproduced in *Kahlil Gibran. Essays and Introductions*, eds. S. B. Bushrin and J. M. Munro, (Beirut: The Rihani House, 1970) p. 165.

SELECTED BIBLIOGRAPHY

Gibran, Kahlil.—*Sand and Foam,* New York: Alfred A. Knopf, 1969.
    The Prophet, New York: Alfred A. Knopf, 1970.
    The Wanderer, New York: Alfred A. Knopf, 1971.
    The Garden of the Prophet, New York: Alfred A. Knopf, 1969.
    The Forerunner, New York: Alfred A. Knopf, 1970.
    Nymphs of the Valley, New York: Alfred A. Knopf, 1969.
    The Earth Gods, New York: Alfred A. Knopf, 1969.
    The Madman, New York: Alfred A. Knopf, 1945.
    Twenty Drawings, New York: Alfred A. Knopf, 1919.
    Jesus The Son of Man, New York: Alfred A. Knopf, 1970.
Beloved Prophet. —The Love Letters of Kahlil Gibran and Mary Haskell. ed. by Virginia Hilu, New York: Alfred A. Knopf, 1972.
Gibran, Kahlil.—*The Wisdom of Gibran,* ed. by Joseph Sheban, New York: Philosophical Library, 1966.
    The Procession, transl. by George Kheirallah, New York: Philosophical Library, 1958.
    Mirrors of the Soul, transl. by Joseph Sheban, New York: Philosophical Library, 1965.
    Spirits Rebellious, transl. by A. Rizcallah Ferris, New York: Philosophical Library, 1965.
    Spirits Rebellious, transl. by A. Rizcallah Ferris, New York: Philosophical Library, 1947.
    Tears and Laughter, ed. by Martin Wolf, New York: Philosophical Library, 1949.
    Thoughts and Meditations, transl. by A. R. Ferris, New York: Bantam Books, 1968.
    A Tear and A Smile, transl. by H. M. Nahmad, New York: Bantam Books, 1969.
    Spiritual Sayings, transl. and ed. by A. R. Ferris, New York: Bantam Books, 1970.
    The Voice of the Master, transl. by A. R. Ferris, New York: Bantam Books, 1967.
    The Broken Wings, transl. by A. R. Ferris, New York: Bantam Books, 1968.
    A Self Portrait, transl. by A. R. Ferris, New York: Bantam Books, 1970.
    Secrets of the Heart, transl. by A. R. Ferris, New York: Signet Books,

WORKS ON GIBRAN

Otto, Annie Salem.—*The Parables of Kahlil Gibran*, New York: The Citadel Press, 1967.

Young, Barbara.—*This Man From Lebanon*, New York: Alfred A. Knopf, 1970.

Sherfan, Andrew Dib.—*Kahlil Gibran: The Nature of Love*, New York: Philosophical Library, 1971.

Naimy, Mikhail.—*Kahlil Gibran: A Biography*, New York: The Philosophical Library, 1950.

Challita, Mansour.—*Luttes et triomphe de Gibran*, Beirut.

Bushrin, Suheil, ed.—*An Introduction to Kahlil Gibran*, Beirut.

Hamdeh, Bushrui, Munro and Smith, eds.—*A Poet and His Country: Gibran's Lebanon*, Beirut.

Bushrin, S., and Munro, J.—*Kahlil Gibran: Essays and Introductions*, Beirut, 1970.

Bragdon, C. F.—"*Modern Prophet from Lebanon*," *Merely Players*. New York: Alfred A. Knopf, 1929.

Knopf, Alfred.—"*News Release*," letter dated November 21, 1961.

Lecerft, Jean.—"Djabran Khalil Djabran et les origines de la prose poetique modern." *Orient* No. 3 (1957), pp. 7 – 14.

Ross, Martha Jean.—"The Writings of Kahlil Gibran," Unpublished Master Thesis, The University of Texas, Austin, 1948.

Russell, G. W. —"Kahlil Gibran," *Living Torch*. New York: Macmillan Co., 1938.

Al Houeyyek, Youssef.—*Zoukriati ma' Joubran*. Written by Edvique Juraydini Shaybub. Beirut: Dar el Ahad.

Jaber, Jamil.—*May wa Joubran*, Beirut: Dar el Jamal, 1950.

Jaber, Jamil.—*Joubran, Siratuhu, Arabuhu, Falsafatuhu wa Rasmuhu*, Beirut: The Rihani House, 1958.

Massoud, Habib.—*Joubran, Hayyan wa Mayyitan*, Beirut: The Rihani House, 1966.

Saiegh, Tawfic.—*Adhwa' Jadidah Ala Joubran*, Beirut: Dar al Sharquiah, 1966.

Naimy, Mikhail.—*Al Majmou' at al Kamilat Li Mouallafat Joubran Kahlil Joubran*, Beirut: Dar Sader and Dar Beirut, 1959.

Ghougassian, Joseph.—"The Art of Kahlil Gibran," *Ararat*, 1972, Vol. XIII, No. 1 – 2.

(Concerning the other books consulted, refer to my footnotes.)